The Award-Winning
Bestseller
THE WIND CHILL FACTOR

THE WIND CHILL FACTOR

"You don't come across a blistering novel of suspense like this one very often!"

—*Hartford Courant*

"If you are a movie buff of World War II epics and if the spy and counterspy intrigue of James Bond's adventures holds a prominent place in your library, THE WIND CHILL FACTOR is for you . . . It leads the reader through a maze of espionage, violence, and intrigue . . . Satisfaction guaranteed."

—CBS Radio, Los Angeles

"A zingy, done-to-a-T thriller, perfectly paced, eminently satisfying . . . I read the book at one sitting, I just couldn't put it down."

—*Minneapolis* Magazine

IS TAKING THE COUNTRY BY STORM

"IF YOU LIKE SUSPENSE, EXPLOSIVE DE-
VELOPMENTS, AND CURIOUS TURNS, *THE
WIND CHILL FACTOR* IS A GOOD WAY TO
START OFF YOUR READING YEAR."
—*Chattanooga Times*

"Full of blood and gore . . . The kind of book
you can't leave alone . . . A grand jigsaw puzzle."
—*Grand Rapids Press*

"Twisting, suspenseful . . . a deftly done thriller."
—*B. Dalton News Letter*

THE WIND CHILL FACTOR

Thomas Gifford

BALLANTINE BOOKS • NEW YORK

For Camille

Library of Congress Catalog Card Number: 74-16598

SBN 345-24800-7-195

This edition published by arrangement with
G. P. Putnam's Sons

First Printing: February, 1976

Printed in the United States of America

BALLANTINE BOOKS
A Division of Random House, Inc.
201 East 50th Street, New York, N.Y. 10022
Simultaneously published by
Ballantine Books of Canada, Ltd., Toronto, Canada

I am not I;
he is not he;
they are not they.

Prologue

THERE weren't many people on the platform. It was cold and the chill felt good, cleansed my pain. I leaned against a pillar. A few feet away a family waited, middle-aged and tweedy with a little blond girl holding her mother's hand. She was smiling with the expectancy and excitement of the very young who are up long after their normal bedtime. She let go of her mother's hand and began to pace ever-widening circles around her parents, until she came close enough for me to see her cornflower-blue eyes. She smiled up at me and I smiled back. She was well dressed: her coat had a velvet collar.

Tentatively she came closer, staring up at me in a child's unrelenting manner, her smile fading. Again I caught her eye through the pain and weariness engulfing me and tried to smile. She reminded me of pictures of my little sister Lee taken many years before.

Finally, somewhat discomfited by her staring, I leaned forward to say hello. That was when she began a high-pitched screaming, a wail, as if I'd attacked her. I felt myself toppling forward, no strength in my knees, and I gripped the pillar. I was befuddled: why was she screaming? Her mouth, a cavern into which I seemed about to fall, reminded me of the wound in Alistair Campbell's forehead.

Her parents turned to stare, her father rushed forward saying, "Here, here," and reaching for his daughter. The woman came closer, her face scowling and full of reproaches, and then she stopped short, covered her mouth with a gloved hand, and I heard her say: "Oh, God, Henry, look at his face, he's all bloody. . . ."

I wiped my hand across my face and it was sticky and my stomach turned; there was blood smeared on my fingers. I tried to hold fast to the pillar but everything was slanting and voices came to me as if from a distant echo chamber. The little girl had stopped screaming and I could see that the rain falling on the railroad track had turned to snow drifting down.

A voice near my ear said tiredly: "Jesus, Cooper, look at yourself, another fine mess."

The voice was familiar, but when I turned, my sight was going quickly and I could see only a shape, a pinpoint of light, a face in the pinpoint, but it was too late and I saw only the snow blowing in great soft gusts, heard only the dim sounds of trains very far away and I was falling and I simply didn't give a damn. . . .

Part One

One

IT began with a telegram.

I had been living in Cambridge, Massachusetts, for several years, since my divorce from Digby, and found that, while I could not recapture the feelings of my Harvard undergraduate days, there was still a certain comfort in the place. I arranged for the use of Widener Library; I came to depend on the Coop for my department store needs; there were several new and used bookstores at hand, stationers, newsstands, tobacco from Leavitt & Pierce, the *Crimson* and the New York *Times* to read with breakfast, walks to take down Boylston Street, past Eliot House, where I had once lived, and along the Charles River, where I had fallen deeply in love with a woman who was destined to go away, who had been the reason for my divorce.

In Cambridge I amounted to myself: there were few aspects to my own definition there which did not stem directly from me. In that sense, it was entirely unlike New York, with its telltale evidence of Digby, who had so many friends and was so much better known than I, unlike—even more significantly—Cooper's Falls, where our family, which had given the place its name, was in many ways public property.

On the morning in question, something past the middle of January, I sat at the table in the front room overlooking the gray, dead grass in the courtyard below, snow in patches like a ramshackle case of baldness. Coffee steamed in a mug, butter dripped into the tiny craters of an English muffin, and I contemplated with some satisfaction a pile of yellow legal pad pages full of my cramped, rather constipated penmanship. A mystery novel—set at Harvard during a student uprising and titled *Tumult*—was coming on nicely. I hadn't had a drink for six months and my physician had almost convinced me that the alcoholism which had nearly ruined me was a thing of the past. I was free of women and growing happily used to it. I was thirty-four and more or less broke and sufficiently well adjusted to feel unafraid of the day ahead, the month to come, the rest of my life.

I was sitting that morning in the middle of an oasis I had made for myself: I'd managed the trick, pulled myself together, survived.

And then, to keep me honest and in my place, the telephone rang.

"Western Union calling for Mr. John Cooper," a woman said.

"Speaking."

"We have a telegram for you from a, hmmm, from a Cyril Cooper?"

I suggested that she read it to me, suddenly aware of that clammy chest-tightening sensation Western Union inevitably produces.

She read: URGENT YOU MEET ME COOPER'S FALLS 20 JANUARY. DROP EVERYTHING. FAMILY TREE NEEDS ATTENTION. CHEERS, OLD BOY. CYRIL.

She offered to repeat the message and I took her up on it, listened with relief: not an overt disaster, anyway. I stared into the street below wondering what the hell it meant. I asked her the point of origin.

"Buenos Aires," she said with a perfected tone of total disinterest. I thanked her and reflexively reached for a pipe and a tin of Balkan Sobranie, stuffed the blackish tobacco into the bowl, applied a wooden kitchen match, and pulled mightily, tasting the mixture and watching the burning shreds of latakia rising above the rim of briar.

First, it was no fake. Only my brother Cyril would have wasted three words on CHEERS, OLD BOY.

Second, urgency in Cyril's life was not a colloquial expression. It meant precisely what it said.

Third, 20 January was not an approximation. It

was precisely when he wanted me back in Cooper's Falls and there was no room for excuses on my part.

Fourth, the message was not only tantalizing: it was intentionally provocative, yet revealed nothing. Cyril never did anything without a reason and if he was being obscure there was a reason behind it.

Fifth, Buenos Aires. Buenos Aires, far from Cyril's normal bases of operation, most of which were European. And yet Cyril would have had an excellent reason for being in Buenos Aires.

After a second cup of coffee, I had made my own calculations. Then I was packing a bag, putting my bits and pieces in order, and heading downstairs for the garage and the Lincoln.

Two

THE Lincoln was a leftover from a time when money was plentiful. I had kept it and taken care of it in the face of an avalanche of personal and economic difficulties, clinging to it as a sort of talisman. The automobile was a joy, humming very quietly, gulping fuel like a Saturn rocket, warm air rising toward its predetermined comfort level. Built in 1966, my Continental reflected a gray world in its gunmetal finish, held me secure in its deep leather interior. It didn't occur to me to get home any other way. I had everything checked: gas, oil, transmission fluid, brake fluid, battery water, air pressure, fuses governing all lights inside and out and all other power assists.

Snowflakes began littering the windshield. The washers were full of winter solvent. The wipers, new, swept across the vast windshield with authority. I was ready.

I spent the first day out from Boston driving a paltry 380 snowblown miles, snow whipping past my vision and skittering across the highway only to disappear without accumulating anywhere. My thoughts naturally settled on my brother Cyril.

Cyril Cooper, two years my senior, was a boy and then a man of extreme affability, determination and, not to put too fine a point on it, sheerest, nakedest greed. His greed, his joy at turning his business life into a series of Harvard Business School case studies, had made him exceedingly rich in his own right. His decency had left him, presumably, without enemies, a rare condition in so rich a man. His business interests included scotch whiskey, two lines of retail clothing shops of trendy persuasion, television taping equipment, advertising, specialty publishing, shipping interests under the flag of Liberia, and land development in Great Britian, France, and Spain. He had taken a loan from our grandfather at the age of twenty-one and systematically built a stairway to tycoondom.

As I drove through the darkening afternoon, puffing on a beautifully seasoned Barling Canadian, my reflections inevitably turned from my brother, always the picture of robust thickchested good humor, to the rest of the family which had, by some peculiar thrashing of genes, produced not only him but someone so utterly different, so bookish and introspective a fellow as myself, to say nothing of our little sister Lee, who had died in the London Blitz.

Cooper's Falls had been founded in the northern part of Minnesota, in a crook of the exquisite St. Croix River, some short distance above the bubbling foamy falls which even in the icecrack of winter never gave up their churning. The original Cooper, my namesake John, had made his fortune in the railroads and the grain which had combined eventually to give the world a goodly number of colorful millionaires and the thriving, energetic city of Minneapolis. But the Coopers were on balance a singularly retiring bunch, until my grandfather hit his stride and made up for a good deal of lost time.

My grandfather Austin was a deeply committed man who grew richer and richer as the nation prospered after the turn into the twentieth century. He knew well and was friend to the more proudly exhibited financial giants of the time: Carnegie, Rockefeller, Ford, Mellon. But at some point, due very likely to an unnamed psychological trauma which, like an old piece of wartime shrapnel, worked its way to the surface and finally suppurated and burst messily through, an unsettling vision overtook Austin Cooper. While visiting Germany during the twenties, he became sympathetic to the plight of the Germans suffering under what he called "the yolk of punishment inflicted by their conquerors following the Great War." He was not alone in his feelings: many humane observers felt the same way and subsequent historians have frequently seconded the view that it was an unjust peace which produced nothing other than a second Thirty Years' War dating from 1914 to 1945. However, reacting in his own fashion, Austin Cooper was not content with simply noting his own point of view in his nightly diary and letting it go at that.

On subsequent visits to Germany my grandfather sought out, with some perception and determination, those men he believed would be the voices of a new Phoenix-like Germany. On the one hand he allied himself with the Krupp family, socially as well as financially, operating as a bridge between various German and Anglo-American moneymen.

But Austin also courted and was eventually courted in return by political leaders he believed to have the gumption—that was his word—to turn Germany around and get it moving once more toward its own particular manifest destiny. As an American, he was useful to these new men. He could move in circles to which they were denied entrance by the force of social convention.

Thus Austin Cooper began his service to two angry and exceedingly able Germans who sought a new world. One, oddly enough was a hero of the Great War, which appealed to Austin's reticent sense of grandeur; the other was a bit harder to take in some ways but was the most hypnotically powerful and brilliant man Austin had ever met, ever would meet.

Hermann Goering.

Adolf Hitler.

Austin Cooper.

Cyril Cooper.

Buenos Aires.

Cheers, old boy.

The names lingered and played across my mind as I lay propped on my motel bed, too tired to read or even pay attention to the television. But I was too wound up to fall asleep: I was tense from driving through the snow and, having thought so long about the family, I was developing a certain apprehensiveness about the whole thing.

It had been a long time since I'd seen Cooper's Falls, a long time since I'd let my mind dwell so pointedly on the family. And I had so many miles, so many hours to go. I had begun to wish I'd taken a plane, but that would not have been true to my nature. Anyone who knew me would have known I'd take the Lincoln.

Finally I climbed under the blankets and listened to the wind whistling at my door until I fell asleep.

The next day they tried to kill me.

Three

THE second day of my trip home was a more intense version of that first afternoon out from Boston. I drove westward into the face of a gray and shifting curtain of blowing snow which cut visibility and speed to a minimum. Shapes were constantly being overtaken and recognized almost as you were upon them, and headlights made lovely but unproductive halos on the snowflakes. The radio warned continually against any travel, reeling off great lists of school closings and canceled meetings. But I gave no thought to stopping, to the possibility of arriving late. Cyril had said the twentieth and the twentieth it would be.

In Indiana and Illinois the weather cleared and

I let the Lincoln off its leash to run flat out for a while, learning by radio that the storm was ahead of me, lying in wait once I turned north from Chicago on the Illinois Tollway and headed on up into Wisconsin. But for now there was hazy sunshine and I tried to ease the tension in my arms which had accumulated during the hours of wheel-gripping zero visibility.

It seemed peculiar in 1972 to be driving along through a country which had developed its own set of new-old problems and crises while thinking back to my childhood in Cooper's Falls with a grandfather whose name had become, through the years of German rearmament in the 1930's, a synonym for the idea of Americans who were admirers of the Nazis, who sympathized for whatever personal reasons with Nazi aims in Europe.

In the mid-30's, before I was born, the anti-Semitism being practiced within Germany was not much known in our part of the country, was not a matter of overriding concern. It was, in a widespread view, a question which would doubtless be with us always and, in the end, each nation had to deal with Jews—and particularly Jewish wealth and leverage—in its own way. In my grandfather's view, Jews were thought of in a business sense exclusively, and if you couldn't really trust them then they weren't that different from anyone else. There was certainly no reason why you couldn't coexist with them. They were a fact of life and while he would not go out of his way to rescue a Jew, neither would he have gratuitously done one any harm. They were simply a group apart and how they handled their problem was their own business. He might have said the same of the Catholics.

Austin Cooper was not, then, a crazy racist or bigot. He was, beneath the glaze of colorful and inaccurate publicity, a rather cool realist who felt that Europe was an ailing, faltering giant which must somehow be made strong again for the long-term good of both the world's and Austin Cooper's economy. It was his bet that Europe would best be served by the emergence of a dynamic leader, or group, which would give birth to a new pride, a new nationalism, a new confidence which would bring Europe back to her feet again. His belief grew with the Depression and so did his involvement with Fascist politics in Germany, Italy, Spain, and England. Nationalism was the answer and if it made for war, so be it. Money survives war, thrives on war. War was no problem. There have always been wars. Mankind loved wars. The point was to make wars pay.

What concerned me, as a child innocent of politics, were the purely personal aspects of having Austin Cooper, America's Number One Nazi as he was called in *Liberty* and *Collier's,* for a grandfather.

My brother Cyril and I were far closer to our grandfather than might normally have been the case. We were too young to have suffered any particular shame at his exploits. For us he was a lean, exceptionally well-tailored elderly man with coins and books for us, a rather sad demeanor, a precise manner of speech, and a surprisingly quick laugh for so serious a man. He played croquet with us on the immense back lawn during the war; he was in his early sixties and wore a white shirt and black tie; by then it was no longer felt safe for him to go out in public for golf or any other occasion.

But if he was only a solemn benevolent figure to us, there were other aspects to having him around, aspects which were a terrible burden to our father, who was a grown man in the company of other grown men. They associated him with the American Nazi photographed on the front pages chatting with Adolf Hitler, riding in an immense open car with Goering and Speer and Frau Goering, meeting behind closed doors with Alfried Krupp and then coming out to engage in smiling handshakes, sealing God only knew what kind of fiendish bargain.

That was what our father had to contend with. Born in 1910, Harvard 1932: a handsome, artistically inclined man who wanted at one time to be a painter. He traveled with his father to Germany in the sparkling days of Berlin's glories in the 1920's, again in the 1930's, when there was a somewhat different aura, met the great men who were deciding how to reshape Europe and, as sons do, he reacted violently against all they—and by association his father—stood for. So, while Austin Cooper came to stand for American Nazism, our father Edward, in his all too brief life, did what he could to oppose the Nazi wickedness. Finally, in 1941, he gave his life flying for the RAF in aerial combat over the English Channel. His Spitfire was never found, his body never recovered. There were articles written about them at the time: one the living traitor to all that America meant, the other his son martyred for freedom. It made hellish good copy, I suppose, if the men in question were not your grandfather and father.

On December 8, 1941, by order of the President, our many-chambered mansion on the estate looking down on that lovely river and the falls which bore our name was put under armed, uniformed Army guard and so it stayed until several months after the war ended. Austin Cooper was cordoned off, protected from all those with reason to wish him ill.

Four

CHICAGO lay smoking and vast, a smudge of industrial haze frozen in the sky above it. As I swung northward against the grain of wind the overcast swept toward me. Soon I was in it again, feeling the two-and-a-half-ton Lincoln take the blasts on its great slab sides. And the snow came swirling across the frozen fields and the sun was reduced to nothing more than a dim grayness behind the howling wind and snow.

I pulled up off the tollway to one of the Fred Harvey emporiums. The place was virtually deserted, cups echoing in saucers: there was an unreal, unearthly quiet about it all, as if, insulated in its cocoon of snow, Fred Harvey had opened a space station. There was a curious moment when I felt as if I'd fallen among automatons and was the only living thing within reach.

The spell was broken when the girl brought my coffee. She smiled past some remnants of high-school acne and commented on the weather. "It seems like night already," she concluded and went away. Two men came in to the eating area and sat down, ordered coffee. One of them, a tall, balding man in a sheepskin coat came over and asked if he could read the *Tribune* lying on the counter beside me. I told him it wasn't mine and he was welcome to it. He smiled and shook his head at the snow blowing across the expanses of glass, obscuring the view of the highway below us.

"Heading north?" he asked with a friendly, gaunt smile.

"All the way to Minnesota," I said.

"You may not make it," he said sadly as if we were all facing this common enemy together. "I hear it's bad, worse the farther north you go."

"I suppose it is," I said.

"Well, it's a hell of a thing." He lit a Kool and folded the newspaper in large, long-fingered hands. He looked like a cowboy, herding cattle home through the drifts. "Thanks for the paper," he said and went back to his companion.

They were quietly drinking coffee when I put my gloves on and went back outside to my car. I was wearing my favorite turtleneck sweater, a heavy oily thing woven by some little old lady in the Hebrides, nothing but thick wool, yet soft as glove leather. The car surged to life immediately, and I ran through the checklist in my mind making sure everything was functioning perfectly. I drove slowly across the service area past a black limousine standing by a bank of pumps. The men inside the restaurant had come back outside. They were standing by the black car, and sheepskin coat waved to me as I passed him and rolled down the ramp to the empty white pit that slowly revealed itself as the tollway.

I was daydreaming without losing my concentration on the road. I would let Cyril dominate my thoughts for a time, then Digby would take his place and I'd be bringing her back to Cooper's Falls for the first time as I'd done so many years ago. My father would be talking to me, the way he'd never had the opportunity to do in reality; my grandfather would address the croquet ball, deliberately, black tie flapping in a summer breeze, and I could hear the solid sound of mallet on ball. . . .

Early evening had overtaken me and the snow was thicker. The roadway had grown slippery with packed snow and ice. Visibility was a joke. I hadn't seen more than a half dozen other vehicles in an hour and I had just passed the state line into Wisconsin when I saw the black limousine suddenly beside me, only a few feet away on my left. It was sliding toward me and there wasn't time to react before I felt the impact, felt the Lincoln gliding off the road unable to grab hold on the hard-driven snow.

Like a pair of gigantic ice skaters, we slid through drifting snow, plowing slowly on down a ridge of crusty whiteness. I spun the wheel, took my foot off the gas, hoped that somehow the snow tires would catch. The black limousine finally detached itself, pulled away and ahead of me, stayed on the shoulder as I slid downward. Finally I felt solid footing behind the rear axle and in an uncharacteristic instant of clear thinking I shoved the gearshift into low and hit the gas, hoping to regain control. Curiously, the maneuver worked and I felt the Lincoln gather itself together, push through the snow below the level of the highway, and claw its way back up to the shoulder, snow rising like waves in front of me, beside me, all around me. I suppose it took only a few seconds from the initial impact until I was back on the shoulder, but it seemed an agonizing lifetime, a nightlong terror which left me suddenly sick to my stomach, shaking, dripping with sweat. I sat clutching the wheel, gulping air in an attempt to keep from vomiting.

The black limousine appeared again out of the snow, its lights blunted against the storm. I could hear it honking, saw the sheepskin coat waving to me, watched as it pulled in ahead of me and stopped.

In view of my own lights, doors opened on either side of the limousine and the two men got out and hurried back toward me, leaning into the wind. I pushed open my door, which creaked sorely at the hinges and stepped out, feeling the full blast of wind and a coldness which had not been there when I'd left Fred Harvey. It cut through the sweater and the gaunt man in the sheepskin coat was shouting to me.

"Are you all right?" His voice was nearly smothered by the wind. Snow bit at my face and eyes.

"Yeah, I'm okay, I guess," I said.

"Jesus, I couldn't help it," his companion said, a short stout man in a blue duffel coat. "I'm sorry as hell, fella."

We stood looking at the damage: paint scraped off, door and front fender badly creased. "Shit," I said.

"I'll look back here." Sheepskin coat ducked his face down behind the fleecy collar and walked toward the rear of the Lincoln. There was no sound but the raving of the storm.

Blue duffel coat beckoned me toward the front wheel, pointing at the fender. He knelt in the snow, seemed to be tugging at the fender, pulling it back from the wheel. I joined him, on my knees in the snow. The fender didn't seem to be rubbing against the tire and I turned to say so.

I never got the words out. I felt instead a blunt, numbing sensation on the side of my head. I heard the sound of something against my skull, heard a man grunt softly with exertion near my ear, felt the snow rushing against my face and then there was nothing.

Five

HOW long can you live lying in the snow in below freezing temperatures? I don't know. But I survived. I was stiff with cold when I awoke and when I lifted my head it bumped against the undercarriage of the Lincoln: somehow I had half hidden myself underneath the car. I had survived the attack for two reasons. Sheepskin coat had done an ineffectual job of bludgeoning me and the warmth from the huge engine, retained against the cold, had kept me from being frozen to death.

Slowly, painfully I wriggled into the open. Our films and television have insulated us against the reality of physical violence because our heroes survive it each week and in each film. I had suspected we were being fed something less than the truth. Standing beside the Lincoln, leaning desperately against its wounded side and puking into the snow, I found my suspicions confirmed. It was more horrible—both the physical reality and the knowledge of menace hovering over me with a tire iron in its hand—than I could possibly have imagined, even in the delirium of drunkenness. Those sons of bitches had left me in the road to die, actually *die*—and I had lived by a quirk of chance. Suddenly I was aware of the weather: I opened the door, hauled myself back up into the driver's seat, and turned the key. The Lincoln fired back to life with me, spraying warm air around the leather interior, defrosting the windshield. The Lincoln was saving my life.

The side of my skull was sticky with blood and terribly tender to my fingertip's pressure. I sat in the warmth trying to calm down and get my thoughts sorted out. Then I got back out of the Lincoln, washed the side of my head with snow, washed the blood off my hands, and set out again. The front tire was not rubbing the fender.

The night was dark. I was back on the road. I couldn't see far enough ahead to push much past forty, and it occurred to me in one of those delayed-action double takes that the black limousine might appear once more, that these bastards might keep doing this to me until they did it right.

It wasn't until I saw through the storm the highway equipment, red lights flashing, pushing a path in the snow, that I began to feel reasonably safe again. There were men in those huge vehicles, men in the trucks full of sand—normal men doing their jobs, trying to protect me from the storm rather than lying in wait to kill me. Slowly, deliberately, I clung to the plows and sanders all the way to Madison, which glowed through the storm like a friendly apparition.

Undoubtedly I ought to have checked my head at a local hospital emergency room, but instead I eased down off the highway, made a cloverleaf to the right, crossed the southbound lane, and pulled up the steep grade to a Howard Johnson's, its orange roof peering out through the snow. After a few polite but mildly perplexed looks at my mussed condition, I was given a room facing toward the rear parking lot, away from the highway and backing against a sheer looming bluff of stone several times higher than the motel itself. The parking lot was well lit, snow in a constant filtering of whiteness, cars parked with six inches and more frosting roofs, hoods, trunks. I lugged my bag out of the rear seat, slid the glass door to my room open from the outside, and discovered the room clerk turning on lights, pointing toward the bathroom. He had a butch haircut, the first I'd seen in a long time. His eyes smiled from behind horn-rims.

"Thought I'd come back and see you got in all right." He nodded his head like the man in the sheepskin coat had done at Fred Harvey's: a weather comment was coming. "Nothing much happening on a night like this. All day long we've been getting cancellations from salesmen snowed in somewhere else. Of course," he said philosophically, "most of our salesmen decided to stay an extra night, so we're back to even, I suppose." He watched me throw the bag on the bed. I pulled the sliding door closed. "Heat's over there," he said, motioning to a wall dial. "Bathroom's in here, color television if you're one of those guys just can't stand to miss the Carson show." He pointed to a blanket folded on the bed. "Brought you an extra blanket."

"Very kind," I said. "Do you have any Excedrin? I have an Excedrin headache, definitely." He went away. Standing at the floor-to-ceiling wall of glass, staring at the white, fluffy parking lot and listening to the wind gnawing at my feet, I realized exactly what I was doing: I was scanning the parking lot for a black limousine with a dented side. I didn't see one and the smiling desk clerk was telling me that here were my Excedrins and didn't I look a little pale?

"Yes, I probably do look a little pale," I said, "but that's only because my head aches, I'm sick to my stomach, and I've been throwing up in the snow on the freeway. Otherwise, I'm fine."

"Well, you'd better get to bed, then," he said. Smiling from the doorway he said: "This flu, it's been going around. Just murder. So get a good night's sleep."

Just murder. Oh, boy.

For a while the Excedrin kept me awake and I kept seeing the man in the sheepskin coat smiling at me and telling me I might not make it to Minnesota. But why had they attacked me? Thrill killers? It didn't seem likely: surely such psychopaths would have enjoyed the act of murder, would have made very sure. Thieves, then? But they had taken nothing: no papers, no money, no credit cards, nothing. Yet, they had painstakingly lured me into a trap and tried to kill me. How else could I interpret it?

I finally drifted off to sleep, the snow scurrying across the glass wall and the shadows falling in stately bars.

Six

AS I left Madison and headed north on January 20, my head ached slightly, a patch over my left ear was swollen and tender, but I'd had no recurrence of vomiting. All things considered, with bacon and eggs under my belt, I felt reasonably well. The man at the Texaco station had checked under the hood for loose hoses and leaks, pronounced everything all right. Aside from her cosmetic damage the Lincoln was purring, giving ample evidence of her fine disregard for the economics of fuel consumption. The sun was bright in the east. The sky was glacial. The temperature had fallen to ten degrees.

January 20. Somewhere Cyril was approaching Cooper's Falls, was perhaps even now landing at Minneapolis/St. Paul. By evening I would know what he wanted, what all the urgency was about.

I knew no more now than I had when I set out from Boston. There was the telegram: URGENT YOU MEET ME COOPER'S FALLS 20 JANUARY. DROP EVERYTHING. FAMILY TREE NEEDS ATTENTION. CHEERS, OLD BOY. CYRIL. I had it memorized.

And it meant nothing to me, nothing I could put my finger on. Decorating the family tree, obviously, was the matter of my grandfather's political eccentricity, but how might that need "attention"? Austin Cooper had died peacefully in his eighties, the family's oldest friend at his side. It was Arthur Brenner himself, in fact, who had written me of my grandfather's death a few years before, had told me how my grandfather had peacefully slipped away with Arthur at his bedside. Arthur Brenner had been my grandfather's attorney, a dear friend of my father's, although a good many years his senior, and had broken the news to me not only of my grandfather's death, but of my father's, my mother's and my little sister Lee's, as well. Arthur had helped my father get into Harvard through his own Harvard connections, had aided him in being attached to the Royal Air Force, and had subsequently helped me go to Harvard. And Arthur Brenner himself had commented upon the death of Austin Cooper that at last the family slate was wiped clean. Time would pass, he'd said, and eventually the memory of my grandfather's Nazism would be gone, and then the memory of my father's heroism would pass, the family would scatter, and Cooper's Falls would be only a name on a map without a living soul attached to it.

I pushed on into the afternoon, farther and farther north, closer to home. By early afternoon the sun was gone, the sky the color of my gray suede driving gloves. The radio reported a blizzard developing in the Dakotas and in the western edges of Minnesota. Swinging north, following the river at the Wisconsin-Minnesota border, darkness began and it was no longer as warm inside the car. It seemed as if the fan blowing warm air had slowed, so I reset the temperature controls upward and stopped to refuel. The service station attendant seemed never to have seen the workings of a Lincoln before and had no theories about the failure of the heating system.

Back on the road, which was now a simple two-lane strip cut between banks of fir trees which grew thickly almost to the roadside, I began thinking of the man in the sheepskin coat, wondering if there could be some connection between two such curious events—the telegram from Cyril in Buenos Aires and the attempt to kill me in a blizzard on a highway in Wisconsin. But that was absurd. Surely, I had been victimized by coincidence, and nothing more. Such violence is terribly complex once you begin to analyze it and realize that there is no apparent motive.

For the last stage of the journey, I turned off on a trunk highway, blacktopped, narrow, totally dark. There was no moon; no starlight; no other travelers. I turned the radio off. There were forty miles yet to go and the fans suddenly stopped blowing altogether.

There was no heat in the car and what little there had been was quickly dissipated. I stopped in the middle of the road and wrestled my own sheepskin coat out of the back seat and struggled into it, afraid to open the door to the harsh wind. Snow eddied across the frozen snow adhering to the blacktop. It seemed as if I'd been engulfed in a thick blowing fog.

Driving on, it became colder and colder. At first my hands hurt, stung with cold, then they began to lose feeling. I tried to stomp feeling back into my feet. My breath began to freeze in my mustache, in the hair in my nose. Passing familiar turns in the road, I knew I had twenty miles yet to go. I turned the radio back on. They kept saying that it was very cold, that a blizzard was on the way, that it was twenty-five degrees below zero in Duluth.

The car was trying to kill me, I thought. Maybe the Lincoln, which was behaving so uncharacteristically, could accomplish what the man in the sheepskin coat hadn't. What in the hell was the matter with the heating, anyway? I fastened my eyes on the Lincoln's hood ornament, pretended that in some miraculous way the chrome ornament was pulling the car through the frozen night. I remembered a movie I'd seen as a child in which there was a motion picture studio called Miracle Productions. Their slogan said: "If it's worth seeing, it's a Miracle."

And finally, in the ragged nick of time, I made the final turn through the trees and eased back off the gas. In front of me were the two stone towers at the entrance to the drive, the gates of my childhood where Cyril and I had waited for the school bus. I sat there, half frozen but forgetting my discomfort for the moment, grinning. Nobody, nothing had killed me. It was still January 20, and I was home at last.

Poplars lined the stretch of road, forming a discreet natural barrier between the Coopers and the curious world: now, in winter, the lights of the Lincoln picked them out against the blackness like gaunt survivors of a death march. Beside the gate on the right was a stone gatehouse with a heavy oak door and long, ancient-looking hinges. During the war years Cyril and I had come down to play with the soldiers who were young and bored and very happy not to be crawling along Omaha Beach. We had touched the Garand rifles and climbed on the jeep and on a few memorable occasions we had gone into town on errands with the soldiers in the jeep, the wind tearing at us as we laughed with the excitement of it all. There are still photographs somewhere of Cyril and me in our regulation suntans, clip-on Army ties neatly in place, properly fitted out with insignia and caps, uniforms our guards had given us one Fourth of July.

The snow was deep and smooth in the driveway. The wind raked off the road, across the immense lawn, and only the vaguest outline in the drifts against the shrubbery indicated the path of the driveway. I chanced it with the new snow tires and slowly but firmly the Lincoln settled into the snow and worked its way forward.

In a while I saw the house, the elms and oaks which shaded the lawn in summer, the veranda which seemed long as a football field, the six squared white columns rising all three stories to the roof with its own tier of cupolas, chimneys rising out of the roof in faint shadows.

The house was dark. There would have been a light for me if Cyril had arrived. He wouldn't have gone to bed, not with me on my way. He wasn't here yet. The snow had held him up. No one was here. I left the car running and plodded calf-deep through the virgin snow. I had decided to spend the night in the cottage down by the little private lake on which we'd sailed and ice skated as children: it had always been my favorite spot. But first, hopelessly cold and tired as I was, I wanted to step inside the great house itself. Five years. . . . I had been away five years and all that time the key to the front door remained on my ring. Turning my back against the wind churning along the veranda, I fitted key to lock and stepped into the front hall.

My footsteps echoed in the parquet-floored entry. Reflexively I reached for a switch, snapped it, saw a dim yellowish light come on against the wall. The yellow shaded bulbs had been fitted into the old gas fixtures. Although the house was no longer lived in, arrangements had been made for Emil Blocker, who had been the caretaker for forty years, to come by once a week with his wife and keep it dusted, clean. I stood looking the length of the foyer as it widened to take in the huge, gently sloping staircase. On either side there were sliding doors, opened, giving on shadowy expanses of drawing rooms. I had grown up running wildly through these rooms, playing tag and hide-and-seek with Cyril, making far too much noise and being hushed by our nanny or grandfather's secretary. Now I couldn't even summon up a ghost. I had never felt more alone in the stillness, listening to the wind and snow outside, the inevitable banging of something that had come loose at the back of the house.

I went through one drawing room, turned on another light, and walked into the library. It had been my refuge in the house from early on, even before I could read the books. My grandfather would let me sit in a huge leather chair, cracked and split and incredibly ancient, while I turned the pages of encyclopedias and historical atlases and obscure magazines which have long since passed out of existence.

Now the room looked as warm and comforting as ever, as if my grandfather had just gone up the stairs to retire for the evening. Logs had been laid in the cold grate opposite his desk with its brass student lamps. Books lining the walls had been dusted. The World War II position map was still punctuated with colored pins. I stepped closer to it and realized that my grandfather had been refighting the German breakthrough in the Ardennes during the winter of 1944-45, called the Battle of the Bulge ever after, when he had died.

Another series of pins, all white, marked the corridor which was to have been used for Hitler's escape at war's end. A realist at all times, my grandfather had always labeled those who thought the escape route might actually have been used as "romantic idlers." Hitler was dead, and in my grandfather's view Hitler's fate had been earned by his own gross excesses and perversity, was richly deserved for having squandered his chances.

But there was still a good deal of wallspace given over to framed and frequently autographed photographs of my grandfather in the company of world leaders. There was even one of him puffing a token cigar with Winston Churchill when Churchill was alone in the wilderness of the 1930's. My grandfather was, of course, at political swords' points with Churchill but admired him enormously. Most of the black-and-white photographs were, however, efforts to capture forever moments with the Nazi leaders: sitting in slatted lawn chairs in slanting late afternoon sunlight with Hitler in some flower garden, chatting with Hitler and Eva Braun at a table laden with the remains of a casual luncheon while a pair of German shepherds drowsed at their feet, peering intently at a bottle of wine being exhibited by von Ribbentrop, who bears an expression of such vacuous arrogance as to be laughable, standing by an immense Mercedes-Benz touring car with a vague smile on his face as if trying to ascertain the reason for Goering's obvious mirth.

There were also a great many family pictures, one of which showed me holding a baseball bat, wearing a Chicago Cubs cap, smiling at my grandfather, who wears a characteristic suit and tie. There were pictures of my father, young and quietly concerned, and my mother laughing, holding my little sister Lee, who died. . . .

The house was moaning in the wind and there was no point in standing in the library getting sentimental. I was very tired. I took a bottle of Napoleon brandy from a cart against the wall by the large, functional globe, and went back outside, turning off the lights and closing the front door.

I let the Lincoln roll back into the whiteness, eating it up, down around behind the house, following the railing barely visible over the snow drifts. Inside the car it was still ice cold. But I was all right. I parked beneath the blackened branches of an oak tree which in summer shaded the cottage.

I got the bags out of the trunk, hauled my gear into the cottage. The screened porch was deep with snow and in the light I could see that the cottage was not kept up as carefully as the main house. It had a mildly stale quality and as I stood in the faintly musty room I realized what was missing, what I'd noticed in the library, in the foyer: cigar smoke. The house still retained the aroma.

The furnishings were wicker, flowered cushions of green and summer yellow against white painted wicker. It was very cold in the cottage and I stacked wood in the fireplace in the living room, checked the flue for snow and birds' nests, and lit it, listened to the dry birch and oak crackle in the flame. Then I went to the bedroom, saw that the bed was made, and laid another smaller fire in the bedroom fireplace, lit it.

While the house was warming up I went around opening all the windows a crack to get rid of the stale smell. Then I went to the kitchen, found that it was stocked with certain necessities, and made coffee in a glass percolator on a gas burner. I lit my pipe of Balkan Sobranie and the two smells, coffee and tobacco, began to fill the house, along with the dry burning wood, getting rid of the closed-up dead smell. I poured a cheese glass of brandy and toasted my homecoming.

It was something past midnight when I took a cup of coffee into the bedroom. I brought with me *Blandings Castle* by Wodehouse, a dog-eared copy which had probably been in the wicker bookcase for forty years, my brandy, and my pipe. I bunched the pillows up behind me and pulled the covers up to my chin. There was a dim bedside lamp and the shadows from the fireplace crackled, danced on the walls and ceiling. I listened to the wind as I read and sipped my coffee and brandy and smoked my pipe and I felt safe and secure, the way I'd felt as a child in the cottage.

I wasn't wondering where Cyril was and I wasn't thinking about the man in the sheepskin coat. It would all be all right and in the morning I'd get it all straightened out.

Then, exhausted, I turned off the lamp and slipped into a deep, dreamless sleep.

Seven

THE morning was good. I felt cold and clean and rested. My head ached only slightly as I stood in front of the glowing embers in the grate. I put my underwear and socks in a bureau drawer, put on corduroy trousers, high-strapped cavalry boots, and another pullover with no bloodstains on it.

The air outside was crisp, triggering an avalanche of memories as I stepped onto the porch. The sky was the same eerie white as the landscape, divided by a ridge of firs in the distance like a piece of abstract art. There was no sound but the wind, no movement but wisps of snow skidding across the crust. The thermometer by the door told me it was exactly zero where I was standing and after a moment I went back inside and put on my sheepskin coat and heavy, fleece-lined gloves.

The Lincoln sat quietly in the snow, graceful, dignified, wounded. Its tracks and my own from the night before were completely filled in by the new snow. It cracked and squeaked as I walked, following the driveway as best I could, circling around the lawn away from the house, past the gazebo and the trout pond toward the other set of stone gates closer to the town.

Standing in the shelter of a grove of firs, I stared back at the house. For a moment I thought I saw a wisp of smoke curl up from the chimney. But no, it had to be snow swirling off the slate roof. When I looked again it was gone, a curtain of blowing snow separating me from the house.

It was nine o'clock and I was going to walk to town. It was dry and cold walking along the road, protected by the thick trees on either side of me forming a natural corridor. Above me snow circled, lashed into the trees. At ground level, it was quiet and the walk of a mile went quickly until I was standing by the great square park at the edge of town. I hadn't seen a car or another human being.

Holidays in summer had been spent at the park. Cyril and I had grown up saluting our fallen war dead and the nation's loftier principles in the park, sweating in the summer sun and drinking frosty bottles of beer from ice-filled washtubs and listening to the town band in the tiny, exquisite shell. Behind the band shell I had made love to a girl from the high school, my first time, tugging at her clothes, full of urgency. In the center of the park stood a bronzed doughboy of the Great War, gesturing countless invisible comrades onward with an arm raised, clutching his rifle. On the base of the statue there were tablets with names of the boys from Cooper's Falls who had died over there, over there. . . .

Walking on, I came to the corner of the park nearest the business district, which lay oddly quiet in the snow. There were perhaps a dozen cars parked along the curbs and finally one passed me stealthily, quietly in the snow. Standing in the corner of the park was a tall nineteenth-century figure, lean and stern and bearded, holding a book in one hand: the first Cooper of Cooper's Falls—one of my ancestors frozen forever, doomed to spend his own eternity watching the sleepy world of Cooper's Falls from the grassy corner of the park.

Not really conscious of what I was doing, I walked past Brill's Drugstore, the Cooper's Falls Cafe, past the imposingly somber Cooper's Falls Hotel, which looked exactly the same as it had in my youth: rich, opulent, more like a club, reflecting the money which hallmarked the town. And there was the tiny frame library, trimmed in gingerbread, a miniature example of the curlicued sort of wooden structure which was so big in Mother Goose's day. The Cooper's Falls library was her "A material," as we used to say when I was in the network television business. I had never been able to resist it.

Almost reflexively I went up the steps and into the

library. A gas heater in the middle of the room was working much too hard: the room was stifling. There was no one behind the rolltop desk, but after I'd slipped out of my coat and draped it across a chair I heard sounds from the back of the building, from behind the racks of Cooper's Falls *Leaders,* which I knew dated back to the very first issue, midway through the nineteenth century.

"Well, John Cooper, how are you?"

I turned around, the voice vaguely familiar, and saw Paula Smithies, a very pretty girl who had one summer gone to bed a great deal with my brother Cyril.

"Why, Paula, for God's sake," I heard myself saying, knowing I was smiling at the sight of her. I hadn't seen Paula in nearly fifteen years and she was not only recognizable but far prettier as a woman than she'd been as a teen-ager. And she'd been pretty then. "How are you? What are you doing here?"

"I'm fine, John, just fine." Her face was pale, hair very dark and long and straight. She wore black framed glasses which were squared off and looked fine. "Would you believe I'm the librarian here now? I've come back to Cooper's Falls in my old age." She grinned openly, looking into my eyes.

"I thought you went off to California, was it California? Married a newspaperman. . . ." I was searching. She picked up a stack of antique *National Geographics.*

"That's right. And he went off to Vietnam for the L.A. *Times* and stepped on a land mine in Laos when he was supposed to be back in Saigon resting and I was a widow all of a sudden." She set the magazines down on a packing crate, pushed her glasses back with a forefinger. "That was three years ago and I stayed in L.A. for a while, working in a branch library but, God, have you ever lived in California, John? It's some sort of updated Dantean inferno—highways, overpasses, underpasses, cars, cars, cars, sunshine, smog, the Dodgers and the Rams, and the Lakers, drugs, and just unbelievable isolation." She reflected for a moment and flashed a nervous little smile. "Unbelievable. People do very peculiar things because they're

[29]

so insanely lonely. Things you're ashamed of afterward, things that eat away at your sanity when you think about them. . . ."

She asked me what I'd been doing and I told her that I'd been up to my ass in all the normal things: marriage, infidelity, writing books, working for the network, occupational alcoholism, divorce, too many pills, a long struggle back. Just the normal things. She laughed, shaking her head.

"Would you like a cup of coffee? Can you stand the heat in here? This damned thing has no idea of the meaning of restraint." She glared at the heater. "I was trying to open the windows in back when you came in."

I picked my way among the cartons of books and opened the windows overlooking the deep drifts between the library and a low stone wall.

"Cream and sugar?"

"Both," I said. It was nice, comfortable. We sat by her desk with a carton propped against the door holding it open. She lit a cigarette, gestured at the cartons, the stacks of file cards. "I've been back since last fall, living at home with Mother. It's very quiet here, boring, but so far I'm pleased by it—it gives me a chance to forget some things which are best forgotten. This job came from the state historical society. A friend of Mother's knew I was coming back and I think they set out to find me a useful, non-traumatic, worthwhile job and there hadn't been a librarian here for years, not since old Mrs. Darrow, you remember her, died. So, here I am, up to *my* ass in books and dust, cataloguing the whole thing." She blew smoke at the stacks. "It hasn't been catalogued since 1925! Christ." She laughed. "I get the feeling it's my life's work, penance for my sins, of which there are far too many." She grinned again, a tense little flicker at the corners of her wide pale mouth.

She was wearing a blackwatch skirt, a kilt actually, with a big gold safety pin, and a blue button-down Oxford-cloth shirt, polished penny loafers, blue knee-socks. It was a Wellesley outfit from the late fifties, when she'd gone to college. Somehow, in the Cooper's

Falls library, it didn't seem out of date: time had a tendency to stand still in Cooper's Falls. That thought surfaced as I watched her and I realized it had been in my mind ever since I arrived at the great house the night before. Time was standing still and as we chatted the morning away I also realized that Paula Smithies was a very attractive woman. I could see what it had been that had drawn Cyril to her: I hadn't even been mildly attracted to a woman in a long time and it was nice to feel it happening, however gently. There was something very pleasant about the fact that she was wearing a Peck and Peck outfit from another decade.

After I'd finished a pipe and the coffeepot was empty, I said that I'd come back to see Cyril. I told her about the telegram.

"I know why you've come back." She had turned serious. I didn't quite understand at first.

"You knew I was coming back?"

"Yes, actually I knew before you did. Cyril told me he was going to contact you, that he wanted you to come back and meet him here." She spoke matter-of-factly, but the hints of nervousness had flowered. She stood up, lit a cigarette, and threw the matches back onto her cluttered desk top.

"You've been in touch with Cyril?"

"Oh, yes, I've always been in touch with Cyril, even when I was married. And after my husband's death, Cyril was . . . very good to me, visited me in Los Angeles." She stood with her back to me as if she were studying the titles on the shelves. "And last week I came across some material here at the library, stuff that had been delivered to the library in boxes when your grandfather died. Books, old things that might fill gaps in our collection of town records, Cooper memorabilia, harmless old stuff that no one had even unpacked until I got into it last week." Finally she turned to look at me.

"I went through those papers very carefully, not at first, but once I realized there was something . . . peculiar about them, something I couldn't quite figure out." She paced past me, around behind her desk.

There was a vague queasiness in my stomach. I

scraped ash out of the pipe's bowl with a pipe nail, packed it again from my leather pouch. "What did you find, Paula?"

"Well, there were some diaries your grandfather had kept, and you can imagine what they were like. Full of day-by-day comments as he traveled through Europe hobnobbing with a lot of men who have passed into history. There were comments on the Nazis, some Italians—Count Ciano, who apparently amused your grandfather, some Englishmen. There were also some letters written in German." She looked back at me: "I don't read German. Do you?"

"No," I said lighting my pipe. "I never had the proper motivation to devote much time to a study of the Germans."

"Well, there were what seemed to be documents, bureaucratic directives, with broken seals, and so far as I could tell they had originated in Berlin. And there was a small metal strongbox, nothing pretentious . . . but it was locked and I left it alone." She stopped and looked at me quizzically.

"Go on, Paula. How did Cyril get into it?"

"Cyril. Yes, all right. Cyril got into it because he calls me every week, no matter where he is—Europe, Africa, anywhere. A couple of weeks ago it was Cairo, before that Munich, before that Glasgow, London . . . every week I get a long distance call and it's Cyril. Last week he called me from Buenos Aires and I told him about what I'd found. . . ."

"What did he say?" I was hypnotized by her recital.

"It was strange," she said, remembering. "First he laughed for a long time and when I asked him why he was laughing he said that it was all very funny because life was so carefully constructed, detail upon detail." She thought back: "Yes, detail upon detail. And then he gave me some instructions. He said I shouldn't mention it to anyone. No one at all." She lit a cigarette and sat down opposite me in the squeaky wooden swivel chair.

"Did he say anything else?"

"Only that he'd get in touch with you and that he'd be back here in Cooper's Falls this week. He said he'd be talking to me in person and he said something else. He said that it was no surprise to him . . . but he didn't say what it was."

I puffed my pipe and she said it was comforting to watch me puff my pipe and I said everyone should have a crutch. She laughed. "What do you think he meant?" We could hear the town clock chiming noon, muffled in the snow.

"Life is so carefully constructed, detail upon detail. . . . Well, I'm damned if I know," I said. "But apparently whatever you found, and God only knows what it means, it fitted with some theory of his. But why was he in Buenos Aires? And why didn't he get here on the twentieth?"

"The snow," she said. "That's the logical explanation."

"Yes, of course it is. The snow." I tamped the ash. "Can you come out to lunch?"

She smiled. "I've got to finish my day's work. I'm very compulsive."

"Well, why don't I stop back before I go to the house? You can come with me. We'll surprise him together."

"All right."

"Did he say anything else?"

"Only what he always says."

"And what's that?"

"That he loves me, John."

Eight

MY head was aching where the man in the sheepskin coat had clubbed me. When I left the library I walked back up Main Street, feeling snow blowing in my face. Trying to sort through what Paula Smithies had told me was making my head worse, so I climbed the steps to Doctor Bradlee's office over the drugstore. My childhood overtook me again as I smelled the antiseptic aroma I remembered so well. Everything was like that, full of emotional responses.

Doctor Bradlee's fingers pressed against the soft, squishy swelling underneath the thick layer of hair. I winced.

"Aha, that hurts, does it?" He had acted as if I'd been in for a visit just last week. He was an old man now, seventy something, but tremendously composed: bald, well over six feet, a serge suit and vest, plain gold cufflinks, nose like a banana, and piercing, intelligent eyes behind gold-rimmed spectacles. He breathed softly, always spoke with a very faint intimation of a smile at the corners of his thin-lipped mouth. Harry Bradlee had seen a great deal in his time.

He probed some more with his fingertips. "Looks as if somebody hit you with a . . . poker, perhaps? Heavy and sharp enough to break the skin. Nasty, but I expect you'll be all right. Any vomiting? Recurring nausea? You'd better tell me how this happened."

As I did, he finished attending to the wound, scratched out a prescription, and arranged himself carefully behind his desk. Through the window I could see that snow was falling hard again. He listened, leaning back, watching me, hands anchored around the arms of the chair.

"You didn't report this to the police in Madison?" There was a hint of incredulity in his voice.

"No." I shook my head. "I know I should have but, my God, it was the middle of the night, I was dead tired, it was over, and I just wanted to lie down and go to sleep. And I didn't want to run the risk of having to stay in a Madison hospital a couple of days."

"Impatience," he said softly. "What a curse it must be. I remember the night you were born out at the house. Your grandfather was very excited and impatient." Doctor Bradlee smiled at me and stood up, his shoulders stooped with age. "When I finally came down those long stairs he was waiting in the foyer for me, waiting to hear the news, and when I told him he took me into the library, where your father was sound asleep on a couch and we toasted you, all three of us, with champagne your grandfather had had on ice for a week."

I nodded. He patted me on the arm and told me to get some extra sleep, take some of the pills if my head got worse, and to check back in a couple of days. He hadn't bothered to ask why I was home after so long a time. Maybe time had no particular meaning for him.

I stopped back at the library in midafternoon. Paula was typing file cards and smiled brightly, saying she had finished her tasks for the day and could be ready to leave in five minutes. While she busied herself in the back I glanced through some mystery novels, noted a couple of exotic titles, and hummed quietly to myself. I saw no point in asking to see the boxes of stuff from the house. It was none of my business: the Nazi thing was ancient history as far as I was concerned.

We drove back to the house in her car, a spiffy little yellow Mustang convertible; she called it her freedom symbol. She'd bought it in California and driven it back to Cooper's Falls. We stopped at a grocery store where I bought a few things for the cottage larder. The snow was positively gaudy, gathering an entire new thickness on the road. What the wind had blown from the trees was being replaced. The soldier in the park was only a vague shape, marching ever onward. My ancestor read his book.

The snow in the driveway was deeper. The lawn seemed to be a glacier. It took several minutes to plow through it but the Mustang was a determined little bastard and made it. Living through storms of this sort was like living through a war, and Paula and I were smiling when we got into the front hall, stomping our feet and shaking snow off.

"Well, he's not here yet," she said. "Let me make some coffee. Or would you like a drink?"

"Coffee would be fine. I just don't drink anymore, except for brandy or port."

"You should be very proud of yourself, John." She walked away from me toward the kitchen. She had long straight legs and I was admiring them when she looked back at me. "Why not lay a fire?" she said.

I put a match to the wood stacked in the library grate, warmed my hands before the flames. Darkness was coming on outside. The heavy drapes were drawn back and what lay beyond was a vast emptiness. When she came back in with the coffee I said: "Paula, I'm worried about Cyril. Why hasn't he arrived?"

"Look, why don't you call the telephone office? See if there have been any long-distance calls. And check the telegraph office. You haven't been here to receive any messages and he may have tried to get hold of you."

We sipped the hot coffee, the fire crackled, and neither the telephone office nor Western Union had any record of incoming messages or calls. There was nothing to do but wait, and our conversation was desultory, random reminiscences.

Finally, to kill time, I said that I wanted to go upstairs and see my old room, go through my books, see if it was all still the same.

"Let me go with you," she said. "I don't want to be down here all by myself. Do you mind? That wind is driving me a little bit crazy."

I turned on the lights in the front hall, flipped the switch that should have turned them on in the second-floor hallway. Nothing happened. The lights upstairs must have been burned out. No one had used the second and third floor in a long time.

"It's strange being back here again," I said. "It gives me goose pimples."

"I know. I haven't been here since Cyril . . . brought me here. Years ago. . . ."

She followed me up the long stairs Doctor Bradlee had descended thirty-four years ago with the news of my birth. It was the same now. The house never changed.

In the hallway we stopped, accustoming our eyes to the gloom.

"John, there's a light down there."

I turned and saw the glow, the strip of light across the floor and on the wall. Something banged against

[36]

the back of the house in the wind. I felt for the wall switch but it didn't work either.

I could hear her breathing as she followed me down the hall toward the light. The light was coming from what had been my grandfather's bedroom. The closer I got the stranger I felt and I laughed nervously. "This is ridiculous. Why are we tiptoeing around?" We laughed in unison and she took my hand, squeezing it. Her palm was cold and damp. We went into the room together.

My brother Cyril was sitting in one of a pair of wing-backed chairs by the windows. His eyes were closed. He had slid or tilted to one side, his head lolling down on his shoulders, left arm extended stiffly over the arm of the chair.

"Cyril!" I shouted involuntarily.

Paula held my arm and bit her lip. "Oh, my God—"

It was perfectly obvious that my brother Cyril was dead.

Nine

DOCTOR BRADLEE arrived out of the blowing snow an hour and a half later, stomping his feet in the hallway, complaining about the intense cold. "I'm terribly sorry," he said as I took his heavy herringbone overcoat, "and on top of it all my car wouldn't start, just too damned cold for man, beast, or machine. Where's Paula? I'd better see her before I examine the deceased." It was an odd turn of phrase: he was talking about my brother Cyril.

Paula was sitting in the library staring into the fire. She had stopped crying and had drunk some brandy. We'd sat together in the library and waited, shocked and saddened, uneasy. My first reaction was one of curiosity rather than sorrow, actually, a result of the shock of coming upon him that way.

I poured some brandy for myself and waited in the parlor while Bradlee tended to Paula. When he came out, his face was drawn and tired; he was not as young as he used to be. "She'll be all right," he said. "She's quite strong. Awful experience for her, though, How close was she to your brother?"

"Quite close, apparently," I said.

"Well," he said, picking up his black pigskin Gladstone bag, the same one from my childhood full of rows of pill bottles, stethoscope, a blood pressure device. "Well, you never know, do you?" He walked out into the foyer and turned to me: "Where is he?" I nodded toward the stairs and he motioned me up, then followed.

Bradlee stood looking at my brother's body for a while. Cyril was wearing Levis, a white Oxford-cloth button-down shirt with the sleeves half rolled up. An identification bracelet he'd worn since his fourteenth birthday dangled from his wrist. On the table between the two wingbacked chairs stood a bottle of Courvoisier and a snifter with traces of brandy in the bottom. The bed was slightly rumpled, as if Cyril had catnapped.

Bradlee was bending over my brother, staring into the dead eyes, pulling the lids back. He was shaking his head, touching my brother's dead flesh. I walked across the room, stood at the window. My eyes flickered around the room, rested on the fireplace: charred remains of a fire, now cold and dead and fluttering in the downdraft. Had it been smoke I'd seen that morning after all, rising through the blowing snow?

"How long has he been dead?" I asked.

"Some time," Bradlee said, eyebrows furrowed. He fixed me from behind his gold-rimmed spectacles. "Might be twenty-four hours, it's really quite impossible to say until we take a closer look."

I nodded dumbly.

"John," Bradlee said slowly, rubbing his great banana nose with a forefinger, regarding Cyril's body, "there's something about this . . . it doesn't ring true to me and I can't quite put my finger on it. Apparently

[38]

his heart stopped beating and he slumped over and died." He shook his head. "But . . . you say you didn't know he was home?"

"No. I thought he hadn't gotten here yet. I was in the house last night and he wasn't here then."

"How do you know?"

"Well, I didn't see him, I didn't hear him."

"I'm going to notify the police. Now don't look that way. I'm merely going to report the death. In a case of this type, when we don't know when or how he died I suggest that we find out." He touched my sleeve. "Just to satisfy ourselves. We'll have to have an autopsy. You'll have to agree to that, my boy."

I nodded.

While Bradlee used the telephone, I fed logs into the library fireplace and told Paula what had happened upstairs.

"Does that mean that Doctor Bradlee thinks there might be something wrong?" She shivered against the back of the chair and drew her legs up underneath her. The wind howled outside.

"God knows," I said.

"I wonder what he was going to do here? It's so ironic. He came all the way from Buenos Aires to talk to you and to me, and now he's dead. So absurd, so futile. . . ."

I put my hand on her shoulder. I'd felt a prickling of my skin as she spoke. Bradlee was standing in the doorway, consulting his gold pocket watch which hung from a gold chain across his vest.

"I've called Olaf Peterson. He's new since your time here, chief of our little police force. He was a detective down in the Cities, made a name for himself in cracking a couple of murder cases, and then married an heiress involved in one of the cases and was suddenly a wealthy man, member of the White Bear Yacht Club, the Minneapolis Club because of his father-in-law, and he said the hell with being an underpaid, hardworking cop. Anyway, he came up here to live on a farm with a house overlooking the river and some of us asked him to help us out with our piddling little police work, on an advisory basis if nothing else, and now we pay him a dollar a year to be our police chief. He seems to enjoy it."

"What did he say?"

"He said he'd come on over and take a look if he can get his car out. It must be getting worse out there."

I put a Beethoven quartet on the phonograph and we all sat in the library, quietly, unable to get the idea of Cyril overhead, slumped, dead in a chair, out of our minds. The Nazis and my grandfather looked down at us from the library walls. Eventually we heard a car through the storm, saw headlights poking at the blowing snow. It was the third car in front of the house, snow piling up on them, and when I opened the door I saw that Olaf Peterson was driving a black four-door Cadillac sedan. He was smoking a cigar as he charged hurriedly up the walk.

"How are you?" he said. "I'm Olaf Peterson." He shook my hand.

Ten

OLAF PETERSON did not come out in the snow to stand around chatting, exchanging pleasantries about the Minnesota weather. He asked Bradlee where the body was and I followed them up the stairway. Paula was staying in the library. Peterson was of medium height, wore a rust-colored suede trench coat cut elegantly with a few strategically placed button flaps. He was dark, almost swarthy, more like a figure from the Levantine than from the fjords. He had a thick black mustache which curled down around the corners of his mouth. He was not at all what I had expected.

Standing in the master bedroom again, I watched him survey the scene with his chin cupped in a dark, hairy hand. His spatulate fingers were well manicured. He'd opened his trench coat, revealing a navy-blue fisherman's sweater underneath and a yellow shirt collar poking up against his chin. He had a very short, thick neck.

"Your brother," he said.

I nodded.

"You found the body," he said. "You didn't move anything."

I nodded.

"Miss Smithics—" He paused. He looked at Bradlee. "What was her late husband's name? Phillips?"

Doctor Bradlee nodded.

Peterson walked closer to the table at Cyril's side, stared down at the snifter and the corked bottle of Courvoisier. He knelt and looked at the lamplight through the bottle of Courvoisier. He pursed his lips and began to think out loud, a quality to which I became inured. "For the sake of argument, let's say he opened this bottle—that it was a fresh bottle. This house has no regular, full-time occupants drinking a bit of brandy now and then, so we have the odds with us there. There is very nearly half a bottle of brandy that has been drunk." He looked up smiling broadly, incongruously, reminding me of a standup comic delighted by his own old and weary joke, laughter in the audience. "Now, there is either a hell of a lot of Courvoisier inside Cyril Cooper or"—he paused for some kind of effect—"or there was someone else sitting here drinking it with him. And if there was someone else here, I'd like to talk to him." He beamed and then immediately dropped his smile and scowled at me: "This is the part of being a detective I simply *love*. The easy part, Mr. Cooper. Obviously, you've had a nasty shock tonight. You didn't kill him yourself, did you? No, I didn't think so."

"I've driven all the way from Boston in answer to a telegram from him," I said. "He wanted me to meet him here on the twentieth."

"You're late, Mr. Cooper." He wasn't looking at me anymore. He jammed the poker into the ashes, clanged it against the grate.

"No, as a matter of fact, I wasn't late. I arrived last night, late last night."

"And why didn't you find him then, I wonder?"

"Because he wasn't here. At least—"

"You were in this room last night, then?"

"No, I—"

"But you were in the house last night? You slept here?"

"No."

"No? I thought you said you arrived last night. Perhaps I am merely confused. . . ." His back was to me. Bradlee was extracting a cigarette from a gold case, tapping it on the lid.

"I did arrive last night. I came into the house about eleven o'clock, poked around downstairs for a few moments, then took a bottle of brandy from the library and drove down to the cottage by the lake and slept there."

"And you didn't see your brother?"

"Obviously not."

"Was it snowing hard, Mr. Cooper?"

"Yes, very hard, and blowing."

"And you saw no automobile tracks leading to the house?"

"No, it was flat snow, drifted."

"But it was very dark?"

"Yes, very. No moon, no light."

"Well"—and he finally turned around to face me—"you didn't see any signs of your brother's arrival because, I suspect, he had arrived earlier, Mr. Cooper, and whatever signs there might have been were no longer visible." He grinned. "And please understand that I am theorizing, merely theorizing." Then the grin disappeared. "On the other hand, I'll bet I'm right." He turned to Bradlee, who was watching him with a hint of a smile. "I've seen a hell of a lot of corpses, Doctor, and I'd say this one has been dead a good twenty-four hours." He looked at his watch, a small, delicate gold square against the black hair. "You, Mr. Cooper, have been home just about twenty-four hours. It's all very ironic, isn't it? You drive all this way, through all the snow, and you may have arrived here within—what?—minutes of your brother's death." He shook his head. "Where was your brother coming from, Mr. Cooper? I know he hasn't been back here in a long time, but where was he coming from?"

"Buenos Aires," I said. "At least that's where the telegram came from."

"My God, Buenos Aires," he mused. "A long way to come to fall over and die, isn't it?"

We were following him down the stairway when Bradlee asked me how my head felt. Before I could answer, Peterson said: "And what's the matter with your head, Mr. Cooper?" He kept on walking.

"Somebody tried to kill him on the road," Bradlee said.

"You're kidding!" Peterson stopped at the bottom of the stairs with a smile of unalloyed amazement on his dark features, beneath the thick mustache. "You are definitely kidding!"

"No, Mr. Peterson," I said edgily. "I'm not kidding. I'm delighted that the revelation amuses you, but I'm not kidding."

Peterson chuckled and went through the parlor into the library, where Paula sat reading a huge volume from a matched set of Dickens, *Bleak House*. He smiled at Paula, made some comment I missed, and sat down in a leather chair by the fireplace.

"Listen, do you folks have a few minutes?" He was all humility. "This is all so interesting. I'd like to ask you a few questions, try to get done by midnight . . . okay?" He was suddenly all folksy warmth. The changes in Olaf Peterson came so fast that it was making my head ache again.

"I could make coffee," Paula said, smiling faintly at me. "I'm the world's champion. Coffeemaker, that is. I seem to do so damn much of it."

"That would be fine, Miss Smithies." Peterson looked at Bradlee and me. "Fix us all some coffee. We could all use some coffee, I'm sure." She went away. "You say she was a close friend of your brother's."

"Yes."

"Very close?" I nodded.

"Oh, boy," he said, lighting up an absurdly slender

[43]

cigar. "Now, tell me all about the attempt on your life, Mr. Cooper."

I told him.

"And you didn't go to the police? Or the hospital? You just went to Howard Johnson's and sort of curled up and called it a day?" His eyebrows, bushy and dark, were inching upward.

"You've got it," I said. "I was tired, the incident was over, and if I felt worse in the morning I could check in at a hospital then."

"But, Mr. Cooper, aside from your own health, you were involved in an attempted murder. You had seen close-up the men who tried to kill you, you had seen their automobile, and you knew what sort of damage it had sustained in bumping you off the road." He stared at me balefully. "And yet you didn't report any of that to the police. Or the highway patrol." He pursed his lips beneath the smudge of mustache. "Mr. Cooper, your behavior in this instance borders on the criminally stupid."

I stared into the flickering fire.

"And you're not a particularly stupid man, are you, Mr. Cooper? Are you?"

"Peterson, I had a good deal on my mind. I was alive and I was moving again. There was a storm going on that night that—I'm not sure I can make this clear—that seemed to make everything different. Another time I'd probably have done all those things I should have done. But that night I didn't. And if your contribution to these proceedings is going to be to tell me that I'm criminally stupid, then you, Peterson, can take your funny little cigars, your suede coat, and your darling little hairpiece and stick them all right up your ass." I stopped for breath, my voice shaking.

"You could see that?" he asked me, his face a map of concern.

"See what?"

"The hairpiece? You could tell?"

"Don't let it worry you. I used to work in television in New York. You get to recognize little rugs like that one. It's a nice one, Peterson."

"Twelve hundred bucks and he sees it"—he snapped

his fingers—"just like that! Christ! Well, anyway"—ignoring my outburst—"what was on your mind? What were you thinking about so hard you didn't report the fact that two guys tried to kill you?"

"Well, I was thinking about my family."

For the first time his eyes moved across the walls, taking in the photographs. Himmler, Goering, Hitler smiled benignly upon us.

"*That* I can understand," he said, making a face. "Go on, what were you thinking about your family?"

"I suppose I was just reminiscing, really. I don't think much about the family, I haven't for a long time. But driving home I had the chance and I indulged myself. And I thought about my brother. I wondered why he wanted me to come home to meet him." I fidgeted with my pipe. Paula came back in with the coffee in mugs.

"You didn't know *why?*" Peterson said. "You came all this way without knowing why? Mr. Cooper, you are just full of surprises."

I looked at Paula as she handed me the cup. Almost imperceptibly she shook her head. All right, I thought to myself, calculating, I won't mention the papers she'd found. Eventually, though, we'd have to tell somebody.

"No, he gave no reason at all. He just said he'd meet me here on the twentieth and I came."

Peterson drank some coffee, smiled up at Paula.

"That's the way Cyril and I are."

"Were," Peterson corrected me.

"Were," I said.

"How's his head, Doctor?"

"He'll be all right, but somebody hit him very hard, Olaf. He's a very fortunate fellow."

Peterson got up without speaking and went through the passageway leading to the kitchen.

Doctor Bradlee ground a cigarette into an ashtray, balanced his mug on the arm of his chair. Paula closed her eyes, her face drawn but expressionless.

"There are certain things to be done, John," Bradlee said. "We've got to get Cyril into town so we can do the autopsy in the morning. And I think we should notify Arthur Brenner. Of all people, Arthur should be told at once. He's been through it all with you Coopers; he's next to being a member of the family."

"Do you think I should call him now?" I looked at the Rolex. "It's nearly midnight."

"I think you should, yes. Arthur will still be up, either playing with his kiln or reading. Call him, you owe it to him."

Eleven

ARTHUR BRENNER was nursing a very bad cold. His rich deep voice showed the wear and tear of coughing and sneezing; he sniffled as I spoke to him. He was a calm and careful man, a fine lawyer and onetime diplomat, an experienced intelligence officer in time of war. Quietly, sniffling, he kept repeating, "I see, I see," asking simple, pertinent questions.

I explained that Olaf Peterson was there, that there would be an autopsy, just to get the record straight, since we had no idea as to why or when Cyril had died. I heard him sip his toddy.

"I see," he said slowly. "Whatever Olaf and Brad think is right should be done. And I think there are certain matters you and I should discuss. Cyril's estate, for one, which is substantial. Try not to let this thing throw you off your stroke. Death is a fact of life, as you well know, and a step we all take at one time or another. So be of good heart and come to see me in the morning. I'll be at my office after I stop by Brad's office for some penicillin. And, John—I'm glad you're here. Thank you for calling me."

Arthur Brenner was a Crisis Man, probably the most methodical and unexcitable man I had ever known. A complete and humane man, intellectually and philosophically sound, a rock, someone to cling to.

Peterson was fumbling around in the kitchen, slamming cupboard doors, clinking glasses, rattling papers. Bradlee was putting on his overcoat. "I'm going home." He yawned. He clasped my arm reassuringly. "We'll get someone out from the funeral home tomorrow morning. Really, there's nothing to be done yet tonight. Everything here will keep." He said goodnight to Paula and I followed him to the door. "I gave her a very gentle tranquilizer. She'll sleep all right." He patted my arm again, struggled with his car for a few moments, and then it came to life in the cold and began pushing through the deep snow.

When I got back to the library, Peterson was in his chair smoking another thin cigar. "Well, Mr. Cooper, I've taken up entirely too much of your time this evening." He was being judicious now; after all, my brother was dead upstairs. "However, there are a couple of curious points before I go. When you arrived here last night did you go into the kitchen at all?"

"No. I poked my head into the parlor, walked through it to the library, stood in the foyer for a minute or two, and left. That's all." My eyes burned with fatigue. My head ached.

"You weren't smoking a cigar?" He peered at the ash on his own, flimsy, gray, delicate.

"No."

"And you didn't drink any brandy while you were here?"

"No."

"Come out in the kitchen with me for just a moment, will you? Excuse us, Miss Smithies."

I followed him through the passageway.

He pointed to a brandy snifter on the counter. Above it the cupboard door was open.

"Without touching it, would you just look at that snifter?"

I looked at it.

"So? I've looked at it."

"That's wonderful, Mr. Cooper. Now just walk down to the end of that counter and step on the foot-pedal of that little trash container."

[47]

I did. There was a dark mess in the bottom of the container: a cigar butt, ashes.

"All right," I said.

"Thank you, Mr. Cooper." His face split into a broad, toothy grin. "That's all. But do remember what you've seen. We may talk about it tomorrow. Ah, don't look so concerned. It's all just a game. A game."

In the front hall he buckled himself into the suede trench coat.

"Drop by my office tomorrow. We'll get this whole thing cleared up, autopsy results, the whole sad business. Will you be staying in the house tonight?"

"No, I'm going back to the cottage."

"Ah, of course. Well, do say goodnight to Miss Smithies for me." He paused in the open doorway. The hallway filled immediately with icy cold air. "And get a good night's sleep. You look like hell."

Back in the library Paula Smithies was staring at the rows of framed photographs on the walls. "My God, John," she said as I came back and slumped down in the chair behind my grandfather's desk, "this is simply incredible. It's like a museum. I've heard all about your grandfather's political connections, the whole Nazi thing, but looking at these photographs makes it all awfully real, like a *March of Time* news-reel, a documentary." I nodded and drained cold coffee from a cup. Her voice grew trancelike. "Austin Cooper and Hitler, Austin Cooper and von Ribbentrop, Austin Cooper and Speer, Austin Cooper and Goering, Austin Cooper and Mussolini, Austin Cooper and I don't know, there should be a photograph of your grandfather shaking hands with the devil."

"Oh, it must be there somewhere," I said.

She turned back to me, flexing her body. "Does it bother you?"

"No, not at all. I never think about it."

She slid back down in the chair, stared at me glassily. "What do you think of Mr. Peterson?"

"He's a smartass. An egomaniac and probably quite mad." I yawned. The sound of the wind and snow beating against the house had become part of my consciousness.

"What do you think he thought about it? What did he want you to go to the kitchen for?" She yawned too, shaking her head.

"I think he was showing off." I wondered if that was what I really thought or only what I wished. "He did a little number upstairs about how much brandy was left in the bottle that came right out of Sherlock Holmes. In the kitchen he showed me a brandy snifter and some garbage. I don't know what the hell he was talking about but he's a compulsive show-off, so he's bound to tell me tomorrow."

It was one o'clock and I went to the kitchen and popped a couple of pain pills Bradlee had given me. Paula heard the water running and came out and took the tranquilizer.

"I should go home," she said.

"All right." As I helped her into her coat I said: "What about the documents, Paula? Peterson's going to have to know, I imagine, sooner or later."

"I don't know why," she said, buttoning up, collecting her leather patch bag and gloves. "What have those things got to do with Peterson?"

"Nothing, if Cyril died a natural death. But the way Bradlee reacted to the condition of the body, and then the way Peterson nosed around . . . well, I don't know, Paula, but if there was anything funny about Cyril's death—then Peterson's going to want a lot of answers to a lot of questions. And one of the questions is going to be, why did Cyril decide to come all the way home from Buenos Aires?" We were standing in the foyer looking at each other. I kept thinking that she was a very attractive woman, that Cyril had known a good thing when he'd seen it. She seemed so self-sufficient.

"Well, we can talk about it in the morning. Arthur would know what we should do."

We went out to start her car. It was deep under snow and I tried to brush it off with my arm. It was dry, soft like dust, incredibly cold. Paula slid in behind the wheel and turned the key, producing that aggravating grinding noise, again and again. I went behind the car to sweep the back window. The grinding got fainter and fainter. I went back to her and she looked up, smiling vaguely. "Well, surprise."

"It's too cold," I said. "It's not going to start, so forget it."

"I'll have to stay the night." Our breath hung in the air before us. Wind chewed at the naked branches of the trees overhead, blew snow in my face. Shaking her head in a spasm, she said: "I can't stay in the same house with Cyril, please, John, I can't."

"We'll go down to the cottage."

The way to the cottage was completely drifted. It was the sort of night you read about people losing their way twenty yards from the safety of their homes and freezing to death in the snow. We sank almost to our knees in it, slogged onward, Paula trying to follow in my tracks. There was almost no moon, no light at all, but finally we staggered onto the small porch. "God," she gasped. "Are we here?" Everything was becoming increasingly unreal. It was as if we'd entered another life, full of cold and death and menace, and we were very tired.

Immediately I laid fresh fires in the living room and the bedroom, poured us brandy, made sure the doors were locked. "You can sleep in the bedroom." I got the fires going. "I'll take the couch out here."

"All right," she said slowly. "I can feel those tranquilizers. They're just creeping right up my spine, or down it." She giggled. "You've got to excuse me. I'm getting punchy." She paused. "We just found Cyril a few hours ago." Tears streaked her cheeks. We were standing in the doorway to the bedroom and I put my arms around her and held her against me.

"It's going to be all right," I said. "We're going to get it all straightened out tomorrow. It'll stop snowing and we'll go to town and get everything straightened out."

"I hope so." She turned her face to me and I kissed her softly on the mouth. Her lips were dry and she clung to me like a child. I stroked her hair. Then I told her to go to bed and I went back into the living room. The couch faced the fireplace and the room was getting pleasantly warm. I found a blanket in a closet and threw it across the couch. I went to the front door, unlocked it, peered outside at the thermometer. The reading was twenty-eight below zero and with the wind God only knew what the wind chill factor must have been. Sixty, seventy below.

I came back in, locked the door again, and went back to the bedroom door. Paula was in bed, smiling at me, covers pulled up to her chin.

"Are you all right?"

"Yes." She nodded slowly, slipping under the tranquilizer. "I'm all right. And thank you for being so nice to me." Her voice was low and soft. "We'll talk more tomorrow."

I went to the chair and picked up my robe. She reached out and took my hand. "Kiss me goodnight," she mumbled. I leaned over and brushed my lips across her cheek and she smiled, young-looking and terribly vulnerable, a woman who had been through a lot in her lifetime and had somehow not been spoiled by it, had handled it all. And my brother Cyril had loved her.

"Tomorrow we'll take this whole thing to Arthur," I said from the doorway, "and he'll tell us what to do. Arthur will take care of the whole thing." But she was asleep and couldn't hear me.

Twelve

IN the bright gray haze of morning Paula and I stood in the snow and watched the men from the funeral home bring Cyril out the front door and slide him into their black van. The young men who were doing the carrying slipped in the snow with their burden, swore under their breath, cheeks and ears whipped cheery winter red by the wind. One of them came over to me, muttered something, and with stiff fingers

I had to sign something. I had to shake the ballpoint pen: the ink was too cold to feed out onto the paper. Then they drove slowly away like a ship carving its way through deep breakers.

The Lincoln started on the second try. It was forty degrees below zero. I let the immense engine idle for several minutes while we went inside and finished our coffee and toast. We didn't say much but she smiled at me rather shyly from time to time as if she was remembering last night's kisses, not Cyril's death.

The heater didn't work, of course, so we huddled in the front seat and I let the 462-cubic-inch engine with its 340 horsepower slowly off its leash. It shimmied slightly in the snow and then began inching forward. It was a long way through snow that was over the bumper but as long as I held back on the gas pedal it just kept burrowing ahead, past the trees in a wide arc and on up the grade to the road. The road to town had been plowed and I accelerated just enough to send us hurtling through the barrier of piled frozen snow.

Arthur Brenner's life was divided into halves, each of which gave him great, enduring pleasure: his office in the Cooper's Falls Hotel, where he was a man of affairs, where he practiced law, where he wrote his articles and advised those who sought his counsel, and his home, which was where he indulged himself in the art of porcelain—the creation of porcelain sculptures, firing, painting, displaying them. I had heard him say, when questioned about his hobby, that a man with the patience and nerve and steadiness of hand to master porcelain was not an altogether inappropriate choice to lead one through the pitfalls and menaces the law sometimes held.

And, now, holding the door for us, he looked all that I had remembered and hoped for. He was a tall man of considerable girth, gray hair thinning over a broad kind face, a face quick to open laughter which made him seem at times younger than his seventy years and at other times implacable and eternal. He smiled now, held out his hand to Paula, then to me.

The office was comfortable: the draperies were pulled back, allowing that bright grayness into the room; the ceilings were fourteen feet and the bay window looked out onto Main Street, commanding an unobstructed view of its entire length.

He led us to a grouping of three chairs in the bay of the window and when we were both seated in the comfortable chintz-covered chairs he lowered his own 250 pounds into the third.

"Let me say first how very sorry I am about Cyril. It's a sad homecoming, a hell of a note." He cocked his massive head and peered at me from behind heavy-lidded eyes. "How are you? You look wonderfully well, but Doctor Bradlee tells me you were set upon and left for dead by highwaymen. Can such things be?"

I related the curious matter of the inefficient thugs and he sat massaging a close-shaven jowl, shaking his head, widening his eyes in amazement at the proper moments. He popped a match on his thumbnail and rolled a cigar on his tongue, lighting it evenly. When I finished he leaned forward and looked from one of us to the other, bushy eyebrows raised. *"Can* such things be?" He sighed. "Of course they can. Life is full of such acts of violence, meaningless, tortured, psychotic. But still . . . I sicken at the thought of it. Are you recovering adequately? Good. You're a very fortunate fellow they were so sloppy in their work habits." He blinked at me as if he were looking past me. "There's really no excuse for your being here after such an elaborate charade." I remembered it; it seemed for an instant to be happening again: I felt the impact, felt the Lincoln slipping away in the snow. . . .

Arthur was speaking again and I hadn't been listening.

"I beg your pardon, Arthur?"

"I say, why did Cyril want you to meet him here? What was the purpose of his summons?"

"That's what we want to talk to you about. You see, I had no idea of the purpose of any of it, none whatsoever." Paula was looking out the window, apparently wrapped in her own thoughts, despair: I

[53]

wondered if she would eventually break down from the shock and what must have been her deeply felt grief. "And I wouldn't have known at all if I hadn't stopped in at the library yesterday morning. Sheer coincidence. I went to the library and found Paula."

Paula came out of her reverie without hesitation; she'd been listening after all. "And I told John two things about Cyril. I told him that Cyril and I had been lovers for years, that we had been in weekly contact for a long time no matter where Cyril had been. And I also told him why Cyril had asked him to come back."

Arthur Brenner leaned back contentedly in the sea of chintz and lifted his right leg up onto an embroidered gout stool. His nose was red from his cold and he produced a wad of Kleenex from his sweater sleeve. He was wearing a heavy cardigan with leather buttons, a tattersall checked shirt, a heavy brown-knit tie. His whole bulk shuddered when he blew his nose and watching him I felt like a small boy again.

"And why was that, Paula?" he asked, his voice soft and reassuring. "Why had Cyril asked John to come home?"

"Because of what I found in the boxes," she said, "boxes from the house, things that had been in Austin Cooper's estate. You see, they'd been packed up in boxes years before, twenty or thirty years before at least, and they must have been stored away in an attic . . . or a basement, somewhere." She cleared her throat, toyed with a slim silver bracelet. "Anyway, the boxes had been shipped down to the library—for the librarian to sort through them. There was nothing but magazines and books so far as anyone looking at the boxes could see. But the thing was, the librarian's job here has always been a sort of part-time thing and instead of being sorted out and catalogued the boxes were stored away in the storm cellar beneath the library. No one ever bothered to look at them until I went down to the cellar a couple of weeks ago."

"But, my dear," Arthur said patiently, wheezing slightly, "what was it that you found in those boxes?" He smiled. "Surely not Austin's old love letters."

He chuckled quietly and took Paula's hand, hid it in his own huge hand. "That would never have been reason to come home."

"There were diaries, Mr. Brenner, diaries of Austin Cooper's trips to Germany, France, Spain, England, and Scandinavia during the 1920's and 1930's."

Arthur shook his head, as if to say *not good enough.* "Well-tilled soil I should say, very well tilled, indeed." He pulled on the huge black cigar. "Nothing else?"

"Yes, there was something else."

"And what was it, my dear?"

"There were documents in German. I couldn't read them, of course, but there were names—very famous names, some I didn't know, and they were addressed to Austin Cooper. There were envelopes with seals and no stamps as if they had never been intended to go through the mails. It was all—I don't quite know—very *official*-looking, if you see what I mean."

Arthur raised himself slowly out of the chair and walked carefully to the window, stared down into the street. The light shifted with the movement of blowing snow but the gray glare remained. His head was wreathed in thick cigar smoke. Paula looked at me inquiringly.

"Yes, I see what you mean," he said finally, "but I don't understand this business of documents. You say this is why Cyril asked John to come home? Curious, I should say. Curious at the very least."

"He laughed when I told him and then he said he thought it was funny, that life was so carefully constructed, detail upon detail. He told me I shouldn't tell a soul. He said he'd contact John and be here in person to talk to me this week." She smiled weakly. "He sounded so happy that he was going to be here . . . we'd been talking on the telephone for so many months." Brenner turned to her expectantly. "He called me each week" she said, "from wherever he was—Cairo, Munich, Glasgow, London, and finally this last call from Buenos Aires."

Arthur thumped his hand on the back of the chair. "I don't understand it. Why in the name of God would he come all the way back here, summon John all the way from Cambridge, just because you came across a bunch of Austin's old Nazi junk? Who gives a damn about Nazis anymore, anyway?" He snorted, Kleenex at the ready. "And that solemn portentous telegram, FAMILY TREE NEEDS ATTENTION, now what the devil does that mean? And then he comes home secretly, goes upstairs, has a brandy, and dies. By gad, if Cyril were here I'm afraid I'd be short-tempered with him. All this obscurity!"

"The point is," I said, "that we don't know why he decided to come back, nor why he asked me to come back. We know certain facts but we don't know the one big fact: *why*."

He slowly levered himself down into the chair. Except for a flareup of gout, Arthur Brenner did not seem an old man.

"You know as well as I do that Cyril Cooper was never capricious, Arthur. If he wanted me back here, well then he had a perfectly good reason. The problem is that we have not been able to figure it out."

Paula looked at me, then at Brenner, touched the huge safety pin on her blackwatch kilt. "Cyril knew something we don't know, then."

"Of course he did, my dear," Arthur said. "He knew why the devil *he* came back—which is everything at this point. Well, there's the will," Arthur said, changing the subject. "Fairly simple, really, John. You get it, most of it. Several million dollars, my boy, and what do you think of that?" A smile split the broad face and his eyes glistened. "You see, there was no one else to leave it to . . . although, and I thought it odd until this morning, there was one other substantial bequest." He fixed Paula with those pale blue eyes. "One-quarter of a million dollars for you, my dear." As I watched him I saw that there were tears welling up in his eyes. Quickly he snuffled and blew his nose, furtively wiping them from the corners of his eyes. The Coopers were his family.

Finally, Paula began to sob quietly, her fingers clenching and working in the kilt. As for myself, I had not quite taken in the fact that I was suddenly a multimillionaire. The whole thing seemed faintly absurd. It was Cyril's money; the family's had been mostly wrapped up in foundations.

"Well, I suppose we'd better take a look at those damned documents," Arthur said grimly. "Damned nonsense and a waste of time." He sighed. "But I can't see what else there is to do, can you, John?"

"No, I can't. We're going to have to look at the damned papers." I hated it, the thought of prying into Austin Cooper's Nazi world. I hadn't realized how much I hated it all, but as I sat there in the chintz, it hit me, waves of revulsion. What had Austin Cooper's peculiar political preferences to do with me? But there it was. In the end you never escaped your past. It lay in wait for you, somewhere in your future.

Arthur looked at his watch, went slowly to the desk, and consulted his calendar. "I have an appointment at one o'clock and I will certainly want a nap after that. What do you say to five o'clock, Paula? John, you could perhaps stop by here at four thirty and we could go to the library together. Paula?"

"Yes, I'll be at the library. . . . I think Cyril would have wanted us to turn to you." She had dried the tears. I was very happy that Cyril had left her some money. At least, she would never have to worry about money again.

We left Arthur together and in the lobby I heard someone call my name. When I turned, the fellow behind the desk smiled obsequiously at a Cooper boy and said that there was a call for me.

It was Olaf Peterson.

"How's the head, Mr. Cooper?"

"All right," I said noncommittally.

"Well, that's good to hear. We'd hate to lose another Cooper. You're the last of the Coopers, you see, the very last one."

"Did you want something, Mr. Peterson?"

"Well, yes, I did. I'd like you to stop by my office over here in the courthouse. We've gotten an autopsy report and I think you'll find the results, ah, diverting." There was a grin implied in his voice. The man had no sense of decency.

"Diverting, Mr. Peterson?"

"More than a little. Why don't you come on over now and I'll buy you lunch, how's that?"

"All right," I said.

Paula and I were walking down the steps to the Lincoln, which still stood in the No Parking zone, against the growing drift. I told her what Peterson had said and she sucked in her breath. "Murder."

"Don't jump to conclusions," I said lamely.

I drove slowly through the veil of snow until I reached the library, standing like something from an Ingmar Bergman film.

Impulsively I leaned across the cold space between us and touched Paula's face, turning it to mine, and kissed her again. She didn't move away.

"I like kissing you," I said.

"It's all my money," she said.

"No, no, I don't believe it is."

"Well, I like kissing you, too. It must be the Cooper charm. I've had the full course, John."

She finally moved away to get out of the car. "It's very strange, kissing you like this. It doesn't seem quite real."

"I know," I said, "but there it is."

"You know when we were trying to figure out why Cyril came back? Up in Arthur's office?"

"Yes?"

"Well, I had a theory about it, too." She laughed reticently. "I thought maybe I was the reason he came back."

I didn't know what to say.

She squeezed my hand.

"See you at five o'clock." Then the door slammed and she was swallowed up by the snow.

Thirteen

PETERSON'S office was on the second floor of the old frame courthouse. Inside, the dry wooden floor creaked noisily underfoot and the radiators hissed and pounded. Snow-soaked overcoats hung on a rack in the front entry. A typewriter clacked away in some records office. Stepping into the hallway, I felt as if I'd entered a tomb.

A middle-aged woman sat at a desk in the anteroom to Peterson's office. Half a sandwich lay on wax paper beside her typewriter. I could smell hot coffee. Like most people in Cooper's Falls the woman was vaguely familiar.

"Oh, Mr. Cooper," she said. "Mr. Peterson is expecting you. He asked me to find out if you wanted a turkey sandwich or a meatloaf sandwich and how you wanted your coffee." She grinned expectantly like a woman of good heart who had at one time many years before tried to teach Cyril and me to dance.

"Turkey, cream, and sugar," I said and walked on into Peterson's office. He was sitting in a swivel chair behind his desk with his feet up on the windowsill. It was stuffy in the room; the radiator was gurgling, sounding as if it needed a Bromo. Peterson was wearing a navy blue turtleneck and his concession to fashion was making him sweat. He was staring out the window at the snow and a copy of Dashiell Hammett's *The Glass Key* lay open in his lap.

"You know, Cooper," he said without looking at me, "this kind of a storm, this really brutish kind of a storm, does funny things to my mind. Do you know what I mean?" He glanced up and grinned, then let his face collapse into seriousness. "I look at all the snow and it makes me realize how insignificant men are in the face of a storm like this. I wonder how important it is to find the person who murdered your brother—what in hell difference does it really make, anyway? We'll all be dead soon enough anyway."

"Murdered," I said.

He nodded. He fumbled for a cigar and didn't have one. "Alice," he called, "do I have any cigars out there?"

"Not unless you brought some in this morning," she answered.

"Ah, Christ." He sighed. "Did you tell Alice what you wanted for lunch?"

"Yes. I thought you were taking me out."

"Not in this weather, Cooper," he said, rubbing his deep-set eyes and swiveling around to his desk, which was cluttered with folders, envelopes, papers. "You'd have to be crazy to go outside in this weather."

"You said something about murder."

"Indeed I did. Your brother was poisoned, very painlessly, with a nicotine derivative of some kind. I know very little of forensic medicine. I just believe what they tell me. But somebody did for him, just about the time you were getting there." He shuffled papers, regarding the mess. "I was quite right about the brandy." He caught my eye, ran his finger around inside his turtleneck. "Very little brandy did your brother drink. Ergo, somebody else did."

I sat mute.

"Curious little thing," he mused. "Damn! I wish I had a cigar. You don't happen—no, you're a pipe smoker, aren't you? Well, it looks very much like whoever killed your brother—and, of course, he could have poisoned himself but that seems somewhat far-fetched—drank some brandy with him, administered the poison, and then cleaned up."

Alice appeared with a plastic tray and our lunch, set it on the clutter between us, and left quietly.

"You recall our little trip to the kitchen last night?"

I nodded.

"And what did I show you?"

"Brandy snifter and some garbage." Fighting my irritation at his insufferable bloody ego, I fixed my eye on a team picture of the Minnesota Vikings hanging on the wall. There was another photograph of a huge black head and the top of a football shirt and it was inscribed "To Olaf Peterson from his friend Alan Page."

"Right, brandy snifter and some garbage. Now—go ahead, eat your sandwich, won't hurt you. Won't taste very good, but it isn't poisoned, anyway. Now—that brandy snifter had caught my eye when I looked in the cupboard because all the other glasses were covered with dust. You see? Only the brandy snifter was dustfree—it had obviously been washed. Which tended to confirm my theory that your brother had not drunk all that brandy himself."

He bit into his own turkey and lettuce sandwich and washed it down with some coffee, making a loud sipping sound.

"As I've said, this is the fun part, Cooper, all this theorizing and what not. This is where I excel. I hate to chase people, shoot at them, arrest them. God! Awful stuff for a man to do. Well, anyway, there was that little bit of garbage, too—cigar butt and ashes. We found cigars in your brother's coat pocket, so they're no lead for us, but obviously he didn't smoke two cigars, then run downstairs and empty them into the trash. That would be hard to believe, don't you see?

"So there was someone up there in the bedroom with your brother, someone who drank some brandy, tried to conceal the fact that he'd been there by removing his brandy glass and washing off any offending fingerprints and by emptying the contents of the ashtray —two rather feeble attempts, but then whoever it was had no reason to think anyone would question the cause of death."

He was right. The turkey sandwich tasted like cardboard but I didn't mind because I was worried about the blisters in my mouth from the hot coffee. Peterson's attitude made it difficult to remember that we were talking about my brother. I fished in my pocket for the bottle of painkillers Doctor Bradlee had given me for my head. I asked him if he had any water and he summoned Alice.

"Head still bothering you?"

"Yeah, it aches a little."

"It's the tension. But you ought to have an X ray just in case. Damn head injuries can come back on you, days, weeks, months later. I got shot in the head once and I had attacks of nausea for a year."

Alice arrived with the water in a paper cone that was beginning to leak. "Hurry," she said, "or you'll get all wet." The water, of course, was warm.

"I just spoke with Brenner," Peterson said. "Tells me that you're all of a sudden a millionaire." He smiled.

"I understand you know that feeling."

"Oh, very nice, Cooper. Touché. But there's one big difference in my newfound wealth and yours."

"And what's that?"

"Mine didn't make me a murder suspect."

I grimaced. "Think of my head, remember the tension theory."

"I'm serious."

"I don't give a good goddamn how serious you are, Peterson, I really don't."

"You told me you didn't kill your brother. Now I've got to figure out something else."

"I'll bet you're going to tell me."

"Are you a liar?"

I laughed because there was little else to do.

"Look at it from my point of view. I have no idea of your relationship with your brother, maybe you hated him, maybe he was a son of a bitch, how should I know? But I do know your family has a bunch of Nazis and God only knows what else skulking around in the closet."

"One Nazi," I said.

"And I do know that you were in the house when your brother was very probably murdered. I do know that his will left a fortune to you and I do know that that makes you one very logical suspect."

"I can't argue with that except to say that I didn't do it."

"I know, I know, you probably didn't, but you see my predicament? You see what I've got to work with here?"

I put the sandwich down, drank some coffee, and stood up.

"Sit down, sit down," he said patiently. "I have to talk about my problems, I'm compulsive about it. Never got around to getting a shrink but too compulsive to shut up. Drives my wife crazy. She's a psychologist. Anyway, sit down and stop looking insulted. It's sure to get worse."

He searched through his desk drawers and found one of his thin cigarettes and popped a gold Dunhill lighter, exhaled, and leaned well back.

"Now, of course, there are other possibilities. Have you considered the fellows who waylaid you on the highway? I can't begin to make any connections between what happened to you and what happened to your brother—except the obvious ones. You *are* brothers and you were both victims of violence within a twenty-four-hour period, give or take a couple of hours. But there are some mighty imposing obstacles in our path, like who could have known you were coming home and like what is there common to you and your brother which would make anyone want to kill both of you? I thought about it all right, and I didn't get anywhere. *No where.* There are just too many things I don't know." He shook his head, puzzled by the effort he had apparently expended without result. "We don't know why your brother came back! That's what's so irritating. We don't know why he wanted you here. And we don't know why he was in Buenos Aires. I asked Brenner about that. He said he knew of no interests your brother had in Buenos Aires, or anyplace else in South America."

"I don't have the foggiest," I said. "I don't know anything about his business life. Only that he traveled a lot, all over."

"Like where did he travel?"

"Cairo. Munich. Glasgow. London. All over. Everywhere. He had lots of deals going on. Work was his pleasure, his holiday. It was a good life and he lived it very well."

[63]

"Cairo. Munich. Glasgow. London." He was disgusted. "Alice," he yelled, "will you please get this garbage out of here!"

He walked out of his office with me and down the stairs without speaking. At the door he stopped and smiled at me. "Look, I have to say this. Don't leave town. We've got a murder case and an attempted murder. I've notified the police in Wisconsin, gave them the description of the two men as you gave it to me, and the description of the car they were driving. Maybe they'll turn up something and we can begin making some of those little connections."

He pulled on his trench coat and we stepped out onto the front stoop of the courthouse. The cold air felt good after the overheated office.

"I'm forty-three years old," he said, pulling on his gloves, which were skintight and had little holes cut out over the knuckles, highly impractical I thought. "I was the boy wonder of the Minneapolis Police Department. I was the boy wonder for almost fifteen years, long time to be a boy wonder. Most of the cops didn't much like me and I wasn't really a very good cop. But I had a flair for murder cases—a couple of big ones, lots of headlines built into them, and some little ones, the kind that usually go unsolved because nobody cares about the people who get killed or the people who do the killing. I always cared, Cooper, not out of any great moral concern or outrage. Not at all. But because murder is such a madly desperate act, a final solution, human beings under some sort of ultimate pressure. I just love murder cases, that's all.

"A murder case," he went on, "is like a computer, a very complex computer that very nearly has a life of its own and it just refuses to work until you feed it the right program. But once you start to figure it out, the case, or the computer of murder, comes to life and begins to squirm and curse and shake its fist at you." He had been staring down at the snow and suddenly glanced up, characteristically quickly. "Ah, you may recognize the fact that I have merely paraphrased two of the oldest clichés of murder literature. That is, that the crime is similar to a jigsaw puzzle and you have to fit the pieces together. And Holmes' delight as he cried, 'Come Watson, the game's afoot.' But both clichés are absolutely true. My computer analogy is merely up to date. And admitting that I enjoy murder is only a little more overt than Holmes."

The Cadillac was parked at the curb, covered with snow. He opened the door.

"I'm going to see Mrs. Smithies, or rather Miss Smithies. Christ," he implored the storm, "who can keep it all straight? Maybe she'll be able to tell me something I don't know. There's so much I don't know." He waved a glove at me and slammed the door.

As I stood watching him, the car wouldn't start.

Eventually he got out, muttering.

"Stop smiling," he said. "Go get your head X-rayed."

Doctor Bradlee took me over to the antiseptic little nineteen-fortyish clinic and X-rayed my skull and we stopped in at the Cooper's Falls Cafe for coffee. It was empty. A few sounds came from the kitchen. A waitress sat at the end of the counter smoking a cigarette.

"In my role as county coroner," he said, "I performed the autopsy on Cyril. Peterson told you the result. People suppose that doctors are very hardened about such things, but it's not true. I was performing an autopsy on a boy I brought into the world and it was a very sad business." He sighed and shook his head. "Somebody murdered him and I suppose we've got to find out who did it. Funny, but I don't think I'm going to feel much satisfaction when we find out who."

"That's along the lines of what Peterson was saying."

"What do you mean?"

"He said he wondered what difference it all made in the end."

"Strange thing for a cop to say."

"Peterson is a pretty strange cop."

"That's an understatement."

I walked back to my car wondering why Cyril had been in Buenos Aires. When I got to the car I changed my mind and walked back across the deserted and glacial street toward the courthouse with its windows patches of blurred yellow through the snow. The wind was giving me one of those instant Minnesota earaches.

Alice was typing something on an official-looking form.

"Is he in?" I asked.

"Well, hello, there," she said, smiling. "Yes, he's here. I'll just give him a buzz." The door to Peterson's office was closed.

When I went in, Peterson was speaking into the telephone with his eyes closed.

"A what?" he asked. "A Jensen Intercepter? Well, Jesus Christ."

I sat down.

"No, the newspapers haven't got anybody here. I haven't told them. I'm not obliged to call the Twin Cities when something happens here in Cooper's Falls. You know that. This is my murder, Danny, and you'd better not let it leak. I don't want all those silly bastards getting lost and freezing to death out there somewhere on the wrong road. Right, bye-bye, Danny."

He looked up at me.

"I have a very eager assistant, Cooper, who has a great many silly ideas. However, while checking for fingerprints out at your place, he looked in the garage and discovered how your brother got here. A lovely little dark brown Jensen Interceptor, of all things." He slapped his palm on the desk and smiled. "Pardon my saying so, but the son of a bitch had real style. A Jensen! Twenty-two thousand bucks for a car they'd fit in the palm of your hand!" His face clouded over. "I suppose you get the car, too."

"I suppose."

"What are you doing here, anyway?"

"I had a thought."

"All right, Cooper, what was your thought?"

"Why not start checking back on Cyril's movements? Why not see when he arrived from Buenos

Aires, what he was doing there, whom he saw when he got there, where he came from. . . ."

Peterson was smiling at me with his hands behind his head.

"Tell me, have I struck you as being an inordinately stupid man? Really, be honest with me. I can take it. Lots of ego at work here."

"No, of course not. For a cop."

"Well, then, what do you think I've been doing today, Cooper? Sitting here abusing my dong, perhaps? Or chasing Alice around the desk?"

"Your wit leaves me weak, Peterson."

"I'm sure. But rest assured that we are trying to find out the answers to all your questions."

"Good."

"You see, I've developed a pip of a theory. Want to hear it?"

"I don't suppose I have much choice."

"I think the reason your brother came home is sitting there in Buenos Aires. I don't know what it is. But if we don't know at this end why he came home there's a mighty fine chance we'll find why in Buenos Aires. Therefore, and toward that end, I'm breaking the budget with my trusty telephone. I'll soon be in touch with the Buenos Aires police and shall we hope they speak English?"

"Let's."

"Go, Cooper, go. I'll be in touch with you."

I stopped in the doorway. Alice was listening.

"Did you talk to Paula?"

"My car wouldn't start, remember? It's very cold out there and my car is only human. There is no telephone at the library. No, I have not spoken with Miss Smithies and, in any case, I don't quite know what I'd ask her."

I shrugged and went back outside. It was four o'clock and pretty dark all of a sudden. I noticed a light on in Johnson's Garage earlier and decided to run the car in and see if Arnie Johnson could take a quick look at the heater. There was a light on in Arthur Brenner's office, which overlooked the street, so I figured he must have had his nap and was up now. I didn't want to get involved in having a drink with Arthur. I didn't want to start having drinks with anyone: it would be too easy in this kind of tense situation.

I got in the car and it wouldn't start.

I got back out and said fuck and shit several times, directing my remarks to the storm rather than to the Lincoln, and stamped off up the street toward the garage.

Arnie was tinkering with a station wagon. "My God," he said when we got done shaking hands, "that's terrible about your brother, Mr. Cooper. You just never know, but my Christ, murder!"

"Yes, it's terrible all right. How did you find out, Arnie?"

"Oh, hell, you know this town. Everybody knows, I reckon. I must've heard it when I was over to the cafe for lunch. You know how it is, hotel switchboard, girls can't help but hear things, nurses up at the clinic, girls over in the courthouse, things like this you just can't keep quiet. Only thing saving us from the boys from the Cities is the snow. First time in, oh, hell, since the Second World War, the highways are closed. That's right, *completely* closed—highway department just threw up their hands, said the hell with it, it's gonna get worse before it gets better, the roads are just clogged with cars, abandoned. So I reckon we're just about the only folks know what happened. But, sure as hell, everybody in Cooper's Falls knows about it."

I told Arnie about my car and he went out in his tow truck and I watched him all the way, hooking it up, pulling it back in. He lowered it while I watched, closed the doors of the garage, and listened while I told him I'd had an accident and that I wanted him to make the heater work. He said he would and I walked back out into the snow and leaned against the wind. It seemed five hundred miles to the hotel and I wondered what the weather was like in Buenos Aires. I wondered if the cops spoke English.

Fourteen

ARTHUR BRENNER and I shoved along in the snow. We had the street almost to ourselves. Arthur was an enormous hulk in a gray belted macintosh which could easily have dated back to the 1920's. The wind had died down and Arthur was grumbling, snuffling.

"You sound like hell," I said. "You ought to be in bed with a hot toddy."

He nodded, grunted. "I'm just too old, John. Seventy, and it's hard to believe. If you ever start feeling sorry for yourself just remember me, eye to eye with seventy years and that's real trouble and not a damned thing you can do about it. And now here I am caught up in all this damned nonsense. Do you think Cyril could have killed himself? Strange terminal disease, perhaps?"

"I don't think so. There would have had to have been a container of some kind, something to hold the stuff that did it, and they didn't find one. And there's all the hocus-pocus with the brandy glasses."

"Peterson told me about that," he grunted. "Sounds damned farfetched to me. But I suppose it makes sense. Peterson's an obnoxious man but no fool, that's certain. But here we are traipsing through a blizzard on a fool's errand if ever there was one and all for what? I know what's in these papers. Nothing but a bunch of personal letters from people like Goebbels and Himmler and Goering. And perhaps even Hitler himself. But nothing of value to anyone but an autograph collector, nothing of historical note, nothing worth all the publicity of reviving your grandfather's unsavory past. Just a bunch of wastepaper that Austin should have had enough sense to throw out years ago."

"Do you have any theories, Arthur? About any of it?"

"No, I don't. I can't imagine why he came home, I can't imagine why someone killed him, I can't imagine who would kill him. It all makes very little sense to me, but then I'm not as young as I used to be and I'm probably becoming senile." He grunted. "At my age I'm beginning to wonder what difference it makes anyway."

At the end of the street the delicate old library stood like a warm and friendly haven. The lights shone brightly through the windows and I remembered how warm it had been when I walked in out of the cold the day before and found Paula Smithies. I was thinking of her mouth, of kissing her as we went up the stairs and opened the door.

I went in first and Arthur was right behind me.

Paula was sitting at her desk, her head resting on her forearm, which lay across the desk blotter, as if she were catnapping. It had been a long night, a trying night, and she must have been exhausted.

"Paula," I said. "Paula, wake up."

I could hear Arthur wheezing with his cold behind me and I touched her shoulder, felt the hair on my neck crawl and bristle. There was something wrong. "Paula," I repeated, shaking her shoulder. There was no life in her, no flicker of movement.

Arthur leaned over me. "Has she passed out?"

I turned her head; her eyes were closed peacefully, her face was calm, and I knew the way you know the worst things that Paula Smithies was dead.

"Arthur," I said, my voice coming from a long way off, "she's dead." I felt him take my arm and lower me into a chair. My stomach turned. My legs were shaking. I was conscious of the heat—I was suddenly dripping wet.

Arthur bent over her. I saw him pry an eyelid back, feel for a pulse. Then he simply stood staring at her. "You're quite right. This girl is dead."

He slid a hammered silver flask from a pocket inside his mac and handed it to me. I sipped the brandy and felt it shock me back to life. He sat down on the library table and unbuttoned the coat; his face had tightened, was no longer the complaining mask of an old man.

"Give me that," he said and pulled at the flask. He wiped a huge hand across his mouth.

"What are we going to do?" I said after a while.

"Well, there's no telephone here and we're going to have to notify Peterson. That is, he's the man you tell this sort of thing to in Cooper's Falls."

"I think we'd better look for the boxes she was going to show us. We'd better find out if they're still here." I paused, but my thoughts were stumbling on, trying to pick out a path. "If they're not still here, if they've been taken. . . ."

"Now, now, John," Arthur said gruffly. "Let's not get ahead of ourselves."

"If they're not still here," I went on, "then we'll know why Paula was killed. Do you see?"

"If she was killed. If!" Arthur sounded very determined. "Don't jump to conclusions."

"You think maybe she had a heart attack?"

"There's no need for impertinence."

"I'm sorry," I said, meaning it. "But let's look for the boxes."

Together we made short work of the main floor and found nothing out of the ordinary. "The storm cellar," I said. "She said she found the boxes in the storm cellar." We couldn't find the door which would presumably have led to the cellar. Frustration set in. "Where the hell—"

Then I saw it: an eight-foot-high newspaper rack seemed to be leaning an inch or two away from the wall. I pulled at it, swinging it out into the room, revealing an opening in the wall leading down into darkness. There was a light cord hanging inside the opening. When I pulled it, a dim light went on at the top of the stairway of narrow stone slabs and another in the cellar. "Come on. I don't want to go down there alone, for God's sake."

He ducked low and followed me down the steps, our hands sliding along the stone-layered wall of the storm cellar. The floor beams over our heads could not have been more than six feet from the dirt floor. We stooped in the middle of the dim room, windowless, musty, smelling of the dirt floor, very cold. Arthur sneezed. "Damn," he said.

Boxes were arranged against two of the walls, but they were uniformly sealed with masking tape. There was a stool in one corner, a couple of old wooden bookcases standing empty, and in the middle of the room were three boxes, brown cardboard, ragged with age, their tops drawn back, tape hanging limply, cut open. On the sides of each of the boxes, carefully printed in black crayon, were the words AUSTIN COOPER.

"Well, there they are," I said.

Arthur bent back the lids and regarded the contents. There was a scuttling sound somewhere in a dark corner and I jumped, startled.

"Nerves," Arthur said, pulling a copy of *Gone with the Wind* out of one of the boxes. "Just a rat, John, just a very cold rat, or a mouse. Not a murderer."

"The boxes have been partially emptied," I said. There was a frigid draft coming from somewhere and I could hear the wind ripping at the old building.

"Yes," he said.

We opened them all and found more books, some family photograph albums. "No packets of Nazi documents. No strange letters, no diplomatic pouches. . . ." He looked at me. "If there ever were any. She could have been letting her imagination run away with her."

I shook my head.

"I know, I know," he said soothingly. "But there's no point in our going off half-cocked."

"We're not." I pointed at the third cardboard box. Under an empty file folder, secure and almost hidden, there was a gray metal strongbox. "That's one of the boxes she mentioned to me. I'd bet on it."

"I didn't hear her mention a metal box," Arthur said, coughing into a fist.

"Well, she told me about it the first time we discussed it. She very specifically mentioned a metal box and I'll bet this is it." I took it out and pulled at the lock. It was shut fast, locked.

Arthur looked perplexed. "Well, I just don't know."

Above our heads the floorboards creaked. At first I thought it was the wind; then they creaked again and I heard a foot fall: someone was standing at the desk beside Paula's body.

Arthur's eyes flicked coolly across mine.

"We'd better get upstairs."

"There's someone up there."

"Precisely. And we can't stay down here forever, in any case. Perhaps some poor patron has come to check out his week's reading."

Cautiously we climbed the stone stairs.

The newspaper rack had swung back against the opening to the storm cellar and as we pushed it away I heard a man's voice, speaking very calmly.

"Step out into the room very slowly. Or I'll probably kill you."

Slowly, the moving panel revealed Olaf Peterson standing ten feet from us, a revolver aimed at arm's length toward the middle of Arthur Brenner's ample chest.

Peterson's face was expressionless until it began to take on a look akin to petty irritation coupled with a weary amusement. He lowered the gun. Brenner stepped into the room and I followed, clutching the metal box.

"This is utterly absurd," Peterson said as if he were talking to himself. "They get my car started, I take a chance that Miss Smithies might still be at the library—just an off chance, a whim. I decide I'll drop in, no particular reason, just the feeling that perhaps she hasn't told me quite everything. Right? I open the library's front door and I'm back in the funhouse. Miss Smithies is dead, strangled I would guess, at her desk, and Abbott and Costello are mucking about in the basement—" He raised a hand. "No, I'm sorry, I didn't mean the Abbott and Costello crack, it's just that it's been a long and trying day." He turned around and walked away from us to the heater, then to the desk where Paula remained as we had left her. "Do you realize that there has not been a murder in Cooper's Falls in forty years, gentlemen? Forty years—until John Cooper comes home and right away he can't turn around without falling over another body. Jesus, Jesus, Jesus. . . ." His volume lessened and he turned to look at Paula's body. "What's the story on this one?"

"We had an appointment to see Paula," I said. "We got her half an hour ago and found her like this."

"What have you been doing for half an hour, Cooper? What? What were you doing in the basement? Brenner, for God's sake, why didn't you come back to the office? What, what, what in hell is going on here? Talk to me, gentlemen, talk to me!"

"There's quite a lot to it," I said.

"I'm sure there is."

"It'll take some time. . . ."

"Oh, God," he said, shaking his head, fingers clenching. "There's no telephone here. Can you believe that, no telephone in the library? You fellows just have a chair, a box, something, and I'm going to call the office, get Danny over here to wait for Bradlee." He stood in the doorway huffing, arranging his thoughts. Then his face cracked into that unexpected grin, sharp and predatory. "The plot thickens, Cooper." And then he went outside.

"We've got to tell him," I said.

Arthur nodded, heavy flesh sagging away from his cheek and jawbones. "No real choice," he said, resigned. "I hope he has enough sense not to let it all out again."

When Peterson came back he was clapping his hands against the cold. "Snowing like hell again. All right, do you want to start your little tale here or wait until we get back to the office?"

"Let's wait," I said. "It's long and I want to get it right."

We waited in silence until Doctor Bradlee and Danny, Peterson's assistant, arrived. Bradlee looked sad and tired, caught my eye, and gave me a weary smile. "I'm sorry, John," he muttered. Danny, all curly hair and bright blue eyes, seemed to be enjoying the excitement. Peterson told him to do whatever Bradlee told him to do and we all set off in Peterson's Cadillac.

Fifteen

THE courthouse was dark as we followed Peterson up the creaking wooden stairs to his office. The building was still overheated. Peterson flipped on the lights, threw his coat on a chair, and jerked open the window facing the street. Snow blew in, silt-fine, rattling on the sill and hissing on the radiator.

"We're all alone now," he said patiently. "So start talking."

"Paula knew why Cyril came home," I said, "and why he wanted me to come home. She found some strange material in boxes of Austin Cooper's stuff at the library. She told Cyril when he called her last week and his response was to say he was going to come home and that he was going to get me home, too."

"Strange material? You're a writer, you can do better than 'strange material,' Cooper."

"She wasn't sure but it had to do with my grandfather's political activity, his involvement with the Nazis. There were letters, documents, official-looking papers. She could identify some names, or so she told me, but apparently they were in German and she didn't understand what it all meant. But when she told Cyril about it he said he was coming back."

"Letters, documents, papers. . . ."

"Diaries my grandfather kept. And she said there was a metal box that was locked."

"The metal box you are holding," Peterson said.

I handed it to him and he put it on his desk, tapping the lock.

"We'll have to get it open. What do you know about this, Mr. Brenner?"

"Only what John has told you."

"You didn't talk to Paula Smithies?"

"I talked with both John and Paula at the hotel."

"But that was the last time you saw her?"

"Yes, the last time."

For almost an hour Peterson went over my every move since returning to Cooper's Falls: my arrival, my first conversation with Paula at the library, the discovery of the body of my brother Cyril, my conversations with Paula during the night, and our meeting with Brenner. Back and forth he crisscrossed everything I said, then switched to Arthur, then asked for a rundown on my grandfather's involvement. Then it was my father, his career, his marriage, his issue, his heroic death. Over and over again. What had we done when we reached the library? Why had we walked? Which of us had seen Paula first? Had we checked the main floor thoroughly? There was nothing but a metal box, none of the other items?

"Do you know what this means, class?" Peterson sat down and took a cigar and sighted down its length. "It means we've got trouble, is what it actually means. It means my wife is going to be very irritated with me because I'm going to have to work late tonight. It means that we've got somebody who has knocked off two people in a couple of days—I mean there's no real point in pretending that the two murders are unrelated, right? Right. So, we've either got a nut on our hands or somebody with a hell of a motive." He paused for effect, lit his cigar, and puffed leisurely, regarding it like a friend whose name he couldn't place. "I don't think it's a nut. Anybody who'd come to that conclusion would in fact, *be* a nut. Nope. Somebody's got a perfectly good reason for killing two presumably harmless people. But then, they weren't harmless to the person who killed them, were they?"

There was in the commonplace setting an unnerving aura of total unreality: murder is such a large fact that your mind simply rejects it. Cyril was dead. Paula was dead. Absurd.

"Now, what do the missing documents mean?" Peterson asked.

"I'm tired," Brenner said. "Must you formulate your theories on my time?"

"I need your advice, counsellor. Be patient."

Arthur sighed, yawned.

Peterson repeated the question, watching me.

"Whoever killed Paula took the documents," I said.

"Is that why she was killed? For the documents?"

"I suppose."

"Are we learning something?" Peterson asked.

"I daresay," I said.

"We have hypothesized that Paula Smithies was murdered because someone wanted some old Nazi documents. She was killed because she may have learned what was in those papers. She was killed because . . . it was better for somebody that she be dead."

"Peterson, this is all reminiscent of some strange kind of therapy. I think it's making me sick."

"Cooper, somebody made your brother and Paula Smithies dead. Better to be sick. But we're going to figure it out, indeed we are." He flicked an inch or so of ash into a glass ashtray. "And why was Cyril killed?"

"I don't know," I said.

"He knew something about those documents. That's why he came home. That is why he summoned you home. 'Family tree needs attention.' But somebody killed him before you got here, before he talked to Paula. Whoever talked to him . . . killed him. Somebody knew he was coming home. You knew. And Paula knew. Now Paula's dead, Cyril's dead, and by all rights you should be dead in a snowdrift on a Wisconsin highway. Aha, piques your interest, doesn't it? Whoever tried to kill you was part of this whole damned thing, I'd goddamn well bet my wife's money on it."

Eventually the interrogation ended. Arthur bade us an exhausted good-evening and Peterson and I watched him lean into the blowing snow. Peterson saw me to the door.

"Take care of yourself. I want you to see this through."

I nodded.

"Big day tomorrow. We may have some news from Buenos Aires. And we'll crack that metal box." He slapped me on the back. "Cooper, seriously—I'm sorry about Paula Smithies. I'm not unfeeling about it. But I'm excited by it and I can't help it. It's my nature. But I am sorry for what you're going through. I really am. Would you like a lift home? Why don't you stay at the hotel?"

"No, I'm going home. I'll pick up my car and go back to the house. Thanks, anyway."

"I'll see you in the morning, then. We've got to make some arrangements for funerals. I hope Danny handled Miss Smithies' mother. Jesus, I've got a long night ahead of me."

I went across and picked up my car from Arnie. He explained what happened to the heater but I didn't care. It was nearly ten o'clock and there were bodies all over the stage. I just wanted to get home, to be safe again.

I felt myself drawn to the big house. I stood at my grandfather's desk staring at the place where Paula had been sitting the night before. What had she hoped for? I wondered. How had she wanted it to work out? Doubtless she'd wanted to marry my brother Cyril: that must have been the end in view. A husband dead in Laos, a kind rescuer in my brother—a romance, a teen-age dream which had somehow come true. And then Cyril was suddenly snuffed out, meaninglessly, and she had had to absorb the shock. Had she had time to understand his death, to begin to search for an alternative? I had kissed her and held her, knowing she was desperate. I had wanted to comfort her, to give her something stable to hold on to in her shock. I thought about the Peck and Peck kilt, the huge safety pin. I had felt something else for her, too. She'd made me realize I wasn't burned out inside. And then somebody had strangled her and closed her eyes and left her for me to find. It was insane,

[78]

and it made my chest ache in frustration and anger and undirected hatred.

I was crying. I couldn't stop crying.

I was crying for Cyril and for Paula and for myself.

I went to the kitchen and made coffee and heard something banging loose on the back of the house. I went back to the library and sat down in my grandfather's chair. The wind howled outside. I walked into the parlor, into the vast echoing hallway, into one room after another, turning on lights. A formal dining room, another drawing room, a music room, the gun room. My grandfather had been a trapshooter, firing out across our own lake. In the music room I stopped and considered the photographs arranged on the tops of the cabinets.

My father in tennis dress: white duck trousers, tennis sweater knotted around his neck, white shirt open at the throat, shaking hands with the great German tennis star von Cramm, the perfectly handsome blond, blue-eyed Aryan who had had no time for Hitler. And my mother. . . .

She was, I suppose, the most beautiful woman I have ever seen and there were dozens of pictures of her in the music room. I was six years old when she was killed in the Blitz: I'm not sure if I actually remember what she looked like or if these photographs of her were what seemed to be my memory. She had a fine long nose, gracefully wavy blond hair, and a slightly angular quality: pictures of her swimming on the beach at Cannes showed long slender legs, a flat belly, small high breasts. She has a frank look in her eyes, unafraid and unimpressed by the camera. On one wall, by itself, was a huge oil portrait of her painted by my father. She is wearing a very simple mauve cocktail dress, low-cut, and she has that characteristic look of unconcern as if she is looking past my father to someone standing in a doorway. My father was a very able painter and his love for her is apparent in the painting.

My father and my mother were dead, too. The delicate little blond girl in the photographs, sometimes laughing, sometimes solemn, sometimes distracted by a small terrier at her feet—my little sister Lee, the image of her mother. I was the unhappy bastard who got left behind.

I went back to the library.

The telephone rang.

It was Arthur Brenner.

"I just took a chance you might be in the house and still awake." His cold was worse. "I'm at home playing with my porcelain and drinking a toddy as you suggested. I'm working on what is the crowning work of my career in porcelain, a re-creation of Flowerdieu's Charge. Do you know the story?" He was trying to take my mind off things.

"No." I slumped back in my grandfather's chair. "No, what's the story, Arthur?"

"Flowerdieu's Charge," he said. "It was a gratuitous act of courage, utterly quixotic. The last British cavalry charge. Took place during the Great War, of course. Charged the German lines with drawn saber, rode through them, wheeled, and rode back again. Lad got the Victoria Cross. Posthumously, of course. Flowerdieu did what he was meant to do and died the death Fate had ready for him. There's a death waiting for us all, John. . . ."

"I know, Arthur," I said.

"Are you all right?"

"I'm all right. I'm just shocked, I suppose. So many people are dead."

"We'll all be dead soon enough," he rumbled. "It's just a matter of seeing it through, trying to believe in something. The difficulty, of course, is that there's not a goddamned thing really worth believing in. At least I'm afraid not. Causes leave much to be desired. . . ." He had had more than one toddy and his mind was wandering.

"You ought to get to sleep."

"Yes, I suppose I ought. I'm an old man and I have a bad cold and I ought to get to bed. You're right."

"I'll be seeing you tomorrow."

"Take care," he said tiredly. "And don't forget to say your prayers."

"Which prayers are those, Arthur?"

" 'Now I lay me down to sleep, I pray the Lord

my soul to keep. If I should die before I wake, I pray the Lord my soul to take.' That prayer."

"I will," I said. "I'll say it."

"Goodnight then, John."

"Goodnight, Arthur."

Sixteen

I WAS sitting at the desk making lists of what had happened since I'd arrived back in Cooper's Falls, trying to make sense of it all. And it kept coming back to Austin Cooper's papers in the boxes at the library. The papers had triggered Cyril's decision to come home and he was murdered before he got to them. The papers made him wire me to come home and I had survived an attempted murder by sheer accident. And whoever had killed Paula Smithies had stolen the papers. Except for the metal box which Peterson was going to have opened.

What could anyone have wanted in those papers? They referred to a period which was now purely historical, a cause which had been buried in the ruins of the Reich. And yet people were still dying.

I don't know how long I'd been aware of the sound outside. And then it stopped, leaving a void in the sea of sound. I noticed its stopping most of all.

I went to the window. The lights from the house made the night too black to see clearly. Staring into that blackness, I was aware first of the sound of the windowpane shattering, chips of glass spraying across my face, and then I heard the brittle, echoing crack of the shot, heard wood splinter behind me on the opposite wall by the fireplace.

Reflexively I ducked and crawled on my knees to the desk, reached up and turned off the light. There was no physical exertion in what I'd done but in a matter of five seconds I was out of breath and frightened. Somebody had just shot at me. As I knelt by the desk I fully realized what I should have known before, what Peterson should have known: just because they didn't get me the first time there was no reason to think they'd give up on the idea. Whatever the reason, they wanted me just as dead as Cyril and Paula. I was a loose end and apparently they felt I was somehow a threat.

And now they had me.

I felt on the desk for the telephone. Lifting it off the receiver, I knew what I'd hear: nothing. They'd cut the line, some time since I'd been talking to Arthur. I was alone. I was cut off. And I was shaking with fear, fighting off the urge to vomit.

I heard nothing but the wind outside. There was a disgusting sour taste in my mouth and, oddly, I began to feel shame. The longer I lay there, remembering the night's dead, the more ashamed I felt. Cyril. Paula. Father. Mother. Little Lee. Paula's husband. . . . We all have a death in store for us. Indeed, Arthur, I thought. And mine is waiting outside in the snow.

I doubt very much that what I began to feel was courage. I am not a brave man. But lying on the floor in the library, I began to realize that I was tired of this, tired of people dying and people hitting me over the head and shooting at me and killing nice, decent people. I began to think that there was some miserable son of a bitch out there in the snow who was trying to kill me, who figured I was some goddamned pushover, nothing but a stupid target, scared shitless, somebody to be cut off from his protectors and methodically butchered.

My hands were clenched into fists, shaking. Everybody else was dead, so what the hell difference did it make? The least I could do was make the son of a bitch work for it.

So, like a child, I crawled across the library floor to the parlor door, reached up and flicked the light switch, sending the room into darkness. Like a chess player, I began to look several moves ahead. Without leaving the darkness I could crawl across several connecting floors, turn off all the lights, move from room to room. From the parlor I reached up and plunged the hallway into darkness; then, across the parquet floor to the dining room, the second drawing room, the music room, the gun room.

The gun room.

There was still no sound but the wind. Now that the house was totally dark, I could see that the clouds had broken, that there was a certain spotty moonlight. Cautiously I edged my way around the gun room to the window, which gave on a wide view of the front lawn. At first I saw only the black outlines and shadows of evergreens in clumps, the skeletal taller trees, the undulating surface of snow. There seemed to be nothing which could have been a man, but of course there was a man. Eventually I saw him.

From behind a clump of something he rose like a specter, a tall man, a hundred yards away, and within an instant I realized what I'd heard: the clump wasn't a clump at all. It was a snowmobile. I had heard its nasty little engine.

I shuddered with anger. He was intent on killing me, this tall scarecrow man with his snowmobile, and I could either accept that fact, say my prayers as Arthur had suggested, and compose myself for eternity, or I could try to kill him. Escape had flickered across my mind for an instant and, in my anger, I had rejected it. If not now, he would find me later as he had found Cyril and Paula. There was no escape. But with nothing to lose, I could try to kill him.

The entire situation began to simplify itself. I walked across to the rack of shotguns, picked out a Browning over-and-under with a pale stock which caught my eye in the dim moonlight, and opened the drawer where the shells were kept. I took a handful of the large paper-jacketed shells and went back to the window.

He was still standing there in the snow. I could imagine his confusion. He should not have missed with that first shot: he had been careless and overconfident, seeing me silhouetted in the window. Obviously he had a rifle with a telescopic sight and he'd missed. And now he knew I'd been warned, put on my guard, but he didn't know what I was doing. He didn't know if he'd wounded me, he didn't know if I was hiding in terror under some bed. He didn't know I'd decided to kill him.

I watched him staring at the house, straining my eyes to keep his shape clear against the shifting shadows, the snow swirling in the wind. I went back into the hallway and put on my sheepskin coat. When I looked again he was on the snowmobile and I heard it come to life. I watched it come closer to the house, moving in a faint zigzag line, leaving a wake of snow snaking out behind it. At fifty yards he stopped again and I watched him get off, fumble with the rifle. I watched him aim at the house and sweep the barrel of the rifle across the frontage.

Then I heard another shattering of glass and the report of the shot, cracking flatly against the wind, finally smothered. He was worried. He didn't know what to do.

I opened the front door, slowly staying behind it, knowing in a peculiarly crazy way that I was controlling the situation. My heart was pumping wildly and I felt curiously lightheaded. I heard a bullet hit the stairway, heard another crack like a bullwhip.

I knelt and crawled through the doorway into the cold. For some reason I wanted to be outside with him: I wanted him to know that I'd decided to play. The Lincoln sat between us and I didn't know if he could see me. But I wanted him to see me. I wanted him to know I was there. I had about ten feet to go to reach one of the great square pillars, so I stood up, looked directly at him, and saw that he still had the rifle at his shoulder and was scrutinizing the house through the sight. He saw me and I stepped behind a pillar, peered cautiously out. The wind blew snow in my face. The gun had never left his shoulder and he squeezed one off and wood splintered off the pillar. At the instant I heard the report I broke the other way to the next pillar. We repeated the process one more time. He'd lowered the rifle and I walked to the end of the porch, stood watching him. He was tall and gaunt with squared-off shoulders and he regarded me in return. At that moment he was very possibly deciding whether or not he should turn tail and forget the whole thing. I desperately wanted him to stay, to come after me: once he committed himself I knew I might win. And I didn't want him waiting for me, waiting for another lonely night.

Slowly he climbed onto the snowmobile and started it again. I stood utterly still, the shotgun concealed by my body. Then, suddenly and with a galvanic effect, the snowmobile surged forward: he was coming after me. I jumped down off the porch into the deep snow and shrubbery by the side of the house. For a terrifying moment I thought I couldn't move in the deep snow, but I managed. I thrashed my way along the shrubbery and made the turn at the back of the house with the sound of the machine churning, gaining on me. I didn't really have a plan. But I did want to confuse him: I didn't want to just take a shot at him, miss, and have him ride me down. I didn't want him to know I had that shotgun. I wanted that to be waiting at the end.

I stood in the shadows as he swept by twenty yards away, curving in a great arc which took him beyond a stand of trees well behind the house. The clouds passed for a moment and the wind held its breath, the snow sparkled.

I ran for the shelter of the evergreens growing along the driveway which led to the cottage. He was turning the machine. I saw it skimming along the snow's crust, occasionally digging in and sending a breaker curling elegantly in the moonlight.

Sucking at the cold air, I inhaled snow crystals, felt my lungs laboring as I lifted my legs high in the deep snow. Hearing the incessant roar of the machine gaining again, I lunged across the shrubbery which was still just visible behind and a few inches above the iron railing which followed the driveway. Panting, realizing I couldn't run anymore in the snow, I watched him throttle down near the shadow cast by the house. The snow glittered. He waited. I had disappeared and he was looking for me in the puzzle of shadows and snow skimming along the surface.

Looking in the direction of the cottage, I saw that the wind had blown much of the snow in the driveway across the lawn, lowering the level in the driveway which lay between us. The snow was deeper again as soon as it got to the railing, which was obscured in the shadow of the bank. The bank itself was now about a foot higher than the driveway.

"You son of a bitch," I yelled against the wind. Standing up, I stepped out of the shadows of the evergreen, holding the shotgun behind me. "Come and get me, you bastard!" And I began to stagger off, slogging, falling to my knees once, struggling back up. I headed off at a forty-five-degree angle from the curve of the drive.

I heard the engine revving up again, looked back to see the skis knife down into the snow as he began to move toward me. I kept moving deliberately toward open ground—open ground where he could easily ride me down and kill me. But to reach me he had to cross that driveway. . . .

I turned finally, gasping for breath, snow caked across me like a snowman. My eyeballs felt dry, frozen. But he was coming and I slid my hand along the stock, cradling the gun against my body.

The snowmobile picked up speed as it reached the far side of the driveway. The tall man was standing, gripping the handlebars as he leaned into the dip of the driveway and I saw him begin to lean gracefully back to lift the front end, to take the snowbank.

And with an awful splintering and grinding of metal the skis hooked under the iron railing, ripped away from the machine which stopped with a hideous finality, slid for an instant along the railing, and tipped across it, the engine churning, snow spewing away in a furious cloud. But the tall man was already gone, through the windshield that must have cut through his coat and on through the flesh on that gaunt frame, hurtling on through the blowing snow with a shriek that died on the wind.

The motor cut out and it was quiet except for the wind and the faint rattle of snow on the frozen crust.

He lay in a broken heap about fifteen feet from me, a black shape like a shadow on the snow. I brought the gun up and held it at my waist, leveled at him.

I was terrified of the shape, my mouth and throat too dry to swallow: what if the shape moved?

Eventually the black mass twitched, made a gagging sound, moved an arm, gagged some more, and I heard wet retching, a flood of something in the snow. Then the head moved, tilted back to look up, and then the torso began to rise too, snow sifting away, until the figure was weaving drunkenly on its knees in the snow, like Neptune rising from the sea.

"Help me—"

The shape gurgled at me, spit, reached up toward its face.

"My face—" The words were mushy, indistinct, sounded like the rush of a sewer. "Something's wrong —with my face." The words were pushed past the gurgling, the product of an awesome effort.

Immobilized I watched as its hands fluttered at its chest, then a leg pushed against the snow and the shape grew taller.

And I pulled the trigger.

The sound was like a bomb going off in my pocket and the recoil almost knocked the gun from my hand. The first blast blew quite a large chunk from the left side of what was the head: bits flew away in the moonlight, seemed to float. The second blast caught him lower and lifted the shape upward and back, out of the snow, until it settled back into the glare of moonlight, legs straight before it, the torso twisted at a peculiar angle.

When I stopped shaking I felt more tired than I knew it was possible to feel and I dropped the shotgun in the snow and walked back across the wide snowy space, feeling desperately small, toward the house. I wanted only to go to sleep. I didn't even look at the thing I had killed.

Seventeen

OLAF PETERSON was standing over me, peering down into my face, a contrail of blue smoke appended to his cigar. It took a minute to wake up. I was lying on the couch in the library and the night was howling outside. A draft penetrated the broken window. My head ached at the base of the skull and when I jerked my hand it knocked an empty scotch bottle onto the floor. I remembered: I'd gone off the wagon, passed out.

"What time is it?" I asked. My tongue felt thick and furry.

"About five thirty," Peterson muttered, shaking his head. He retrieved the empty scotch bottle, held it upside down. "What the hell happened here, Cooper? How did the window get broken? Why did you leave the front door open? Why doesn't your telephone work?"

"They cut it after I spoke with Brenner," I said. "Which wouldn't have given them much time—" I sat up on the couch. Peterson was standing by the broken window: blue duffel coat, gray turtleneck, black cigar, snow melting on his hairpiece. "Why are you here?"

"I worry about you, Cooper. I got to worrying about you tonight when I finally got home. I said to my wife, I'm worried about that dumb son of a bitch and she said which dumb son of a bitch is that and I said Cooper and she said why don't you call him and that's when I found out there was something wrong with your phone. I mean, everybody else is getting killed, at least everyone who is involved with you, so why not you—and why not Arthur Brenner? So I called Arthur, told him to make goddamned sure his doors were locked, told him to take precautions—he was asleep, naturally, sounded half snapped on toddies, but I felt better. But I wasn't going to take any chances with you. It should have occurred to me right away." He regarded me sourly.

I told him what had happened. It came back to me in an unexpected rush of awareness, like a dream hitting you in rapid fire while you're taking your morning shower. The telephone call, the shot, the terror and the crawling, the gun room, the stalking, the shape rising out of the snow, the shotgun going off. . . .

Peterson sat staring at me after I'd finished. He said nothing, he smoked his cigar, he stared. I got up and went to the window. The eastern sky was beginning to get a little grayer than the night around it, which was still black. The moon was obscured, the wind ranted. The window was icing up at the edges. I felt sick to my stomach, cramped.

Finally he sighed and stood up.

"Let's go find what's left of this guy you killed." As I buttoned my coat he said: "Jesus, I hope he hasn't been buried in this fucking snow."

They say that when it gets sufficiently cold you can't tell as it gets still colder. That's wrong. It was forty degrees below zero out there and the wind was gusting to thirty miles an hour and I can't imagine ever having been out in such cold before. The sky kept easing toward morning and as it lightened it revealed what could have passed for another planet, long dead. The treeline was shrouded in snow and stood behind a mist of snow. The lawn was crusted and cracked like breaking ice underfoot. The bleak, broken snowmobile sat upended in the snow like the wreckage of a plane crashed thirty years ago in the Libyan desert. Snow driven across the crust eddied around it, hurried on.

The man was just a hillock of snow but I knew where to look. Peterson went to work, scraping snow away, found a frozen hand bluish and brittle and naked. The snow was rust-colored and Peterson furiously continued to work. I joined him to keep from freezing to death. It was like unwrapping a particularly hideous present. I wasn't even curious about the man. But I kept wiping snow away. Peterson was muttering to himself. The sky was almost completely gray when we finally saw him.

Half of the head was gone, one whole side: no eye, no cheek, no ear, strings of frozen matter protruding stiffly from the stump of throat and the pellet-chewed shoulder. The half of the head that remained had been butchered as it went through the machine's windscreen, but the contours were there, it was recognizable. His thick sheepskin coat had been blown to tatters by my second shot: it was caked with frozen blood and there were shreds of flesh stuck to the fur lining.

"Incredible," Peterson said, straightening up, shouting over the wind. "This is just an incredible mess." The figure lay on its back, legs broken and canted at peculiar angles, like a marionette at rest, arms cruciform, its middle hollowed by one shotgun blast, its head half gone in another: blood in the snow, frozen crystals, random bits of flesh.

"It's the tall man who tried to kill me on the highway. There's enough left of him, I can tell, I'm quite certain."

Peterson looked at me to make sure he was getting it all. Then he picked up the man's rifle, which he had apparently clutched until the end. I went back and picked up the shotgun I'd used. We began to walk back to the house.

"Cooper," I heard him shout over his shoulder, "you sure as hell are a lot of trouble."

"Christ—" he went on back inside—"I don't know how the hell we're going to get a meat wagon out here in this snow. I've got four snow tires on the goddamn Cadillac and it took me two hours to get here last night. God, what a pain in the ass."

We were drinking coffee. I had found aspirin. My stomach was still unsettled from the scotch. I wasn't used to it and I wondered if somehow I was going to start drinking again.

Together Peterson and I went over the events of the previous night which had led to my killing the gaunt man. He assured me that it was a matter of self-defense, that I had nothing to worry about, but that I would be required to make an official statement. Identifying the body might take some time if he had no papers on him but there was time to worry about that later.

What perplexed Peterson was the possible connection between the frozen carcass outside and the murders of Cyril and Paula. Were they connected at all? And if so, how? What did Cyril, Paula, and I have in common that would make them want to kill us? And who were they? Clearly, the attack on the highway could no longer be considered an isolated, random act of violence: I had been pursued with intent to kill.

"It's unsettling, Cooper," he said, blowing on the coffee, toying with an immense gold signet ring, "because I've got to believe these are very determined people and so far you've eluded them. It is probably very annoying for them, botching the job so badly."

"What can I do about it?" I was weary: I hadn't slept enough.

"Get out of this house for one thing. Get into town—or you can stay with Brenner—can't you?"

"Not forever," I said.

"Until we can think of something, Cooper."

He went outside to the Cadillac and radioed for the ambulance and they said they'd try.

He came back looking sour; he wasn't the same old Peterson, laughing and playing games and being a smartass. He sat down in my grandfather's desk chair.

"We got the metal box open last night. It was full of pages of numbers, a good deal of fairly harmless-looking pages of German prose, more pages of numbers and random German words, some charts of an organizational nature which had a very military look about them, lists of American cities, lists of corporations, graphs. None of it made the slightest sense to me. But still, we're positive—well, relatively positive—that Paula died because of this stuff, this old crap." There was heat in his voice I had not heard before.

His mouth curved down, framed by the dark crescent of mustache, and I was reminded more than ever of the Levantine.

"I'm getting sick of this whole thing, Cooper, sick of having citizens killed on my doorstep, sick of being pissed on by these bastards and I don't give a goddamn who they are. There's a time when I enjoy the excitement of something new, it reminds me that I'm still alive, my mind feels alert again. But that time is over. It's really over because this is no fun, is it?"

I wasn't sure how rhetorical his question was, but I answered: "It was never any fun for me."

He cleared his throat, nodded. "Of course not. I realize that. It's no fun when you're *involved*. I wasn't involved. I was being presented with a peculiar situation and it was fun. Now, I'm beginning to be involved. I know you people—you're not characters in this little play being performed to keep me occupied." He made a fist, ground his chin against it.

"Does it make any sense, Cooper?" He moved around the room, warmed himself staring into the fireplace, peered into the bullethole in the wood paneling. He lifted the rifle the dead man had used on me. He studied it, turned it, read whatever was inscribed on its underside, and grunted.

"Mauser 7.65 mm. Nice gun, well cared for up until last night. Made at the Mauser Werke at Oberndorf am Neckar. Good action, hinged floorplate. Release button here on the trigger guard, nice square bridge. Hell of a rifle." He went back to the wall and inspected the hole, touched it with a fingertip. Then he sighted through the scope. "The scope is a Zeiss 2-1/2-x Zielklein and the bullet . . . the bullet about 180 grains nipping along at 2,700 feet per second. That is more velocity than you can shake a stick at, Cooper."

He went back to the desk and sank down in the chair. It creaked in the stillness: the fire crackled, snow rattled on the window.

"A bullet can kill you in a couple of ways. It can hit in some vital area, the brain or the spinal column near the top or the heart, and that's the end of your story. With that kind of a hit a .22 rifle can kill a grizzly, but the margin for error is much too great.

The other way of killing you is by one kind of shock or another. In this case you need enough gun, enough velocity for tremendous impact, and a bullet which expands very quickly once it hits you and gets inside you—do you follow me, Cooper? You want a bullet that will destroy as much living tissue as possible. If you destroy enough tissue you've got a kill. You can hit a deer in the paunch with a high-velocity rifle, carrying expanding bullets, blow most of the abdomen away, and it dies though its vital areas go untouched. The messages from the lacerated nerves short-circuit the brain, and zap, death.

"There are other kinds of shock. The sheer impact of a bullet if it's going fast enough creates a kind of hydraulic shock not much different from the mechanism of hydraulic brakes. The pressure created by the bullet's impact is so great and so sudden that it blitzes the veins and the arteries leading to the brain—death, again.

"Now, our dead friend was leaving nothing to chance. If he missed your vital areas, he had a soft, thin-skinned bullet which would explode inside you and destroy enough tissue to kill you even if he hit your shoulder or thigh, and the bullet was going to be traveling fast enough that any substantial hit was almost certain to cause hydraulic shock."

Peterson's recitation made me sicker to my stomach.

"How the hell do you know all that?" I asked.

"I've been around," he said. "Grisly, isn't it?"

As he had spoken so matter-of-factly about what the killer had wanted to do to me, my mind was instead going over what I had done to him. The first shot must have blown away much of his brain, a vital area, causing immediate death. The second would have created extensive tissue shock—but he was already dead.

Peterson was sitting at the desk making a list with a fiber-tip pen. I knew what he was doing before he said it.

"All right, while we wait, let's go over what we've got here, Cooper," the voice began again, insistent, determined. "There are certain questions we've got to ask ourselves. I'm not boring you, am I, Cooper?"

"No, I'm just tired." I didn't want to argue with him; there was no spirit in me for that. "And I'm thinking about what you've said. I'm very docile, Peterson."

"Now, was this guy who tried to kill you the same guy who killed Cyril? And Paula? Wait a minute, I'm not saying he was, damn it, I'm asking. It is possible. He could have kept right on driving after they left you for dead, gotten to Cooper's Falls ahead of you, and killed Cyril before you got here. It is *possible*, Cooper, and we've got to start thinking all this is connected. And he could then have killed Paula this past afternoon, taken the boxes, stashed them somewhere or given them to his buddy, the little guy in the blue duffel coat, and come out here to kill you in the night.

"The question now is, why? What was the motive? What did Cyril and Paula have in common? What, Cooper?"

"They both knew about the boxes," I said. "They were the only people who knew about the boxes when Cyril was killed, if he was killed on the twentieth before I met Paula and she told me."

"But if that is what ties Cyril and Paula together, what ties you—the third victim, and the *first* on the schedule—to Cyril and Paula? What do you know in common with them? Nothing, Cooper, not a damned thing, at least not about those boxes. You've never seen any of the contents, you're utterly harmless, aren't you?"

"I don't know," I said, trying to sound tough. "Ask the guy out there in the snow."

Peterson stood up and stretched, went through the passage to the kitchen and came back with the coffeepot. He poured us both some and took the pot back to the kitchen. When he came back his eye was caught on my grandfather's World War II position map. He studied the pins. "Do wars ever end?" he mused.

"I don't know," I said. "It's peculiar but for some people they never end, every so often they find some poor bastard holed away in a Berlin attic or a Jap somewhere on some Pacific rock who still think there's a war on. People are funny, as the man on the radio used to say."

He stood at the window drinking his coffee.

"But the people who want you dead don't know that you don't know . . . anything, really. After all, you're Cyril's brother and he knows about the boxes, he knows enough to bring him back from Buenos Aires. Put yourself in their shoes. Since Cyril knows about the boxes—whatever there is about those boxes, and we still don't know—he *may* have told you and as long as that possibility exists they figure that you'll have to die, too. Cyril may have told you in his wire for all they know. He *may* have telephoned you from Buenos Aires, he *may* somehow have gotten the word about the boxes to you.

"Those boxes, which had been sitting around that library for years, are terribly important to someone, Cooper. Whether or not Paula knew anything about them, she had them—and they killed her to get them. So we're left with those boxes. What's in them? And what's in the one they left behind? And who was the man who tried to kill you? And who else is in danger? Anyone you've talked to? Doctor Bradlee? Brenner? Me, for Christ's sake? I've got the goddamn box—I may be next on their goddamn list. And, believe me, Cooper, this piece of frozen hamburger out there in the snow didn't do all this by himself—not by a long shot."

Perspiration was standing out on Peterson's forehead and he wiped his face with a handkerchief. It was the first time I'd noticed any evidence of nerves. By talking through it to convince me of the danger, I believe he had opened up some new vistas for himself. I think he was just getting an inkling of the enormity of what was happening, an inkling which had not reached me in my tiredness and sorrow and revulsion at what had happened.

We didn't say much more until the ambulance came and then I heard Peterson giving orders to the men who were going out to get the body. "Be careful not to break him," Peterson warned. "He should be pretty damn brittle by now."

It took us an hour to get my Lincoln and his Cadillac free of the driveway and then I followed him into town. It was twenty-five degrees below zero and the wind was blowing snow everywhere. You couldn't see anything but snow when you looked away from the taillights ahead of you. It was one thirty in the afternoon of January 23.

Eighteen

THE attack on Arthur Brenner was already over by the time Peterson and I were driving into Cooper's Falls. It had begun about noon and continued until one o'clock without interruption and then stopped.

With the storm making travel next to impossible, we might have gone even longer than we did without knowing what had happened. But Peterson had begun to get nervous about Brenner in midafternoon. When he tried to call him there was no answer at his home, no answer at his office in the hotel, and he had not been seen by anyone at the hotel all morning. Peterson looked at me.

Together we drove toward Brenner's house, which sat on the outskirts of town overlooking the river, masked from the road by a hill covered with firs and evergreens and pines. The path had been plowed, was one-car wide, but the tremendous gales had partially refilled the way with powdery snow. We said nothing as we drove. My stomach burned with a bilious nausea; my knees shook. The Cadillac with its four snow tires got stuck at one narrow turn, the front end buried in a wall of snow which extended well above the top of the car. I'd heard of such walls caving in and burying cars, leaving the passengers, with no way of pushing the doors open, to die of carbon monoxide poisoning or freeze if the motor was turned off. Peterson rocked the car back and forth and finally it freed itself as a portion of the wall cascaded down across the hood with enough impact to be felt inside, enough impact to send a shudder through almost three tons of Cadillac.

Coming around the final corner, we saw the house dimly through the curtain of snow, a shapeless mass blending into the grayness of the storm which hung over the river below. As we moved closer, with an agonizing slowness, we saw that the house was dark.

"My God!" There was a quality of awe in Peterson's voice.

An explosion had ripped a hole in the front of Arthur Brenner's white Colonial house. Where there should have been a door there was a jagged cavity, blackened. Windows on the front of the house were blown in.

Peterson stopped the car and we ran as best we could across the snow, sinking to our knees through the crust that bit at us like ragged edges of broken glass.

"Brenner," I heard him calling. "Brenner!" There was desperation in that cry, sorrow and fear and despair.

The front door had been snapped off its hinges and lay smoking in the front hall. A mirror was shattered, a vase of flowers in pieces on the snow-covered hallway floor.

Directly in line with the door and the hole in the front of the house, Arthur Brenner lay face down on the carpeted stairway as if he were trying somehow to crawl up the stairs. He was wearing a heavy wool bathrobe and seemed to be in one piece. He lay very still.

Miraculously, Arthur Brenner was not only alive, but almost untouched. His cheek had been bruised and he had been knocked unconscious by the impact of the blast. But Arthur, huge and elongated on the steps, fluttered open his heavy-lidded eyes, stared up at us, and moved his mouth slowly without making sounds.

[97]

"They booby-trapped the door," Peterson said. "Get him some brandy."

The brandy seemed to revive Brenner and he nodded, swallowing. "I heard the door chimes, I opened the door, and there was an explosion and the next thing I knew you were here."

"I can't tell you how lucky you are," Peterson said.

"I know, I know. They wanted me dead."

Apparently there were no ill effects. In a few minutes Arthur was on his feet, shaking his great head, leading us into his study. While Brenner went to his basement workroom to check his porcelain figures, Peterson quickly built a fire in the grate and had it roaring when the old man came back. He was smiling and had a Band-Aid on his cheek. Not a single piece had been broken.

After giving Arthur a detailed report on what had been happening in the hours since he had bade me goodnight with the suggestion that I say my prayers, Peterson leaned back in the chintz-covered armchair and finally lit a cigar.

"It all adds up to one rather startling fact. Almost impossible to believe. *We are under siege.* This is a war and we are cut off by the elements, under attack from unknown forces. We have killed one of their number. They have killed two of us and tried to kill two more. They have attacked us in our homes with rifle and explosives." He looked at us and I had the feeling of unreality you get when watching a certain kind of movie, when the danger is part of the movie and not of your own life. Of course I was wrong: this was no movie.

"Why?" Brenner asked softly.

"They want that box," Peterson said.

"More," I said. I was terribly tired. "They want to kill anyone who may have seen the contents. Anyone who *may* have seen the contents."

"They are frightened," Peterson said.

"So am I," Brenner said.

In the late afternoon we all climbed back into the Cadillac, negotiated the narrow canyon of driveway, and laboriously made our way back to town. We were at war.

The mayor of Cooper's Falls was waiting for us when we finally got to Peterson's office in the courthouse. He was wearing a purple Minnesota Vikings snowmobile suit and holding a visored purple helmet in his left hand. He belonged to the purple snowmobile standing at the courthouse steps. His face was pale, he was forty-four years old, he owned an insurance agency, and his name was Richard Aho. He was a Finn.

"Peterson," he said calmly as we stood in the outer office with Alice watching us. There was the overpowering reek of strong coffee. The radiators sizzled. It was five o'clock. "Peterson, what is going on here, in this town? I come into the office to try out my new snowmobile, a Christmas present from Phyllis, and I start hearing all sorts of shit."

"What shit, Richard?" Peterson slid out of his coat and hung it on a hook. "Sandwiches, Alice, get 'em over at the hotel, an assortment. And, Alice—you're a dear." He walked through to his own office. "What shit have you been hearing, Richard?" We all went into the office. It was stifling.

"Dead people? That shit." Aho looked persistently at Peterson. "One of the Coopers, of all people, and the librarian, Paula . . . Smithies. Are they dead? Murdered?" He unzipped the purple quilted suit: "Christ, it's hot in here."

"Yes, they've been murdered. And this fellow here"—he pointed at me—"is another Cooper, John Cooper, and they've tried twice to kill him and last night he killed one of them out at the Cooper place. This afternoon they rigged a bomb to Arthur Brenner's house and blew the front off."

Aho took the news with a quiet, staring amazement. Though I had never heard of him, Cooper's Falls was his town, too. From time to time he looked at me. Finally he said: "Mr. Cooper, trouble seems to follow you."

Peterson grinned. Aho's coal-colored eyes bored into me.

I yawned.

"Seems to," I said.

We all ate the sandwiches and learned that our telephone connections to the outside were gone. The storm had taken lines down all along the St. Croix as well as in many rural areas across the state. We could contact the Twin Cities by short wave but so far our little war was ours alone: no word had been sent. Peterson argued that it would do no good since we were unreachable. The highways were all blocked, all airplanes were grounded. Snowmobiles could get through, at least in theory, but the cold was too intense and the visibility in the storm was nil. Unlikely as it seemed, we were cut off from the outside world. Aho nodded his agreement.

There was no word at all from Buenos Aires in response to Peterson's inquiries.

The box sat in the middle of the desk. Peterson nudged it. "The problem is this thing. We've still got it. And they still want it. It's no good to us because we don't know what it means."

"Are they prepared to kiss us all?" Aho pursed his lips.

Peterson shook his head. "I don't know."

"They think they've killed Arthur," I said. "They must have figured that he might have seen the contents of the box and understood what it meant."

Brenner blew his nose and coughed. His cold was worse than ever. He looked his age just then, slumped in a chair in the corner, his muffler wrapped around his throat. Peterson pulled a flask of brandy from his desk and handed it to him.

"They don't know where the box is," Peterson said. Alice brought more sandwiches and coffee. "Why don't you go on home, Alice? It's late."

"I'm afraid to go out," she said. "It's cold, murderers are lurking in the streets, and I'm not going out. I'm staying right here until the storm is over." She was determined.

"Take a room at the hotel," he said. "On the town treasury."

"Well, thank heavens. I will, but I'll wait here awhile yet. You may need me." She went back to the outer office. We could hear her talking to other women who worked in the building, gathered now around her desk.

"Cozy," Brenner said.

"They don't know where the box is," Peterson said. "I think we had better leave the damn box here, lock it up, get to the hotel, and as John Wayne used to say, make our stand there."

No one had a better idea. So we piled back into our gear, closed up the courthouse, and fought our way through the storm to the hotel across the street.

I bedded down in a double room with Arthur. We all drank brandy and stayed together until midnight. The talk was desultory. We were all tired. At midnight, when I could no longer keep my eyes propped open, Peterson insisted that we all get to bed.

Arthur was snoring almost immediately and the close air smelled of the lemon toddy he'd drunk in bed. I was so tired that it was impossible to think. It was a good thing.

Nineteen

THE night came undone with a racketing explosion which brought me awake, sweating in the overheated hotel room. Brenner lay breathing deeply in his bed. I shivered with a chill. My stomach turned. For an instant I wondered why I had wakened; then I heard the continuation of the explosion, which was no quirk of my imagination. It was real and I unwound myself from the bedclothes, went to the window. The streetlights shed a yellow light through the falling snow, and past the snow the courthouse was burning. I heard the whine of snowmobiles, saw only the jagged flames at the windows of the courthouse. There was another detonation, the window before me rattled, new flames were jerked up out of the dim shape of the courthouse.

Brenner stirred. I went into the hallway and began rapping on Peterson's door. He called to me to come in. He was sitting in an armchair by the window staring out across the street. Past him, I saw the flames in the night. Aho stood in the doorway to the white-tiled bathroom, where a light reflected brightly.

Peterson did not turn to me.

"Well, Cooper, what do you think of that? They just blew up my goddamn courthouse." He chuckled bleakly. "Tenacious bastards. I'll give them that. They come out of the night with the weather ready to kill them, forty below zero, they come out of the night on their snowmobiles and they go after that box. And they blow up my courthouse."

Aho sneezed and swore.

I didn't know what to say.

A match flared, I smelled Peterson's cigar.

I looked at my watch; it was three fifteen. My body ached; my head hurt. I shook with a sudden chill. The hotel was beginning to produce sounds as townspeople trapped for the night by the storm came alive, began emptying into hallways.

"Come in here, out of the hall, for Christ's sake," Peterson said. Brenner was up, sniffling behind me, wrapped in his heavy overcoat. He followed me into the room without speaking.

Silently, the four of us stood watching the fire grow through the storm. Flames ate their way through the structure. A wall, damaged by the blasts within, made a crunching, sliding noise and slipped away. A furnace was revealed, yellow and orange, flickering away into the night.

"I wonder if they got the box," Peterson mused. "I put it in the safe in my office. I wonder if they cracked the safe first, got the box, and decided to blow the place up as a kind of gesture. Or if they just blew it up and figured they'd get the box that way? I wonder. . . ."

Aho said: "I do not believe this. Cooper's Falls is being destroyed. That courthouse was over a hundred years old."

"There's nothing we can do about it," Peterson told him. "We don't even see them. They use the snow. They come and do their work and disappear and the snow covers their tracks. Anyway, there must be several of them, at least two more than the guy you killed, Cooper." He puffed the cigar. No one spoke. The fire burned on. "I don't think we'll ever find them. They're operating on us and getting away with it is part of the operation."

Aho sneezed again.

From far away there was another sound like an explosion.

"What was that?" Aho said. He was beginning to sound timid about the whole thing. "Did you hear that?"

"I'd say it was the library," Peterson said, standing up and stretching. "I'd bet they just blew up that lovely little library. They're not taking any chances."

"What the hell should we do?" Aho said.

"I'm going to get dressed and go see what happened at closer range. This town must look like one hell of a Fourth of July."

Arthur Brenner wisely decided to go back to bed. His cold was bad. He was stiff from being flung about by the explosion at his house. He was not as young as he once had been.

"There's nothing you can do, John," he said as he pulled the covers up to his chin. "Why don't you go back to bed, too?"

"I don't know, I just want to see this through, Arthur."

"I should say the world has gone mad," he wheezed. "This is utterly insane, the devil's handiwork."

There was nothing tremendously instructive to see. The night's cold and wind chopped at us; we gasped in the cold. Three walls of the courthouse had collapsed, the inner stairways had created an inferno, the street between the hotel and the courthouse was littered with wreckage and black soot and ashes had discolored the snow, were thickening the atmosphere with acrid smoke, bits of debris. The fire roared over the ripsaw of the storm. It looked like a photograph from World War II.

At the end of the street a glow colored the snow, giving it the look of a pink halo. Peterson had been right; jogging, slapping our bodies to keep warm, we found the exquisite gingerbread library demolished, scattered across the snow crust, burning out of control. Everything was lost, all the books and newspapers, all that Paula had left behind her. Books, intact, lay on the snow, something salvageable. Bits of molding had been driven into the crust like stakes.

No one said anything against the wind.

When morning finally came the snow had stopped. The sky was a clear metallic blue, and the sun shone with a blinding intensity. The surface of the snow glared like a polished stone. We gathered for breakfast at the hotel. The dining room was full: the world seemed to bustle, cars moved in the streets, the people of Cooper's Falls stood in the bitter glare looking with astonishment at the smoking husk of the courthouse, the blackened crater of basement where the library had been and where the mountains of books burst into random flames at odd moments.

Peterson's assistant joined us for breakfast, his mouth agape at what had been happening while he'd taken to his girlfriend's bed with flu the day before. Together we all seemed to sense that the siege was over. Whoever they were, they had the box, or had destroyed it, and there was no way to pick through the wreckage of the courthouse. The volunteer firemen had given it a try at daybreak but the water from the town's mains supply had frozen in the hoses, had never reached the nozzles, and several hoses had snapped like kindling, the rubber instantly frozen. In the morning's gleam automobiles sat in banks of exhaust, motors left running; there was no assurance a car would start once its engine stopped.

Peterson swung into action with an easy sense of efficiency. With the wind and snow abated, the crews were out repairing telephone lines and he immediately got in touch with the Minneapolis FBI office, the state police, and God only knew what other law enforcement agencies. He prepared for the influx of television and newspaper reporters which was bound to follow and took long involved statements from me, from Arthur Brenner, and from Richard Aho.

He continued trying to check with the Buenos Aires police as to Cyril's movements while there. He contacted Doctor Bradlee about the matter of the bodies which had been accumulating. He released the bodies of Cyril and Paula for funeral arrangements, met with Paula's mother, consulted with Wisconsin officials about the attack made against me on their highway system. He set about reducing the horror and carnage of the days of the storm to recognizable, factual events expressed on official forms, in official files. Alice fairly jumped from typewriter to telephone to filing cabinet, all set up in a suite at the hotel.

In the late afternoon official cars began to arrive from the Twin Cities. The governor of Minnesota arrived by helicopter with several aides. The reporters arrived by car and helicopter. They were joined by a mobile television unit. Peterson was swept away from us in this flood of humanity which had so quickly filled the empty, desolate, frozen world of the past few days. But before he gave himself over to public officialdom, Peterson sequestered me in Arthur Brenner's office suite in the hotel. And once he was gone, Arthur and I sat in his bay window overlooking the Breughelesque panorama of the crowded street below us; sat where Paula and I had gone to him for advice, and we talked and smoked and sipped sherry and had food brought to us. It was a warm, snug world; it took time to adjust to the quiet, to the end of the war. And that was clear: by reestablishing our contact with the outside, by surviving the storm and coming out in the clear sunshine, the siege, the war, the attack at Cooper's Falls was over.

Shortly after our dinner, Doctor Bradlee dropped in for coffee and to check our various conditions. He noted acerbically that we both, in all probability, would survive, but as we began our coffee I found myself yawning uncontrollably.

"The best thing you can do," he said, sipping, "is to get to bed. You're physically exhausted. You've been operating under terrible pressure, emotionally and physically, John, and about all that will get you back in any reasonable condition is rest."

Finally under the covers in one of Arthur's twin beds, I lay still with my eyes closed, listened to the murmur of voices from the other room. The two old friends were chatting over their coffee, quietly, undoubtedly considering the altogether unheard of events of the past few days. I lay quiet but sleep was beyond my grasp.

I knew that I was going to do something, take some positive action. I had decided that the gaunt man was not the only murderer, that he may not have killed anyone at all—having failed with me. There was, I felt sure, far more to it than what had been revealed so far. The fingers of the past were reaching out toward me as sleep finally came and I welcomed them. There was comfort in the past, and danger, but that was where it all would end. I knew that as I went to sleep hearing the low voices from the other room and, for me, the past held no fear.

Twenty

THEY used jackhammers to dig the graves. The graveside service was mercifully brief: no one could stand the cold for long, even with the tents that had been erected over the two grave sites, and the electric heaters from the funeral home. The crowd was very small: most of us moved from one burial, Cyril's, to another, Paula's. The sun was bright. A harsh wind cut like a scythe. Flaps on the tents whipped; cars were left running on the path. They were buried on a high bluff overlooking the falls itself. We had come from a very brief church service directly to the cemetery and, the icy wind hurting our lungs, directly back to town.

In the town smoke still rose from the courthouse and the library. We had seen it, like a mist, from where we'd stood at the cemetery. Someone said the fires would burn for days. Everywhere, even at the cemetery, there was no escaping the smell of burning.

Peterson asked me to stop at his improvised office. He stared at the graves, his cheeks burned by the wind. He wore huge sunglasses against the snow-glare.

Later I followed him down to the hotel dining room. He shook his head at two newsmen who started across the lobby toward us. We went in for coffee.

"What are your plans?" he asked.

"I'm not satisfied with all this," I said. "You and I know . . . it's a Swiss cheese, it's all holes being held together by some acts of violence. There must be an explanation."

"Of course." He nodded. "But it's not your business."

"Well, that's debatable, isn't it?"

"So what do you think you're going to do?"

"I'm going to Buenos Aires."

"Why? What for?" He toyed with his spoon.

"Because something rather significant has occurred to me," I said. "About the box, about all that stuff that Paula found, about the men who tried to get it back."

"And what is that? Tell me, what has occurred to you?"

"I can't figure out how these people, these killers—"

"Go on, Cooper, I hang on your words."

"I've been wondering how they found out about the boxes in the first place. Paula told Cyril and that was all, Cyril made no mention of them to me. Paula told no one until I got home. But I've been thinking of the boxes as the key—to everything—" I searched his face. He nodded slowly, eyebrows beetling together. "They tried to kill me but it wasn't because of the boxes. All they knew was that I was coming home and the only way they could have known that was to have known the contents of the telegram. And the only way they could have known the contents of the telegram was to have been watching Cyril. And Cyril was in Buenos Aires. In Argentina, for God's sake. We don't know why he was there but he was there and they knew it; they knew the telegram's message. The boxes didn't come into it until later . . . unless they tapped his telephone and heard the conversation with Paula. Surely they wouldn't have Paula's telephone tapped, she was nothing but an innocent bystander, an accident.

"So, whichever way I look at what happened, I keep coming back to Cyril in Buenos Aires. It had to start there, at least for the rest of us. And I want to know what it all means, Peterson, I want very badly to know. I don't see any other way to find out. I'm going to Argentina, I'm going to find out what Cyril was doing there. I'm going to search for Cyril's past."

"You're very foolish," Peterson said.

"But I'm right."

"You probably are but wouldn't it be safer to leave it alone?"

"Why?"

"These are dangerous men. They have very nearly destroyed a town in the middle of the world's most powerful nation, they have murdered and looted and . . . and you want to find out why." He shook his head. "More guts than brain."

"But I am right."

"Oh, yes, I expect you are."

The coffee cups were empty.

It never really occurred to me not to go to Buenos Aires once the idea had presented itself. Why not? I was in a state of psychic shock, of course, and I had gone off the wagon. It seemed to me that the worst thing I could do was get in the Lincoln and drive back to Cambridge and try to reestablish my normal schedule. My novel could wait but I didn't believe I could simply turn off my thoughts about the war I'd lived through in Cooper's Falls. I didn't want to start thinking the lonely death thoughts. I didn't want to start drinking again. I was going to keep busy. I was going to Buenos Aires and calmly try to find out what my brother had been doing there. There was no plan beyond that. Curiosity was feeding me.

The inexplicability of what had happened confused me. I had myself done an awful thing: I had killed a man. That, coupled with the murders of Cyril and Paula, seemed to have soiled me. It had sucked me in to this remarkable situation and revealed an aspect of myself which I could not have believed possible; I did not want to leave it unfinished.

And I was haunted by the sight of the man in the snow, the wind sifting the snow down from his broad shoulders, the echoing explosions of my shotgun, the wreckage of the man, the frozen shreds of matter from the stump of neck and shoulder. I had done that to him and I could not shake it from my mind.

Peterson told me he was totally unidentifiable. The black Cadillac had disappeared. No one had been found: no snowmobiles, no trail, no evidence of anyone at large in the storm, no trace of camping, nothing . . . except three dead bodies, a house with a door blown off, a courthouse and a library burned to the ground.

My gaunt man was beyond recognizing. *He doesn't exist in any official sense,* Peterson had told me, *and most of his face is scattered all over the snow in your front yard.*

I wanted the answers and I was going to Buenos Aires. Perhaps they were there. I had no place else to begin.

I spent my last night in Cooper's Falls with Arthur Brenner. The storm was over, the night air was clear and glacial. The wind chill factor was seventy degrees below zero, but the Lincoln had been attended to by Arnie Johnson and purred in the cold. Carpenters had been at work boarding up the front of Arthur's house. The wings of fire blackling extended beyond the patchwork, streaking the white front of the house. A temporary door had been installed and Arthur greeted me in a cheery Pendlèton plaid shirt and heavy corduroy work trousers. He was smiling and reassuring, settling me on a comfortable couch before a flickering fire of birch logs with their white bark peeling away, turning to flame.

He was generous with his best sherry. Actually, Arthur's only sherry was the very best. He had been working on Flowerdieu's Charge in his workroom, eagerly explained the various steps of working with porcelain. The warmth of the room lulled me and he had prepared a roast himself, a hearty meal buttressed with vegetables and homemade bread and robust burgundy. We ate almost without speaking of the horrors the week had brought. What we did say was circumspect, judicious; an act. We were both tired. But as I listened to him at the table, it occurred to me that he was somehow remote, untouched by the tragedies. He was old: death had less sting for him. He doubted, perhaps, the ultimate worth of life in the last resolve.

It was late and we heard the wind chewing at the makeshift work at the front of the house. The brandy was warmed, cleared my head.

I told him I was going to Buenos Aires and he looked at me sideways.

"You shouldn't go there. You're making a mistake."

I told him I wanted to find out what it all meant, why Cyril had come home to be murdered. I told him what had occurred to me: that they must have been watching Cyril or they would never have known about the boxes.

"Those blasted boxes," he said gruffly, with sudden conviction. "Better they'd never been found, left to gather dust and mold until we were all dead and forgotten . . . out of their reach. Whatever the hell was in them." He whipped a match along a fireplace brick and lit a cigar, flung the match into the fire.

"Death," he said. "Those boxes meant death, John, surely you see that—for your brother, for Paula. Stay out of it now. These men, these murderers are gone. They've got the boxes. There's nothing left to frighten them, they're satisfied, they've gone. Leave it, John. Let Peterson do his job, let him do what he thinks best, let the FBI do their best. But you, you stay out of it—it's serious."

He threw another log on the fire and poured more brandy into my snifter. We sat quietly. The clock on the mantelpiece chimed midnight. Arthur began to talk about my grandfather, about the times they had spent in Germany in the twenties and thirties. Austin was a practical man, he said, a pragmatist, but not a political man, not a theorist. I wanted to know, as I always had, what my grandfather really thought of the Nazis. I suppose I wanted to hear that he had despised them, yet I knew he was not an emotional man who despised anyone or anything. My grandfather asked only one question: Does it work? What worked fascinated him. It was simple but I never had known that Arthur Brenner thought about such things. I asked him as the wind blew, the fire's shadows flickered on the wall.

"I can't say I was fond of any of them individually. Your grandfather didn't even think of them in a personal sense. For him they were politicians, no different from other politicians except that they seemed more efficient, more determined. They were undeniably impressive men in their own way. . . . Of course, your father had to try to live it all down. A tragedy, that. As for myself . . . as for myself, I felt a grudging admiration for them. Not a moral admiration, of course, but something else. I tended to try to look at them with a certain detachment, tried to see them in the long view—of history, a long view taken by some rather brilliant men. . . ."

He went on in this vein for some time. I had never heard him speak so reflectively on the past. In my mind's eye I saw him as a young man, massive and blunt faced, eyes narrowing as he took the measure of men like Hitler and Goering, weighed them on the scales of historical urgency, and noted in his little book the results. By seeing them straight on rather than from behind a screen of moral righteousness, Brenner must have been of great use to the Allies during the war. I remembered how we would see him from time to time in Cooper's Falls, how he invariably came to visit my grandfather, how the New York *Times* once published an article about him in which they pointed out the curious friendship between this highly placed government intelligence man and the nation's most prominent Nazi sympathizer. It was a curious bond; surely it stemmed from Arthur's ability to keep self-serving moral judgments from intruding on friendship.

"Everyone becomes, in victory, obsessed by the moral factor," he said, swirling brandy in the snifter, turning his face to the fire, "and then a great deal of pure hokum is given wide currency. War, however, has never been considered immoral at the highest levels of responsibility—merely wise, or unwise in the event you lose or your aims are not fulfilled. Hitler's war was not immoral, his attempt to bring Europe to heel—my God, it's a perfectly rational idea in the sense of political and economic reality. Psychologically it was sound, the Teutonic peoples being what they are." He caught my eye. "The idea of their superiority is not exactly new, nor exactly unfounded, John. Read your history. . . ." He turned back to the fire. "Hitler was the embodiment of a certain national will, the result of the Peace of Versailles. The thing I had constantly to argue was the absence of any moral question in his widest aims. Morality came into it with the Jews, the Gypsies, any of the people he set out to exterminate. That is, generally speaking, morally reprehensible and the one gigantic error in the thousand-year plan. How could he have blundered so badly, when the world was in his grasp? The mind quakes at it, John, the immensity of the flaw. Obviously, he ought to have included the Jews, with their enormous wealth, intelligence, acumen. By absorbing the Jews into the Reich, Hitler would have united Europe and created the most powerful economic and political union in the history of the planet.

"Then there were the mystical elements of the entire endeavor, the conception of the young Siegfried sleeping, awaiting the time when he would rise again. These, of course, bypassed your grandfather completely." Arthur smiled, nodded tolerantly. "Myth, music, the energy harnessed at the great rallies. He was totally unimpressed, embarrassed by what he felt was 'show,' a vulgar display.

"I was somewhat more interested in all that. It

was the use of energy that impressed me, the way the Nazis controlled the spirit of obedience. The potential for accomplishment was unthinkably immense. There is something fascinating about fanaticism, John, something compelling about men who believe deeply that they have the answer and are willing to do anything for it." He sniffled, blew his red nose. "Nothing like that over here, of course. People are not so obedient."

I said: "But, Christ, Arthur! They were all crazy!"

He said calmly, smiling: "Oh, no, John, they weren't crazy. They were a half-step out of line, they possessed the great flaw, but they were far from crazy. They were strong and daring men, somewhat off course, but in another time there's no doubt of it, they would have ruled the world. They were not thugs, John, take my word for that, and they understood a great many truths—they understood that death is not so much, after all, and they knew, *knew* there was truth in a kind of social Darwinism. I spent a great deal of time with them, devoted many years of my life to bringing them down, I know them well . . . and much of what they said is very hard to argue with."

Before I left, Arthur tried again to talk me out of going to Buenos Aires. It was no use.

"These men may be still watching," he said, but he spoke with a dying fall.

"Why? They've got the boxes. Or destroyed the last one if they didn't actually take it."

"Perhaps you're right, John, perhaps. . . ."

"Arthur, you were my grandfather's closest adviser. Do you know what was in those boxes, why anyone would want them?"

"No. But then that's the mystery, isn't it? But as you say, they've got them now."

He was standing in the window waving to me as I drove away down the path. He was a warm man. I hoped I would see him again.

Peterson drove me to the International Airport just south of Minneapolis. He gave me a letter to give to a police captain in Buenos Aires with whom he'd been in contact. Nothing had been added to fill in the blanks: no traces of the attackers, no identification of my dead man, no information about his rifle. No further clues at the Cooper house, no light on my brother's murder. As we drove up the long hill leading out of Cooper's Falls, the smoldering ruins of the library and courthouse blotted the snowscape behind us.

We had little to talk about; everything had been said.

We drank coffee at the lunch counter; the planes taxied past the bank of windows. The weather had warmed: a thick gray fog obscured the end of the runways so that the huge machines seemed to materialize, be upon us from nowhere.

"Do you know what that stuff in the metal box was?"

"No."

"So we'll never know, then."

"Oh, I expect we'll know."

I stared at him. "What does that mean?"

"It means that I left the box in the courthouse that night, Cooper. And the box was empty. The papers I put in my overcoat pocket. I'm taking them to the cryptographers in Washington myself. The Feds have set the whole thing up. They got tremendously interested at the mention of Austin Cooper. They haven't forgotten him."

"The box was empty," I said.

"The box was empty." He smiled.

"So our friends don't have the papers. They know they didn't burn. . . ."

"I'm afraid they do, Cooper. We located the safe in the ashes and debris. The door had been taken off. The box was gone."

"They know. . . ."

"They know."

He saw me to the boarding gate. We shook hands and he smiled, his mustache curling down around the corners of his mouth like a bandit. As the jet lifted off into the fog the terminal disappeared, there was nothing but moisture beading up on the windows, streaking across them past my face. The stewardesses began to bustle about with lunch. "I'll be seeing you," Peterson had said. But what clung in my mind was something else, echoing in my brain.

They know.

Part Two

Buenos Aires

FROM my window at the Plaza Hotel on Florida Avenue I looked out across a green park, past jacaranda trees and vivid flowers, and felt soft, warm summer breezes. I sat in the midafternoon warmth watching Buenos Aires spread out beneath me like a green blanket.

While waiting for Peterson's policeman to return to his office, I turned it over in my mind. They knew the box was empty; they knew they had destroyed half a town and failed.

"These men may still be watching," Arthur had said.

Whoever they were, they had not wanted the boxes to find out what was in them. I was positive of that: they knew what was in them. They wanted to keep us from finding out.

And I was full of the unfeeling, unemotional impulse which had been growing inside of me ever since I had killed the gaunt man. Everything that followed had come so fast, so brutally: I felt as if normal reactions had been washed away. When I chose Buenos Aires and the search instead of Cambridge and the novel I had pretty well sealed it.

The telephone rang.

Ramón Roca looked like a dignified, imperturbable floorwalker in a 1930's movie but he was, instead, a captain of detectives for the Buenos Aires police. His office was on Moreno but we met at nine o'clock that evening at the Claridge Hotel Grill on Tucumán where, he had assured me on the telephone, we could enjoy an excellent and quiet dinner.

The temperature when I left the Plaza was ninety-four and so was the humidity. There was no breeze: I swam to the taxi. The night was full of bright life, people moving, well dressed and handsome. There were flashes of color in the flower stalls. The paradise and jacaranda trees lined the streets, purple and yellow. I left early enough to go for a ride down Ninth of July Avenue, with its ten lanes of traffic, the widest thoroughfare in the world.

Roca was waiting for me at a dim corner table and rose as I was led toward him. He was wearing a very dark suit, gold-rimmed spectacles, and offered a small, fine-boned hand I was afraid I'd crush. He was about sixty, with fine white hair combed back and worn moderately long. He was drinking scotch and his voice was faint and precise: he was used to being listened to.

"Mr. Cooper, it is so good to meet you. Your friend Mr. Peterson has set us an interesting task and it is now so pleasant to connect the task with a human being." He smiled very thinly and formally beneath his fine gray mustache and lit a cigarette and exhaled neatly as if he didn't want the smoke to impinge on anyone else. I ordered a drink.

He had ordered dinner for us: Edward VII steak, which turned out to be a mixture of *pâté de foie gras,* ham, and steak. While we ate and drank he talked as if he were lecturing me on a little-known smidgen of Argentine exotica.

"Your brother was in Buenos Aires for the full week ending on the seventeenth of January, when he left for Los Angeles via Pan American. At Mr. Peterson's request we have reconstructed your brother's visit as best we could. And, let me add," he said, patting his thin mouth with white linen, "you have my sympathy."

He produced a manila folder from a black briefcase and placed it unopened on the table.

"Everything I have to tell you is noted in the enclosed dossier, Mr. Cooper. But let me summarize it for you." He opened the folder like a conductor with his score.

"We know when he arrived, that he came to us from Cairo, Egypt, where he stayed, and when he left for Los Angeles. We have learned of meetings between your brother and one Martin St. John. They were seen dining at the Jockey Club, which is our most exclusive such facility and of which Mr. St. John is, rather curiously, a member." He tasted his wine and went on.

"Mr. St. John cuts an extraordinary figure in Buenos Aires. He is a sort of informational miracle. He knows everyone in politics and power and politics and power are his"—he shrugged, eyebrows raised—"games, you might say.

"He is an Englishman by birth but dates well back here in Buenos Aires, almost thirty years to the beginnings of the Perón period. We are not altogether certain as to what he was doing before Perón took him up. He is said to be a Cambridge man. He is said to have been seen in India and Hong Kong and Egypt before and during the war. Mr. St. John's past is exceedingly shadowy. When he appeared in Buenos Aires he could not have been more than twenty-six or twenty-seven years old. What, or who, recommended him to Perón I have no idea. I have been fairly well aware of his career, particularly following the fall of Perón, since his protection has been somewhat less complete than before." He finished his wine and constructed an interlocking bridge of slender fingers across his narrow, vested chest.

"Why were you interested?" I asked. "Was he a criminal or something? And what did Cyril want with him?"

"St. John saw the Perón regime from the inside, Mr. Cooper. He was not a criminal. He was, as far as we can tell, a security expert, a kind of unofficial but indispensable counterintelligence officer, yet enough of a chameleon to go unharmed after Perón's fall. Presumably, he was useful elsewhere, too useful to suffer an ignominious death and an unmarked grave—as occasionally happened in those days." A bleak smile faded quickly, dark eyes flickered downward to his papers.

"What one knows with some certainty is that he was important in the scheme which brought so many Germans—Nazis, of course, but many others as well —to Argentina during the latter stages of World War II and shortly thereafter. St. John, however, has always struck me as a singularly apolitical man, regardless of Perón's admiration for Mussolini among other gentlemen of that persuasion." Roca's eyes skittered across the dossier again, replaced the top sheet with one from below.

"St. John saw these escaping Germans as sources of rather substantial income . . . but for whom?" He spread his palms open. "For St. John, no doubt, and for Perón himself—and, I am firmly convinced, some of it found its way into the national treasury. After all, we are speaking of very large sums of money and Perón was not what one might call an economic success. He needed all the revenues he could find."

The meal had been cleared away and coffee and Napoleon brandy served. Roca also arranged for cigars and we lit them in comfortable silence. It was past eleven o'clock.

"How," I finally asked, "do we know what my brother wanted with St. John? All this past history."

"I suspect that you'll find youself asking Mr. St. John that question. However, there are other points we have yet to discuss concerning your brother's visit to Buenos Aires, points which tie him rather closely to St. John's past." He consulted his papers and made a check mark with a ball-point pen.

"Your brother left Buenos Aires after being here only one week. It has been difficult to retrace all his movements but we were surprisingly successful with a taxi driver whose primary source of fares is here, the Claridge Hotel. Twice this man took your brother on lengthy trips." The papers got a sharp glance across the tops of his spectacles. "Once to the polo matches at Palermo Park and once to the estate of Alfried Kottmann."

"Kottmann—a German," I said.

"In addition to being a deft polo player for a man

of his age, Kottmann is one of the leaders of our German community. He arrived here in 1943, on Christmas Day, actually, in the height of summer, and he has been here ever since. Immensely wealthy. And thought to be St. John's first big catch. Perón had not yet come to power but he was an immensely influential figure behind the scenes and St. John was well in with him.

"In June of 1943, President Ramón Castillo was overthrown by army generals. The army during the 1930's had come under very widespread Nazi influence, you see, as the Nazis tried very hard—very hard, Mr. Cooper—to make Argentina part of what came to be called the Axis powers. Argentina was to be the foothold, the Germany of the Americas, the beginning of the New Order in the New World. While the attempt never ultimately succeeded, within the army the Nazis had a considerable effect. The army became a very Teutonic institution—right down to the uniforms and emblems and organization, to say nothing of its attitudes.

"However, once the generals had got rid of Castillo, they proved to be utterly disunited. Rawson, the first of the army presidents, endured one day. General Ramirez followed him and lasted nine months. It was during this period that St. John arranged for Kottmann's arrival. In any case Farrell followed Ramirez and lasted until 1946 at which time Colonel Juan Domingo Perón himself emerged, accompanied by his movie actress wife, Eva, and together they ruled the country for nine years. During those nine years, Mr. Cooper, Juan Perón and Eva stamped this country with their own image, for better as well as worse, and only now are we emerging from their shadows." He swirled brandy thoughtfully on his tongue before continuing.

"Of course, Perón lives in exile in Spain and there are those who would bring him back. But during those Perón years, Martin St. John was never far from power. And, since Perón was a great admirer of fascism, the German emigrants—many with immense wealth at their disposal—were welcomed.

Perón grew immensely wealthy himself, St. John got his share, and the Germans found a safe harbor in a war-torn world which did not for the most part look on them at all kindly." He stroked cigar ash into a glass bowl.

"As for Kottmann, he was a wealthy industrialist in Germany, got out when the time was ripe, and has lived very discreetly here for more than a quarter of a century. Utterly impeccable, Mr. Cooper, no nasty Nazi connections . . . at least none have ever been found."

Dinner was over, the brandy gone, the cigars burned low. Roca patted the folder and removed his gold-rimmed spectacles. He folded them and inserted them into a black leather case. "It's all here in the dossier." He smiled, signed the check, and we left. The night was heavy and warm and struck like a fist when you left the air conditioning.

From the shadows a small, white-faced man appeared to open the door of a black Chevrolet sedan. We settled into the back seat and the small man climbed in behind the wheel.

"There is no particular reason," Roca said as we slid through the night, "why you should concern yourself with the intricacies of life here in Buenos Aires. Merely exercise discretion and prudence yourself and all will be well. Argentina is a moral conundrum, Mr. Cooper. Don't judge us. You would go mad in the attempt. Simply go about your business here, satisfy your curiosity, and enjoy our summer. All will be well."

Roca was a serenely sophisticated man and I liked him. He was a good host. He was full of good advice. And he was scaring me.

"I have arranged an appointment with Mr. St. John for you tomorrow. The details are noted in the dossier. Please, let's meet again before you depart Buenos Aires."

"Of course," I said. "I'll look forward to it." I meant it. I watched the black Chevrolet disappear in the flow of traffic.

I was sweating in the night.

[124]

"Sinjin is my name, Mr. Cooper." A laugh full of the gravel of good tobacco and good liquor rumbled in his thick chest. "Pronounce it Sin-Jin. Americans always call me Saint John—makes me sound quite awfully Biblical, doesn't it? And that won't do, will it?"

He was broad and wore a rumpled, soiled white suit with a flower in the buttonhole. He balanced a broad-brimmed straw hat with a bright band and a flat crown on his knee. There was a network of laugh lines spraying out from the corners of his soft brown eyes, and his thick unruly hair was whiter than the suit. His overall untidiness made him look older than he was: he ought to have been in his late fifties by Roca's reckoning.

"I hope this was a convenient meeting place, old boy. When Roca got through to me I'd already scheduled a board meeting here at the Opera earlier this morning and I couldn't very well scratch it, could I? In any case, you oughtn't miss the Opera." His eyes swept the empty auditorium with a sense of pride. "Lovely, isn't it?"

I followed his expansive gesture. "Yes, it is lovely. Magnificent."

The smile turned to concern. "Roca tells me of your family tragedy, Mr. Cooper. The least I could do was give you some time."

From the outside the Colón Opera House is Grecian, elegant and graceful. Inside it is all red plush. We were sitting in the middle of the auditorium, where he'd led me from the lobby. Apparently St. John was one of the governors or trustees: someone responsible.

"I was damned sorry to hear of your brother's misfortune. But he was a troubled fellow when he came to see me. Wary, damned wary . . . of me, perhaps. He came to me with a peculiar story, I might say an intriguing story. He had a newspaper clipping he showed me, a photograph of a strikingly beautiful young woman and a somewhat older man." His eyes twinkled like two mice in the broad, friendly cheese of his face. "He asked me if I knew them but I'd never seen either one of them in my life. And he wanted to meet Alfried Kottmann. I asked him why and why he'd come to me and he hedged, said that he was sure I knew damned well why he'd come to me.

"Well, I mulled that one over a bit. After all, who was he? What did he know about me and Kottmann? Not that any of it's a secret, of course. But for just a moment I thought he was one of Simon Weisenthal's eager lads hot on the trail of Martin Bormann or another Eichmann. You'd be surprised how many of those chaps I've treated to lunch while they interrogated me as if I were some sort of Nazi flunky." He frowned. "But I try not to be irritated. They are merely doing their work and the breadcrumbs seem fairly often to lead to old Martin St. John in Buenos Aires. I point out to them that all Germans are not necessarily war criminals and we go round a bit and they eventually toddle off." He slid comfortably down in the red plush and let it roll forward on its ball bearings. He crossed his short thick legs in front of his comfortable potbelly, rumpling himself all the more.

"But then he mentioned his grandfather, with whom I was familiar as anyone my age would be, and I decided he was not a fire-eating Israeli after all." Bushy eyebrows drew together. "He never told me directly why he wanted to see Kottmann but he seemed surprised when I said that it would be no particular problem, that I would call Alfried and arrange a meeting."

St. John's presence was strong, that of an actor playing a part. He was at home in the ornate, gilded theater.

"We met several times—he was a persistent devil —your brother," he said, grinning. "He asked me a good deal about the old days, about Perón and Eva, and I then got the idea that he might be writing a book. About his grandfather, perhaps, or the Nazi movement in the hemisphere. He wanted to know all about the Nazis. However, I'm afraid I was a disappointment to him. Finally he had to be satisfied that I had arranged a meeting with Alfried Kottmann."

We walked back up the aisle, through the forest

of red plush and out into the sunshine and humidity. He offered me lunch and I accepted. We strolled along the crowded avenue with its ten lanes of traffic, found a small open-air restaurant. We drank cold lemon squashes with gin. I was tired; it was the heat. I urged him to continue.

"Well," he went on, sipping the drink and removing his splendid hat to let the breeze at his white hair, "yes, I was involved with bringing certain Germans to Argentina, anyone who cares knows that. I was rather closely involved with Colonel Perón in those days and he was quite smitten with the German style, and with Nazism, too. There's no point in pretending he wasn't. But Nazism has come to mean a good many things in the years since then—exterminating Jews, for example, slave labor and concentration camps and so on. That is not, however, what Nazism meant to Perón. To Perón it meant efficiency, effective leadership, discipline, and, above all else, nationalism. Nazism, fascism, whatever—it meant pride in one's nation, the subordination of everything to the greater good of the nation. That was what impressed Perón about the Germans and he even gave it his own name . . . . *justicialismo*." He motioned for another drink and I thought of Brenner, who had said some rather similar things that last night.

"Perón thought it would be just damned jolly to get some of the Hun to Argentina and I was to act as a conduit. And I was an eager young chap on the make." He grinned, roguishly, candid.

"And Kottmann," I said. "Where did Kottmann fit into it?"

"Alfried Kottmann was one of the first and one of the richest. He let it be known in certain circles that he wanted egress in 1943—actually, it wouldn't surprise me if he were a stalking horse for those who followed, rather in the way of finding out how well it would work and precisely where he would be welcome." He flashed me another grin, crinkling the corners of his eyes, as if we were both men of the world who understood such things. "And how much it would cost, of course. Argentina was a natural possibility because of the Nazi success here with much of the public in the thirties and with the army right on through the forties. Perón wanted to make the deal and I handled the negotiations because, presumably, he trusted me. Eventually, Kottmann was delivered to Buenos Aires and that was that. The case was regarded as proven and a flourishing little traffic was begun. But"—he smiled deprecatingly—"as I told your brother, Mr. Cooper, that is all ancient history. A game played by young men in the long ago." He wet his thick lips with the lemon squash. The traffic on the avenue seemed far away.

"But Kottmann was nonpolitical?" I asked.

"Such men are almost always nonpolitical. The politicians need them, rather than the other way around, so there is no pressure to affiliate oneself with politics. The Kottmanns of the world always outlast the Hitlers. That is a basic law of history. The Kottmanns deal in Hitlers."

The sun was being smudged by cloud cover. The air had grown perceptibly cooler, if no less humid, and the waiter brought sandwiches. The wind tweaked St. John's yellow buttonhole flower.

"I never discussed politics with Kottmann. Politics!" He popped the word contemptuously. "All those hysterical and utterly bogus moral judgments, winners always having God and Right, to say nothing of Might, on their side and scurrying about hanging losers from every available lamppost after the war. All of that is trivial shit in the manipulation of real power, Mr. Cooper. Shit!" He fixed the grin but it was cold.

"Perón was the victim of such judgments before his exile, but they were foolish. He did some of the right things and some of the wrong things, he was far from infallible, but moral judgments are hollow and false." He pushed out his lower lip and regarded me in the manner of a sage.

"Well, surely," I said, "there are such things. Morality is a palpable fact of conduct—"

But he brushed me away with the meaty hand, shook his head, said only: "Winners and losers, Mr. Cooper, nothing else. I believe in nothing else." The hand was a fist.

"In the end, Perón, the great leader, was the victim of what must be called a popular revolution. The country came almost in half but rather more turned against him. It was a very close thing . . . but it was enough." He raised his eyes to heaven.

Lunch was gone and we were standing back at the curb and Martin St. John was engulfing my hand in his. There was a smattering of lovely fresh lemon squash dribblings on his white suit. He squared the straw hat on his large head.

"Well, Mr. Cooper, I hope I've been of some help. Your brother didn't keep his last appointment with me. He did go to see Kottmann but he never came back to see old Martin St. John. As a matter of fact, I've still got that clipping." A taxicab pulled over. "I'll arrange an appointment with Kottmann and call you at your hotel. The Plaza, isn't it?"

"Yes, the Plaza," I said. "That clipping—I'd like to see it."

"Of course, you will—we'll be in touch, won't we?"

I nodded and he was gone. The thunder was louder now and the clouds were purple. I was very tired. I got my own cab. The day was almost gone and I felt as if I'd spent it with Sidney Greenstreet.

I bought the Buenos Aires *Herald* and the airmail New York *Times* as I walked through the Plaza lobby and ducked into the ritzy, famous American Bar for something tall and cold.

On an inside page of the *Herald* I was mildly astounded to find a brief story about "the siege of a small Minnesota town," which they had picked up off the wire. It was brief, but the facts were there: two murders, the courthouse and library blown up, one of the attackers killed. My name wasn't mentioned, nor was anyone else's but Mayor Richard Aho, who had apparently made a statement. The idea of a siege was news anywhere, no doubt.

Curious, I went carefully through the *Times* and there it was, right before the cultural coverage. DEATH, DESTRUCTION VISIT MINNESOTA VILLAGE: that was the head. The story said the attack was motiveless, occurred during the winter's worst storm when the town had been totally isolated. Cyril's name was used and the connection to our grandfather duly but objectively made. Aho and Peterson were named. Peterson was in Washington, D. C., and was unavailable for comment. Aho had obviously been instructed by Peterson to keep his mouth shut and I could imagine the reporters flocking to the scene, frustrated, angry.

I finished my drink and went upstairs to my room. I opened the windows, took off my clothes, and stretched out in a lukewarm tub. I tried to fit all that Roca and St. John had told me into some framework with what I knew about Cyril and what had happened in Cooper's Falls. Roca merely played his cards properly, survived several regimes, and lived to preach discretion to inquisitive young North Americans. Yet he had led me to St. John. . . .

And St. John had been quite willing to go on with the story. But why not? It had all happened so long ago. They spoke of the Nazi phenomenon as if it had been cast in bronze and placed under glass. Yet, it was all I had to tie Cyril, Buenos Aires, and Cooper's Falls together.

The telephone woke me and I struggled dripping from the tub. It was eight thirty. St. John was speaking to me and I recognized a Beethoven quartet in the background. He said Kottmann would see me at breakfast. A car would be sent to the Plaza, if that was acceptable to me, six o'clock in the morning.

"Of course it is," I said, staring down at Buenos Aires in the late, slanting sunshine seeping past the dark clouds on the horizon. "Of course."

When he rang off, the telephone produced a click followed by another almost simultaneous click, an electronic echo. St. John was gone.

The Mercedes limousine was forest green, longer than a small parade, and dappled with raindrops. When I came through the doors the rain-washed cool of morning touched my face. The jacaranda and paradise seemed to be the invention of a gifted watercolorist.

Rolling through the wet, fresh six o'clock streets of Buenos Aires, I wondered if the New York *Times* had a man in the snow talking to Peterson and I wondered, then, if Peterson was back from Washington and what the cryptographers had learned from the contents of the box. It seemed peculiarly far away: I felt my life split in two, divided by the flight to Buenos Aires.

We wound north from the city toward El Tigre. The sun was beginning to shine tentatively through the bunkers of rain clouds rolling from the South Atlantic to my right. On my left the greenery was thick and deep. Somewhere out across the Rio de la Plata was Montevideo. The sun came and went, rain splattered the window.

At seven thirty we reached the estate. We had swung back from the road and up a steep incline, leveled out in a tunnel of greenery, and suddenly there was a huge iron gate towering above us, guardhouses on either side. At the approach of the Mercedes the gates began the rather tedious job of sliding open and a man in one of the buildings nodded to my driver as we eased through.

Bright flowers exploded in color on either side of us as we proceeded on up the narrow drive of finely crushed gray stone. It silently pulled away again as I was led up the walk between the flowers and across the portico, into the echoing hallway. There were several gigantic paintings of horses and castles on the Rhine in rich dark frames and the floor was stone. The furniture was European, silk, antique.

"Follow me, please." The butler was far older than he at first appeared. He walked very straight but his voice was dry and cracked. "Herr Kottmann will see you in back, if you will be so kind."

I followed him through French doors and out across a veranda, along another gray path between more flowerbeds. Five or six people in robes were sitting around a large white wrought-iron table near a swimming pool. A maid in a black dress which looked twenty years out of date was serving them breakfast. The mist was clearing. They did not look up at me as I was led past: an older woman, a man and woman who seemed to be in their late twenties, some children. Their voices were low. Spoons clicked on china.

The butler led me to a spot beneath a shade tree.

He produced a towel from his pocket and wiped the rain from another wrought-iron table and chairs. "Herr Kottmann will join you here, if you would be so good as to wait." He held the chair for me and when I was seated I heard his heels come faintly together. "Coffee will be served." He went away listing slightly to starboard but erect, holding on to his illusion of youth. I wondered how long he'd served Herr Kottmann.

Across a tremendous expanse of emerald grass, wet and thick, a man was riding a pale horse in the shifting sunshine. He was far away and rode well, wore a helmet, and leaned down from the saddle to stroke a ball. In one fluid movement he would cantilever himself away from the horse and swing the mallet in a graceful arc through the heavy moist morning. Later the sound of the smack would come floating toward me as I watched him move off in the path of the ball, tracing it across the turf. As he came closer I saw the hooves spray divots, heard the snorting of the pony as it wheeled and accelerated.

He finally reined in about twenty yards away and sat patting its pale neck, talking to it. Then he dismounted, shucked off the helmet, tucked it under his arm, and a groom appeared to lead the horse away. He strode toward me purposefully.

"Mr. Cooper," he said, extending a hand. "I am Alfried Kottmann." He smiled through a thin mouth, white teeth glinting. He smoothed his black hair straight back. His skin was tight and tanned and fit. He turned and gave me an aquiline profile with ridges at the corners of his mouth. "Here comes the coffee." The woman in the out-of-date black dress, her hair in a suitable Teutonic coil, carried a silver coffee service. "I'll pour, Hilda," Kottmann said. "Thank you."

He carefully poured cream into my coffee and spooned sugar. It was bitter and thick, bracing.

"Your journey was satisfactory?"

"Yes, it was very beautiful."

"I am prone to these early meetings because I seem to be an early riser. I work the ponies most mornings, enjoy my beautiful environment, my flowers, have my coffee, shower, and find that I am really quite primed for the day." He leaned back in his chair, crossed his legs, held his cup and saucer on his thigh. He wore whipcord jodhpurs and high brown riding boots, a red polo shirt with a towel draped around his neck. His boots were creased with age and toned with years of polish; they were flecked with moist black earth and wet grass. The only things missing were the dueling scars and monocle.

"I was terribly sorry to learn of your brother's untimely passing, Mr. Cooper. He was here such a short time ago and now, so abruptly, I learn he is dead."

"Someone murdered him."

I could hear the wind in the trees. It carried the voices of the people by the pool: a child leaped into the water, there was a splash, children shouted happily. I had not thought of the fact of Cyril's death for several days and now, for some reason, it came to me with a jolt. He was gone.

"Your brother called on me here, Mr. Cooper, chairs. . . . My life has changed so little, I still ride the ponies each morning and have my coffee . . . and your brother is dead." He shook his head gravely. "In the midst of life, eh, Mr. Cooper? We never know." He looked at the back of his hand. "I stay fit, stay out of doors as much as possible. Yet, there are liver spots on my hand. I am sixty-eight and there's no pretending with Father Time, is there?"

"You look younger," I said.

"It is my young wife." He smiled briefly, gesturing at the group over his shoulder. I had thought it was his wife, his children, his grandchildren, but I'd been wrong.

"In any case, Mr. Cooper, I understand that you are curious as to what your brother was doing here in Buenos Aires. Mr. St. John arranged for him to meet me. I saw no reason to see him at first but then my curiosity prevailed. I am not a particularly public man. I live quietly, see my old friends. But I decided I might as well meet your brother. Perhaps it was because Mr. St. John had told me who Cyril Cooper actually was, the grandson of Austin Cooper. Now,

I certainly knew about Austin Cooper's friendship with Herr Hitler and all the rest of those fellows. Your grandfather was not looked upon as an American traitor in Germany, by Germans—on the contrary, he was felt to be simply a friend of Germany, a man of vision who saw a strong, rebuilt Germany as the key to the strength of Europe. Many sophisticated Germans saw your grandfather as one of the bulwarks in our hope of staving off the Russians, you see . . . quite apart from the Second World War."

"What did my brother want from you?" I asked.

"So I saw him," Kottmann went quietly on. "It was not so simple discovering why he wanted to see me. I had the feeling he was not being perfectly frank with me. He said he was a journalist, that he was interested in the German community in Buenos Aires, how we all got here, how we managed to live down the Nazi stigma. . . ." He sipped the coffee, tweezed a piece of turf from his boot. He caught my eye and seemed to be looking through me.

"It was my duty to inform him that I felt there was no Nazi stigma to live down, that Germany and Argentina had enjoyed close relations for a great many years, and that if there was a stigma to live down it was a stigma borne by South Americans generally for the hideous manner in which Germans of all sorts were persecuted during the late thirties and early forties. You see, that was the truth of those years, Mr. Cooper, an unpleasant fact ignored in your country. All Germans were looked upon as agents of Herr Hitler, regardless of their own beliefs—being a German was enough. You see, Hitler claimed that even if your blood was only one-quarter German, you were all German, all Nazi, surely poised to take up arms for the Nazi cause . . . anywhere in the world. He said there were three hundred thousand Germans in Argentina in 1942, each of whom sympathized with Nazi aims, and the world actually believed him. He said that there was the framework of an entire Nazi state within the borders of South America and the rumors spread and were frequently reported in the press. Even *La Prensa* here in Buenos Aires swallowed some of it—secret airfields in the Andes, immensely powerful jungle radio stations. Nazis high in the various governments. In Montevideo, if you were a German, you were lucky not to be jailed on mere principle.

"In reality," he said, plucking the end from a croissant and moistening it with coffee, "what you actually had was a band of swaggering would-be SS and Gestapo boobs hanging around cafes loudly letting it be known they were German agents and discussing absurdities along the general lines of taking over the Panama Canal from secret bases in Colombia and going to war with the United States." He smiled a trifle sadly and ate the morsel. "Can you imagine that? Those blithering nincompoops were the Nazi threat in South America." He shook his head.

"Why did you come here, then? If it was such an inhospitable place?" I was beginning to feel secure. I knew he was lying, or at least embroidering the truth to his own benefit.

"Ah, well, Mr. Cooper, I'm exaggerating the peril and, in any case, by Christmas of 1943 the situation had calmed down a good deal. Argentina was still neutral, but within three weeks the United States demanded that she give up her neutrality and come in on the Allied side . . . and there was relatively little opposition. Argentina did as she was told and the people realized that the Nazi threat, if there had ever been one, was over.

"When I decided I had to leave Germany, I believed the war was lost. And I knew enough history to realize there was a more than passing chance that I might be considered a war criminal during that curiously vicious period which follows the arrival of peace. And I did not relish the fate of war criminals. I once had a rather oblique conversation with Krupp about it but Krupp's attitude was one of total arrogance. Whoever wins, he said, they'll need me—and not in jail. Well, history gave its own answer to Krupp." The wind stirred the treetops, sun flashed through the leaves. "And he turned out to be more or less right." He sipped at the coffee, tasting it before swallowing. The children laughed.

"So I cast about for ways to escape with as much

money as possible. That was the hardest part, I assure you. But I scraped a bit together and instituted a few discreet inquiries. I began to think quite seriously about Colonel Perón, whom I had met a few years before when he had been military attaché to Rome."

He slid a pair of tinted aviator's glasses from his pocket, put them on, and turned to stare in the direction of the pool. A child began to cry. The older woman had begun to comfort him.

"My wife's mother," Kottmann said. "She's younger than I am, oddly, but she is my mother-in-law. Life," he said to no one in particular, "is marvelously peculiar." He enjoyed another bite of croissant.

"Perón. . . . Yes, I did tell your brother something I thought might interest him. And you, too, perhaps, if all this antique matter doesn't bore you. I once met both your grandfather and father . . . and curiously enough Perón was there, as well." He paused to watch the expression on my face. "That surprises you, Mr. Cooper?"

"You mean that my grandfather and father actually *knew* Colonel Perón and you?" I felt myself grow pale and I drank a sip of coffee to draw attention away. I tried to smile. "It's a small world."

"Knew . . . no, that is too strong a word. They may have *known* Perón, I cannot say, but they did not *know* me. We merely met at a party and Frau Goering introduced me to all three of them at one time—"

"My father was killed in the Battle of Britain," I said. "Flying for England. We are not all Nazis in our family."

He smiled, nodded his head. I saw myself looking pinched and tiny in his opaque glasses.

"I know all about your father, Mr. Cooper. An exceedingly brave man, I am sure. In any case, I was interested in meeting your famous grandfather, who seemed, I must say, rather austere. Goering kept slapping him on the back and laughing but he did not seem to find Goering terribly amusing." A smile on the thin mouth. "Your grandfather struck me as far more of a Junker than was normally found at such gatherings.

"But I was intrigued by Perón. He seemed a clever, alert fellow. He must have been about forty then and somehow he impressed me as being . . . crafty, you see? So, in 1943, with craftiness in mind, I thought of Perón. I felt he was sympathetic and accessible and clever. Shortly thereafter Martin St. John, who really defies classification, entered my life, arrangement for passage and payment were made, and so"—he sighed—"I am here today."

"You were not a Nazi, I take it?"

"Oh, my, no," he said, a glimmer of surprise gone at once, barely recognized. "I rather sympathized with their war aims, of course, and at the beginning they seemed very competent men. After all, the going was easy and I was making a great success—or, more accurately, my father's firm, and my firm by birthright, was doing very well out of it. But the war didn't continue at the level of an operational training maneuver, you see. And with stiffer resistance it seemed a less good idea and our leaders no longer had immunity in my eyes." Irony clung to each word. "They were all rather unsavory, quite suddenly, and I saw that they were losing the war—well, I have no patience with that sort of thing. Then I began to get fairly accurate reports on the extermination camps —so impractical, so perverse, so childishly malicious. It was time to leave."

A small boy came running across the grass. He was wet, holding a towel. "Excuse me," he said with six-year-old gravity. "Papa, when may I ride? You did promise, Papa. Mama said I should ask."

He clapped his son's arm affectionately.

"Very soon, Hans, very soon. You have one more quick dip and then—"

Kottmann stood up, lean and hard.

"My family requires my attention." He ushered me ahead of him onto the path. His boots crunched. "Is there anything else? Let me see. . . . Your brother had some very nonsensical notions about the Nazis, I'm afraid. He attributed some very grandiose schemes to them, saw one lurking behind every jacaranda tree. He was pleasant about it, talked about the young Siegfried only sleeping and waiting to come alive again.

[137]

Terribly Wagnerian. He said he felt Argentina would be the home of the Fourth Reich." He spread his hands in the air before him and shrugged. "I didn't know what to say."

We walked across the veranda and into the hall. There was music coming from concealed speakers. It was the second time I'd heard a Beethoven quartet in two days. I recognized it: the same Beethoven quartet.

"Is there any chance Perón may come back?" I asked.

Alfried Kottmann looked at me patiently.

"Juan Perón is seventy-seven years old, Mr. Cooper. He lives in Spain with a young wife, his third, and his half a billion dollars, whatever it is. Why in the world would he come back to Buenos Aires?"

We stood in front of the immense house. The forest green Mercedes was waiting. The sky had darkened again and smelled like rain.

"I am sorry I haven't been more help," he said. "But that's all there was to my meeting with your brother."

The door was open; the chauffeur was waiting.

"One last thing," I said. "Did my brother show you a clipping? A newspaper clipping?" Kottmann's face changed; it was as if he'd slipped a mask over his friendliness.

"Yes," he said.

"And did you recognize the people?"

"No, I did not." He bowed slightly. "Now I must go. Good-bye, Mr. Cooper." His heels clicked across the stone as I slid into the back seat. It rained hard all the way back to Buenos Aires.

The air was heavy and hot and wet when I got out of the Mercedes. I went into the bar, drank a quick gin and tonic, congratulated myself on the way I'd been handling my liquor, and went back outside. There was a thick haze, but the Plaza San Martin was crowded, people moving slowly. Even the pigeons were droopy and tired. They staggered. I joined them, sat on a bench, looked back across the Calle Florida to the beginnings of the shops. In the afternoon, motor traffic was prohibited and people swarmed in the thoroughfare.

I tried to collect my thoughts. I loosened my tie.

Unless there was a run on Beethoven quartets, St. John had not only lied to me about having seen Kottmann after meeting with me, but had in fact been with him when he called me. I remembered the second echoing click when he hung up the phone. Kottmann? If so, why? Whatever was the reason for lying? Disassociation from one another perhaps.

And why had my question about the newspaper clipping so obviously irritated Kottmann?

I still didn't know what prompted Cyril's visit to Buenos Aires.

It was thundering again. A little girl aimed a thoughtful toe at a pigeon and missed. The paving was wet and the rain gentle. The clouds made it dark. The lobby was bright coming in from the purple afternoon.

I sat at my window thinking, watching the rain and hearing the breeze blowing it. Cyril had wanted to know about the Nazis, the Germans in Argentina, about Kottmann in particular. What else was there? If it hadn't been the Nazis, what had he been after? I drew a blank trying to cope with alternatives. But everyone was chuckling indulgently over the Nazi thing. St. John had called it "ancient history." So had Brenner. It was romantic nonsense, product of an overworked imagination, an obsession with one's grandfather: the Nazis were a part of history, something quaint, as unlikely in the far greater dangers of the atomic and computer age as something from another century.

Cyril's newspaper clipping bothered me. I wanted to see it. St. John would have to show it to me.

The telephone rang. It was Ramón Roca again. I thanked him for arranging my meeting with St. John and told him I had been to see Kottmann.

"It was helpful then, seeing Kottmann?"

"I wish I knew," I said. "But I don't."

"Well, we have come up with one more lead." His voice was restrained, very quiet, sibilant. "Your brother made another call in Buenos Aires. He saw

Dr. Hans Dolldorf, a professor of economics living in retirement here in the city." He gave me the address. "Perhaps you will want to contact him. I leave it to you." I wrote down the telephone number and thanked him. He said it was nothing.

The apartment building was very high, very new, and very expensive. I checked the tenant listing. Dolldorf was on the nineteenth floor, but no one answered my buzz. I asked the doorman if he had seen Professor Dolldorf go out. He fixed me with a supercilious smirk and said that yes, in a way, he had. He spoke with a Middle European accent which seemed to contain a well-practiced insult.

"In a way," I repeated. "What does that mean?"

"What I said." He busied himself with a pigeonholed cabinet full of keys.

"Look, you silly shit," I said conversationally as two elderly women approached, "explain yourself. Or I'll have your balls for breakfast, make no mistake." I stepped up close to him as he reached for the door. The ladies passed. I pushed him back into the corner of the entryway. "Talk to me. Now."

He looked at me as if I were insane. I stared at him.

"He came out dead. On a stretcher with a blanket over him."

"When?"

"Day before yesterday."

"Open the goddamned door," I said. He held it open.

Her eyes were huge and dark beneath thick dark eyebrows, long brown hair curling on her shoulders, and she was biting her lip and had lipstick smudged on a white tooth. She was wearing a black sleeveless dress and behind her the drapes were drawn across the window. She listened as I fumbled through an explanation. I was flustered by the eyes. There was a tracing of wetness on one cheek.

"A couple of weeks ago my brother, Cyril Cooper, an American," I ended, "visited your father. I wondered why, that's all. And just now I heard of your father's death. I'm sorry. My brother is dead now, too. . . ." She turned around and walked away from me. She was tall and strong and her name was Maria Dolldorf. She stood by the window in the shadows. The room was lined with books and there were papers and magazines everywhere.

"I have just come from my father's funeral," she said formally. "I wasn't expecting visitors."

"I'm sorry. I had no way of knowing."

"It's all right. I am stupidly emotional. We are given to excessive grief here." She tried to smile and shivered. "You have come a very long way to ask your questions. I must ask you why is it so important, Mr. Cooper?"

"I can't see you," I said. "It's so dark."

"I'm sorry, but it's a sedative. The light hurts my eyes. Please sit down." We sat side by side in two chromium and cane chairs, very expensive. "Why?" she asked again."

"My brother was murdered and I think what happened to him was involved with what he did here in Buenos Aires. We don't know who killed him." I felt faintly foolish; it had become such a long story. She sat with her hands in her lap; tanned fingers in the dim light, plain nails. "So I'm trying to find out what he was doing here before he came home to be killed. Do you see?"

"Your brother was here, yes. He talked to my father. My father told me about it. My father was terribly upset. Terribly."

"Why?"

"His health had been failing, his eyesight going. He was nervous, almost afraid . . . of everything. I came in the evenings after my work and we would have dinner together or go out to Palermo and sit in the evening sunshine. And we would talk or I would read to him. The night after your brother was here he was very nervous, hadn't slept, his hands were shaking. He'd been drinking brandy all day and he babbled on about the American who'd come to see him. . . ." She was twining her fingers, turning several rings.

"I asked him why he was so troubled and he said this man had asked questions about the past . . .

about Perón and the Nazis and Alfried Kottmann." She closed her eyes, forced the last bit.

"Why should that have upset him?"

"My father had been an adviser to Perón in the old days, one of the few intellectuals whom Perón trusted. My father was an economist and a German and Perón listened to what he had to say. He made a hash of his economic policies but my father at least could tell him what was going wrong and why. They were very close. Some"—she paused and turned to face me, her eyes searching my face—"some people used to say that my father slept with Eva Perón because Perón . . . failed her. I don't know if my father did that or not, it doesn't matter. But my father knew all those men intimately and having it all dragged up now out of the dark, by this unknown American made him afraid. When Perón fell it was not easy for my father. There were those who kept him from the university position he deserved on merit. Alfried Kottmann helped him. But my father grew weaker, sadder as the years went by. He was a sad man. . . ."

There were tears streaming down her cheeks. She excused herself and I heard water running, a door closed, the toilet flushed. I was standing at the window with the drapery held back when she returned. The sun had reappeared.

"If you want to talk more let's leave this place. It smells of him. I cannot think of anything but him." She looked at the cluttered desk. "I'm not ready to clean all this up. Let's go to the park."

She drove an expensive sky blue Mercedes 280SE convertible. Apparently, whatever indignities Herr Professor Dolldorf had experienced, poverty had not been among them. She turned the radio on and moved with a certain panache through the late-afternoon traffic.

Palermo Park stretched wetly green away toward the gray and glass towers of Buenos Aires rising up through the haze over the trees. She knew her way; she had taken her father there. We sat at a table with gin and tonics and watched the golfers strike the golf balls, watched them arc white coming toward us, then plummet to the greens. It was reminiscent of a country club, but we were sitting in the midst of a huge city. Yet it was cloistered, quiet. Finally she spoke.

"My father was killed."

"I beg your pardon?"

"You said your brother was killed by someone." She was watching the golfers, speaking tonelessly. "So was my father. Three days ago—or was it four?—someone came to his flat, took him in his robe down the hallway to the service stairway in back, cracked his skull, and threw him down a flight of concrete stairs. A janitor found him half choked on his own vomit, his hands tied behind him with the belt of his robe. He never came back to consciousness. He died in the hospital." She lit a cigarette from a black and gold packet. "Someone did that to an old man who was nearly blind and very weak. And terribly sad."

There was a decorous cheer from the green. Someone had holed a long one. Maria curled her lips around a lime and sucked it.

"Detective Inspector Roca, please."

The telephone clicked several times, resulting in a pause and then the soft sibilant voice.

"John Cooper," I said.

"Ah, Mr. Cooper. . . ."

"I saw Hans Dolldorf's daughter, Roca, I couldn't see the professor because somebody dragged him out of his apartment the other day, beat him just about to death, and threw him down a stairway. He died without regaining consciousness. They buried him today."

There was a lengthy silence, then: "I see."

"Now you're going to tell me you didn't know a damn thing about it. You sent me to talk to a corpse, by coincidence. Is that right?" I was beginning to feel the way I did the night I shot the gaunt man: there was no reservoir of patience. The fuse kept getting shorter.

"Please, Mr. Cooper. You're upset. I assure you I did not know anything about Professor Dolldorf's misfortune. I'll look into it—are you free this evening?"

"Yes, of course," I said. "Quite free."

"There is a roof garden at the Plaza. Meet me there in two hours. At nine o'clock."

The sun was still shining but the shadows lengthened across the carefully manicured grass. In the distance I could see the sun glinting on the Mercedes-Benz rooftop symbol and the golden shimmering reflection of the Fiat building. Beneath us the city moved into the busy nighttime.

"I looked into the matter of Professor Dolldorf," Roca reported. "Your facts were quite correct, Mr. Cooper. He was beaten to death, in effect, by a person or persons unknown. There seem to be no clues, no leads, no witnesses. Whoever they were, they came, did their work, disappeared. No motive established yet . . . that is, no specific motive. He had enemies. He was an old-time Peronista, a key figure, a power behind the throne. He got out of it with a good deal of money judging from the way he lived. Or someone was paying him as he went." He extracted a cigarette from a black leather case. He lit it slowly and exhaled. "We can check on all that."

"Are you interested?" I asked.

"Of course, particularly interested because—how to put this?—murder seems to have followed you to Buenos Aires."

"He was killed before I got here."

"Yes. But he was visited by your brother. Before you could get to him, somebody killed him."

"You make a connection, then?"

"The temptation is certainly present, Mr. Cooper."

We strolled around the garden. I told him how upset Dolldorf had been after my brother's visit. He raised his eyebrows. Finally he said: "I did make some inquiries. Alfried Kottmann and Martin St. John attended the funeral today. Did Kottmann mention it this morning?"

"No. He said he was going to ride with his son."

"I see. Well, Mr. Cooper, you must understand that this entire matter is very delicate." He gestured economically with his hands. "These people are not

[144]

normally interfered with—the Kottmanns, their friends. People like Dolldorf. We try to leave them alone. They very nearly belong to history at this point and if they are still acting out some destiny which is rooted in the past—well, we choose to let them. It is all among themselves, don't you see?"

"No, I don't. Murdering Dolldorf is not an historical footnote. It happened now—it's homicide."

"Try to see my point. And whether you can or not, I suggest you accept the conventions of my country." His mood never seemed to change: behind his flat eyes, Roca was thinking, figuring the odds.

"What are you saying? You're speaking in code."

"I'm saying the past casts very long shadows, Mr. Cooper, and we must feel our way very carefully. We must not be imprudent or indiscreet. We are dealing with volatile men." He dropped the cigarette on the grass. The rooftop was windy; the awnings flapped.

"Tell me one thing," I said.

"If I can."

"Where does Perón fit in to all this? After all, he's gone. He's been gone for a long time."

"But not forgotten, you see."

"It doesn't make sense. It's unrealistic. Everything seems to keep coming back to the Nazis and Perón. My God, this is 1972 and I don't see how we can seriously be standing here gravely discussing the Nazis and Juan Perón."

"I agree." Roca smiled faintly beneath the gray mustache. "It is a curious situation."

"All right." I sighed. "Are they bringing Perón back?"

"They? Who?"

"Anyone."

"Ah, come now, Mr. Cooper, come, come. . . ." Roca's grin was fading with the sun.

I was in bed, half asleep when María Dolldorf called. I looked at the Rolex. It was nearly midnight.

"Can you meet me? Tonight?" She sounded out of breath.

"Well, I—"

"I've found something," she went on urgently. "I've

[145]

been going through my father's papers this evening and I found something. It is about your brother. I don't know what it means but it frightens me." Her voice was husky. I remembered her full mouth and the remarkable eyes. I remembered Paula Smithies finding something among other papers, a very long time ago. And dying.

"All right," I said. "I'll meet you."

"Listen, then. Do you know Mitchell's Bookstore?"

"No."

"Get a cab, then. Tell him you want to go to Mitchell's Bookstore. The address is 570 Calle Cangallo, which runs east and west. He won't have any trouble. It's the largest English-language bookstore in South America. Wait in front for me. I'll pick you up. Be quick about it," she said and hung up.

The blue Mercedes convertible was waiting when I arrived and I made the switch without a word. She pulled away and we drove through a maze of side streets, turning again and then again.

"Where are you going?"

"Where I live," she said. The top was down and her hair was held in place by a headband. I turned to watch the houses, remembered she had buried her father that afternoon. She was still wearing the black dress.

She pulled the Mercedes into a driveway. Well back from the street she pressed a button in a handset and the garage door slid open. The car rolled quietly in and the door slid down behind us with another push of the button. She lived in the carriage house over the garage. I followed her up the stairs. A wind had come up but it was still and warm.

She pulled the windows open and pulled the curtains across; they swayed and rippled in the breeze. A dim lamp burned on a table and she told me to sit down, she had something to show me. I heard her filling glasses with ice. She came back with gin and tonics and sat down beside me. She placed a black book on the table.

"My father's diary. I found it this evening at his flat. Perhaps it was morbid, I don't know, but I began to leaf through it, reading a bit here and there, nothing of any importance at all, then I was nearly at the end. And I came to the day your brother visited him. . . ." She had a slip of paper marking the place, ran a finger through the pages and opened it, showed it to me. I sipped at the drink and looked at the diary.

"I don't read German," I said.

She pursed her lips, slipped her tongue across them, and began to read a translation:

"I am old and impotent and very tired and still there is no peace for me. Pains in my chest today were aggravated by a visitor and I have felt ill ever since he left. I had never seen him before. And of course, I could only see his shape today. Eyes are worse each day. A young North American who said he was the grandson of Austin Cooper. Was I to believe him? How could I know? He was full of questions about the past, about the old days. I cannot bear to think about it. But it came so soon after my meeting last week with Siefgried. P. haunts me but there is no escaping. And now Siegfried tells me the time has come for Operation Cataclysm. Cataclysm! I said it was a mistake. I told them I was a sick old man but it was no use. Siegfried said there was no turning back now. I told him that I could stop it. I should have said nothing. He said Barbarossa had told him the time was now. They are afraid to wait. I don't know why—could it be this—"

"Wait a minute," I said.

"That's all, no more references to it." She looked at me inquisitively. "It ends in the middle of a sentence."

"What the hell does it mean?" I felt impatience bubbling in me again. "Who are these people he's talking about? These names." Was it as obvious as it seemed? But who was Siegfried? Barbarossa?

She shook her head. "I don't know. I never heard him mention any of it, never a word." She repeated the names in the diary: "Siegfried. Barbarossa. P."

"Code. Or he was rambling on without meaning. Does that seem—"

"No," she said emphatically. "No, he wasn't one to ramble. He was very alert and quick. He wasn't in good health but he was perfectly competent, as quick as ever."

"Well, then, it referred to someone in code. Christ."

"It frightens me. Your brother, the diary, they meet, they die . . . now you come." She lit a cigarette. "It's not difficult to wonder what comes next, is it?" Her hand was shaking and she clasped her bare knees.

"No. I suppose not. It's only difficult to know—"

I paced the room for a time. There was only the sound of the wind outside. It was one o'clock.

"May I take the diary?"

"Why?"

"I want to show it to a friend of mine, a captain of detectives here in Buenos Aires. There's always the chance it might mean something to him. After all, he's going to be involved in the investigation of your father's death. It's his job, Maria."

"The police!" she laughed, hollow, bitter. "The police don't give a damn about my father. Just an old German Peronista out of the way. They're not going to do anything about it. They'll say, why not let all these old bastards kill each other? They're afraid to poke around in this kind of thing, I assure you, Mr. Cooper."

"Let me take it anyway," I said.

"All right. It makes no difference."

She shrugged. Her fear seemed to be gone. Her face looked heavy and tired, her features smudged downward.

"It makes no difference," she repeated.

In the morning I called Roca and told him the story of Professor Dolldorf's diary. He calmly arranged for one of his men to pick it up from the Plaza's security officer. He was hardly elated but he was curious.

I called Martin St. John at the number he had given me. He suggested I meet him in his office within the hour. I asked him if he had the clipping my brother had left. He said he did.

St. John's office could have been worse. It could

have been on fire. As it was, it simply sat there and reeked with cigar smoke and liquor and sweat and musty stacks of papers and books. There was an antique oscillating fan constructed of black wires forming a cage around huge blades; the result just blew the smell and papers around you like a lazy hurricane. St. John was sitting behind the desk. He wore the same white suit, with a tired yellow flower in the buttonhole. I recognized the stains. It was probably the same poor flower. The panama hat rested on top of a wooden filing cabinet. He struggled to his feet, took off the half-glasses perched on the end of his short, round nose, and motioned me toward a cracked leather chair.

"Forgive the clutter, Mr. Cooper. I am a creature of clutter, a cluttered office and a bloody cluttered old noggin, but I remember it all, know right where I've stowed it, don't you see? Sit down, sit down."

"I hope I'm not inconveniencing you," I said. I moved a pile of bloated manila folders from the chair arm to the floor. The carpet was worn through. It was not a large office. The building itself had a look of shabby gentility long outdistanced by the sky-scrapers of Buenos Aires, which were new, with-it places to be. St. John was not a with-it type at all. Ths fan massaged the hot air, St. John brushed the long white hair back from his forehead.

"How bad was it here for Kottmann?" I asked. "Being a German, I mean."

"Ah, you mean the persecutions?" He chuckled, perspiration beading on his forehead. "They never reach men like Kottmann, do they? The wealthy Germans who came to Argentina by way of our little pipeline were not likely to suffer at all. Who would dare persecute them? The masses, the rabble might do a little gutter persecution but how would that affect people like Kottmann? After all, their whole class is basically opposed to the masses, to any kind of democracy. And the mass never even knows who they are. They are unreachable, Mr. Cooper, and that is the way of the world."

It was very hot in the little office. The one window was apparently caked shut with the grime of decades.

St. John wiped his face with a faded red handkerchief, stuffed it back in a pocket. An old alarm clock ticked on a bookcase.

"Would it hold true, his being unreachable, for —let's say—a German professor? A teacher?"

"It is difficult to say, isn't it?" His eyes narrowed and he stared at a gold pencil in his thick-fingered hand. "It would depend, one assumes, on the professor."

"But, hypothetically, could being a German, a Peronista, have cost an academic his job? His career?"

"Anything is possible, old boy. Absolutely possible. Old St. John's law." He sighed and slowly let his eyes follow a fly around the little office.

"Mr. Cooper, you're growing wary now. You remind me of your brother." He smiled, almost kindly. He was reading my mind. "I hardly knew Professor Dolldorf. But I had known him many years ago, and when I heard of his death . . . I could not resist paying my last respects. It's that simple." He stood up with a puffing noise, brushed the long white hair off his forehead again, and went to a bookcase. "And now that clipping." He shuffled through folders and loose papers, fat fingers riffling. "Aha, where, where . . . I know it's here . . . somewhere, somewhere. . . ."

I sneezed with the dust. I was sweating, felt my shirt cling to my back.

"Here it is," he said, going back behind the desk, mopping his forehead with the red bandanna. The piece of newsprint hung limp from his fingers. He sat down again and stared at the picture.

"I have no idea why he showed me this picture, no real idea. . . . Mr. and Mrs. Gunter Brendel, from a Glasgow paper, dated last October. Glasgow, of all places. He made no mention of how he'd come across it, only that he wanted to find Alfried Kottmann. He said—let's see—he said that it had all begun with this picture—whatever 'it' may have been." He shook his head and handed me the picture.

A second later my entire life had changed.

I stared at the picture and my hands were trembling, the paper fluttered. A man and a woman were standing in a receiving line, she much younger in appearance than he. It was a large picture; she was looking at someone not in the photograph, smiling distantly. The man was handsome, head inclined, smiling, as if listening to what an unseen man was saying.

"Can I get you some water, old boy? You don't look at all well. I say. . . ."

"I'm all right."

"I took the liberty of showing this photograph to Herr Kottmann after your brother made his departure. Alfried told me he'd never seen the woman but he had known the Brendel family years ago. He said Gunter would be about fifty now. Gunter's father had been tried as a war criminal and had died in prison. Gunter, a steadfast lad, had picked up the pieces and restored the family fortune with some business ventures.

"But then, all that is past, isn't it? It's wiser to leave it all in the past, I should think. Perhaps we should simply let the past take care of itself and bury its own, what?"

"But is it past?" My voice was shaky, my throat dry.

"Aha, there's the rub of it. Is the past ever past?"

The dots on the newsprint separated, blurred together, seemed to move and come alive. I had been studying the photograph all afternoon.

My first reaction was that it was a photograph of my mother, as if she had been frozen in time as she had been when my father painted her so many years ago. It was true: the woman in the photograph bore a striking resemblance to my mother, yet there were differences. The corners of the broad mouth turned abruptly down even though she was smiling; the upper lip was even thinner than my mother's, the lower enough fuller to seem exaggerated in the network of newsprint dots. The hair seemed tawnier and longer, the eyebrows more of a flat line, less arched. There was the same broad flatness to the forehead. It was all so familiar, as if I had been waiting all my life to see it.

It was my little sister Lee.

I now knew why my brother Cyril had begun the long journey which led all the way back to the snow piling up in Cooper's Falls and death in the master bedroom.

He had held the same clipping in his hand. I knew it had fluttered the same way as his hand trembled. He had seen Lee's face and he had set out to find her. I knew I had to find her.

I had the beginning and I knew the ending. But what had come between?

Buenos Aires. But there was more. There was the list Paula had recited. Glasgow . . . and I knew what Cyril had found in the Glasgow newspaper. From Glasgow he'd gone to Munich. Deep into Germany, deep into Bavaria. I shivered in the heat, thinking about Lee.

The phone rang. I picked it up.

"I'm afraid."

It was Maria Dolldorf. A message had been waiting for me at the Plaza when I returned. I was to call Miss Dolldorf. She was still at work. There was a tremor in her soft, bitter voice.

"I'm afraid. Something is happening. I don't know what, but it's not right. . . ."

"What do you mean?"

"I got a call today, here at work. It was a man, but not a voice I recognized. He told me I was being watched, that I was never alone. He said I should be very careful whom I saw, what I said, and he asked me if I understood what he meant."

"Did you?"

"No. He said old friends were best, that I should be careful about making any new friends. He meant you, John. He must have meant you. You're virtually the only person I've seen outside of work—in a long time. And they knew it." She paused to clear her throat. She was nervous; her voice trembled. She couldn't keep it steady. "John?"

"Yes?"

"They're watching you too. I've spent the afternoon thinking about it. That's how they got to me . . . I was nothing until I met you. There could have been no reason to watch me."

"There was a reason to kill your father."

"Your brother—"

"What language did he speak?" I asked her, knowing the answer.

"German," she said.

"Look, are you afraid to see me?"

"I don't know . . . I'm not making sense."

"Come here, then. We'll have a drink and get things calmed down."

After a couple of drinks and a light dinner during which we thrashed our way back through the matter of her father's death, his diary, and the warning she'd received—all more or less to no avail, she pursed her lips and cast her huge eyes downward. She was embarrassed: would I see her home? I understood. If someone had gone to the library with Paula Smithies she'd not have died.

The sensations came all at once, held to the earth by the heavy, water-soaked air: the sound of fire engines, the smell of burning, the sight of thick smoke billowing over the trees.

"My God," she said softly and the Mercedes lunged ahead. The street was clogged with two fire engines trying to make the turn into the narrow driveway leading to her carriage house. She pulled the car over and I jumped out, followed as she ran toward the driveway. A crowd had gathered from the neighboring houses. Flames jerked up over the trees, bright orange and yellow against the rich darkness.

Maria had been stopped by a fireman halfway up the drive. She was talking to an elderly man in shirt sleeves. "It was too far along," he said, "when I noticed it." He spoke English. "I called the firemen but it's too late."

The carriage house was an inferno. The heat struck in a wave, the air was filling with pieces of ash, sparks. He acknowledged me. "I am Maria's landlord." He nodded toward his own house. The firemen were on his roof wetting it down. Maria clung to my arm.

"My books," Maria said. "My books are all burning up."

She stood there staring at the fire, tears welling

up and lacing her cheeks. Her mascara ran. It wouldn't have happened to her if I had not found her. It was my fault as much as if I'd struck the match.

Shadows danced against the house. I could smell the flowers by Maria's windows burning, the honeysuckle shriveling, curling, blackening to ash.

"Did you hear or see anyone at the carriage house?"

He stared at me. "No."

There was no stopping the fire; all that could be done was to keep it from spreading to the main house. The shadows of the trees and shrubbery cavorted on the lawn as the flames licked out through the windows. Standing down wind from the carriage house, I smelled gasoline, faintly but distinctly. It was incredibly obvious. It was obvious because they wanted Maria, and through her me, to know they could do whatever they wanted with us. The fire was a display for our benefit.

I drove the Mercedes back to the Plaza, with Maria huddled in the passenger seat, giving me directions. She was still shaking when we got to my room. I had her lie down on the bed and covered her with a pink blanket.

It was almost two in the morning. She had been threatened, her house had been burned down, her father murdered. Now she was having trouble keeping her eyes open. Her hair drifted out across the pillow. She licked her dry lips and I poured her a tumbler of ice water. "John, I'll have to buy new clothes. . . ." I wiped dried tears away with a wet washcloth. She was breathing deeply.

I sat back down. I tried to fall asleep but it was no good. I stared at the clipping for a long time. Could it be true? I wondered. Could little Lee somehow be alive? Or was I coming apart, dreaming? After all, it was nothing but an imperfect newspaper reproduction. And countless people in the world looked exactly like one another. How could I possibly tell? My earlier confidence waned. My head ached unmercifully, throbbing, moving around toward my eyes from the base of my skull.

But Cyril had seen the photograph, too. And he

had carried it with him through one city after another until he showed it to Martin St. John and Alfried Kottmann in Buenos Aires. I unfolded it again and spread it out on the desk top. Cyril had actually held this piece of paper. . . .

He must have seen Lee in it as I did:

Gunter Brendel and his wife are shown above at a reception celebrating the new arrangements initiated between Brendel's firm and a Glasgow exporting company. The agreement was reached during the Glasgow Trade Fair now in progress. See story.

Until I was proven incorrect, I would believe the woman was Lee. Everything about her was absolutely right. I yawned: the hours had passed and the sky was lightening. Maria was sleeping soundly and I stretched out on the bed beside her, closed my eyes. I wasn't doubting at all as I went to sleep.

It had to be Lee. It explained so much.

In the morning Maria took her car and went to put her life back together.

Roca was in his office and asked me to come by.

It was a functional room at the Moreno Street address. The walls were pale green, the furniture modern and institutional. In his elegantly tailored dark blue suit he seemed out of place in the drab surroundings. There was an official photograph of the President on one wall. He shook my hand, smiled, and sat primly in a large leather desk chair with a high back that was obviously his own idea. The top of the large desk was bare except for a black telephone and Professor Dolldorf's diary.

"We have several matters to discuss, Mr. Cooper. I suggest we get to them."

"Fine. But I have something new for you."

His eyes narrowed and he ran a fingertip along the thin gray mustache. He seemed tense, careful, wary—to use St. John's word. He had begun to fear me, I thought. He wasn't quite sure what I'd brought to Argentina with me but he damned well didn't like it. I told him about the threat Maria had received; the fact that it had been made in German. He listened, then put a legal pad on the desk and made a few notes with an old Shaeffer white dot fountain pen. When I brought up the fire his eyes darted up and he knitted his brow. His head looked like a peanut resting on hunched shoulders.

"Miss Dolldorf's home was actually destroyed by fire?"

"Yes."

"And you smelled gasoline?"

"Yes. There was no doubt of it. Gasoline."

He leaned back from his desk and stared at me.

"Interesting," he whispered, "but very difficult to quite believe. In fact, I'm inclined to agree with your assessment of the situation—it was set to frighten Miss Dolldorf and, very probably, you, too. But, still, it is a terribly overt step."

"Apparently they are very confident people," I said. "They kill my brother, an innocent girl he knew, burn down half a town, try to kill me, murder a professor in Buenos Aires, and burn down his daughter's apartment and threaten her about me. . . . Yes, they do seem confident to me."

"Ah, well, you make many connections, Mr. Cooper."

"Do you mean you don't believe it's all linked to my brother, my family? Look at this," I slid the photograph toward him.

"The woman—she is a duplicate of my mother at that age. But the picture was printed in a Glasgow newspaper last fall and my brother brought it to Buenos Aires with him. And showed it to Mr. Kottmann and St. John. Kottmann knew the man, according to St. John, but lied to me, told me he'd never seen either of the people before. Why did my brother carry it with him?" I drew a deep breath. "Because the woman, I am convinced, is my sister Lee." Roca started again, squinting at me across the desk.

"Your sister?"

"She supposedly died in the Blitz. In London, with our mother, thirty years ago." I took my pipe from my pocket while he stared from me to the picture and back to me. I packed the large bowl. "Well, I don't think she died after all." I lit the tobacco, waved the match out, dropped it in an ashtray. "I think she lived through it. I think she is Gunter Brendel's wife. And Gunter Brendel is the man Kottmann told St. John he knew in Germany. The man Kottmann told my brother he'd never heard of, and has now emphatically told me he'd never heard of!"

"Well, well . . . I don't know what to say. . . ."

I drew on my pipe, savoring Roca's uncharacteristic confusion.

"And that's the one connection we have between my brother and Buenos Aires. He came here with that picture. He damn well knew it was Lee and somehow the picture led him to St. John and Kottmann. The question is how."

Roca said nothing.

Finally I said: "It seems to me you ought to get some straight answers out of Kottmann and St. John. Between them, they've told me a good many lies since I've been here. Not big lies, just some little ones . . . but outright lies."

"Have they?"

"I've said they have. Maybe they'll tell you the truth."

"That is going to be difficult, Mr. Cooper."

"Why?"

He reached into a desk drawer and withdrew a file folder, placed it carefully, squarely, in front of him. Ceremoniously he opened it and flattened back the cover. He took two sheets of white paper with typewritten notations on them and placed them side by side meticulously.

"Your inquiries here in Buenos Aires have set me thinking—the English would say you've set a cat among the pigeons." He smiled faintly. "And I have been reading through a bit of our material on Mr. St. John and Herr Kottmann. I have also had them watched, very discreetly and at a distance, the last twenty-four hours. No particular reason—simply because you put me in a mind to do so. Fortunately, I am in a position to make no explanations to anyone." A ghost of another smile, gone before it arrived.

"I read Professor Dolldorf's diary yesterday." He touched it with a fingertip. "Paying paticular attention to the section you mentioned in your note. Oddly enough, nowhere else in the diary is there any of that sort of thing—it is truly pedestrian for so intelligent a man. Depressing. Obsessed with his various aches and pains. And then, after your brother descends on him, he makes the one interesting entry, the one enigmatic reflection . . . and we are left to decipher it." He took a cigarette from a case in his pocket and lit it. Everything the man did was a ritual.

"So there I was. Kottmann and St. John under surveillance. The diary before me with its references to P—Perón?—and Siegfried and Barbarossa, waiting to be decoded. Was it hysterical babbling? I don't know, Mr. Cooper, I don't know and I tell you that in all candor . . . but I doubt that it was.

"Finally I decided I wanted to find out exactly what Kottmann and St. John were doing, where they were. I was thinking about Dolldorf's funeral. In my mind, I saw them there in the cemetery paying their final respects. And I was becoming very interested." He shrugged. "Being interested is my profession."

"Go on," I said impatiently. "Why is it going to be so difficult to interview them?"

"Because they are gone."

"They're gone?"

"Indeed," Roca said. "Gone." He paused and I sat nonplussed. *Gone.* "You recall that in the note which you left with the diary you asked me if there were any records of Alfried Kottmann traveling out of the country. I checked on that, Mr. Cooper."

"And?"

"Alfried Kottmann returned to Buenos Aires one month to the day before your brother checked into the Claridge here in Buenos Aires. Kottmann was coming back from Egypt. Cairo." He made a check mark next to some typing on one of the white sheets. "Your brother came here from Cairo, Mr. Cooper." He sighed, a tiny, buttoned-up little sigh. "It seems to me we're building a peculiar little edifice, doesn't it? Odd little coincidences.

"So I thought I would enjoy a conversation with Herr Kottmann. But he was gone."

"Where have they gone?" I asked. It was airless in the little office, antiseptic, organized, but my mind was in chaos. Every time I turned around there was something new and disagreeable.

"They left in the very early hours of this morning from a small private airstrip north of the city. The airplane was Herr Kottmann's Lear jet, the pilot was Helmut Kruger, a professional pilot for hire who often flew Kottmann on little jaunts around the country. Their destination was filed as Patagonia . . . do you know Patagonia, Mr. Cooper?"

"For God's sake, of course not."

"It is the end of the world. Desolate, bleak, at the end of South America. Ah . . . no one goes to Patagonia for a good time." He sighed and daintily killed his cigarette. "Yet it is the sixth visit Herr Kottmann has made to Patagonia in six months."

"Surely you can interview him when he gets there," I said. "Or when he returns."

"Well, not necessarily." He pursed his lips and drummed his fingertips on the file. "Let me explain. He, St. John, and the pilot set off for Patagonia. They . . . never arrived. The Lear has landed nowhere, nowhere between here and their destination, and nowhere in Patagonia. They cannot be raised by radio. They have not been seen by any other airplanes along their flight path." He pursed his lips again, as if to blow me a kiss. "They have disappeared. I've already ordered an air and ground search. I'm not quite sure why, but I have the distinct feeling that we're not going to find them." He smiled gravely.

Glasgow

THE last leg of the flight to Glasgow ended in the dark and the rain. I had tried charting the events since my departure from Boston in a notebook but it quickly became too involved. I couldn't organize it. I was no Roca.

When I left him at the Moreno Street office he had been perplexed but far from confused. He faced his new difficulties with dispatch and discretion. By evening he would surely have each in its own manila folder.

He told me he would keep Maria Dolldorf under protective surveillance until what he termed "this period of instability" was over. He was also ordering some very thorough research into Professor Dolldorf's financial condition and any continuing involvement he might have had with Kottmann or any other leftovers from the Perón years.

The diary Maria had found among her father's papers particularly fascinated Roca. He informed me that inquiries would be made into Barbarossa and Siegfried; into circles of Peronistas who from time to time worked up a sweat about bringing the deposed President home.

So I gave up on my chart.

All I really cared about was my little sister Lee. I had to find her. Innocent and childlike, I was convinced that when I found her it would all begin to come clear. I would understand . . . once I found Lee.

I felt a hand on my arm.

It was my seatmate, a small, solid man with a red face, dressed in a Harris tweed suit. He had a

Clara Bow bee-stung mouth that looked as if someone had yanked it shut with purse strings.

"I say, that's Glasgow down there," he said primly. "We're here at last." He pointed out the rain-flecked window as the 707 banked slightly: Glasgow squatted below, asleep and grimy. The purse strings crinkled open in a tight little smile. "I didn't want you to miss that first look." He looked away shyly.

"That's all right," I said. I yawned.

"Have you had a long journey?"

"Rather. From Buenos Aires."

"Oh, my! That is a long way." He made an effeminate gesture with pink, pointed little hands. "I thought I'd come far . . . from Rome and Madrid. But you've beaten me with Argentina, haven't you?" He smiled. "Oh my, yes."

I nodded. I was hoping he wouldn't try to pick me up. He pulled a pigskin briefcase from beneath his seat and straightened it on his lap, across his fastened seat belt. I fastened my own and he stuck out a pink, soft hand.

"MacDonald."

"Ah, yes," I said hesitantly. "Cooper."

"Well, it's nice to meet you, Mr. Cooper. I always like to meet people I travel with—it's a superstition, I realize, but I always think of the chance of dying, a plane crash . . . it's a good idea to know who you might die with, don't you see?" He smiled at me brightly and withdrew the little hand. "Is that too awfully morbid? I suppose it is. Well, so be it, so be it . . . it's my way." He patted his moist shining forehead with a handkerchief.

The 707 was dropping lower through the rain. I was conscious of the engines throttling, the vibrations of the fuselage.

"Staying in Glasgow long?" he asked.

"I don't know," I said. "I shouldn't think so."

"Not a terribly cheery place, Glasgow. Awfully commercial, industrial, not at all like Edinburgh. On business I suppose?"

"No, no. No business."

"Well, if it's a holiday you're on, Glasgow is bound

to be a disappointment, Mr. Cooper. Edinburgh, now there's your tourist spot."

The plane was coming in much lower now, gliding over a deep serene blackness, landing lights ahead of us.

"I'm on a personal matter, Mr. MacDonald," I said wearily. "No vacation, no holiday." My eyes burned from the stifling air in the cabin.

"Insurance, myself. Business, business, always business." He shrugged narrow shoulders and brushed a hand nervously across his egglike cranium, eyes squinting behind his plain plastic spectacles as if he were about to receive a blow. There was perspiration on his forehead. It finally occurred to me why he'd begun the conversation. He was afraid. Taking off probably affected him the same way. Now, waiting for the wheels to touch down, his pink little hands gripped the armrests, knuckles blanching. Then came the thud, the slight jolt, and we were earthbound. MacDonald released his grip, wiped his forehead again, and I saw color returning to his face.

I saw him again at the baggage pickup. He smiled with the camaraderie of the born insurance salesman, made his way to where I waited.

"Where are you staying?" he asked, now full of relief and not so worried about dying. I suddenly found myself enjoying this harmless man after the fellows I'd been running across.

I named the hotel and he nodded approvingly. "Top of the heap." Our bags came down and we hoisted them. "Well," he said before climbing into a taxi, "we must have a drink. I can unhesitatingly recommend a pub I'm sure you will enjoy." He waved and was gone, the image of his bee-stung lips lingering in my mind.

The wind blew the February rain in slanting sheets, cold and penetrating. Ground fog clung in patches to the tarmac. I wrestled my own bag into a taxi and we swung off into Glasgow. Cold and wet and shivering, I could not have been farther from Buenos Aires.

When I left the Lorne Hotel early the next morning, Sauchiehall Street was thick with a grimy winter fog.

I felt refreshed, nervous, ready. The shock of Lee's photograph had begun to ease and I was ready now to start searching for her in earnest.

I took a taxi to Cyril's office. The fog closed in, smelling wet and dirty. I rather liked it.

The offices were on the second floor of a respectable, quiet, prosperous-looking building in West Regent Street. All Britain Distributing, Ltd. offered a very restrained face to the world, polished brass and dark shiny doors. The reception room was small, gleaming, carpeted, presided over by a middle-aged woman in sensible tweeds. A radiator hissed out of sight, but it was cool in the room. I told her who I was, she blinked, disappeared through a heavy door that closed with a sound, and came back saying Mr. Dumfries would see me right away if I'd kindly follow her.

Jack Dumfries was tall and slender, turned out in a vested dark blue suit, white shirt, narrow striped tie below the spread collar. It was the British uniform for the business day. A signet ring glinted on his little finger. He was an ageless man, fresh-faced but slightly stooped, in his thirties. Or forties.

We shook hands, he poured us tea from a dainty little pot with a pastoral scene painted on its plump sides. A fire struggled with wet logs, hissing and popping in the grate. It was a marvelously elegant office, typical of Cyril's concern for surroundings.

Dumfries took up his stand by the mantelpiece, stirring his tea, smiling officiously. I hoped to God he wasn't going to turn out insufferable.

"What's your title here, Mr. Dumfries?" I asked. I sat down in an oxblood leather armchair and looked gravely up at him. The fire warmed me; I hitched closer.

"I am the managing director, Glasgow," he said, sipping tea into his large mouth, staring at me with wet blue eyes over the rim. "I report to Mr. Cyril Cooper in writing, twice monthly, to the London office." His voice was edged with defensiveness. "As far as Glasgow is concerned, it's my own show."

"Sit down, Mr. Dumfries," I said, "please."

The china was rattling as he lowered his elaborate

frame into another leather chair. Rain clattered on the casement, flung by the wind through billowing fog.

"My brother Cyril is dead, Mr. Dumfries."

"Oh, no. . . ." He looked very sad, but wheels were turning behind the wet blue eyes, calculating instantaneously.

"He died quite suddenly in the family home, back in Cooper's Falls, Minnesota." I pulled out my pipe and began filling the bowl. "Now, his interests in All Britain Distributing, Ltd., pass to me. I am somewhat unfamiliar with them but my attorneys are straightening all that out now. I will need recent audits and inventories made available in the relatively near future." He looked normally disconcerted as I struck a match and lit my pipe. I smiled, watching it all sink in on him.

"Of course, whenever you wish them, Mr. Cooper. I'm certain you'll find everything in perfect order." He leaned forward, elbows on knees, preparing himself for any onslaughts from the new management.

"I have every confidence in you, Mr. Dumfries," I said, "every confidence. My brother was an excellent judge of men and if he chose you to take charge of things here in Glasgow I'm certainly not going to change things. You may rest assured." I puffed on the pipe, got a good fire going, sipped some tea.

Dumfries sighed, sagged inside the expensive uniform.

"This is a shock, Mr. Cooper," he said, relaxing a bit. "How did your brother die? He seemed in excellent health last fall, which was the last time I saw him. We seldom saw him here—a very silent owner. We never knew where he was. We're really just an investment for him."

"He did die of an illness, Mr. Dumfries—he was poisoned. Someone murdered him."

The color seeped from Dumfries' face. It was turning into an unpleasant morning. He got up and stood staring into the fog, the street below. "That's incredible. I don't know what to say." He looked back sharply. "Do they know who did it, then?"

"No, I'm afraid not. All very mysterious, very

sinister. You see, there have been two attempts on my life as well . . . and several other people are already dead."

I gave him an abridged version of what had happened. He hurried through two cups of tea and lit a cigarette. The façade of reserve had pretty well crumbled. I liked Jack Dumfries. When I finished he stared at me and said: "Jesus Christ and company. . . . By rights, if the pattern continues, old Glasgow is in for a crime wave, what? Now you're here, I mean."

"If the pattern holds.

"There are some questions I'd like to ask you and we might as well get to it. First, there's something I'd like you to take a look at." I took one of the Lorne's envelopes from my pocket and handed it to him. When he opened it and fetched out the clipping he snorted in surprise. "You have seen it before?"

"Of course I have," he said. "I arranged to have this picture taken." He stroked his chin. "Odd, though, what you two chaps have seen in it . . . you see, the day this photograph appeared in the Glasgow *Herald* was the same day your brother arrived in Glasgow last fall, the same exact day, and he brought it with him to the office. I'd never seen him in quite that mood but I'll never forget it, that's certain."

The Glasgow Trade Fair was in progress at the time and Dumfries was quite pleased with himself for having arranged the photograph of Herr Gunter Brendel and the accompanying story by Alistair Campbell which made special mention of a business arrangement contracted for between All Britain Distributing, Ltd., and Herr Brendel's firm of importers in Munich. In the normal course of things, All Britain had been trying to crack the German market with a new brand of scotch whiskey called Thistle and Heather. This was the breakthrough which Dumfries had been working on for some time. To celebrate it, he had prevailed on Campbell, whom he had known for several years, to treat the deal as an example of expanding trade relations with Germany and thereby gain publicity for Thistle and Heather. All in all, it had worked perfectly. Together they had arranged for the photograph to draw attention to the story and it was understood that from then on as much of the new whiskey was Campbell's as he could possibly consume—a not inconsiderable gift given the journalist's capacity.

When Cyril arrived at the All Britain offices that morning he was unusually excited. Shooing everyone out of the office, he and Dumfries had sat before the fire and Cyril had begun questioning him about the photograph, the story, and the events leading up to the agreement with Brendel's firm.

"He was very persistent," Dumfries recalled. "He particularly wanted to know how the whole thing had been initiated, whether they had come to us or we had gone to them. Of course, I had made the initial contact with Brendel because the word was out that his firm was in the marketplace."

"Did you go to Germany to pursue it?" I asked.

"No, Herr Brendel came here from his offices in Munich. He wanted to see if we were in the trade to stay, don't you see?"

"Did he know that my brother owned All Britain?"

"Aha, you see, that's another point which fascinated your brother—once he was absolutely certain that I had initiated the negotiations and not the other way round, then he started in on that angle. Was there any way Brendel could have known of his involvement? Had I ever made mention of it? Could it have come to Brendel's attention in any way that I knew of?" Dumfries lit another cigarette and peered into the teapot, which was empty. He went to the door and summoned more tea, which appeared almost instantaneously.

"Well, I could only speak from my own knowledge," he went on, "and based on that I told your brother that the name of Cooper had never come up and, actually, why should it have? I am the managing director. Brendel would not be interested in remote ownership."

"You satisfied Cyril on that point, then," I said. The fire was baking my shins. I got up and stood with my back to the window. A brass ship's clock struck eleven o'clock. The fog outside was thick as ever.

"Well, then, what about Brendel's wife? Frau Brendel? Did you ever meet her?" My breath was short. I couldn't help it.

Dumfries shook his head like a man trapped into a magical show. "Same damned thing your brother wanted to know. He was more urgent about it, though . . . yes, the answer is yes, I met her. The second time Brendel came to Glasgow, to visit the Trade Fair, I dined with them, just the three of us—that would be three days before your brother arrived. It was at Guy's"—he recognized the curiosity in my face—"a very nice restaurant, Mr. Cooper, our best, actually. Brendel treated, too, and insisted on tying the business knot, so to speak. Altogether a memorable evening. Champagne . . . and, thank God, no Thistle and Heather whiskey." He made a face.

"All right." I interrupted him. "Tell me about Frau Brendel, whatever you remember about her."

"Ah, Frau Brendel. Lise was her name. Lise. . . ."

I flinched inwardly at the name, the similarity to Lec. "She's not an easy woman to forget, I assure you, Mr. Cooper, but rather difficult to describe. Quite exceedingly beautiful . . . but quite remote. Not in the least unfriendly, but, this sounds absurd to say after one meeting—I realize that—but she seemed a rather sad woman." He caught my eye. "Do you know what I mean by that? Not sad-sad but not a happy person. She smiled and carried off all the amenities of entertaining one of her husband's business friends, but when she didn't think you were looking, when her face was in repose, there was a rather sorrowful expression."

"Sorrowful?"

"She is a good deal younger than her husband, very solicitous toward him, more like a daughter, actually." He leaned back and crossed his long, thin legs and blew a smoke ring which hung before him like a mobile before drifting away, disintegrating. "It's rather awkward, saying this—"

"Yes?"

"Herr Brendel is a very elegant man, bits of jewelry,

excessively well tailored, speaks in hushed little whispers—very effete—I don't want to say more than that."

"He's a homosexual?"

"Well, not in so many words, no," Dumfries said, clearing his throat. "But he blurs the line, if you know what I mean. He's handsome, well preserved like a woman of a certain age. He has that kind of artificially tanned face. It looks creamed and kneaded and so extraordinarily immaculate—as if he's had his eyebrows trimmed." Dumfries laughed nervously. "What I mean to say is simply that that might explain Frau Brendel's aura of loneliness, solemnity, the frown that comes over her in repose. It is as if she is anesthetized against laughter, the normal gaiety, silliness. She does not have an absolutely overwhelming sense of humor, you know."

"You told my brother all this," I said.

"Yes. He was very persistent and wanted to know where he could find Brendel—"

"And—where can I find Brendel?"

"I can only tell you what I told him. Namely, that Brendel's home office is Munich. And I know that his firm also has offices in London. He was no longer here in Glasgow when your brother arrived."

"Did Cyril say what he was going to do about Brendel? Did he tell you why he was so interested in this photograph?"

"No, and I didn't pry into it. But it did make an impression on me, you know. I thought about it afterward and I wondered if it wasn't the woman he was curious about—was it a former lover? Someone he knew or had known, who had meant a great deal to him." He smiled calmly. "Which is about what I would conclude from your questions." The smile faded. "But now, I don't know. His death. Or the other people you say have been killed. Are they all connected? Is this photograph a part of it?" He picked it up again and seemed to be searching it for new meanings.

"Mr. Dumfries, you'll probably be much better off not knowing."

"About the firm," he said. "Is there anything you want done right away?"

"Not a thing, Mr. Dumfries," I said. "Carry on as you have been."

"Well, take care of yourself. . . ." He hesitated, touched the knot of his tie.

"Do you know what Cyril did after he left you?"

"No, I never heard from him again, which wasn't usual. My reports were filed but there was no word from him personally and I simply assumed that he was wrapped up in something important."

"Well, he was," I said.

The newsroom of the Glasgow *Herald* was artificially bright and hot and smelled of sweat and typewriter ribbon. There was a steady clatter of typewriter, teletype machines, the throb of presses somewhere in the building's innards. The floors were dirty, the desks old and battered, the conversation salty and harsh, and I felt as though I'd walked into a performance of *The Front Page*.

Alistair Campbell was leaning back in a wooden swivel chair, staring morosely into an antique black typewriter. Smoke climbed steadily from his corncob. He was wearing heavy tweeds and a cardigan underneath his coat. His hair was wiry and red, his head tiny, his face crimson, his tie brown: he gave the immediate impression of having been left too long in the fog and rain, of having rusted.

There was a vague aroma of scotch in his vicinity, mixing with a peculiarly acrid tobacco. Apparently he was making good use of his Thistle and Heather.

"Mr. Campbell?"

He bit off a cough. "Aye, Campbell. And who might you be?" He cast a fisheye my way from beneath enormous bushy eyebrows which were sandy like his hair. Behind the smoke his eyes, tiny and nut-brown like glittering Spanish peanuts, flicked across me.

I told him my name and asked him if my brother had called on him

"Cyril Cooper, eh? Yes, indeed, Mr. Cyril Cooper did call on me, all in a lather, said he'd come directly from Jack Dumfries. And I suppose you've done the same."

"I have, yes. I want to ask you a few questions."

"About the scotch deal with the Germans." He

nodded the little head and took the pipe out of his mouth, flashed yellow, stained teeth.

"Right again," I said. "You have a good memory, Mr. Campbell."

"I do have a good memory, laddie, right enough, but any bloody twit could remember what I'm remembering. This is definitely not the sort of thing you forget." He shook his head and stood up, a diminutive man not five and a half feet tall. He brushed his hand across his freckled forehead and we shook hands.

"Can we talk, Mr. Campbell?"

"Ah, by all means." He looked quickly about us. "But not here. I suggest we repair to a friendly and inconspicuous pub of my experience. Where we're not so likely to be overheard. This place"—he gestured in disgust—"you never know who's listening."

He gave me the name of a pub which sounded vaguely familiar and told me directions. "And, a word of advice." He fixed me with those bright ferret's eyes. "Be careful, very careful. Take a taxi to your digs, lay low until it's time." He winked a beady eye, avuncular, and squeezed my arm. "Word to the wise, eh?"

Campbell's melodramatic warning brought on a nervous stomach.

Be careful of what, for Christ's sake? It sounded as if he knew how violent my life had become. Yet he obviously hadn't known of Cyril's death or any of what had happened.

Finally the hour came and I stood at the polished bar in the appointed tavern. I was a few minutes early, fussing with my pipe and matches, watching the door with its leaded glass when he came in. He stood inside the doorway, in the smoky haze, wearing the foulest mackintosh I'd ever seen. Recognizing me, he elbowed his way up to the bar and ordered two pints of bitter, knocked the bowl of the corncob into an ashtray.

He frowned and sucked foam from his bitter. At last he said: "The kind of thing I've got to tell you"—he shook his head—"I don't know. . . ."

"Did you tell my brother what you're going to tell me?"

"Aye, I did that—and come to think of it why don't you ask him?" The eyes glittered cannily past the smoke.

"He's dead. Murdered." He blanched, what had been pink about his face turned a dirty gray, his tongue wetted his cracked lips.

I explained briefly and he listened, subdued, as if a bad headache had got the better of him. I told him how I'd learned his name, why I'd come. He eventually recovered his composure and lit the corn-cob.

"It's dangerous people you're fussing with, laddie." He kept on repeating it. "You've no idea. . . ." He stared at me across the pints of bitter and jerked his freckled hand at the doorway of the tavern as it swung open for a moment. Outside, the mist and fog were thick, erasing for a moment the dirt which was Glasgow's trademark.

"It's dangerous out there." It was his theme. His bushy eyebrows drew together in a scowl. He sucked at the pipe. The tavern was thick with smoke and smelled of soaked Dundee woolens.

"Your brother," he resumed, "wanted to know about Brendel, Frau Brendel, whatever I knew about them—and I knew a good deal, most of which I'd come upon by sheer chance, things I'd pieced together . . . things I've never mentioned to anyone but your brother." He sniffed. "Mainly because I'd just figured them out. The stuff of nightmares, laddie." He squinted up from his bitter. "But who'd believe me?"

He peered into the pipe's dead ashes, drew the sleeve of his mac beneath his nose, and drained the last of his pint. He snuffled, cupped his hands around the hot stained bowl of his pipe. He spoke very quietly, staring straight ahead past the barman into the steamy mirror. "Now, listen carefully. Buy a ticket on the midnight train bound for London. Check out of your hotel and leave your bag at the railway station. Get yourself some chupper, eat hearty. Then meet me and we'll go over it."

He gave me an address scribbled on a greasy scrap of paper: a tenement in the area called the Gorbals. He told me that Glaswegians insisted with perverse

[171]

pride that it was the worst slum in all Europe. "Ten o'clock, exactly," he said, getting his scarf straightened, turning his pipe upside down. He jammed his soiled tweed hat down on his ears, shoved the folded newspaper into the pocket of his mac, and disappeared in the crowd arguing soccer near the door, a small and wet and grim figure.

I finished my own pint feeling weighed down by the residue Campbell had left. "The stuff of nightmares," he'd said. I swallowed the last bitterness and pushed past some brawny lads between me and the door. A hand grasped my arm, a voice spoke my name, "I say, Mr. Cooper—" It was MacDonald, the nervous man from the airplane the previous night. His red face, flushed in the heat, split with a Clara Bow smile. His eyes watered and he dug a fist at them like a small child.

"MacDonald," I said. We shook hands.

"I see you took my advice." He beamed.

"I beg your pardon?" His voice was too soft. Everything about him was soft but the wiry Harris tweed.

"This pub," he said as I bent to listen. "The one I recommended and here you are, first night in Glasgow and we meet here. Join me in a pint before you go, won't you? Can't leave me to drink alone, can you?"

I was sweating and so was he. The mirror behind the bar was steamed. MacDonald's head gleamed. We had the pint at the bar and I strained to hear: he seemed to be talking about insurance, the calls he'd made during that day. "And how's your stay going?" He loosened his tie.

"All right, it's all right."

He offered up the bitter. "Well, happy days!" He smiled. "How did you find the pub, for heaven's sake? It's off the beaten track."

"A friend brought me here."

"The little reddish man? Looked like a monkey?"

"That's the one."

"Ah, well, then—he's a good friend, bringing you here. I like the smell of the place." He chatted on. We had another pint, drowning in our own sweat.

MacDonald finally bade me goodnight with the

hope that we'd meet again what with things coming in threes and all.

The rain had turned to snow, had slowed traffic, and that was why I was late for Alistair Campbell. The taxi driver gave a curious snort. "Gorbals," he muttered and pulled away from the curb, but immediately we were trapped in a series of minor traffic jams, wheels spinning on the cold wet streets. Two automobiles with dented fenders sat at odd angles to the curbstones. Without uttering a sound, he was regarding the inconvenience with a singularly dour Scot's gaze.

Darkness overtook us. The buildings were dense and dark behind a thick curtain of snow.

"I have an appointment—" I began. My throat was sore from the abrupt change in climate, jet lag was creeping up on me with a mallet, I was cold and tired, and the bitter left a rank aftertaste.

"Aye, you've an appointment and you saw the traffic, as well, din't you?" he said and I slumped back on the seat and shut up.

The tenement was indistinguishable from the rest. Standing on the sidewalk when the taxi was gone, I felt awesomely alone. It was dark, the snow hung like tinsel scarves in the dim glow of a streetlamp at the end of the block. There was no welcome here. My footsteps were muffled in the snowfall. It was colder.

The low doorway opened two steps up off the entryway, which smelled like a sewer, like urine and garbage and poverty. Water dripped at the end of the entryway. Odd, low shapes loomed in the courtyard beyond. I opened the door which squeaked shrilly in its warp and rust, went inside, and stood in the silent hallway. One bare light dangling from the tip of a frayed black cord burned halfway along the hall's length. It swung in the draft I made. My shadow leaped, enormous, against the wall. Upstairs, rear, Campbell had said.

My flesh felt clammy inside my clothing and I had a stitch in my side, under my heart. I felt feverish behind my eyes.

I made my way in the half-light down the hall toward the stairway. Who lived in such a place?

Whispers came, then silence, a horn honking, the squeal of a cat tracking in the new snow. I smelled cooking and beer and I went up the stairs, which creaked angrily.

As I reached the top of the stairway, the door at the rear of the dim hallway swung open with a bang and the short figure of Alistair Campbell appeared half in shadow, arm raised in welcome. I waved and stepped toward him.

Slowly he seemed to collapse, clinging to the wall as if it were the facing of a cliff. I stopped and he lunged forward. As he came into the light I saw that his hand was red, leaving a trail along the wall like a bleeding, wounded slug inching its way toward a safe hole.

My breathing had stopped. My knees and thighs clenched weakly. His breath rasped in the quiet. The front of his mac was soaked with blood. His eyes stared through me, the glitter and gleam long gone.

"Stains," he gasped with tremendous effort. "Find stains. . . ."

A figure blurred out of the shadowy stairwell at the back of the hall, am arm was raised, and there was a sound like the sucking of air, twice, and Alistair Campbell leaped jerkily forward, his wet red hand just reaching my raincoat, clutching the belt, clamping it in his hand. The back of his mac was blown open in two places and the sucking sound came again and the plastered wall beside me exploded, showered me in chips, filling my eyes with gritty dust—

I lost my footing going backward down the steps and, before his grip loosened, Alistair Campbell's body slid partly down on top of me. The smell of blood covered me like a sheet in a morgue. The sucking sound came again, a rush of hot air past my hand as I fell, plummeting back down the stairs into the dark.

I could hear the man in the upstairs hall fumbling to get past the body, which lay crossways in the narrow stairway. A door opened a few feet away from me as I struggled to my feet, an unshaven man in a dirty undershirt stuck his head out and told me to fuck off, and I ran the length of the hallway, ducked through a doorway into the entryway, turned right away from the street, and headed into the courtyard.

I could hear him pounding down the stairs, charging along the hall. He was coming after me; he'd shot Campbell full of holes and taken a couple of hurried shots at me. Adrenalin surged, my heart skipped, my side ached.

The courtyard's looming shapes became a junked automobile, a rusting truck with a flatbed carrier, stacks of tires, trashcans, and I dived among them, felt a bit of wire slice my cheek. Snow sprinkled my face; it was turning back to rain and the wind was blowing. I tried not to make any noise. This was the third time they'd tried to kill me.

Feeling my way along the length of the truck, I heard him reach the entryway. He was undecided. Kneeling, I saw his legs and feet dimly from between the undercarriage. He turned away finally and walked toward the street. I crouched there, waiting. He did not reappear. At last, I made my way back past the tires and trashcans looking for an exit. I opened a metal door and stepped into a dark corridor, ill-lit, with water standing in puddles on a dirt and gravel floor. A broken wooden door swung open at the other end: rain and snow glistened in the lamplight. There was the smell of engine oil and gasoline.

I pushed past the broken door and was back in the real world: a wet street, loud boys at the corner swearing nastily. I walked the other way: my face burned and ached, I kept imagining I heard the sucking sound of the silencer and the meaningless cry of *stains, stains* as he fell smearing the wall, my coat, with his blood. I wiped cold rain across my cheekbone and felt the ridge of the wire cut. My hairline was sticky and I pulled my tweed cap down, brushed plaster dust away.

Twice I asked directions. It took me a long time to reach the railway station on foot. I missed a couple of cabs, zig-zagged in an inefficient attempt to avoid any would-be pursuers. Obviously they hadn't followed me. They were making a bad job of it again.

I took my bag from the locker. It was 11:14. I went to the men's room, feeling weak-kneed and faint. My eyes burned intolerably from the plaster dust and my head had begun to ache. In the mirror over the washstand my face looked back at me like something from a set of atrocity photographs: haggard, worn, pale yellow. My cap was stuck to my head and when I peeled it away I saw that one of the puffs of air I'd felt go past my head must actually have just caressed it. Christ. They were getting closer . . . and it was always my head. The soggy beginnings of a scab came away, stuck to the cap's silk lining, and the blood began to seep down out of my hair. I dabbed at it with watersoaked paper, prayed that no one would come in and find me.

Nausea flooded me suddenly, and I vomited into a toilet, sank to my knees, and fainted across the seat.

I was still alone when I blinked my eyes open, and after sitting there with my head hung down between my knees for a few more minutes I felt well enough to finish cleaning up my face. It was a ridiculous job, patting and drying, and I finally stuck a piece of toilet tissue in the gouge and held it in place by pulling my cap down over it. My head throbbed like a Buddy Rich riff, drowning out other sounds. All I wanted was to get on the train, collapse in my compartment. Eventually, I would have to think over what had happened and mourn Alistair Campbell along with the others. But I was too tired just then, too hurt.

There weren't many people on the platform. It was cold and the chill felt good, cleansed my pain. I leaned against a pillar. A few feet away a family waited, middle-aged and tweedy, with a little blond girl holding her mother's hand. She was smiling with the expectancy and excitement of the very young who are up long after their normal bedtime. She let go of her mother's hand and began to pace ever-widening circles around her parents, until she came close enough for me to see her cornflower-blue eyes. She smiled up at me and I smiled back. She was well dressed: her coat had a velvet collar.

Tentatively she came closer, staring up at me in a child's unrelenting manner, her smile fading. Again

I caught her eye through the pain and weariness engulfing me and tried to smile. She reminded me of pictures of my little sister Lee taken many years ago.

Finally, somewhat discomfited by her staring, I leaned forward to say hello. That was when she began a high-pitched screaming, a wail, as if I'd attacked her. I felt myself toppling forward, no strength in my legs, and I gripped the pillar. I was befuddled: why was she screaming? Her mouth, a cavern into which I seemed about to fall reminded me of the wound in Alistair Campbell's forehead.

Her parents turned to stare, her father rushed forward saying, "Here, here," and reaching for his daughter. The woman came closer, her face scowling and full of reproaches, and then she stopped short, covered her mouth with a gloved hand, and I heard her say: "Oh, God, Henry, look at his face, he's all bloody. . . ."

I wiped my hand across my face and it was sticky and my stomach turned; there was blood smeared on my fingers. I tried to hold fast to the pillar but everything was slanting and voices came to me as if from a distant echo chamber. The little girl had stopped screaming and I could see that the rain falling on the railroad tracks had turned to snow drifting down.

A voice near my ear said tiredly: "Jesus, Cooper, look at yourself, another fine mess. . . ."

The voice was familiar, but when I turned, my sight was going quickly and I could see only a shape, a pinpoint of light, a face in the pinpoint but it was too late and I saw only the snow blowing in great soft gusts, heard only the dim sounds of trains very far away, and I was falling and I simply didn't give a damn. . . .

London

THE voice I heard when I came to was the same I'd heard as I passed out, but it took a moment for my eyes to focus.

"Cooper," it said. I felt a gentle tug on my shoulder. "Cooper, can you hear me?"

It was Olaf Peterson.

I had been more or less unconscious since I had fainted into Peterson's arms at the railway station. He'd got me to a police medical aid station for repairs and then to a private clinic for some sleep. When I saw him it was three o'clock in the afternoon and he needed a shave. I asked him why the hell he was in Glasgow. He smirked with characteristic self-satisfaction and told me there would be plenty of time to discuss that later.

We were ticketed on the sleeper train to London, one day behind my schedule. We would talk then. In the meantime a short man with fuzzy gray hair and gold-rimmed spectacles appeared, a doctor giving my poor aching head a once-over.

I winced at the probing of his fingers.

"Lucky," he said tersely beside my ear. "Scratch. No dressing required. Let the air get at it. No comparison to what I usually get." He looked over at Peterson. "You should see the lads I patch up after a football punch-up." He looked back at me as if I were a severe disappointment.

In the early evening we went to police headquarters, where I explained my connection with Alistair Campbell. A newspaper lay on the desk with a picture of Campbell taken years before, a story of the shooting, a picture of the man who'd stepped into the hallway and told me to fuck off.

I went through the story several times. The detective's name was MacGregor and he looked like a carnival pitchman and spoke like a funeral director. Finally, having got the facts straight, he shook his head, frowned. He could make nothing out of the Gunter Brendel part of it; he clearly didn't want to open it up in all its complexities, at least not until he'd made the most of sheer facts.

He thanked me for my trouble and I was taken into an anteroom where I waited. Eventually Peterson came out and told me we were free to catch our train. One cop to another, Peterson could apparently work wonders.

He looked at me as if deciding to keep me or throw me back. "Jesus, what disgusting sandwiches," was all he said.

The night train traversing the four hundred odd miles to London was extraordinarily luxurious and once we settled back in the compartment I began to feel something like my normal self. Granted, my head had taken far more punishment than was good for it, but the pills helped. So did Peterson: he was as ironic as ever but it felt good not to be alone. It was almost as if his broad, thickset body was a shield for me, as if he could protect me.

Peterson produced a bottle of scotch, summoned ice and squat tumblers, and lit a cigar. Through the smoke he regarded me with a faint, tolerant smile.

"All right," I said, "what are you doing here?"

"The room clerk at the hotel told me you'd bought a ticket on the midnight sleeper to London. I went to the station and found you covered in blood, scaring small children, learned to my chagrin that you continue to be involved in murder wherever you go, and of course found you in desperate need of someone—anyone—to keep you from disgracing yourself." His voice trailed off; he shook his dark head. Some sort of plaid hat with a gaudy feather in the band lay beside him, beneath it a pearl-gray cashmere topcoat.

"But why did you come to Glasgow at all?"

"Because something very strange is going on, because I'm curious, because I feel this peculiar need to keep you alive. Because I should never have let you go to Buenos Aires. Because I wanted to have a vacation from my wife.

"Look, Cooper, remember the boxes—the empty boxes? I took the contents to Washington, to the government cryptographic center. But before I delivered them for decoding I stopped at a branch library and spent several dollars Xeroxing them, every page. Once I had my own copy I could feed them into the bureaucracy and not worry.

"What happened in Washington was that I got the classic runaround. I was debriefed by the FBI and by the CIA, because of your grandfather's career. I met with men who were described as being from the Pentagon—nothing more, and the cryptographers came up with nothing. They said they'd need more time, that it was a 'toughie.' That's what they called it, Cooper, a 'toughie.' Christ, it was insane." Peterson took a deep drink of scotch and put his feet up on the seat, stretching out with a pillow behind his head. The train rocked gently on the rails.

"For three days they went over what had happened in Cooper's Falls, hid me from reporters—Cooper's Falls has been a very big story, front page stuff, the network news, the works. Anyway, when they got done with me I checked in with the cryptographers and they were still mumbling and farting around and shaking their heads.

"I decided they weren't going to get anywhere so I flew up to New York to see a friend of mine from the old days, a guy named Ernest Harnetz at Columbia. He's a physics professor but he's also what we used to call a puzzle man when I was on special duty, a guy who could break a code like a pane of glass. I laid the stuff on him and we had a couple of drinks and he looked through it and began to doodle on some Columbia University stationery.

"About three hours is what it took him to crack it from corner to corner. 'They're bullshitting you in Washington,' is what he told me. 'They don't want you to know what's involved, so they're bullshitting you.' So he started telling me what was in those boxes."

I drank some scotch. "And—"

"It sounds funny, Cooper—"

"I'm sure."

"Plans, Nazi plans to occupy, take over, countries and major cities and huge corporations all over the world—once the war was won." He stopped and chewed the cigar.

"Or if the war was lost, either way, win or lose. They had plans, page after page of specific plans. For RCA and General Motors and utility companies, power and gas and all that, government agencies, cities—Chicago, New York, Miami, Detroit, Los Angeles. . . . They had divided the United States into six sections, all absolutely clear-cut and precise."

"Win or lose," I said. "What do you mean win or lose?"

"If the war in Europe was lost, that was only a temporary setback—a delay of a generation or two, and they allowed for that, apparently, because there was a second plan full of steps for taking over all the nations and cities and agencies and corporations slowly and from within. They already had their people placed inside these organizations. A vast, really enormous network of men who would make Quisling in Norway seem very small potatoes, indeed. Harnetz said you could read between the lines and see that Quisling was a sort of trial run, an experiment on a relatively—ah—inconsequential level.

"And it wasn't just the United States, Cooper, it was everywhere. Africa, South America, Russia, Mexico, Canada, England, hell's bells, they had it down pat. This was all contained in an outline of several pages. The United States was handled in great detail. Projections about time, the order in which things were going to happen—they had a timetable and they were in no hurry.

"In 1976, the President of the United States would be a Nazi . . . and no one would have the vaguest idea. No one would even care. By the mid-eighties, Europe would be totally Nazified—they seemed to feel the U.S. would be the easiest target—and by the year 2000, the Nazis would truly rule the world.

"Harnetz and I talked all night. They wouldn't be called Nazis by then, or at least probably not, but it would be the victory of a philosophy, the triumph of their ultimate will, the justification of all that had gone before. The last section of the coded stuff, a black book, not very large, concerned the post-2000 era, the resurrection of Hitler as the New Christ . . . the father of us all."

Silence in the compartment: the countryside dark beyond the window, the rails shifting us gently from side to side. Peterson was sweating below the rim of his hairpiece. His face was curiously relaxed, he stared blankly into the night.

"It sounds like a child's fantasy," I said at last.

"Of course. But you've never seen the documents, the seals with the eagles and swastikas, the aged parchment, the mildewed edges, the signatures—the ink that was put there by him, Hitler himself. You see them and you smell the age on them and, believe me, Cooper, the bottom falls out of your stomach—it's no child's fantasy and the guys that put it together were no comic-opera characters in funny uniforms." His eyes came back to me, his voice came back to life. "It was a long-range plan and they weren't kidding. They were men, historical figures, and they weren't pretending. They had their men—and that's the only part Harnetz said there was no way of decoding. The code names of the men involved. They were chosen symbols which could only be known through a key, Striker equals so-and-so, Sprinter equals somebody else, Red Breast is another guy, Vulture, Siegfried, Skylark, Panther, Shark, Barbarossa, Sphinx, dozens and dozens of names coded like that—I can't remember. . . .

"Harnetz thought that the plan was intended to be more or less inviolate, that while the original men connoted by the code names might grow old and die, the code names would never change. New men in each generation would assume the old names."

"Who was the man in America? Could you tell, was there a key man at the top during the war?"

He was right: my stomach was sliding like an accident in a gravel pit.

"Siegfried was the American."

"Asleep, only waiting to be summoned again. . . ."

"It was your grandfather, Cooper. It had to be Austin Cooper."

It was quiet for a long time in the compartment. Rain spattered the window, lights flared and were gone.

"Washington must have it figured out," I said.

"I suppose," he said. "But the question is, is it just a piece of history that came to nothing? Or is it still alive? I don't know. But several people have died because someone took those old boxes pretty damned seriously. You just can't ignore that one, can you?

"We're alone, Cooper," he said quietly. "You started the whole thing, or your brother did, and now I'm afraid there's no way to back up and get off. We're alone and I'm in it, too, up past my ass. And"—he sighed—"and everyone we touch is in it. Alistair Campbell was in it for a few hours—and now he's out of it. What I can't account for is just this: why aren't you dead? Surely, they could kill you with incredible ease if they really wanted to."

"I know, it occurred to me, too."

He lit a new cigar and turned on a fan. "Now, tell me what you've been up to. All of it."

And I did. Peterson had found out I'd gone to Glasgow from Roca so I traced all my actions from my arrival in Buenos Aires.

Roca. St. John. Kottmann, Maria Dolldorf. Professor Dolldorf's diary. The clipping. My little sister Lee. Brendel. The burning of Maria's flat. The disappearance of St. John and Kottmann en route to Patagonia. The lies and half-truths. The constant shadow of Perón. The code names—Barbarossa and Siegfried.

"Your sister, Cooper? Your *dead* sister?" He was incredulous in his own theatrical way. "Your *sister?*"

"That's what ties Cyril to it. That's where it all begins. Cyril would be alive now if he'd never seen that clipping. I'm convinced that he began in a simple attempt to find out if the woman, Frau Brendel, was our sister. Somehow that led back to the house in Cooper's Falls and to death." I was caught up in my own enthusiasm for Lee. Which was more important, what Peterson had learned or what I had stumbled on? Godforsaken Nazi gibberish or Lee? But they were indivisible, one led to the other. And people died finding out.

"Everywhere you turn it's Nazis," Peterson grumbled sourly. "Nest of vipers. Jesus. I thought that war was over. Christ, everybody you touch. . . ." He shook his head, repeated the German names from Buenos Aires: Kottmann, Dolldorf, Brendel. . . . "An English brigand, St. John." He made a face. "What scares me is that the whole thing makes a dubious kind of sense. I wish I could get hold of it properly."

We finally settled in to our berths in the dark.

"There's no progress at all in the murder investigations," Peterson said. "And Arthur Brenner has had a stroke."

"What?" I'd gone rigid: Arthur was always supposed to be there, safe, unchanging.

"At the hotel in the dining room. Just slumped across the table, Bradlee told me. Happened when I was in New York. I flew back to Cooper's Falls for one day before I set out for Glasgow and Bradlee told me he was in a coma. He said it might have been brought on by the strain of the attack on him, or by the constant struggle with the cold and snow. Bradlee says he's in bad shape. . . ." Peterson's voice was fading.

"I see," I said. There were tears in my eyes.

"What did Campbell say when he came toward you in the hallway, just before he died? Something about spots?"

"No. He said something about finding stains. It didn't make much sense. He was staining the wall with his blood."

A rain-shiny black taxi dropped us at the corner of Oxford Street and North Audley Street. A bright-red London bus was reflected in the black metal. I turned my coat collar up against the gusty wind and rain.

Peterson paid, blew his nose, yanked his muffler tight at his throat. Rain beaded on his black leather trench coat, clung to the epaulettes.

Beneath the dull gray cloud cover, Mayfair did not seem overly enthused about going on with the whole nasty charade. Grosvenor Square waited it out, black umbrellas bobbing above hunched shoulders, diplomats in bowlers, Eero Saarinen's American Embassy bleakly brooding in its stark modernity over the patience of history at its feet. Leaves wilted on the pavement, clung to my shoes. In the center of the Square, Dick's statue memorializing Franklin Delano Roosevelt stood manfully in the rain.

My brother Cyril had lived in Curzon Street, not far from Berkeley Square. Up some stairs from the street, through a polished door, in a dim and gleaming hallway, there was my own waxen image mirrored in a brass nameplate engraved with the single word, COOPER. Peterson stood behind me, his features oozing down the nameplate. Abruptly he began to shake rain onto the carpet like a wet dog.

The quiet hallway, carpeted and wallpapered and very discreetly lit, smelled faintly of wood polish and the evidence of its use reflected the bits of light from every satiny surface. Peterson surveyed the eye-level lock, bared his teeth a trifle fiercely in the manner of Emiliano Zapata, and popped the door open with a credit card properly inserted.

The foyer emitted the slightly stale quality common to unused rooms, no matter how frequently aired and dusted. There was no smell of food and drink and smoke and sleep and rain and open windows and perfume. There was instead a quality of absence, perhaps loss. A gilt mirror in an elaborate frame, umbrellas lingering in a brass boot, motes of dust dancing in the shaft of gray light between nearly closed draperies.

The flat was dim, quiet, waiting for Cyril's return. Even Peterson seemed inhibited by the solemnity of the place, the fact that Cyril was never going to return. Finally, he reached for a pull in the shadows and yanked the draperies open with a clatter. Rain streaked the windows in the bay overlooking the street. He threw a sash up and there was the sound of the water running in the spouts, dripping off the eaves.

We moved like security operatives through the rooms, the austere bedroom with a few spare garments hanging in the closet, the cluttered expensive living room mixing trendy steel-framed posters and Queen Anne furniture and a huge carved banker's desk, a dining room with tubular steel and glass everywhere, a kitchen with everything built in, a chopping-block table in the middle, pots and pans and cutlery lining the walls like sentries.

"What do we do now?" My voice sounded high, boyish in the stillness. The draperies rustled in the wind, rain speckled the sill.

"The desk," Peterson said, walking around it. "It's got two complete sets of drawers, one on each side. As if for two people," he muttered. He pulled a drawer; it slid quickly out. Methodically we tested them all; they were all in use, none locked. "We might as well start."

"What are we looking for?"

He gave me a sour look. "I don't know. We're just looking. We're snooping. Follow your instincts. Act like a detective, for God's sake. You're the one who started all this poking around—"

"All right, all right, you're making my head hurt."

After an hour of sorting, Peterson straightened up and fluttered a piece of paper from his broad, black-haired hand. "Clipping," he said. "Frau Brendel again."

It was the same clipping I carried in my wallet. I felt a twinge inside and nodded.

"He must have been as convinced as you are," Peterson mused. He stared at the picture. "It looks like your sister?"

"No, it looks very much like our mother. Or like what our sister could look like today—"

"If she were alive."

"Obviously, she is. I might have had my reaction to the photograph because I knew my brother had been carrying it around with him. But Cyril—he just saw it in the paper. And that was enough for him."

The drawers on my side proved useless. I slumped

in the chair, stared across at Peterson. His brow was knitted and he frowned beneath his mustache. He held his palms open and shrugged: nothing.

I dug in my pocket for the pipe, knocked the bowl into a heavy glass ashtray. Next to the ashtray lay an envelope addressed to *Cyril Cooper, Esq.* I looked at it without thinking, then the engraved return address registered:

> Ivor Steynes, Bart.
> Cat Island
> Cornwall

I looked up at Peterson.

"Stains," I said. "I've found stains. Campbell was talking about a man named Ivor Steynes."
Peterson looked at me in disbelief.
The letter, on cream vellum, was brief:

> *My dear Mr. Cooper,*
>   *I shall look forward to meeting you here at Cat Island per our telephonic conversation.*
>   *Cordially,*
>   *Ivor Steynes*

It was dated late the previous fall, obviously after my brother Cyril had visited with Alistair Campbell and presumably been given the same lead the poor cagey little Scot had tried so desperately to give me.

"We'll have to contact him," Peterson said.
The telephone on the desk was fully operational and after nearly an hour of negotiating I learned how to get a call through to Cat Island, by no means a simple task. There was only a single line on the island, I was informed, and I would have to wait to get my call through. The operator would ring back when she had my party.

I lit my pipe and we sat in the gathering afternoon gloom. Now the spidery connections traced a random pattern across all my thoughts, like an unfamiliar road map in an unknown land. I had stopped trying to make lists. I had stopped worrying about the connections because I could no longer keep them straight. There were so many names, so many threats and dangers and deaths. When my guard was down, it occurred to me to seriously wonder if I was going to get out of it alive. When I was tired, as I was just then, I wasn't absolutely sure that I cared.

We both flinched when the telephone rang. The connection was crackling, as if the wind and rain were blowing themselves out in the earpiece. Finally a voice came faintly across the wire.

"I wish to speak with Sir Ivor Steynes," I shouted. "My name is John Cooper."

The static began to clear after a few more words and then there was nothing until a metallic click and a reedy voice, itself metallic, came on: "Ivor Steynes here, Mr. Cooper. Can I help you?"

"I'm Cyril Cooper's brother—"

"Aha, I see . . . and Austin Cooper's grandson. Where are you, old man?" The thin voice was almost gleeful.

"I'm in London. I want to see you, if at all possible."

"I see. And how is your brother?"

"He's dead. That's why I'm here."

There was a long pause. "Repeat, please."

"My brother Cyril is dead. That's why I want to see you." Peterson was staring at the rain blowing across the sill. His cigar was dead.

"Ah. A natural death, then?"

"No."

"I'm very sorry, of course. Can you come to Cat Island?"

"Yes, we can if you'll tell me where it is—"

"We?"

"I have a friend with me."

The voice at the other end had lost its tinge of friendliness. "Come to Land's End in Cornwall. Cat Island is off the coast. You will reach Land's End tomorrow afternoon by rail or by motor. My man will meet you with the boat at six o'clock. Dawson is his name, the boat is the *Lear*. He will bring you to Cat Island and we will talk then. Is that clear?"

"Utterly," I said.

"Until then," he said. That was all.

Rain was still blowing, slanting in the gathering darkness: clouds skudded like watercolors above Berkeley Square, where the nightingale had once sung. We walked back through the Square, along Mount Street to Park Lane, stood wetly staring at the slick green of Hyde Park. Peterson took a deep breath. Headlights flared in the slicks of rain.

We made our way among the palatial Grecian columns of the Grosvenor House, obtained an enormously expensive room overlooking the street and the park. Peterson stood staring into the rain. "Cat Island . . . I suppose it pours all the time on Cat Island."

Early the next morning, fortified with eggs and kippers and muffins, lugging a thermos of coffee, we rented an Audi and set off for Land's End, desperately dependent on a road map and Peterson's ability to drive on the wrong side of the road. Any change in the weather was clearly for the worse. The windshield wipers beat steadily. Headlights were on all day.

The man at the car rental had told us that Cornwall was like a foreign country. Turning left at Morwenstow to follow the coastline, I spotted a MEBYON CURNOW! chalked on a brick wall: home rule for Cornwall! The rain was beating in off the Atlantic, washing the chalk down the dirty wall.

Sharpnose Points, Marham Church, Dizzard Point, Cambeak, Fire Beacon Point, Tintagel Castle. . . .

The rain and fog to our right rolling in from the sea blended sea and sky into a deepening gray void. Blotting out the light. Through rips in the fog, breakers from the Atlantic punished the shattered headlands far below us. The cliffs of granite dropped away like the walls of a skyscraper miles in length.

At Tintagel Castle we stretched our legs. King Arthur's birthplace stood alone, devoid of tourists in the brutish weather, being slowly reclaimed by nature over the centuries. The towers and walls rose like mossy men guarding what lay inland beyond. Below, the Atlantic crashed wildly against the causeway. The ruins were carpeted in wet green turf and in the mist your mind played tricks.

Peterson had his hands over his ears; rain dripped from his nose. He beckoned to me. The breakers drowned out his voice. We got back in the Audi. It was three o'clock and darkness was creeping all around us. We were forty miles from Land's End and Dawson and the good ship *Lear*.

The place-names crept by, wetly, wearily. My back was beginning to ache from the long hours. Doyden Castle, Pentire Point, Wadebridge, Trevase Head. . . .

At Newquay the hotels brooded darkly over the wet gray beaches as we sped past. I was driving while Peterson dozed; everything blurred through the steady rain. The wind along the coast had gathered velocity. Water exploded like pebbles on the windshield, then slacked off to nearly nothing, then the cycle repeated itself. The radio crackled relentlessly.

The narrow streets of St. Ives were almost deserted. A man in a beret and a heavy sweater stood on a corner, drunk, pissing in the gutter. He stared into the glare of the lights, wiped a hand across his beard, and continued his duty.

Down toward Land's End, the fading remnants of daylight revealed only the bayonet-steel granite, severe and bleak, an exposed fist of stone flung angrily into the sea. Gurnard's Head, Pendeen Watch, Cape Cornwall, St. Just. . . . Penzance to the left and you between it and the ocean coast with the countless coves and inlets and rock-shrouded bays, chinks nibbled out of the mainland.

Land's End. Beyond it, if your brakes fail, you plummet from cliff top into the churning sea. There is no more England once you've got to Land's End.

Peterson peered out of sleep warily.

"Christ. End of the world." He yawned.

Before us, a lone hotel clung to the edge like an outcast, banished forever from the company of others. The gale whined around the car. Sea gulls wheeled and dipped into the void, like phantoms swallowed in the fog.

A fire roared in the grate; a woman brought us

brandy and cakes and coffee. My throat was raw; the brandy burned it, fired my stomach.

"I wonder, Cooper, I really wonder. . . ." Peterson frowned. "I think I have a temperature. Some madman thinks he's going to get us out in a boat in this god-damned hurricane. We're headed for some nickel-fiction place called Cat Island. There can't be any-thing out there, it's just not possible."

The youngish woman reappeared, threw a log on the fire. "It is a blustery day," she said simply. "Will you be staying the night?"

"No. We're going out there." I gestured toward the coast.

"To the Scillies?" She seemed surprised. "It's not a good night for it, is it?"

"Not the Scillies. A place called Cat Island. Do you know it?"

"Mr. Dawson is coming for you, then?" I nodded. "Well, he's a dandy sailor, my father says. And the *Lear* is a lovely craft, too."

She smiled again. "They sometimes come here for dinner in the summertime. Dawson fancies the girls, the young people who come down for the surfing at Newquay and St. Ives." Peterson tried to stifle a yawn, gave up on it.

"And doesn't Steynes fancy the girls?"

"Goodness, no. He has no use for the girls, I'm sure."

"And why is that?"

"You'll see, won't you?" She picked up the tray after giving the fire a severe poke. "Have a nice journey." She smiled formally and went away.

We huddled in a shed at the tip of the wooden dock, oily slick with the pelting rain. I wiped my eyes, Peterson cursed. A light blurred like a tiny cold moon through the fog and rain, an engine throbbed against the constant thundering of breakers. The *Lear* bumped solidly against the timbers. A large, exceed-ingly agile man in a dark slicker was making the ship fast to a piling with a coil of thick rope. The lamp swung from a hook over our heads, creaking. Finally he jumped onto the dock and leaned into the rain, making for the shed.

"Cooper?" he yelled over the fierce whine.

I nodded. "And Mr. Peterson." A black turtleneck curled up over his chin and a rainhat was pulled low. I smelled oil and sea water.

"Well, come aboard then," he said good-naturedly, "and don't fall in the sea." He gave us a hand on the slippery ladder. The rope strained; the *Lear,* which seemed to be about thirty-five feet in length, with a large cabin, quivered. Peterson came up behind me and we headed down the stairway into the cabin while Dawson cast off.

He came into the warm cabin and slipped out of the slicker, took off the rainhat, hung them on a hook. It was an immaculate room, polished brass and wood and built a long time ago. Rain beaded on the windows.

"Bad night," Peterson said.

"We're used to it." Dawson's mouth was crooked, his nose flattened, his eyebrows snarled like a hedge, everything dark brown. "Here, a tot of brandy'll do you good." He poured from a flask into coffee mugs. He moved a switch, the engines throttled up, pounding beneath us.

"Still it's a bad night in my book," Peterson grumbled.

"Choppy, it's choppy, I'll give you that, but the *Lear* can handle it like a knife in cakes. Hold on . . . I'm taking her out. . . ."

Waves chopped across the deck, foamed at the windshield, coiled like snakes across the deck. Peterson slumped in a pile on the bench, clutching his mug of brandy. His face was paling rapidly.

"How long will it take us to get there?"

Dawson stared straight ahead. "An hour, give or take a bit. It's not far, you know, but it'll be slow going, fighting the seas."

I drank some brandy.

"Have you been with Sir Ivor long?"

"Let's see, I met the Colonel in forty-two. He was back from Africa by then, working for CIGS and I was seconded to him on some special assignments." He glanced my way, drained off his brandy. "Been with him ever since, the way it turned out."

Later he said: "Don't be alarmed—the *Lear* is sea-
worthy. Like the old pirates. The coastline harbored
more pirates in its day than any other in the world."

"Are you a pirate?" Peterson asked.

"No, no, not a pirate."

"Jesus," Peterson muttered, "thank God for the
small favors."

"But we fitted out the *Lear* to go U-boating in
the old days. Used to run the Channel looking for
the bastards. Good recreation, it was."

"Ever find one?"

"Oh, yes, we found two of them. Wounded from
one thing or another, unable to submerge. Came across
them in the fog."

"What did you do?" Peterson's interest was
fanned.

"Well, the Colonel's blood was up, you know."
Dawson poured another measure of brandy. "We
mounted cannon. We opened fire, no damned warning
shots, shot hell out of both of 'em. Sunk 'em both, you
know."

"Good God," Peterson muttered.

"Water was full of Jerries, yelling and waving,
quite a sight. . . ."

"You took prisoners, then?"

"Prisoners?" Dawson smiled, wolfish, deep ridges
at the corners of his mouth. "No."

"Well, what did you do? You couldn't leave them
to drown."

"Oh, no, we didn't leave them to drown. No, the
Colonel ordered me to run them down. And he made
use of a machine gun." He was staring ahead again,
into the fog. "No, nobody drowned, I'm certain of
that, sir."

Sick, weak-kneed, exhausted, we finally felt the
clunk against the jetty. It was old, constructed of
splintered timbers, soaked with the rain. That structure
itself finally petered out and after Dawson had secured
the boat in a covered hutch we followed him across
the pebbly shingle of sand, encountered scrub and
bracken and finally, gasping, reached what he called
the Beach Road. A lengthy, gleaming, rain-spattered
pre-World War II Rolls-Royce sat squarely in the mid-

dle of the road. We bundled into the back seat, teeth chattering.

"There are only two vehicles on Cat Island," Dawson said as he arranged himself behind the wheel. "And I'm the only one who drives them. So I can park wherever I damned please." He put it in gear and we began to move cautiously forward, headlights poking fingers of light into the mist and fog. "This road was built in 1760, according to the official history. The Colonel had it repaved when he retired here." He gestured into the darkness at the vaguest of shapes. "Disused old carriage house there, some stables, tennis courts all caged in . . . but the vines have pretty well taken over. None of that has been used since the whole family came often to the island, a long time ago, before my time. Now there's only the Colonel left."

Peterson swore under his breath, stared into the dark. "Jesus," he said suddenly, "what the hell is that?" The lights had tweezed an angular, gaunt shape at the roadside, plunged into the turf like a huge dagger. Dawson stopped the car. Water coursed down the beam of his flashlight playing across the shape.

"It's a German bomber. It crashed here during the Blitz, badly shot up, on fire. No survivors, by the way. The Colonel likes it, says we should treat it like a piece of lawn sculpture. So there it sits." He flicked the light off. "The Colonel's funny about it, likes things that remind him of the war." The Rolls began to ease forward. "He left the remains of his own Hurricane on the other side of the island, out near the cliffs. Quite a story, that. He was pretty badly riddled over the channel and just barely got the aircraft back to Cat Island—ten feet lower and he'd have caught the top of the cliffs. As it was, he skimmed in over the top, belly-landed it, and blacked out. The Messerschmitt chasing him came in too low, couldn't see the cliffs in the fog, and flew smack into the granite." He chuckled quietly and I found myself straining to hear him. "That one is still there, too, driven like a big rusty nail right into the island. That's a lot of wrecked airplanes, three of them, on an island only a mile long and three hundred yards wide. But, hell, it's an unusual island in lots of ways."

"The Colonel sounds like a strange man," I said.

"Bit eccentric, you know. But that's the English all over, isn't it? You Yanks always get a chuckle out of eccentric Englishmen." He laughed, continued: "Bertie Wooster and Jeeves. Well, the Colonel's an eccentric, all right. And more power to him, I say."

A massive stone wall rose out of the fog.

"This is the castle's outer wall." Dawson left us, beaten by the wind.

"Cooper, Cooper," Peterson growled. "What in the name of God have you gotten us into now? This is insane."

"It's only the weather."

"Goddamn Colonel's obviously a nut case. Broken airplanes all over his playpen. This Dawson is his keeper. He's got that tolerant sound when he's talking. It comes from taking care of crazy people."

Dawson came back and eased the car through the gate, past the wall four feet thick.

"Main house is about two hundred yards up the hill. We're in the keep now but it's all ruins. Things a thousand years old arc pretty often in ruins." Dawson enjoyed his role as guide. "We've got a Stone Age hut here. Think of it. And a graveyard from Roman times."

He braked the Rolls before the large, three-tiered, square house. It was absolutely symmetrical: window for window, column for column. Dim yellow lights shown from deep inside and I thought of Roman campfires and soldiers huddled in the brutish night.

Dawson took our bags and left them in a porter's cubbyhole off the entrance hall. The yellow light came from ornate wall brackets which had once been converted to electricity. The hallway gave onto murky depths where the paneled walls became all but invisible. The floor was stone and cold. He took us into a library toward the back of the main floor. The walls were immensely thick; books rose like the face of a tor into the darkness. Peterson made for the fireplace, where flames leaped hungrily from huge, blackened logs. Outside, the Atlantic wind screeched along the plateau; rain beat on the windows.

"I'll go check on the Colonel," Dawson said, "if you'll just make yourselves comfortable. Brandy, whiskey, soda—"

Peterson poured a brandy into an oversized snifter with a coat of arms cut into its side, hurried back to the fire. "Cold," he grumbled, "so damned wet."

A table contained framed photographs, ranging in subject matter from family outings in tennis gear that had a twenties look to pilots grouped around a Spitfire in some corner of a forgotten English aerodrome. Propped in a corner was a huge propeller—from such a plane, I supposed, and on the wall I saw a striking antique-looking crude black-and-white drawing on framed, glassed-in parchment. A body with an expressionless face was being dragged behind a horse and a man appeared to be dancing beside the body, but he, likewise, possessed an utterly disinterested face. Beneath, in perfect penmanship, was an inscription several lines long:

An early Steynes, suffering the not surprising fate of a man who felt he might himself make a good King, died in June of 1242, being first dragged from Westminster to the tower and thence to the Gibbet, when he had there breathed out his wretched soul, he was suspended on a hook, and when stiff in death was lowered, disembowelled, his bowels burnt on the spot, and his wretched body divided into quarters which were sent to the four principal cities in the Kingdom, by what pitiable spectacle to strike terror in all beholders.

Peterson was reading it over my shoulder. When he finished, he looked at me. "Do you suppose it worked?"

Dawson appeared in the doorway. Peterson jumped when he spoke: "Colonel Steynes."

And through the wide opening came a man in a wheelchair, motor whirring, wide, thin mouth smiling and pale eyebrows arched high over blue-gray eyes.

A Sherlock Holmes nose protruded like a hook from the narrow face: gray-blond hair fell lankly across the high forehead. The voice, freed of the bad telephone connection, still had a flinty, metallic quality, cold like the drafts on the stone floor. A heavy steamer blanket lay across his legs.

"Good evening, gentlemen, good evening and welcome to a rather inclement Cat Island. You," he said, rolling handily toward me, "are surely Mr. Cooper. A distinct family resemblance, through the eyes, and let me tell you how very sorry I am about your brother. . . . And you," he said, looking at Peterson, "you are an associate of Mr. Cooper's?"

Peterson introduced himself and Colonel Steynes motioned us to deep leather chairs before the fire. He summoned Dawson to bring a tray of glasses and brandy, whiskey, and soda and suggested that he check the larder for some dinner for us. We settled in. I lit my pipe with a wooden match, and built a weak whiskey and soda.

While we waited for Dawson to return, Steynes showed himself a bright, sharp-tongued commentator on the present English political problems and leadership. He found them decent enough but "pathetically weak." But he smiled when he spoke and showed full use of his arms and hands. There was an elegant gray-blond mustache laid along his upper lip, deep ridges in his cheeks, and his face was weatherbeaten from the Atlantic gales.

Dawson appeared with a tray of cold roast beef sandwiches, a wheel of Stilton, mustard, fruit tarts, a pot of steaming coffee. Colonel Steynes urged us to fill our plates. Dawson was dispatched to ready our rooms and Steynes fitted a Dunhill cigarette into a black holder, and began to tell us what we'd come to hear.

"Cyril Cooper came to me directly from his meeting with Alistair Campbell in Glasgow. I have known Mr. Campbell since I was associated with him in Cairo before the general outbreak of the Nazi war. Your brother showed me a newspaper cutting—a photograph of a man named Gunter Brendel and his lovely wife, Lise, Frau Brendel. As it happens,

I have an extensive file on Herr Brendel and Campbell was well aware of that, but we will come to that later.

"Cyril explained to me who he was, grandson of Austin Cooper, a fact which I found rather more interesting and satisfying than he could possibly have imagined. Your brother knew only that I could give him information regarding Herr Brendel. And he explained to me that he was, in fact, not interested in Herr Brendel himself but in the young woman, Lise Brendel." Steynes fixed me with a pale eye through a veil of cigarette smoke. "He suggested a unique hypothesis. He believed that Lise Brendel was his sister, long presumed dead. I naturally asked him what prompted this belief and he very sheepishly informed me that she looked like what he thought his sister would look like today, very much like his mother looked to him when he was a child. But he was very, very insistent.

"In point of fact, however, I would almost certainly not have gone into it with him but for the one tremendously salient fact—that this young man was Austin Cooper's grandson . . . and, gentlemen, that Herr Brendel was and is a Nazi." He spoke with that same metallic calm, but the last word echoed in my mind. Steynes leaned forward, sipped his whiskey. Peterson stared at me, eyes alive, then went on chewing on the rare beef.

"That connection—Austin Cooper and Herr Brendel, two Nazis—that connection bore down on one like a runaway lorry on an empty street." He smiled at the turn of phrase. "That 'coincidence,' if indeed it was a coincidence. That, my friends, is something I have learned to distrust, the coincidence phenomenon. I have found too often the existence of a meaningful pattern beneath the untroubled surface of what the laity may conveniently call coincidence. As I listened to your brother, considered who his grandfather was, and who Herr Brendel is, related these facts to my own sphere of interest—which we will discuss somewhat later, I began to discern that pattern, like a school of sharks, beneath the unflurried surface of the vast sea of sheer coincidence." He sighed. "Mr. Peterson, would you jostle those logs? I know perfectly well that I have no feeling in my legs, but I swear that I can feel the drafts on my feet—like the old salt who can feel the changes in the weather in his pegleg."

The sparks roared up the flue, sucked by the wind. Peterson stroked the drooping dark mustache, stood watching the fire. Steynes fixed another cigarette in the holder and went on, snapping a wooden match on his thumbnail with a long finger.

"Now, it seems to me that my distrust of coincidence is justified. You tell me your brother is dead. Is he dead because Austin Cooper and Gunter Brendel, two Nazis, are calling to one another across the years? It seems possible, doesn't it?" He stopped and stared at me with those naked eyes. "Tell me about your brother, Mr. Cooper. Tell me why you have followed his trail to Cat Island."

I tried to lay it out carefully for Colonel Steynes. It took considerable time. I concluded: "And three nights ago in Glasgow Alistair Campbell was shot and killed by a man who also tried to kill me. I escaped and realized when I saw your letter on my brother's desk in London that Campbell spoke your name to me in that dim hallway as he died and I misunderstood him. We're here, Colonel Steynes, because Campbell wanted us to come and because my brother was here . . . and his path is the path we're following."

Steynes had blanched behind his weatherbeaten exterior and a quick tightness yanked at the corners of his mouth. He took a stiff measure of whiskey, said quietly: "So Campbell is dead. . . . Rum fellow, rum . . . and the most recent victim in a very long war. They have killed him because of you and your brother, of course. He will be avenged, I assure you."

Peterson caught my eye, mouthed the word "avenged" with raised eyebrows. Peterson was not impressed. I was beginning to break into a cold sweat.

Colonel Steynes' pale eyes flickered at us from behind the sandy blond lashes, banked and freezing fires in the maimed body. His eyes frightened me because Peterson could just be right: Steynes might be mad. The metallic voice was going on.

"Now you tell me—if I may sum up this altogether extrordinary tale—that your brother is mysteriously murdered, that some awesome species of document has been sought by strange and homicidal men who choose to handle all matters with a maximum of violence, that these curious documents are in fact old Nazi plans for world domination—historical trivia, at this point, heh?—that a town has been sacked in a manner worthy of my ancestor Bevil Steynes, Bevil the Red, as he was known by his chums, that a harmless old professor is murdered in Buenos Aires after meeting with your brother. . . ." He paused for breath. Outside, the wind smote the house and it creaked and whirred like a machine.

"You tell me that Martin St. John and Alfried Kottmann, both of whom are known to me—a point which we'll come to in good time, that both St. John and Kottmann met with your brother, met with you, and subsequently vanished from the face of the earth. You tell me that my old friend Campbell is shot to death in a Glasgow slum in an attempt to keep him from directing you gentlemen to me. . . ." He sighed again, leaned back in the wheelchair, cosseted by chrome and steel and leather, the King of Cat Island.

"I suggest that my first distrust of coincidence was correct, that we are dealing with a very specific pattern.

"Let me further suggest that the only coincidence in this entire business was your late brother running across that photograph in the Glasgow *Herald*.

"From then on, I suggest that Cyril Cooper was a doomed man, doomed because he was driven by something in his own character to find his sister. Once he set out to find her, he no longer had a chance to escape with his life.

"And why? Why must that be so?

"Because your brother had come too close to them, to Brendel, to Kottmann, to St. John, to all the rest of them. . . .

"Who are these men?" A faint smile came and went. He poured himself another whiskey and soda, wet his thin, dry lips. "That is what you are wondering, inevitably, and let me say that if I thought I could save you . . . I would simply refuse to tell you. But even now, only the grace of God has kept you alive.

"In light of that and the nature of the situation you find yourselves in, I will tell you even more than I told your brother. I owe it to his memory as well as to you. I will tell you who I am and what I am, how I came to be the man I am at this moment—

"But it is much too late in the day to begin all that now—we will start in the morning." He smiled at us, turned the wheelchair around, and began to move off, beckoning us to follow him. "I trust that I have piqued your interest." In the entrance hall he rolled to the bottom of the wide staircase. A chair attached to a track on the wall waited at the foot of the stairs. Laboriously he levered himself out of the wheelchair into the lift. Peterson and I stood watching. The exertion tightened his face into a grimace of effort, pain, determination.

"Now," he said, once he was situated, "Dawson will see you to your rooms for the night. And, gentlemen, you can sleep soundly. As long as you are here with me on Cat Island you are entirely safe. And now," he concluded as the chair slipped from view into the darkness at the top of the stairs, "goodnight."

Seabirds, gulls, wheeled against the gray wet sky hovering low over the Atlantic. Occasional bursts of rain spattered the windows in the room crowning the lighthouse which was built on a tiny outcropping of rock reached by a stone causeway that was crumbling slowly away over the centuries. At eye level, through the fog and mist, the shape of the high walls of the castle keep loomed over the plateau. The smell of wet ferns and moss and saltiness seeped in at every crack, the wet pungent odor of the sea. Peterson stood glumly, subdued, staring at the evidence of a distant horizon slicing like a jagged knife wound, separating the grayness of the sky and the slate flat sea which grew choppy and angry as it approached the island.

Dawson poured us steaming midmorning coffee from an old thermos. Peterson sipped loudly, burrowed deep into his black leather trench coat, pulled a white muffler tight at his tonsillitis, sniffed. I was trying to keep my pipe lit, gave it up, burned my mouth on the wickedly strong black coffee. Colonel Steynes, in a plaid Burberry cape, was settled in the swiveling wooden chair beside the mechanism controlling the lights.

Waiting for Colonel Steynes to begin, I tried to pick out landmarks visible on the nasty sledge of granite, like the exposed head of a hammer crashing up through the surface of the Atlantic, that was Cat Island. The Stone Age hut huddled remarkably intact on the sheltered landward side, shielded from the weather, surrounded by wet green turf like sponge, encroaching bracken, the odd thicket of bramble and remembered hedge which dotted that side of the island. Moss clung to the walls. Down the Beach Road a quarry lay like an explosion from an ancient war, eaten out of the granite. And above it the vine-covered tennis courts and the rusted fuselage of the German airplane. Driving from the main house to the lighthouse road, Dawson had swung the old Rolls on a miniature detour, stopped above the cliffs, pointed with a smile of real enjoyment at the ME 109 driven like a stake into the cliff—the plane which had pursued the Colonel through the fog and rain back to Cat Island more than thirty years before. It too had begun to green with sea moss.

Over a hearty breakfast, accompanied by Peterson's sneezing, the Colonel had reminisced about his career. He was half-German, had served as a courier and special operative based in Cairo before the war, had gone on to Whitehall, had engaged in the Battle of Britain, flying Spitfires and a limping old Hawker Hurricane. It was in the Hurricane that he'd run afoul of several Messerschmitts on his last flight.

The crash of the Hurricane had crushed much of his spinal column, broken his legs, burned his body badly, left his carcass leaking blood like a sieve. He had remained comatose for several weeks while the effort was made to save his rapidly waning life. In time, of course, he'd come around. A year after the crash he'd come back to Cat Island, paralyzed from the waist down, weak as a child and almost hairless, like an aged, decrepit baby. Dawson accompanied him, had stayed on, had brought him back to health.

At breakfast, Colonel Steynes had discussed the murder of his German half-sisters by the Nazis in 1945 as the Russians pushed toward Berlin. Their deaths were singularly senseless and the news came to him shortly after hostilities ceased. Subsequently, his health having sufficiently improved, he was invited to join a team of British officials sent to Germany to engage in the investigations of a few, very specific war crimes. Among them were the murders of his half-sisters: the killers, though identified by witnesses who survived, were never found. Eventually he returned to Cat Island, alone. His entire family, German and English branches, had been wiped out by the war. By the Germans. By the Nazis. "An extraordinary coincidence," he had said, tucking into his toast and eggs, "but I have never found the pattern in it—except in the chance result."

Now, in the lighthouse, with the electric-heater bars growing red, he began to elaborate on his story.

"So I watched the world in convulsion after the war. I saw Germany sick and reeling, cowering in defeat, hostile and pathetic and resentful, even more crippled than I was. I was, I believed, more or less helpless, a physical derelict—but the longer I remained in Germany the more I began to see that there was a moral difference between my weakness and theirs. And I began to harbor a more than normal distaste for the Germans. I saw my reaction for what it was—the seed of an irrational illness, an obsessive hatred for an entire race of people, the Germans.

"I was aware that my attitude was splitting—part of me stood back and realized the unhealthy nature of my thinking, the other part was wickedly enjoying this new outlet for anger, hatred, the beast of frustration within me. I responded by summoning up my resolve and leaving this banquet for my hatred, returning to Cat Island, to solitude, to a space and time for easy reflection.

"Now, to continue in this frame of mind would have been to court a dangerous kind of madness, an obsession about an entire nation. It would have been antecedent to further frustration because I would surely not have been able to inflict any widespread hurt on an aggregate people. So I carefully began to desensitize myself about Germans, to think of them as individual human beings who had undergone hideous suffering themselves. I finally managed to expunge this feeling of group hatred.

"Instead of spreading my obsession, my madness across several millions of Germans—I aimed it at a manageable number. . . ."

Dawson busied himself refilling coffee mugs. Peterson prowled restlessly around the circular room.

"Colonel Steynes," he finally said with a trace of impatience, "you mentioned avenging Alistair Campbell's death last night. And this morning you're talking about something you call your madness, your obsession." The tone of his voice stopped Dawson in his tracks. The Colonel smiled at Peterson. "How the hell are we supposed to know that you are not totally crazy? I mean, my God, I'm standing here in the top of a lighthouse somewhere off the nastiest damn bit of coastline I've ever seen, talking to a man I don't even know who thinks he's an avenging angel. I have the very hell of a sore throat, I'm up to my ass in unsolved murders, and everywhere I turn somebody draws a Nazi across my path. Your personal psychological problems hold little fascination for me except insofar as they pertain to the sad story of Cyril Cooper. Now let's get on with it. Let's cut the crap, as we Yanks say."

Colonel Steynes was listening patiently to Peterson, sipping the fresh coffee. When the tirade finished Steynes said: "Anything else, Mr. Peterson?"

"Not right now."

"All right. Dawson, tell Mr. Peterson to shut up until I have finished. Tell him that you will throw him out of the top of this lighthouse if he doesn't shut up."

Dawson laughed.

Peterson rolled his eyes. "Jesus, Jesus, Jesus. . . ." He turned to look out to sea. Defeat and madness stared him in the face.

"Mr. Peterson," Colonel Steynes said somewhat more pleasantly, "all will become clear to you shortly. My story is such that you must understand the background—otherwise you will have a good deal of difficulty comprehending my rather peculiar role in this matter."

The rain outside had begun drumming steadily on the roof and windows. Fog was rolling on, growing thicker.

The story told us by Ivor Steynes challenged our credulity and intelligence.

Having returned to England and the quiet of Cat Island, Steynes struggled to control his mania. He began to study Germany closely, its history and literature and music and humor. He also made use of his extensive contacts in the military, at Whitehall, even in Downing Street. He had access through paranormal channels to highest security files, the advantage of the old boys' system, his family, his own lavish heroism. So, to his study of the Teutonic past, he added an unprecedented fund of information about the present, what was actually going on inside postwar Germany.

The more he learned the more effectively he was able to plan how he might sate his desire for vengeance.

Germany was full of Nazi war criminals who had eluded recognition and capture. In fact, the world was rapidly becoming a refuge for these sewer rats, picking their way past human detritus, the bodies of the innocent, holding enormous sums of treasure looted from the vaults of Europe. No one was stopping them, no one was even trying very hard to bring them to any bar of justice. In the event, Sir Ivor Steynes decided that he would do precisely that.

He began carefully. Movement was not simple, given his physical condition, but Dawson was there. And there were friends, a vast network of friends. Even in Germany he had his sources, men who had been close to Himmler, men in the upper reaches of the SS, and clerks who happened to know where the bodies were buried, even a man who had microfilmed much of Reinhard Gehlen's intraparty files. The information Steynes received was frequently one of a kind. He procured one of the East German Brown Books at a time when it was one of the most closely guarded documents in the world.

To test his sources of information he carried out a reconnaissance mission on Doctor Rademacher, one of those involved in the extermination of Jews. Not only had Doctor Rademacher not been brought to trial, he had been concealed and protected in an elaborate Foreign Office plan. Documents and records had been falsified to save him from prosecution. If Doctor Rademacher had been revealed for what he was, then German postwar diplomats would have been implicated by the dozens—not only in the Rademacher cover-up, but in their own criminal actions during the war. Steynes knew all this and watched the machinations developing to protect Rademacher.

Finally the doctor was accused of one of his lesser actions—the extermination of 1,500 Jews in Belgrade. He was convicted, drew a prison sentence of three years and eight months. Steynes' resolve to take certain steps himself grew, but he held carefully to his plan: he would merely watch the Rademacher case, testing the quality of the intelligence he received from his informants.

And, bearing out the word he received in advance, the court allowed Rademacher his liberty while his appeal pended. During this time, one of the escape apparatuses went smoothly into action and Rademacher joined the steady stream of war criminals emptying into Argentina. Once he was safe in Buenos Aires, the Nazi publication *German Honor* applauded his safe arrival, hailing his escape as an "extraordinary feat of rescue from the clutches of the Jewish jackals." It was only one case, but Steynes had known what was going to happen before it happened. His system of informants had worked to perfection.

Steynes provided us with several more very similar cases he'd followed less closely than the Rademacher affair. The cicumstances were always cut to the same pattern; in his redoubt at Cat Island the research dossiers grew fat. The evidence of Nazi control in peacetime, postwar West Germany was overwhelming. In the Bundestag, October 23, 1952, Chancellor Adenauer acknowledged that two-thirds of the upper-level diplomats in the Foreign Office were former Nazis. He could not, he argued, build an effective Foreign Office without stocking it with such skilled men. And the world swallowed the story. But not Ivor Steynes, crippled and alone on his island; he saw it for what it was: the birth of the Fourth Reich.

With the success of his surveillance of Doctor Rademacher's flight behind him, Steynes was ready to go one step further. His subject was Oskar Eugen Lober, alias Hans Kruger.

A native of Regensburg, Bavaria, Lober had become a Nazi party member early on, worked his way diligently up the SS ladder, and during the war had held the rank of colonel. His specialty was internal party politics, his career a small work of Machiavellian art. Allying himself with Himmler, he worked as an aide, a backup man and late-night confidant, was entrusted to carrying out subsurface diplomatic missions in Italy, Spain, and Sweden at various times.

He slipped through the Allied nets following the war: he boasted that a false mustache had done the trick. Having acquired a sturdy little art collection during the sacking of Jewish homes and estates, Lober had read extensively in the field of art history, made the acquaintance of certain art dealers who had counseled Goering, became a passable imitation of a dealer himself. At the same time he was establishing a false identity as Hans Kruger.

In late 1952 Ivor Steynes' sources informed him that Hans Kruger, resident of a modest villa overlooking the Swiss shores of Lake Lugano, owner of a fashionable art gallery, might in fact be someone else. Researches were undertaken, Kruger's movements plotted by faithful observers. Kruger was a frequent visitor to Madrid, Cairo, and Vienna. His mail came from all those cities and many more: Buenos Aires, Rio de Janeiro, Mexico City.

Further discreet inquiries revealed that Kruger was in fact in constant contact with what were known, in certain circles, to be the headquarters of the international Nazi movement in Madrid. Steynes knew that Madrid was the European center of the reborn movement, that its vaults were crammed with money gotten out of Germany long before the war ended.

From Madrid, the Nazis operated and funded special departments for Africa, Pan-Europa, and Latin America, as well as for a general unit called the International of Nationalists, a propaganda organization with arms in nearly every nation in the Western Hemisphere. By 1951 a secret UK report had indicated that the perimeters of the IN stretched from Malmo and Helsinki to Tangier and Cairo to Rome and Buenos Aires and Dallas. From Madrid came the funds which were carefully reinvested throughout the world—and Hans Kruger was a messenger, a courier, a functionary, moving about the globe from one museum or private collection to another, dealing in old masters and new Nazis.

Oskar Eugen Lober/Kruger was only one of many. Most were in import-export businesses; many were employed by German automobile manufacturers who were quite naturally seeking new international markets. Behind the curtain of legitimate business organizations, the Nazis moved vast sums of money from area to area, feeding the new party, building it up wherever the climate was receptive.

The dossiers piled up on Cat Island.

Dr. Johann von Leers. Anti-Semite inciter to riot.

SS Colonel Otto Skorzeny. Scarface Skorzeny, almost seven feet tall.

Luftwaffe hero Hans Ulrich Rudel.

SS Colonel Oskar Eugen Lober. Art lover.

In January of 1953, Lober/Kruger was one of a delegation of ex-SS officers and principals of the Condor Legion who gathered in Cairo to meet with Haj Amin el Husseini, once the Grand Mufti of Jerusalem and longtime Hitler loyalist and personal friend.

At the conclusion of the week-long conference, Lober/Kruger retired with three of his co-conspirators to a private home in an elegant Cairo suburb. The night before they were to return to Spain, they were visited by two quiet-seeming gentlemen who produced Bren guns and executed them without much deliberation. The house was then burned to the ground and the crime was never solved.

Sir Ivor Steynes had brought his first subjects to the bar of his own rather primitive brand of justice.

After his first long-distance success, Steynes began to step up the pace. With Dawson at his side he wheeled his way back to Germany to observe the Nazis who were beginning to make themselves heard, and rather loudly at that. The illegal NSDAP (National Socialist German Worker's Party) was officially winked at, and as early as 1951 claimed more than a quarter of a million members. In Lower Saxony at the same time another neo-Nazi party, the Socialist Reichs Party, polled 367,000 votes—more than 10 percent of the total. And Steynes was there, Dawson behind, watching their rallies, hearing the speeches.

It was familiar ground, the straight Nazi line and the people loved it. The war had been lost only because of treason. There had been no atrocities. The gas chambers at Dachau had been built and stocked with corpses of Allied victims after the war. Count Wolf von Westarp, former journalist and SS officer, flailed his one arm against the unjust peace. Major General Otto Ernst Remer screeched insults at the British and Americans; and one of the SRP leaders, a Dr. Franz Richter sitting in the Bundestag, turned out to be plain old Fritz Roessler, a Nazi official from the good old days.

When the SRP was banned it merely gave the Nazis more grist: through the back door, they said, we will infiltrate all existing institutions. You will not know who we are but we will very soon control the economy, the government, the military. They called it "the cold revolution, a revolution carried out quietly from the top." Ivor Steynes listened and the dossiers grew.

The Adolf Hitler Action Group
The Deutsche Reichs Party
Wilhelm Meinberg
Gustav Schroer
Adolf von Thadden
Herbert Freiberger
The simple fact of the matter was that the SS had

effectively returned to power in peacetime Germany. Whether you called them ODESSA or the Bormann Brotherhood, or *Die Spinne,* as Steynes called them, it was the remnants of the SS once again obeying a handful of masters.

For years, unchallenged and undetected, Steynes had gone about his business: the execution of surviving Nazis. Killing people, he explained to us, was singularly simple business once you had the proper apparatus. The idea was to have either no discernible motive at all—or a motive so obvious and commonplace that you, the murderer, are indistinguishable from all the rest. Many people wanted Steynes' victims dead. How many victims? Only a very small percentage of the Nazis available. Steynes modestly deprecated his efforts. Just a beginning, on the average ten a year, just over two hundred.

Peterson was hypnotized by the story. The only sounds were the gulls, the wind, the breakers, the occasional patter of rain, the metallic voice of Colonel Steynes.

Then, sent by Alistair Campbell, who had acted as an information gatherer for Steynes many times, came my brother Cyril. An outsider asking questions: not an appealing prospect for the Colonel. He wanted to know about Gunter Brendel and his wife. Why had Campbell disturbed Steynes? There was no answer: something he had sensed in Cyril's urgency had triggered the forbidden impulse.

And something unprecedented had driven Steynes to share Brendel's dossier with Cyril. Perhaps it was Cyril's claim that Brendel's wife was his sister. And perhaps it was the character of Herr Brendel, whose dossier was thick, whose turn had almost come.

Gunter Brendel's history was archetypal, almost too perfect.

Gunter Brendel's history could not help reminding you of one of those exercises in which you peer through the wrong end of a telescope: there he was, tracking across the bloody wastes of history, a tiny figure, scurrying past the smoking heaps, the victims, averting his eyes, tweezing his nose closed, scuttling to the next green oasis, leaving it too smoking and in ruins. A microcosm of the rise of National Socialism, never quite dirtying his hands, but his boots caked with the muck.

In 1938, at the age of seventeen, he reached real, recorded prominence in the Hitler Youth, and that was where Ivor Steynes' dossier began. During the war he was shuttled from post to post, conducting himself meritoriously at each one. He was attached primarily to command posts, eventually finding himself going from Kesselring to Keitel to Goering at staff level, then to the Reichs Chancellery as liaison to the SS. There were photographs of him, slickly, smoothly handsome with Himmler and Goering and Skorzeny.

There were letters from those who had known him, testifying to his homosexuality and how it had clearly been of use to him while moving up the military-political ladder. Because, clearly, he was one of those who bridged the gap between the Nazi hierarchy and the professional military caste. By inclination he was attracted to the one, but by birth a near-member of the other. Apparently he'd been accepted by both.

Somehow, Steynes had come into possession of a series of letters from Martin Bormann to Brendel, friendly notes, surprisingly chummy for what the world knew of Bormann, and formal letters of commendation.

As the Reich was methodically being blown to bits by the Russians in the last weeks of the war, Brendel was dispatched to the Bavarian mountains to help establish *Festung Europa,* the final redoubt where the ultimate stand would be made and from which the Werewolves would strike terror into the hearts of the occupying power.

After one abortive Werewolf raid in which the mayor of a village was murdered and left dismembered on his doorstep as a warning to those who cooperated with the victors, Brendel faded from view and Steynes' informants lost him. He reemerged in the late forties without a single blot on his official copybook and took his place in the family business. He had officially been recovering from "severe wounds suffered in the service of the Homeland" in a private hospital.

In the intervening years, through the fifties, he remained a spotlessly respectable businessman, never dabbling, however slightly, in politics. But Steynes had seen Herr Brendel in the provinces, quietly standing in the shade of village bandstands or lifting a stein in a quiet corner—while the Nazi rallies of the fifties gave proof of the rebirth of the old spirit

Grosstreffen. The weekend reunions were called *Grosstreffen.* Always in provincial towns, the old soldiers and their new admirers gathered together to sing the old songs and hear the old speeches. A Panzer division here, an SS formation there, the Afrika Korps somewhere else. Steynes saw and secretly photographed Brendel, in a heavy tweed suit, the bright Bavarian sun shining in his eyes, as he leaned against an old Mercedes at the Afrika Korps rally in Karlsruhe, September of 1958. He was thirty-seven. He was rich and fit and unaccompanied, apparently unnoticed.

In Würzburg, at a paratrooper outing, Steynes had watched five thousand of the old "Green Devils" go quite mad at the appearance of Field Marshal Kesselring, carrying him about on their shoulders. And Dawson had surreptitiously snapped a photograph of Gunter Brendel slipping into the back seat of the Field Marshal's limousine early Monday morning, in the rain when the rally was over.

The record was copious. At reunions of the Gross Deutschland, the Viking, Das Reich, and the Death's Head divisions Brendel was spotted. Not by reporters, not by the public, but by Dawson and Steynes. Another snapshot: Brendel in dark glasses, raincoat, umbrella above, turning away from the hidden camera, behind him a banner nailed to a building, the huge initials LAH—*Liebstandarte Adolf Hitler.*

The guard regiment whose sworn duty was the protection of Adolf Hitler. The *Treuegefolgschaft*: the loyal followers. They met in Verdun to reminisce, to search for missing comrades, to acknowledge once again that "they were ready to do their duty for the Fatherland."

And Brendel was there in the rain, turning to the young woman at his side. Blond, eyes wideset and clear, an eager smile on her face as she looked up at her new husband. I searched the fresh young face for a clue. Surely, it was Lee. It had to be Lee. Men had died because it was Lee.

But suddenly, listening to the rain drum on the windows of the lighthouse turret as it had beaten down on Gunter Brendel's black umbrella, suddenly I could not feel so sure. It was a very pretty blond girl. But was it Lee?

Dawson laced our coffee with brandy and Peterson coughed. No wisecracks: he had fallen under the otherworldly spell Steynes had been weaving. These were not the babblings of a nut case—these were documents, bits and pieces of Martin Bormann and Gunter Brendel and the Nazis past and present. And Steynes was not finished. His hand was white and cold. We all held our coffee against our palms to stop the chill. Steynes opened another thick folder, spread it across the plaid blanket on his knees.

There were, he explained, several organizations devoted to smuggling the biggest Nazis out of Germany. ODESSA, the old SS group, had been one, and *Die Spinne* had been another. *Die Spinne*—the spider—had been immensely more effective, but it had worked in unison with ODESSA and HIAG, as well, another SS organization whose initials stood for the German "mutual assistance."

Two major escape routes had been open to the Nazis. One, through the Alpine Fortress, flew captured American planes out by way of Switzerland and Spain, then on to Africa and Egypt. The other was termed Project North and was operated by *Die Spinne* closest to Sweden. This was the U-boat route. It was saved for the most prominent transportees and it was the method by which *Die Spinne* got Martin Bormann to South America. Gunter Brendel had helped to coordinate *Die Spinne*'s activities inside Germany. It was *Die Spinne*, Project North, which got Eichmann to Argentina . . . got Alfried Kottmann to Argentina long before the war ended.

I felt almost physically the tumblers clicking in

my brain. The names, the men, the paths which had seemed connected only by my brother Cyril's search and death were tightening like the drawstrings of a purse. But what was being choked off, locked inside?

"Did Brendel run *Die Spinne,* then?" It was Peterson: he punctuated the question with a sneeze into a sodden handkerchief and actually apologized.

"No, Brendel didn't run it," Steynes said. "He might be considered the vice-president in charge of traffic. He delivered the bodies to the transport branch and went back for more.

"The man who had overall responsibility for *Die Spinne* wasn't even a German. He was quite young then, a soldier of fortune, an adventurer, not even a Nazi. Utterly apolitical, I assume, his type always is. He was a technician, a skilled and clever fellow I've been told, though I never had the pleasure of meeting him. He was, of all things, an Englishman. But then we are supposed to be a calm race, good with details—"

"His name?" I asked.

"Martin St. John," Peterson said.

Steynes' head swiveled sharply. "No grass growing under your feet, I daresay." His eyes bored into Peterson: a dark smile stung the corners of his tight, ridged mouth.

"St. John?" I said.

"A guess," Peterson said, reaching for his brandied coffee with one hand, feeling for his handkerchief with the other. "Who the hell else is left in this puzzle, anyway? Everybody keeps turning up again and again, if you've seen him once, you're sure as hell going to see him again. Thus, St. John—the man who got Kottmann out before the roof gave in on all of them."

"Perspicacious, indeed," Steynes said against a sudden howl of wind. Fog rolled around us. "Martin St. John was, indeed, *Die Spinne.* The Spider. And you," he said, turning to me, "have had him buy you your lunch in Buenos Aires. *Die Spinne. . . .*" He mused into a fist for a moment, blowing into it. "The man who got Bormann out of Germany. . . ." He motioned to Dawson. It was time to leave the tower. Slowly, following Dawson and his burden down the twisting stairway, we slipped into the fog that clung to Cat Island.

A fire blazed in the dining room when we assembled for dinner. Peterson's voice had begun to go and his nose was stuffed. He kept pulling in on a Benzedrine inhaler. "Never travel without one," he croaked. "No goddamn Kleenex, though." But there was no more complaining about our host's mental state.

Dawson had roasted a joint of leathery mutton and we drank a robust claret, slashed our mouths on thick-crusted bread.

Steynes explained how *Die Spinne* had moved the cargo across the Atlantic.

"This is the tricky part," he beamed, the pleasure of special discovery easing the harshness of his countenance. "Not at all widely known—oh, a bit of random theorizing here and there, but those who knew always make sure to pooh-pooh it. And once again I make no explanation of why I'm telling you all this—I don't actually know." He drained his claret, stared into the faint blotch of sediment. "But I slept on it all last night and here it is. . . ."

Dawson refilled the glass, attended to ours.

"Separating myth from reality about *Die Spinne* is no easy task. General Paul Hausser was the more or less 'public' head of *Die Spinne,* assisted by Hasso von Manteuffel. Few realized that young St. John was actually doing the work. The same kind of confusion surrounds the means by which *Die Spinne* worked its wonders. And how efficiently. There are those who insist that it existed mainly in theory. Others believe that the Swedish connection or conduit to the outside world was used with some degree of effectiveness. And still others insist that the main exit route was through Spain using captured American Flying Fortresses.

"The truth includes aspects consistent with all these theories—but they are only minutiae. The real story is somewhat more difficult to fully take in."

He motioned to Dawson. "A sweet, Dawson? Do we have an afterdinner sweet? A tart? Would you gentlemen enjoy a tart?"

"A plum tart with sweet cream," Dawson suggested.

Peterson rolled his eyes at me: his flu had blunted the edge of his impatience. I was immensely tired. My shoulders ached and the claret had precipitated a volleyball game behind my eyes. I wished that it had never started. I was having difficulty assimilating it all, yet I knew my life dangled from *Die Spinne*'s web, was being pulled up into its mesh.

My forehead was damp in the fire's heat. I dabbed it. Dawson placed a huge tart before me. He looked fresh, tireless, cheerful. He gently slapped my back. "Hang on, Yank."

Steynes sampled the tart, smiled, wiped cream from his chin, sucked coffee noisily, happily: he was enjoying himself.

"Certain activities of the northern-based U-boats are well known. After all, as the war was drawing to a close there were approximately four hundred of them at sea. Or able to get to sea. And Admiral Doenitz had ordered his submarine commanders to fight on and never give up. An amazing number of them shared his belief and desire. They simply did not give up once the war ended. After all, the sea is large and was theirs as much as anyone's.

"U-977, commanded by Heinz Schaeffer, came out of the Norway-Scotland run and ran for Australia. It was a specially equipped ship, no longer had to surface to recharge its batteries what with the snorkel breathing device. It took fourteen weeks, but he made it to Argentina. And he was only one of many. But, you see, we had ways of knowing rather much of what he was doing. And eventually we picked him up. He wound up in Hertfordshire, actually, but the point is that he got to Argentina in the first place.

"U-530, under Oho Wermuth, was sitting off the coast of Long Island—yes, Mr. Cooper, Long Island —when the war ended. Two weeks later, he, too, arrived in Argentina.

"U-239, U-547, U-34, U-957, and U-1000—they were never found. Some evidence indicates they got to Japan, to the northern shore of Massachusetts, to Africa. There were leads as to the human cargo they dropped in various places. But much of it remains mysterious even to this day.

"But these vessels, while well equipped, were still normal U-boats. Bormann was not taken out on one of these—*Die Spinne* was using something else altogether, a kind of U-boat which we have never officially admitted existed at all. Let me tell you about these rather marvelous things.

"They were huge, first of all, and their range was incredible. They could go where they wanted.

"Thirty-one thousand five hundred miles at ten knots—*thirty-one thousand five hundred* miles." He smiled at our faces. "A very long way, that."

He munched more tart, licking plum and cream from the corners of his mouth.

"Each could carry nearly three hundred tons of cargo. And there were supposed to be one hundred such ships."

"Supposed to be?" Peterson wheezed from the end of the table.

"*Officially,* they were never built. Stalin was sure that they had been built. We—the British and the Americans—told him that they were only scheduled to be built, that they existed only on paper, that air raids on the production facilities had made their construction physically impossible.

"There were no documents at all beyond those plans—no indications of completion, no stop orders. And we told Stalin that there were no stop orders because the plants were destroyed and stop orders were thereby rendered superfluous.

"Stalin did not believe us.

"Stalin was right."

Steynes stopped for effect. Peterson shook his head. Dawson offered us cigars and Steynes took one, clipped the end, warmed it, lit it slowly, ritualistically.

"Do you realize what the existence of these ships meant? The survival of Nazism, nothing less—not an offshoot, not an ideological neo-Nazi movement. But a direct lineal continuation. Not only in the person of Bormann and others but in the survival of the documents, whether you call them the 'Bormann papers' or something less dramatic.

[217]

"The survival of these textual bases for the Fourth Reich frightened the Russkies, who had sound ideological justifications for fearing them. Afer all, Nazism and Communism are conflicting ways of ordering things, quite unlike the Allies' reasons for joining the battle.

"There were Englishmen and Americans, among others, who were eager and receptive, who wanted this testament—rather like the Dead Sea Scrolls of National Socialism, only more so.

"And now you know"—Steynes sighed through a cloud of blue smoke—"what was in those precious boxes your unfortunate librarian found."

Peterson had a low-grade fever the next morning when we set off in the Audi from Land's End. I let him sleep and drove slowly through the shifting gusts of fog and rain. There was no hurry and I wanted to think, to sift through the mountain of information Colonel Steynes had provided. It was hard to shake the feel of the island but it was crucial to make sense of it all.

As Steynes had continued well on into the morning hours, I had jotted some notes on a pad Dawson had given me. I fished it from my shirt pocket and rested it on top of the steering wheel, watching it jiggle.

Apparently, according to the Colonel, a power struggle was going on within the Fourth Reich, as it was called, Steynes said, "in certain circles." On the one hand was the Old Guard, the men who had lived through the Second World War, who may have known Hitler and others at the top. Martin Bormann would be included in this group and Steynes felt he was probably still alive in South America somewhere though he had no reported sightings of him for nearly three years. Alfried Kottmann, Professor Dolldorf, my grandfather—these men were part of the old bunch, cogs in the old machinery.

There were new, younger faces, Steynes had said, but he was cautious about discussing them. Peterson felt that Steynes simply did not know who they were, that his information was confined to those left over from the Hitler period.

Between the two groups were certain key figures, bridging the gap, holding the factions together. Both groups were commonly financed out of Nazi treasure which was continually being increased. Holding that middle, Steynes said, were Martin St. John and Gunter Brendel, natural placaters and compromisers.

Brendel's postwar activities had not been confined to showing up, shadowy and unnoticed, at party rallies in the provinces. In addition to expanding the family import-export business, which was a convenient cover for almost any kind of transaction, Brendel had moved deep within the inner circles of the SS revival organizations, the HIAG and the *Sicherheitsdienst* (SD). His activities, and those of these and several other related groups, included forgery of foreign banknotes and passports, the control of factories and management in key industries, ownership of nightclubs and brothels used as fronts and sources of blackmail, on and on. The arms and legs of the Spider were everywhere: there was no escaping its reach.

Brendel's influence had extended, as well, into the judiciary and law enforcement facilities of West Germany, both of which were liberally stocked with old Nazis, the faithful who had with the Spider's help covered their tracks. It was Steynes' opinion that no single individual was more responsible for the Nazification of the New Germany than Gunter Brendel.

Peterson had asked him why, if that were the case, had he not sent one of his avenging angels to murder Brendel? Steynes had pursed his white, cold lips and poked at the remains of his plum tart. Brendel was still alive, he said finally, because he was more of the postwar world rather than a criminal of the war itself. Vengeance was the fate of the old Nazis: Brendel was in the gap and Ivor Steynes had other business to finish.

"What really pisses me right off," Peterson croaked across the rich roast beef that room service provided us that evening at the Grosvenor, "is that we still don't know who is doing all this killing. It's all well and good to say, hell, it's the Nazis, and be done with it—but that won't cut a lot of ice with the rest of the world. The sane world, out there," he snorted, motioning past the rain-streaked window at the street below. "The Nazis are just a little out of date to them, a bit of mid-century exotica. Christ! They'd lock us up." He thrust an inhaler into his nose and pulled in until his face matched his ascot and his eyes crossed.

"Nazis," he said again. The room smelled of Vicks and Benzedrine and an English throat spray. "And who the hell was the gaunt man and his little round helper? Did the gaunt man kill Cyril? We could have a different murderer for each body, do you realize that? Do you? Wake up, Cooper—"

"I am awake. I'm resting my eyes." I heard him eating. He was having a hard time breathing and eating since his nose was plugged.

"And I wish I felt better about Steynes. I just decide he's sane and I start to remember him and I figure he must be nuts. Which makes us nuts for spending all that time listening to him." He pushed the rolling tray of food away. "I mean, can he be absolutely for real? Somebody has got to have a line on him. I've got an old friend at the Yard. I'm going to make inquiries." He sniffed and sneezed mightily, bringing me fully back to consciousness. "At the same time, while I'm at the Yard, I'm going to get hold of Roca and see if those bastards, Kottmann and St. John, have been found. And call Cooper's Falls and the Bureau." He yawned. "They're going to be wondering where the hell I am, I suppose. Unless they're following us.

"And the Feds," Peterson mused, reaching for a chocolate mousse. He peered up, curious. "Look, Cooper, if they are interested, really interested—and federal records have been destroyed in this mess, even if the murders didn't attract them—they may be watching us. It's a fact of life. The problem is, you're never quite sure why until it's too late. Sometimes they've got their own axes to grind. The Bureau or the CIA or some Special Branch guys—they all operate with just as much power and authority as they need to do what they want to do." He bolted the mousse and licked remnants out of his mustache. "Fact of life."

I said I wanted to check on the addresses Steynes had given us for Brendel's office and for the Belgravia flat, where Brendel and his wife lived.

"So, she's 'Brendel's wife' now, is she?" Peterson's eyes glittered at me as he wiped linen across his mouth. "Having doubts, are you?"

"I don't know."

"Maybe she just looks like your mother," he said.

The next morning I came out of the Grosvenor, through the Grecian lobby onto the paving of Park Lane, into a steady drizzle, persisting from a light gray sky not unlike the Cheviot pinstripe Peterson had been wearing at breakfast. I'd never seen him dressed so formally: he was heading for the Yard and I suppose he wanted to look the part. Watching him move from costume to costume was an impressive series of changes. Just perceptibly, his character changed too. This morning there was no sniffling, no ornate whining. Regardless of how he was feeling, he was quick and businesslike and a trifle fearsome. "I'm going to cut through some of this bullshit, Cooper," he said as we parted. "I've been coasting and I goddamn hate coasting."

Beneath my umbrella I entered the rainy quiet of Hyde Park. Dawdling because my mission was so unnerving—mechanically, the closer I got to Lee the more I wanted to wait, reconsider—I slowly made my way through the park, unaware except peripherally of others, heading for Kensington Gardens. The Serpentine got in my way and I turned left, winding with it, turning right as it ended, crossed Rotten Row, stood on Knightsbridge staring through the rain at Hyde Park Corner and the corner of Wilton Place. There was nothing for it but to push on.

The town house fronted up against the street in Belgravia Place. The building was brick, pristinely trimmed in white with a bow window, a brass knocker on the gleaming white door, an elegant, uneventful-looking, quiet exterior. I waited and after a half hour they came out and I caught my breath.

Frau Brendel led the way: tall, honey-colored hair, a waist-length leather jacket, tan baggy slacks with thick cuffs and platform shoes with soles two inches thick. She waited at the top of the narrow steps, hands in pockets, shoulders hunched forward, tinted aviator glasses. Behind her Brendel came into view, tall and broad in a Chesterfield and homburg and gray gloves. He turned, picked up a tan overnight bag with a blue-green stripe around it, said something to her, and followed her down the steps to a black Mercedes sedan. It struck me as odd: they might easily have been mistaken for father and daughter. At that distance she looked twenty. I felt odd: I'd expected someone older, somehow not this *Vogue* fashion model.

Quickly they were into the Mercedes. Brendel pulled it away from the curb and they passed directly in front of me, slid around the bend toward Knightsbridge, and were gone.

I walked back through Hyde Park feeling weak and tired although it was not yet midmorning. I wasn't thinking of the Fourth Reich or Ivor Steynes or Lee or any of the people who had died. I was just tired and wet and empty.

I picked up the Audi at the Grosvenor and clumsily thrashed my way through London until I found Brendel's office, the address Steynes had provided. I slid the car into a space near the entrance and waited.

Within ten minutes the black Mercedes appeared in my rearview mirror, oiled its way past my shoulder, and parked ahead of me in a no-parking zone directly in front of his office. She opened her own door, turned to face me for an instant, brushing her hair back, went in to the building with him. His arm circled her shoulders, broad and square, and they were gone again.

An hour later they came back out. He took the small tan bag out of the car and together they set off down the street, briskly, purposefully.

I got out of the Audi and followed them. The rain had subsided to a fine mist. There was no wind and it was balmy. Stopping at a corner, Brendel bought her a spring bouquet of flowers and she carried them in a paper spill, color between them as they walked, his umbrella tip clicking on the sidewalk.

They turned in at a restaurant, Eduardo's, and I paused, figured the hell with it, and went in.

Eduardo's despite its name, could not have been less Italian. It was in fact an oldish pub, full of old varnish and mahogany and the smell of lemon polish, appointed with yards and yards of etched Victorian glass, a stack of the day's *Financial Times,* and men in white shirts with spread collars and agonized little knots in their ties. There weren't many women in the dining room and I spotted her at once, sitting by a front window, leaning forward for Brendel to light her cigarette.

I got a table on the side wall, which provided a good view of them, opened my own *Financial Times,* ordered a grilled chop and stout, and watched them through the jumble of businessmen going at their briskets like trenchermen.

There was nothing for me to do but observe. Brendel had a look of well-tailored fitness. The spill of flowers lay on the table. She spoke, sipped wine, ate small bites, methodically cut her beef and speared her salad. My mind spun treacherously, one moment drawing me into a feeling of kinship with this woman I'd thought about so intensely, the next turning me cold and distant and uncaring. She was not what I had expected—but then whatever I had expected was blurred by emotion and had possibly never existed at all. But the fact was that this woman seemed unmarked by fate, not a sorrowing, fey, remote creature, a romantic heroine, if that was what I'd been expecting. She was instead a real woman; perhaps that fact frightened me a little. The thoughts I had lived with, the turning of Lee into the object of a quest and the key to several murders, seemed faintly absurd when related to this woman lunching with her husband. Yet, the dead were nonetheless dead and the subterranean world Peterson and I had stumbled upon was—apparently—real.

She lit a cigarette and leaned back, hooking a long

arm over the back of her chair. Her eyes were moving across the room and the thought of meeting them terrified me quite suddenly.

Abruptly I got up, left money on the table, and went back outside and across the street to a tobacconist. Being in the same room with her had somehow struck me as a risk; and I had panicked.

They came out of Eduardo's within a few minutes and stood talking by the entrance.

Brendel handed his wife the tan bag. She squeezed his arm and they went off in opposite directions. Adrenalin pumping, I waited until she was half a block away and crossed the street. She was tall. It was easy to see the streaked hair moving through the noontime crowds.

She went first to Kutchinsky, the jeweler, in New Bond Street and emerged with a tiny package she slid into the pocket of her jacket. Then to Jaeger in Regent Street. I followed her inside. Suddenly I was sure I'd lost her in the acres of woolens. Fearing the worst, that she'd somehow eluded me, I turned a corner and bumped into her.

Her eyes behind the large, ominous glasses flicked across me as I looked downward, muttering my excuses, trying to retain my anonymity. Backing away, fumbling, I felt myself dismissed by her. Fortunately, she couldn't have cared less about the clumsy oaf who had bumped into her.

On her way out she floated an air current past me, leaving a scent of garden flowers unlike any other perfume I'd ever smelled. She didn't stop but nodded faintly as she passed, acknowledging our collision. I pretended I hadn't seen.

On the street I lagged farther behind her and waited across the street, just another man in a raincoat, when she went in to Christian Dior on Conduit Street.

She polished off Dior in a few minutes and set off back down Regent Street, across Piccadilly Circus, through Trafalgar Square and past Nelson's Column to The Strand. I was wearing out when she stopped before a run-down building on a slightly disreputable side street angling back from The Strand toward Leicester Square and Covent Garden. She checked her watch, took a deep breath, and disappeared into a narrow doorway.

The ancient wooden stairs creaked beneath me. Their centers were hollowed out and worn smooth from centuries of panting climbers. They seemed endless, mounting two stories, surrounded by shabby, smudged walls and the smell of sweat. At the top of the stairs a lettered door stood ajar, a gray, unlit room beyond. I tilted the door enough to read the inscription: MACOMBER SCHOOL OF DANCE. And as I read it, I heard a piano begin banging away, drilling.

I walked toward it, came to another door with BALCONY lettered in tattered gold paint. The balcony was dark, deep in shadow, and the theater seats, four rows of them, were empty. Below me the class was in session.

Twenty or thirty girls who looked to be ten years old or so stood at the bar along the side wall limbering up. A gray-haired woman with glasses on a chain was at the piano. Frau Brendel walked slowly along beside the girls, stopping to speak with each one, pointing, advising, demonstrating. Her hair was pulled back tightly into a bun and she wore a black leotard over pink ballet tights. She was too tall for a ballerina but her body looked fuller than I'd expected. Her legs were muscular, her buttocks firm and powerful, her chest boyish, flat. She moved slowly, gracefully, controlled, her arms liquid in the air. The music stopped and she spoke to the girls in French.

She was very good with the girls. They clustered around her eagerly when she called a break, and I almost forgot who she was, why I was there. Near the end of the hour three women in raincoats joined me, mothers come to watch their daughters.

When the class ended I got out quickly, down the creaking stairway, into a doorway across the street. The sky was growing orange-gray toward the Thames and the afternoon was dwindling. The girls came tumbling out, met mothers and nannies, and melted away toward The Strand. I knew she would follow and I waited, skulking as I had been all day, feeling more and more like a ferret sneaking after its prey. Then she was on the sidewalk again and I set off after her. Her hair was still in the bun, she still carried the tan bag with her dancing gear.

She retraced her steps back to Trafalgar Square, took a left, and headed toward Charing Cross and the Embankment. Finally she slowed, stood staring down into the Thames and across at the Royal Festival Hall, and strolled slowly along the riverside. Leafless trees like stick men kept her company along the Embankment. Ahead of us—I was only fifteen yards behind her now—Westminster Bridge loomed in the haze turned orange by the late afternoon sun's glow beneath low-hanging clouds. The Houses of Parliament just beyond, the Thames dark brown. . . .

Watching Lee again leaning over the river, watching her as her gaze traveled from the water up to the bridge and to the huge low buildings which housed Parliament and on to the sky, I remembered as a child looking in awe at Turner's paintings of the rioting sky over the dark and muddy Thames, seeing how Pissarro and Manet and Monet had gone to school on his canvases. Watching Lee and watching the sky change and burn beneath the rainclouds, I remembered that it was a battlefield, a battlefield where my father—and hers, I felt sure in that instant—had died defending Britain from the Hun. . . .

She was alone and at rest and I sagged on to a bench and knocked ashes from my pipe. I was exhausted, my head ached from being constantly alert to her moves. I felt a great warmth for her, possibly just because I had spent a day with her, with her constantly in my mind. I felt close. I was attracted to her, to her life, to her attitude in the ballet class, to her walk and to her style and her life as I had seen it. I was tired and my reserves were low and I envied Brendel his closeness to her. . . . I was sure she was my sister Lee.

Near the Westminster Bridge she stopped and stared at something chalked against the bridge's facing. Once she moved on, I reached the place where she'd stood and peered at the printing in white. The words, in German, were, incredibly, a quotation from someone, perhaps the only words of German I could have translated without a dictionary: *I have not understood but I have lived.*

What seemed like hours later I hurried panting through St. James's Park, along Birdcage Walk toward Buckingham Palace. Rain spattered onto dead leaves. There were more people about now and streetlamps were flaring.

Exhausted and sweating, I stood in Belgravia Place, looking up at the windows as she snapped second- and third-story lights on. I imagined her undressing in the bedroom, stepping into a hot shower, washing her perspiration in rivers down her strong, slender body. I huddled in a doorway.

Only a few minutes later a man in a black trench coat turned past me from Pont Street, stood for a moment in a wedge of lamplight in front of me, nipped across the street, and let himself in at the Brendels' door without hesitation. He had moved quickly but I'd seen his face: blond long hair, a strong, long-nosed profile, full, chiseled lips, a broad mouth, a hard face, handsome, indeterminate age. A spoiled, rich face, a cliché, too pretty to be taken seriously, a male model's face putting you in mind of exquisitely groomed, bickering homosexuals.

Cold and wet, the street deserted before me, I trudged off. I wasn't thinking: I was registering the sights of Green Park, while the fog seemed to grow up from the ground. An occasional figure sat on a bench like a sodden lump of clay, umbrella canopied, still.

"Oh, I say, Cooper! Mr. Cooper, hold on—"

I turned abruptly, startled, and one of the lumps came to life, disengaging itself from its bench. Stubby, squat in a Burberry with a Henry Higgins slouch hat, it came toward me repeating my name, puffing.

"MacDonald," I said. "Is it MacDonald?" I peered under the rim of black umbrella. It was a small world.

"Of course it's old MacDonald," he said, clapping my arm, pulling me toward him so that we were both sheltered. "What a small world it is!" he exclaimed, eyes pinched together by his smile.

"Out selling insurance?" I was unreasonably glad to see someone I knew, however slightly, after the extraordinary isolation of a day spent peeking covertly at someone else's life.

"Trying, old man, trying. Making some calls among the idle rich, following up some leads—we call it 'prospecting' in my trade—you never know what might turn up. Belgravia, Mayfair, some large policyholders. Damned nasty weather, though, could die of influenza, that's certain. Ah—thank God I'm a policyholder myself, won't be leaving any loose ends when I depart this life, struggle, treadmill. . . ." He looked up at me, chuckling merrily in the face of impending doom. Whether on an airplane with whitened knuckles or sitting in the rain, MacDonald seemed never far from death, but then, that was his business.

"Always love to stop for a moment in Green Park," he went on, walking beside me, "been doing it for years. But the day's gone all nasty, hasn't it? Lovely sunset not so long ago, but now look at it. Nasty." He thrust a hand out, palm up, to demonstrate the effects of the rain.

I told him where I was staying when he asked. He nodded knowingly and unwrapped a raspberry-flavored throat pastille which bore an unmistakable aroma. He said he was probably already late for an appointment with a potential client and really must be off. I nodded. "But I'll be getting in touch with you, old man. We'll bend an elbow together. I know all the good places. . . ."

He scuttled away in the rain, his coat too long on his round frame. The fog erased him like a formula which hadn't quite worked out on a schoolroom blackboard. He was the only insurance man I'd ever seen without a briefcase.

"Nothing like Havana leaf," Peterson growled hoarsely, blowing a gust of blue smoke toward me. "Civilized English realize that. Probably the main reason they still trade with Castro—no point in cutting off your supply of Havana leaf over sillyass politics. Sense of proportion—"

He was threatening to continue the rhapsody but my uncontrollable need to yawn cut him short. His throat was still sore, but he argued the medicinal value of expensive Cuban cigars.

He watched me bring my yawn to a successful conclusion and switched his attention to the lengthening ash.

"All right, all right," he puffed, "on to business. First, the credibility of Colonel Ivor Steynes. I guess I'm happy to say that it's very high—I was circumspect, of course, didn't want to give him and his games away altogether, but my friend Bertie Redmond at the Yard gave me a hell of a queer look when I asked him—and then went on to say that Steynes was held in very high regard at Ten Downing among other less-imposing addresses and could be trusted. I got the feeling that we were both being cagey as hell, pussyfooting around the Colonel, but he said Steynes' fascination with Nazis was well known to the Yard and the Foreign Office, that Steynes had in fact been used on more than a few occasions to help fill in serious blanks which led to people the government wanted to—ah—question.

"Bertie gave me a rundown on Nazi activities in England since the end of the war. Concrete examples but no real significance. Bertie says they're dying off, that they're curiosities now—old men, a few fanatics, no followers to speak of. I couldn't tell what he was holding back but he seemed pretty open about it all. He showed me a slender little picture file of known Nazi supporters still alive. Of course, it meant nothing to me. Except that I've pretty much committed them to memory." He sneezed. "You'd better have a look at them—you saw those two men in Illinois before they tried to kill you."

"I saw the gaunt man. The other one—I'm not so sure. I don't think so."

"Well," he said impatiently, "well, take a look."

I nodded.

Peterson went on to tell me that he'd called Buenos Aires. Roca told him that there'd been no progress: the airplane which had carried Kottmann and St. John northward had still not been found. But a friend of Roca's in Santiago, Chile, reported seeing a man he thought was St. John with a prominent Chilean general. Roca was following it up.

He also talked with Doctor Bradlee back in Cooper's Falls, checking on the condition of Arthur Brenner, who was still in a deep sleep, but strengthening steadily, life signs good, slowly coming out of it. "Bradlee called it a healthful rest," Peterson summed up slowly, inspecting his ash again. "Remarkable man, Brenner, been through a lot for a man his age. As long as I've known him, I've always thought of him as a god-damn rock—what these bastards did to him makes me about as mad as any of this crap.

"I also talked to the FBI and the Minneapolis boys and none of them knows what the hell is going on. The confusion was just satisfying as hell—they don't *know*. And Washington is just leaving those government men out there on the vine. One of them asked me if anybody new had tried to neutralize you—no, honest to God, that's what the guy said. Neutralize. . . . Wanted to know if we knew who was trying to kill you." He sighed and shut his eyes against the smoke. "And now, tell me about your day, Cooper."

I went through the recital, slowly because I was terribly tired, and Peterson listened, head back, eyes closed.

I told Peterson about MacDonald.

"The same man who sat with you on the plane to Glasgow?" Peterson's eyes were still closed but there was a sudden rather intimidating edge to his voice and his arm had stopped on its way to the ash-tray, cigared with its chimney of smoke trailing away. "The same man?"

"Yes, short, chubby fellow—sells insurance, scared of planes."

"The same man you ran into in the tavern in Glasgow?"

"Yes."

"Now you run into him in the fog in London. . . ."

"It's a small world."

"Cooper, it's not that small."

"What do you mean?" My mind was turning over, but slowly. "What else but coincidence?"

"When MacDonald calls you—and pray that he

calls you—you arrange to meet him for a drink. I want to see Mr. MacDonald." He pulled on his nasal inhaler. "Because Mr. MacDonald is no coincidence."

The morning sun hung low, a metallic disk beyond the haze, and water stood in placid springlike pools in the street. It was early, but we'd finished breakfast and were drinking the last from the silver coffeepot. We were arguing and tension clawed at my shoulder blades, the base of my skull. Peterson wanted me to go around to New Scotland Yard to see Bertie Redmond and look at the Nazi picture file. I wanted to get back to resume my surveillance of Lee.

"I wish to hell you would begin seeing this for what it is," Peterson said, eyes narrowed and oddly disconcerting. "Your brother didn't get murdered because he found your sister—if she even is your sister. *If*. . . . That's not a reason for killing anyone, Cooper, not if she's just your long-lost sister. He might have been told to go to hell, to stop bothering her—but he wouldn't have been killed, for God's sake. People just don't kill people. Do you see that? Are you with me so far?"

I nodded, scowling.

"If he didn't die because he found your sister, then he died for something else, some peripheral matter he stumbled on in his search for your sister. It appears that we now know what that peripheral something is—the survivors of Nazism, or the New Nazis, or the New-Old Nazis, whatever the hell they are. Now, it's not *Springtime for Hitler*, not a comic opera, it's not the *Harvard Lampoon*, it's not a joke, it's murder and God only knows what else.

"So we've got Cyril and a woman who may be your sister and a pack of Nazi remnants. But we've also got a network, Buenos Aires and London and Munich—your brother visited each city; there are apparently Nazis in each city. Then we've got the avenging angel of Cat Island and your brother was there too.

"Now, goddamn it, let's just see it straight for a minute. There's only one sane conclusion to be drawn from all this—these Nazis, crazy as it sounds thirty years after their big sendoff, are killing people . . . they are killing anybody who gets too close, anybody who threatens them. I mean, my goodness, what the hell else can we assume? Jumping to conclusions is one thing, but we've been steadfastly jumping away from conclusions. And now, Cooper, I'm scared. . . .

"I couldn't sleep last night. I can *always* sleep, always. But not last night, not the night before. And I wake up sweating and scared. I'm scared of this situation and I'm scared of these people—I'm scared because I'm not doing anything, because they're watching us run from place to place, waiting to see what we do, if we'll finally give up and go home.

"And more than that, I don't know if going home will save us either! And I say 'us' because it's my ass now, as much as it is yours. We've been poking around in their little hole and they don't know for sure how much we know but they're worried. You know what I think, Cooper? I think they'd like to know how much we've found out before they kill us. That's what I think. They don't know what we may have told other people." He sipped loudly at his coffee. "God," he muttered, "how I love cold coffee! Love it, love it. . . . Life's little pleasures and I want to keep having them.

"The Nazis are trying to kill you and they're doing it badly. Maybe they don't want to kill you—I don't know. Maybe they only want to scare you off. But I don't think so. I don't think they want you to go on living knowing what you do."

"But what do I know?" I asked. "Really?"

"Not important. You may not even know that you know it. Alive you're just a terrible, unnecessary risk. You'd almost think you're being protected by some-one—simply because you're still alive. God, maybe."

He got up and paced the room, flexing his muscles, doing his little isometrics routine. He stopped at the bureau and threaded a striped tie beneath the collar of his white shirt. Both items had been purchased the day before: he found time for everything and I always wound up hot and sweaty.

"Now is that all—what we see right up here on the surface—is that all there is?"

I didn't know what to say.

"Think about it for a minute." He zipped his pants back up and smoothed the tie down over his shirtfront. The pinstriped vest came off the rack next. "Nobody bothered you until you were headed for home. They didn't kill Cyril until he got home. They killed Paula. Who never left home once she returned. Home. Cooper's Falls. I don't know—but there's something there. Maybe those boxes. They were stolen and to get the one they missed they damned near blew up the town. Sounds to me like a hell of a murder motive, if motive is what I mean. . . ." He slid the vest on, fitted it snugly across his chest, buttoned it up, and reached for his coat.

"Which leaves those papers my friend at Columbia deciphered, that old plan for taking over the United States from within once the Germans won the war, the whole Austin Cooper thing.

"Now, I didn't set a hell of a lot of store in that. Oh, I believed they planned it and so on, but it seemed like childish stuff—be the first Nazi in your block to rule the world, crap like that.

"But—now, listen to me, Cooper, damn it, what if they all believed it all, what if it was all a long-term reality? I mean Jesus, what if Steynes isn't just mopping up survivors, like shooting German sailors in the cold, black water? What if Steynes is trying to *stop* something? What if Cyril was going to blow the whistle? And Dolldorf? What if something, something *real* is happening *now*? Well, I mean to tell you, you'd better get your ass over to the Yard and look at those goddamn pictures and get your head in the game. And cut out spending all your time thinking about the woman in the case."

I went with Peterson to the Yard, clasped Bertie Redmond's thin cool hand, and looked at the Nazi file. Nothing. No familiar faces, no gaunt man, no stubby helper. But I tried. Peterson had shaken me.

We left the Yard and taxied back to the street where Brendel had his office and where I'd left the rented Audi. Having obliged Peterson by accompanying him to see Redmond, I had some arguing room. In the back of the cab I made my case.

"You think I'm making too much out of the woman—Lee," I said, trying to repress the emotions I felt when I spoke of her.

"My point is that Lee is our handhold, the place we can begin to pry things loose. Cyril must have felt the same way—after all, she's one of us, even if she doesn't know it. And Cyril pushed closer and closer to her. We just don't know how close he came. He may actually have confronted her—"

"And that may be what got him killed," Peterson said flatly.

"Well, they already know about us. We can't make our situation any worse."

He nodded, grumbling. He was wearing a bowler. New. If they killed him they'd be killing a well-dressed man.

"Don't forget the telephone calls to Paula," I said. "Munich. He called her from Munich. Brendel and Lee live in Munich—that's Cyril's only connection with Munich."

Peterson kept nodding as we paid the driver and marched briskly down the street to the Audi. I pointed out Brendel's office but he ignored me. "Okay, okay," he said abruptly when I got in behind the wheel. "Let's see this woman. I want to see her."

I looked up, focused out of my reverie, and saw them.

She was wearing a forest-green pantsuit with a matching band in her hair and he wore a dark-green sportcoat, black slacks, black turtleneck, and they were headed for a matching dark-green Jaguar XKE with the organlike exhaust signifying the new V-12. It was the man from last night, the handsome model-type in the black trench coat. Together now, laughing, they looked like lovers from a television ad. They were young and beautiful and rich and they were happy because they didn't smell bad and if you would stop smelling so rotten you'd be just like them.

"Okay," Peterson said, all business, "let's tail them. Maybe they're off to blow up the Tower of London, strike a blow for the Fourth Reich." He snorted, but he wasn't kidding. His face was tense, grappling with the situation. I could see him changing during the morning: he was going on the offensive and I hoped I could stay free of flying debris. Looking at him in that instant before I switched the ignition, I was more frightened of Peterson than I was of all the rest of them.

They wandered among the French Impressionists at the Tate, moved on to the Wallace Collection in Manchester Square, and stood transfixed before one Canaletto after another and then strolled into the street, his arm around her shoulders. She didn't laugh, or even smile often, but occasionally she presented her face for a kiss and his lips nonchalantly brushed hers and then her smile would come, her arm would curl around his waist, and the Jaguar would slide off into the traffic.

In Burlington Street they visited a small gallery and somberly inspected an exhibition of Francis Bacon's visceral, brooding nudes. She spoke with a man, indicated one of the paintings, spoke to him while he wrote down instructions. They left talking seriously, animatedly. Art lovers.

"Lovers, too," Peterson said. "Just plain lovers. Herr Brendel goes back to Munich to mind the store or the Reich and his wife gets it on with a handsome stud. Not exactly a new story. Unless—" He paused to light a cigar. We were sitting in a small restaurant where they were lunching, hands touching on the linen. "Unless, this guy is a fag—which is possible from the looks of him. Some women—married women—hang around like this with art-loving homosexuals and the busy husbands don't really mind. Figure it's safer than having a young wife on the loose."

"Possible," I granted. "But it could be just the opposite. Homosexual husband gives wife a bit of freedom—equally old story."

"She doesn't look her age," he said, "if she's your sister."

"Nobody does anymore."

"No, I suppose not."

They returned to Belgravia Place late in the after-

[235]

noon and we went back to the hotel. The telephone was ringing when Peterson pushed the door open.

I picked up the telephone.

"Ah, you see, I've not forgotten you, have I? I promised I'd ring you up and, lo and behold, here I am." Followed by a cascade of chuckles.

Peterson stared at me, mouthing the word "who?" with elaborate impatience.

"MacDonald," I said into the mouthpiece. "How nice of you to call." He chatted amiably, much of which I missed because Peterson was, if not exactly dancing, doing an animated prowl punctuated by tiny leaps, his fist slamming into his palm, whispering, "Hot damn! Hot damn! Leave it to good old Mac-Donald," he muttered happily and disappeared into the bathroom. His head jerked back into the doorway. "Make that date. I want to see him. Tonight."

The pub, if not actually squalid, lacked any sense of flair or style other than that attributable to the curry parlor next door. It wasn't far from the docks and the smell of the Thames and fog and rain and unwashed barges hung over the premises like Fred Hoyle's black cloud. Through the smoke, MacDonald clung to the bar surrounded by taller and presumably disagreeable ruffians.

He waved jovially, his red-faced smile verging on the forced, his hand pudgily clamped on a pint of brackish-smelling stout. The odors of the place were in constant battle and I rather liked it after a moment of getting accustomed.

I introduced Peterson, who shook hands with a warmth so uncharacteristic and phony that I expected strangers to stop and stare. MacDonald bought it, though, and Peterson hovered, occasionally bumping into him, excusing himself, reaching for the counter, buying drinks, throwing bills around like a maddened keeper of revels. Peterson was bubbling with conversation: How did MacDonald find Argentina? Oh, you weren't in Argentina, well, it must have been Cooper, then, I know *someone* was in Argentina—his voice slightly drunken and gravelly, his speech slurring like someone in a bad play. But in the stifling air and noise of the pub Peterson must have seemed to MacDonald a gregarious, friendly, half-drunk American.

"Have another," Peterson kept saying, filling his new friend with stout. From time to time I caught MacDonald's eye. He winked, a desperate smile playing, then Peterson was at him again, asking questions about the insurance business and what was MacDonald's territory and did he ever get to Germany and what was Germany like?

"Like any other place, I suppose," MacDonald said. He flashed a soiled, once-white handkerchief across his round glistening face. "You hear a lot of rubbish about the Germans, of course, but they're like everyone else, I'd say."

"Ever meet a Nazi?" Peterson asked curiously. "I mean, hell, Cooper and I are just leaving for Germany in a couple of days and I was wondering. . . . Missed that war, too young, but I've always been fascinated by the period. Now, I hear there are still Nazis in Germany. . . ."

"Well, really, I travel there so seldom," MacDonald said, his face beginning to blanch. He licked his lips and he came away dry. "But I think the talk of Nazis is bunk. There was a new Nazi party, called something or other, a few years ago, that had people worried." He wiped his face again. He was quite pale. Peterson pushed his stout at him. "But, but—" MacDonald lost the thread of his remarks for a moment, then pushed on, lower lip trembling. He did not look well. "But they got point-oh-six percent of the vote in the last elections—"

"Remarkable you should remember that," Peterson said admiringly. He wiped his face with his hand. Sweat seeped at the edges of his hairpiece, his mustache drooped. He was the bandit again. "Remarkable! Are you interested in politics, MacDonald? Or history?"

MacDonald was ashen by now and I couldn't make eye contact. His eyes had gone fishlike.

"MacDonald," I said, grasping his sleeve. "You don't look well. Are you all right?"

"Not feeling too chipper, old boy," he muttered.

[237]

"Have another stout," Peterson said, almost shouting into MacDonald's fading gaze. "You're off your feed—some nice hot curry'll put some life back in you!" He slapped MacDonald on the back and shouted to the barkeep down the line that we needed more stout. "Come on, Mac, drink it up, nice warm stout good for the tummy. . . ."

MacDonald's hand was shaking as he reached for the mug Peterson was shoving at him. He opened his mouth but was too dry to get the words out. He loosened the blue scarf at his neck and flung back the coat. It was inevitable. "Excuse me," he muttered and pushed back through the crowd, urgent but weak, with one saddened backward glance.

"Jesus, you were hard on him," I said. "He really looked awful—what was your performance supposed to prove, anyway?" I was irritated. I'd never seen his manic routine before but MacDonald, even in our conversation about him at the hotel, had served to excite him.

"Tut, tut," Peterson observed laconically, sliding a long bulging black leather billfold on to the counter. "I do not trust nor do I much like your Mr. MacDonald. So I put some rotten stuff into his awful warm stout, awful rotten stuff that makes your mouth and eyes and joints dry up like they'd been calked—always leaves you just enough strength to get to the crapper where you puke up everything down to your shoelaces. And then you collapse. Puts a great strain on the old ticker and generally renders the recipient pretty well *hors de combat*—"

"What? It doesn't make you go blind and your cock fall off?" I glared at him.

"No, Cooper, it's jerking off that does all those things. And worse." He opened MacDonald's wallet and slid a handful of cards into his heavy hand with the black tufts on the knuckles. "MacDonald!" He spat in disgust. "Christ. His name is Milo Keepnews, he lives in Madrid . . . and he, heh, heh, works for something called Mendoza Imports. I'll bet Mendoza Imports—"

"Keepnews," I said. "*Milo* Keepnews. . . ."

Peterson thumbed through more cards, scraps of paper.

"The question is, who the hell does he work for? Us—that is, the CIA, or them—the Brendel bunch." He glanced up. "I'd say those are the primary alternatives." He saw the puzzled look on my face. "Big leagues, Cooper, and I'd say offhand old Milo Keepnews here is either in the market to watch you and kill you . . . or watch you and keep you from being killed. Either way, he's dangerous because he can't possibly protect you and he draws the opposition and tough guys like me like flies to shit." He tilted his stout and drained it off.

I stared at him because I didn't know what the hell was going on. "CIA?" I muttered.

"Fingers in everything. They look at each other on Monday mornings and they say, well, hell, somewhere out there there's somebody doing something bad. And then they start poking around and they notice a murder here or a town getting blown up in Minnesota or an old Nazi professor gets knocked off in a Buenos Aires high-rise and they say now, there's something bad, and away they go. So maybe old Milo is one of them. Organization man, whoever he is. Look at all these credit cards, Eurail pass, airlines, oil. We just don't know whose organization. But he's holding iron, I know that, and I think we'd better go see how he's doing."

I followed Peterson's thick back as he bulldozed through the glut of people. The door to the toilet was chipped and the spring was broken on the outside, hung loose from a nail. Keepnews had remembered to lock the door. Ear to the thin wood, we heard him retch, heard him move and groan.

"MacDonald, old boy," Peterson called. "Are you there?"

No answer.

Peterson stared at the doorknob, which rattled when you leaned on the door, but would not turn. Then he grabbed the knob, gritted his teeth, and with a short, stiff yank ripped it through the door, held up both knobs for me to see, and pointed to the jagged rip in the door. "Strong, huh?" he said with a nasty grin. "Come on, MacDonald, you old sumbitch, how you keeping in there?" He pushed the door open and the first thing I saw in the dim light was the muzzle of a revolver pointed at my guts.

Keepnews was sitting on the floor, which was a damp layer of dirt accumulated since Shakespeare's youth. He was wedged between the filthy toilet bowl and the wall, his arm resting on the excrement- and urine-stained receptacle. One fat leg was thrust out before him, the other bent under him. Vomit—and food and the foam from stout—covered the front of his coat. His round face had a greenish touch to the pallor and was sunk into the folds of the muffler. The tiny room reeked. Keepnews' eyes rolled, trying to keep us in focus, the gun wavered. I stood still. Peterson closed the door and told me to lean on it.

"Going to shoot us are you, Milo? Well, pull the trigger." Peterson stepped closer and the gun tried to track him but fell short, wound up pointing at the wall between us. "Ought to be ashamed of yourself, Milo. Really." Savagely, from an excess of energy, Peterson kicked the gun out of Milo's hand, the toe of his shoe pinning the hand backward against the washbasin. A strangled cry from Milo, vomit foaming at the corners of his mouth, speckling the muffler. The sight and the smell made me want to vomit: I didn't know if I could hold it back.

"Who you working for, Milo?" Peterson asked conversationally, reaching down and calmly lifting the round man to his feet, which flailed hysterically for a foothold. Peterson held him against the wall, the round head lolling forward into the muffler. There was something. . . . I moved closer, my hand over my nose. Something. . . .

Peterson's hands ripped the coat all the way back, buttons popping against the walls. He fumbled in another inside pocket, then another, came out with a worn-looking passport case.

"Why, Milo," he said. "You have so been to Buenos Aires, you little devil." Milo's head hung lower. Again, without warning, Peterson slammed him against the wall and the tiny mirror jumped off its nail and shattered in the basin.

"Wake up, Milo," Peterson said. His hand swished past Milo's cherubic face and when it came away the nose looked funny and a gout of blood spread along the upper lip, outlined the corners of his mouth. "Who do you work for, Milo? Do you work for Brendel?" His hand flashed again and the lip split open, a row of bloody teeth showed. I turned into the corner and threw up, trying to lean away to keep it from getting on my clothes. "Or do you work for the Agency?" Peterson harped.

Finally he said, "Oh, shit," and I heard Milo collapse down the wall. I turned and immediately recognized the face, round and sunken against the navy blue scarf, the hair plastered down with sweat like a tight-fitting beret.

"I know him," I said.

"What?" Peterson was rinsing his bloody hands, beginning to curse because there was nothing to wipe them on.

"I said I know this man," I repeated. It was almost the same kind of shock as when I recognized Lee's picture in the clipping.

"So?"

"He's the man on the highway. He was with the gaunt man when they tried to kill me on the highway."

Peterson looked at me and then down at the man.

"He was wearing a navy blue coat that night and I remember its collar coming up around his chin—and now, look at him, the muffler, the way it frames what's left of his face. It's the same guy."

"God, he must have been confident you wouldn't recognize him."

"Well, it's him."

Keepnews groaned, his hands fluttered briefly in his lap like birds too heavy to fly. Peterson watched him. Finally he said: "He's had it, Cooper. He's broken. I've seen it happen before. Go back to the bar and bring me a mug of stout."

Not knowing why, I went and got one and returned to the toilet. Peterson was leaning against the wall going through the wallet and the passport. "Buenos Aires. He was there when Dolldorf was killed. Glasgow. He was there when Campbell was killed and somebody tried to kill you. United States. He was there when your brother got it. He's been moving fast lately. Dangerous man, Milo Keepnews. I wonder where he's from? London, maybe. I wonder what he was like as a little boy?"

"He didn't seem so bad," I said. "He was frightened on the plane." But he was the gaunt man's companion. No doubt now.

Peterson was grinding a powder between his fingers, letting the stuff sift into the stout. When he finished, he set the mug down on the washbasin, crunching bits of mirror. He handed me a piece of folded newspaper. "Look at this."

I unfolded it, the creases greasy, the newsprint smudging back on itself.

It was the photograph of Lee from the Glasgow paper. Everybody seemed to have them. And this one tied Milo Keepnews tighter than Peterson's vest.

"It was in his wallet." Peterson leaned down by the inert, crumpled figure, so helpless, tubby, inoffensive-looking. One of Peterson's blows had smashed Keepnews' round spectacles and driven a spoke of metal into the bridge of his round and now shapeless jelly of a nose. I'd never seen anything like that happen to a man.

And then I remembered what I'd done to the gaunt man that night in the snow.

"Come on, Milo, old boy," Peterson said, lifting the mug of stout to the limp mouth. He cradled Milo's head and leaned him forward. "Down the hatch." He tilted the mug and the stout ran down the vomit-caked chin. Reflexively Milo sucked some of the stout into his dry mouth with a gasping, wheezing sound.

Eventually the mug was empty and Milo had sagged back against the wall, groaning softly, eyes closed. The stench was stomach-turning. I went into the dim, chipped hallway. A door at the back stood open a crack. When I peered back into the little room to see what was taking Peterson so long, I saw him sponging at spots of vomit on his coat where he'd brushed against Keepnews. Finally he finished his dabbing, folded the damp handkerchief, and replaced it in his pocket. He appraised himself in a long, thin splinter of mirror. He touched his hairpiece, adjusting a lock or two at the front, and stood back to look down at the body. One of Milo's sleeves had slipped off the toilet bowl and his hand was amorphous, a blob, in the scummy water. His eyes were open. He stared unblinking at the floor, mouth drooping.

"Good-bye, Milo," Peterson said matter-of-factly as he pulled the string on the one bulb.

A wet fog had come up outside, scurried along the pavement. I followed Peterson numbly, unsure of what to say. We were walking away from the river.

"He's dead," I said.

"Oh, yes, I'm sure of that." Peterson was calmly puffing on a cigar, hands in pockets.

"Something in the stout."

"Mmm." He nodded.

"My God."

I felt myself getting queasy again and Peterson, sensing it, pulled me into a brightly lit coffee bar and got us two hot cups of coffee. I sipped coffee and listened closely, because he was speaking very softly.

"Milo Keepnews was our enemy, John." I could not recall his ever using my name before. "I'm sure he killed several people—probably including Paula and your brother. He killed Professor Dolldorf, set fire to Maria's apartment, and killed Alistair Campbell. At least twice he tried to kill you, both times very nearly succeeding." He paused and dripped cream into the coffee. "He was not a nice man. He was setting you up for something. He was following you—he was following you while you were traipsing around after Brendel's wife and he was probably following us today. He was carrying a gun and I found the silencer in his coat pocket and tonight he would almost certainly have killed us both. So, please, try to see this thing the way it is. Naturally, normal people don't go around having this sort of thing happening to them. But you're not normal, not anymore, and my normality is not even a faint memory." He sipped the coffee, his dark eyes boring into mine, his voice strong and reassuring. "Our lives are out of kilter, John. There's nothing left for us now but to see it all the way through, survive or die. It's very basic—but we can't remain passive. That's terribly important. We can't let things happen to us anymore. We have got to start happening to other people. Keep them wondering what's going on." He sighed into his muffler and put his hand briefly on my arm. "Tonight we happened to Milo Keepnews. And that's going to bother hell out of them. The idea now is to keep the pressure up. They know you've been watching Lee—Milo certainly got that word to them. And they may know I've been to Scotland Yard. And they may know that we've deciphered most of what was in those boxes. And they know we've been to see Steynes. And I expect they're nervous about all of it. The one point of strength we have, John, is speed and surprise. The fact is, I don't believe they're ready for our full-fledged counteroffensive." He patted my arm again. "Now, come on, we've got to keep moving. We can't slow down to think about it now." He was smiling at me, but I kept seeing Keepnews gaping at the floor.

Peterson talked all the way back to the hotel and I heard his voice, the tone and enthusiasm and thrust of it. He was happy, almost bubbling over, and I was sick. Sick of what I had just seen, sick of what Peterson had done. But, God knew, sick of what Milo Keepnews or MacDonald or whoever the hell he was had done. I was confused and nauseated and whatever happened to right and wrong? More casualties, I supposed, just more of the night's dead. . . .

Peterson uncorked a bottle of Courvoisier and settled back on the bed, pillows plumped up behind him. He splashed some brandy liberally into a snifter, rolled a mouthful around on his tongue, and gave me a grin. The knuckles on his right hand, which he had clamped around the snifter, were raw where Keepnews' glasses had sheared through the skin. He crossed his boots at the ankle and lit another cigar.

A happy man.

I woke up and heard his voice: "What?" Incredulous, cigar ash dribbling on the flyfront of his forty-dollar shirt. "What are you saying to me?" He was whispering at the top of his lungs. I blinked and shook myself, stiff from napping in the chair. He saw me and pointed at the other telephone.

A thin, metallic voice was speaking on a crackling, snapping line. It was Colonel Steynes.

"Calm yourself, Mr. Peterson," he said patiently, "calm yourself and listen while I explain it again. It will be of rather considerable interest to you." He chuckled bleakly and there was a pause. "In the early hours of this morning, during one of our incessant foggy rainstorms, alarms were tripped alerting us to an invasion of Cat Island. Dawson and I, of course, have several systems of defensive action—and the alarm system in our War Room kept us informed as to the invaders' stealthy movements. For the better part of three hours Dawson and I sat in the War Room, having secured the house itself, and considered our situation." I could hear Peterson breathing. I glanced up and saw him staring at his cigar, which had gone dead on him.

"We knew there were three of them and damned if they weren't taking their time about it. They were advancing with impressive care. By plotting their progress on our alarm map we knew when one of them had entered a clearing visible from the wall of the keep. I dispatched Dawson with a rifle, silencer-equipped, and a quarter of an hour later, in relative quiet, one of the three died. Dawson returned and we waited. Light had come and our intruders had stopped, doubtless confused by their inability to raise the third on their wireless devices.

"Then, while Dawson was preparing us a breakfast, we heard an explosion, which we discovered blew a hole in the wall of the keep. A rather large explosion, too. We did not realize that it was a diversion, unfortunately. When Dawson positioned himself in a second-floor window to shoot the man, he was himself shot by the third man, who had gotten to the top of the keep wall on the opposite side. Even as he took the bullet, Dawson fired on and killed the man coming through the hole in the wall." He paused again. He sounded like a written report of an action in another war, another time.

"With Dawson wounded we had to rethink our

plan. It was an unforeseen event. I stanched the flow of blood, once we realized it was a flesh wound, administered a painkiller, sterilized the area, and considered our options. It would have been interesting to take the third man alive. But it seemed a luxury which we could not perhaps afford. We did not know for certain the intent of our guests, or our one remaining guest, but their operation seemed a radical one. We presumed that the mission was to kill us and thereby put an end to our Nazi hunting. Without us, without me, the apparatus would die. The remaining Nazis would live. Do you follow our thinking, Mr. Peterson?"

"Yes, of course. I follow you."

"The rest turned out to be very simple. I wheeled myself out on to the wall of the keep. I was protected by the fog, you see. I sat and waited. A matter of nerve. Nothing more. And I have more nerve than you could possibly imagine. You see, the third man was trapped on the top of the wall. Dawson was covering the wall with a machine gun. We sat there for three hours, fog all around us, no sound. Waited. Quiet. And then the breeze freshened and began to blow the fog away and I saw him in front of me, about forty feet away, crouched along the parapet, and he saw me, raised his gun in a kind of wild-eyed fright, and I shot him. I am an excellent marksman and instinctively I shot to kill and killed."

There was silence on the line, the crackling stopped, as if the connection had been broken. Peterson stared into his brandy.

"We identified two of the three from our files. Nazis, of course, men in their fifties." He sighed. "And I thought you and Mr. Cooper should be informed."

"I appreciate that, Colonel," Peterson said. He was more shaken by Steynes' story than by what he'd done to Milo Keepnews, and there must be, I thought, a moral somewhere in that.

"Specifically, I thought you should be informed," Steynes pressed on, "because of the identity of the three men. Two—the two we were able to identify—were associated with Gunter Brendel, *your* Gunter Brendel. One was employed by Brendel's firm as a security man at the time of his death. The other actually appears in a photograph we have of Brendel taken a few years ago in the Tirol. The connection seems rather marked—"

"Yes, yes," Peterson interrupted. "We found out today that Cooper has been followed. He was surely followed when we went to Cat Island. And our friends began to make the connections."

"I would suggest that Mr. Cooper is in very grave danger."

"Well, yes—but not quite so grave as it was. You've done a hell of a job, Colonel."

Steynes gave the metallic, cold chuckle. "Surely, you would have expected nothing else, Mr. Peterson. After all, I have never met my match."

"You and I—we're a lot alike," Peterson said. And incredibly, Steynes laughed deeply, as if another man were there to do his big laughs for him.

"Well then, be warned," he said.

"And how is Dawson?"

"He is well, if just a bit chagrined by it all."

"We're going to Munich," Peterson said.

"The woman? Who is she?"

"We don't know yet. We found her but we just don't know for sure, not yet."

"One more thing—" Steynes said.

"Yes?"

There was a moment's hesitation.

"I've fired one of my little arrows."

"The target?"

"Herr Brendel, I'm afraid. He is a dead man. I have sent my man. It's time he died."

"Oh, Christ!" Peterson said, sucking in his breath. "No!"

Germany

ABOVE us the brightly colored people began to move in the clear cool breeze, the sky beyond the ornate, needlelike Gothic spires so blue it threatened turning white. The bay windows high above the Marienplatz arched over the figures, framed them as they began to move in the Glockenspiel. It was eleven o'clock. The coopers danced on the lower of the two levels; above them a tournament was taking place and far below we stood, along with some other tourists, and stared up at the tower of Munich's New Town Hall.

"It represents an event from the Landshut Princely Wedding. Duke Christoph of Munich raised hell with the Count of Lublin and carried the day." Peterson turned to me deadpan.

I stared at him in surprise.

"Don't worry, Cooper," he said, beginning to move away. "It's nothing to worry about. Happened in 1475. But I know these things." He called back over his shoulder: "I've been here before."

We had flown to Vienna rather than directly to Munich, a maneuver Peterson had said would help to confuse any tails which had been assigned to us. In Vienna, we had switched to rail and arrived shortly before in the gleaming station in the center of downtown Munich. It was all a gamble, according to Peterson: if we were able to shake any would-be followers it was worth the lost time. We had to bet that Colonel Steynes' assassin would be in no particular hurry. Once the hit was made on Brendel, Peterson was convinced that entirely new rules would govern the game and the problem was that we were just beginning to learn the old ones.

The people in the clock tower, pretend people

though they were, frightened me. Their tournament went on, each day, in the wind and the snow, and old Count Lublin came out and took his daily whipping from Duke Christoph, history being skewered on the Gothic needles and shafts. They were pretend people up above but I was becoming a pretend person, too, my humanity slipping away from me.

I followed Peterson through the crowds in the Marienplatz but my mind was being allowed the dangerous opportunity to wander and catch a brief, realistic glimpse of what was happening to me. The brutality and danger of it all moved in a blur, in a sphere just beyond my grasp. There was so little left to cling to. There was Cyril, dependable, smiling, successful. There was the memory of my father. Brenner, the rock for the father I'd never really known, was there to set my compass by, to prove that I did in fact possess a reasonable past. But Brenner was in a coma, a sick old man whose time had finally begun to slip away.

All my anchors, few as they were, proved absent and frail and insubstantial. And I had tried to replace them as best I could with new ones, with Peterson and with the idea of my little sister Lee. That was what I had to count on. Peterson and Lee.

And I had seen Peterson coolly kill a man in the toilet of a London waterfront pub. I had seen the excitement, the power moving in his face as he did it. Milo Keepnews was undoubtedly a killer and he had, in the game which was perhaps without rules, deserved to die. But there was the killer animal in Peterson and it had surfaced in that nasty, filthy death chamber.

So what was left to cling to? Lee. . . .

We were standing before a church.

"Der Alte Peter," Peterson said. "Saint Peter's Church. Oldest in Munich, built it for the first time in the eleventh century. Look up there." He pointed to the north side of the tower, plunged like an ancient dagger up to its hilt in the pale sky. "See the white disk? It means the view is good. We'll see all the way up to the Alps." He led the way. "It's a long

climb up Old Peter but worth it. Hell of a view."
I sighed, jolted out of my morose comtemplations.
"Come on, Cooper, we've got to talk. Follow me."

In the end I stood gasping in the thin cold air while
Peterson prowled the perimeters of the platform. The
wind whipped at us in sudden, unexpected bursts.

Across the square, towering into the sky, were
the twin blunted towers of the Frauenkirche, the worldwide symbol of the city. The cupolas were green with
tarnish and age. We were alone at the top of the
church but no nearer to God.

Peterson clapped his arm around my shoulders
in an uncharacteristic moment of warmth, but I shrank
involuntarily. "Well, John, it's time to do your stuff.
You've come a long way to find your sister and you've
been through more than you could possibly have
bargained for. Well, now's the time—she's here, left
London by plane with her blond young friend about
the time we were having our interview with Mr.
Keepnews." He smiled. "No grass under my feet,
thank you. While you slumbered I was on the blower
to whatsisname at the Yard. A little checking—she's
here. And there's no time to wait, not with Steynes'
little helper on the move. Contact her. Get it out of
the way. We can't really be in any deeper and since
it's what you've come for let's get on with it. You
can't afford to be mooning around here in a daze
anyway. Now. Right now."

I walked away, looked back at the Alps. Winds
were shifting the blur between them and Munich.
The sky was blue behind me, white toward the mountains.

"Well, I'm scared. I'm frightened of calling her—"

"It's because you put it on such a personal basis.
You think she knows how much it means to you,
how important she has become to you, but of course
she knows nothing of the kind. Who the hell knows
what she may be? But, I'll tell you this, the longer
you fuck around preparing your ego for the plunge,
the better the chance we go out of here in a box."
He cuffed my arm and walked away, disappeared
down the stairwell.

He was waiting for me at the bottom, clapping his gloved hands together for warmth. My legs shook from the descent.

"Germans make lovely churches," he said. "Too bad they keep wanting to rule the world." Everywhere I looked spires pointed toward the sky.

"All right," I said. "I'll call her."

There were fresh flowers in a colorful, gilded papier-mâché vase on the desk next to the telephone. The Bayerischer Hof was another exercise in Peterson's hotelsmanship. My stomach felt as if I'd been poisoned and at the other end the telephone was ringing.

To the German-speaking woman who answered, I said with an awful flutter: "Frau Brendel, *bitte.*"

A pause, silence, another telephone lifted, a click from the first being replaced. Peterson sat by a window looking out into the early-afternoon winter shadows in the Promenadplatz. Particles of dust hung in the room's still, warm sunrays.

"Lise Brendel."

"Hello." I swallowed. "We've not met, Mrs. Brendel, but my name is John Cooper. Do you mind speaking English? I'm a failure at German, I'm afraid."

"English is all right, actually—mine is very good. Your name is . . . Cooper?" She spoke with a distinctly English accent which took me by surprise.

"Yes, John Cooper. I'm an American. And what I want to discuss with you is—well, very difficult to go into over the telephone."

Silence.

"But I've come to Munich only to see you. It's a highly personal matter, you see." I sighed. Peterson's eyes were closed. I felt innocent and silly. "Ah, might we meet soon? At your convenience, of course, but . . . soon." I stopped to breathe and left it to her.

"Important? Important to whom, Mr. Cooper?" There was a mocking quality but it was impossible to tell if she was smiling.

"To me, Mrs. Brendel. But possibly also to you."

"Yes, of course, I know . . . important to both of us. I fully understand." There was a long pause.

"You are the second man named Cooper who has called on me."

"Cyril Cooper—he spoke with you?"

"Oh, yes, just as you are."

"Did you see him?"

"Yes, naturally I saw him. Are you a relative? A brother, then?"

"Yes, his brother."

"Look, we'd better get this settled, hadn't we?" She was sounding less distant, more matter of fact. "Do you know Munich, Mr. Cooper?"

"No." My heart was fluttering again.

"I certainly can't see you here, at our home. That's impossible—my husband was very patient about Cooper Number One, but another complete stranger coming out of absolutely nowhere?"

"You saw my brother at your home? He met your husband?"

"Of course. But I think twice would be pushing things a bit." She paused. "I don't quite understand what it all means."

"Are you my sister, Mrs. Brendel?" Peterson's head snapped around; he'd been rubbing his eyes, now peered at me from between spread fingers.

"I really can't speak to you over the telephone, Mr. Cooper. There's a section called Schwabing, the old artists' section. There's a man who lives there, Doctor Gerhard Roeschler. He is my dear friend and I can meet you there. Let's see, this afternoon I have my dancing class. Ah, this evening, is that soon enough, Mr. Cooper? Nine o'clock?"

She gave me the address and I wrote it down on Bayerischer Hof notepaper. I was about to say good-bye when she stopped me.

"How is your brother? Well, I hope."

"We'll talk about it, Mrs. Brendel. Tonight. And thank you for . . . you know, for taking me seriously."

"And why shouldn't I, Mr. Cooper? You're not joking with me, are you?"

"I'm serious," I said.

She hung up and I looked at Peterson.

He smiled at me, the sunshine bleaching the color out of his face.

The street was lined with rickety, makeshift stands and wobbling trestle tables. Paraffin lamps glowed softly in the cold, clear night. Poplars, black like solid shadows, had clothesline strung between them, and paintings and drawings hung from the line by hooks and wooden pins. Artists stood by the tables wearing navy peacoats, leather-fringed jackets, and worn, faded denim. Beards curled over collars, long hair drooped on shoulders, an occasional whiff of marijuana hung in the near-freezing night. The crowd was thick-chested and hearty, the artists thin, young for the most part. A sign in English hung between two trees: THE SOUL OF BAVARIA=MADNESS AND ECCENTRICITY. A good deal of English punctuated the German conversation. Many women were beautiful and fashionable and from the back a dozen of them might easily have been Lee . . . Lise Brendel. It was like a freezing festival. People laughed and made jokes as we passed.

We turned off onto a sidestreet of espresso bars, ice cream parlors, small nightclubs. Tinny music from rock bands filtered out, people spilled onto the street, and we kept moving away, into the darkness. There was a clammy quality to the night as if rain or snow was readying itself somewhere. My own apprehension grew. Lee was waiting.

We turned again as Peterson followed the directions, up a slight incline of paving stones, the noise very faint behind us.

Roeschler lived in half of a flat-fronted two-story building, very old and plain, lights dim behind heavy draperies in a downstairs window. My stomach was turning over: something in me longed to flee, be gone.

The door opened as we knocked.

He was a large old man with a shock of unruly white hair, wearing an open-necked plaid woolen shirt, baggy pants, and carpet slippers. "Come in out of the cold," he said, guiding us through a drafty, dark hall and into the warm, cluttered sitting room. A fire crackled. Antimacassars clung to heavy old rocking chairs, books stood behind glass doors, a couple of fat old tabbies stretched and gave us long, disinterested looks and settled back where they lay. The wallpaper bore a small, complex pattern and there was the faint aroma of schnapps and cabbage soup.

"I am Gerhard Roeschler," he said, taking our coats and hanging them on an old floor-stand by the door, "and you must be Mr. Cooper." He shook my hand, smiling widely, his hand dry and thick. "And you"—he turned to Peterson, without breaking stride—"must be Mr. Peterson—aha, you're surprised!" He chuckled and shook his head, lowering himself into a huge rocker, motioning us into deep chairs. The room was parched from the fire. "Well, your reputation precedes you, Mr. Peterson, it truly does, though I must have my secrets. And I have so many—" He slapped the arm of the rocker, smiling. He adjusted round spectacles and peered at us, the smile fading.

He poured us schnapps in tiny cut-glass goblets and a fat tortoiseshell cat leaped soundlessly into his lap. His shirt was covered with cat hair. He lifted his glass. "To your long journey, gentlemen, and may it bear fruit."

We drank and he grew serious, wiping his great wide mouth with the back of his hand, skin wrinkling.

"Lise just called me, Mr. Cooper, and asked me to apologize for her. She cannot leave her home this evening. Tomorrow, however, she will meet you in the English Park and I will give you instructions." He saw the disappointment in my face, stroked his cat's ears while it purred, said: "Perhaps it's just as well, Mr. Cooper. This way we can talk quite freely among ourselves—you must not expect me to tell you why, but I'm prepared to give you a good deal of information about Lise Brendel."

A clock ticked loudly in another room, cat hair clutched at my throat. It was so dry. The schnapps tasted like childhood's candy.

"Is Lise Brendel my sister?"

"It is possible. When two men come to Munich, two brothers, and ask the same question a few months apart—ach, the likelihood of such a happening seems to increase." He sipped from his glass. "Let me say this, I do not know who Lise Brendel is. And neither does she," he concluded. "Nor do you. . . ."

"What are you saying?" Peterson broke the silence like a sledge.

Roeschler seemed to be addressing his cat, stroking its whiskers.

"Lise Brendel has been undergoing a kind of identity crisis for several years, that is, a psychological search for who she might be, what her life is all about—that is what brought her to confide in me. For her, I became a substitute for the father she never knew." I quickened at that. "Then your brother Cyril Cooper appeared out of the blue to present her with his question: Was she, in fact, his sister? Now her problem became a concrete reality, you see. Now she was not alone with her thoughts—where she had been questioning the purpose of her life, wondering who the real Lise was, there was now someone else with a shattering new question: Who was she *actually?*

"Was she Lise von Schaumberg as she had always assumed . . . or was she somehow another person, back from the dead, someone called Lee Cooper, an American of all things? And why would such a question arise? Where was the logic of it?"

He wet his lips with the schnapps. "For you, for me, for anyone who knows perfectly well who he is it is difficult to imagine the confusion of the orphan. Lise had always been told that her parents had died in an automobile accident, there were records to prove it, a trust fund waiting for her on her twenty-first birthday, a family of uncles and aunts and good friends. Then your brother came to Munich, sat with her in this room, and showed us photographs of his mother and a newspaper photograph of Lise, and very pleasantly asked if such a thing was possible. He poked through what records there were that survived the war, made inquiries in Dresden, took too many people very much by surprise. He created rather a stir in certain circles and in the end he learned some things, some truths, which many people here wanted to remain secret. He was a problem, Mr. Cooper.

. . . Fortunately, he was able to leave Munich before it was too late."

Roeschler took a carved wooden bowl from a table within his reach; the cat only flicked one eye open to see what was going on. He lowered the bowl lightly onto the cat's side and took out a brightly painted walnut and a nutcracker Tchaikovsky would have loved, a troll or a Black Forest dwarf with a hooked nose and a predatory grin. He squeezed it around a walnut, splintered the shell, and dug the meat out with a thick finger.

"But I am much too far ahead of the story," he said, "the story which began during the war. It begins there because that was when I met Gunter Brendel." He stroked the cat and told us a very sad story.

Gerhard Roeschler had wanted to become a psychiatrist, an analyst, and with that in mind had been studying in Vienna when Hitler came to power and annexed Austria. In his studies he had worked with many Jews and had in fact married a Viennese girl who was one-quarter Jewish. There was a baby about a year after the Nazis murdered Dollfuss. And Roeschler's money was running low. Finally, he left his studies to become a science writer for a newspaper. The offer of a better job brought him back to Munich, where he set up his family in Schwabing because of its proximity to Munich University and because it had been for a very long time the bohemian colony, the natural home for artists and writers. It was also the center of a good deal of anti-Nazi sentiment, and, in fact, some action of a more overt kind.

"Those of us who both hated and feared the Nazis here in Munich, here in Schwabing, centered in the university—my hatred and fear stemmed from my wife's Jewish connection, small, fractional though it was. We didn't think they knew but there was always the fear that they might find out. We had heard stories about Dachau, just outside of town. We weren't sure, but in our hearts . . . yes, we were sure . . . and I became involved in what was called the White Rose. And my life was . . . never the same again."

During the war the White Rose grew up around Hans and Sophie Scholl, a couple of students at the

University of Munich, and one of their teachers, a Professor Huber. The group was small, not really dangerous to so oppressive a regime, but an embarrassment at the very least. They felt a commitment to fight against the Nazis in any way that they could and about all they had was the ability to turn out a certain amount of secret propaganda. Anna Roeschler threw herself into the group's efforts with the kind of enthusiasm which had drawn Gerhard to her in the first place. She wrote leaflets, spent early morning hours delivering them, chalked slogans on walls in the dark of night. She began to feel more Jewish, more of a part of the group than her husband did. But, still, she drew him farther and farther into the machinery of the group. He didn't mind, he shared her sentiments, but by nature he was no activist. Frequently, he stayed home with the baby, Heinrich, while Anna was on one of her missions. He would work on his own writing while she worked on hers.

He never knew how they learned of his marginal involvement in the White Rose but one night they came, no uniforms, no fuss. There were only two of them in their trench coats, standing in puddles of rain, asking him if they might have a few moments of conversation.

They knew that his wife was partly Jewish. Which, of course, made young Heinrich Jewish. And made Gerhard guilty of harboring two known Jews. They acknowledged that sometimes these things happen, that love can lead anyone into shadowy paths, and not infrequently, illegalities.

The taller and more distinguished-looking of the two men did all the talking. He was calm, well mannered, smiled in a friendly way. He told Gerhard Roeschler that they knew of his and Anna's involvement in the White Rose; he suggested that unless he cooperated with them in breaking up this "minor irritation, this pimple on the Führer's behind"—and he had chuckled man to man with Roeschler—it would be necessary to interrogate Anna. And, of course, Heinrich too would be taken to be with his mother. It was a conversational threat. Wife and child. Taken away.

On the other hand—and the man had offered Gerhard a cigarette and lit both of them with a Hermes lighter while the other man leaned against the door—on the other hand, there was a way out, wasn't there?

"It was all incredibly painless," Roeschler said, his hand embedded in fur, the chair creaking, "or so they made it seem. I was doing the right thing—what were my principles, my disgust with Hitler and the war—when compared with the life of my wife, the life of my child? Naturally I said nothing to Anna but I did increase my involvement with the group. Anna was very proud of me—of course. My increased interest was the result of the need to be able to report to my newfound friend in the trench coat. And it wasn't purely blackmail, oh no, he actually paid me for my information and for some time there was no result that I could see. The group continued and I kept meeting the man in the trench coat in the English Park nearby, passing odd bits of information.

"Then, in November of 1943, the group planned a big night, an extravagant night. I tried to keep Anna from going but my man assured me that there would be no trouble, that she would be absolutely safe. I believed him. So Anna went with them while the White Rose painted DOWN WITH HITLER seventy times—all along Ludwigstrasse. Seventy times! And—this will surprise you, gentlemen, no arrests were made, no trouble, my Anna returned safe and sound.

"A few days later Hans and Sophie Scholl were arrested passing out leaflets, which Anna had written, and Professor Huber was picked up almost immediately. They were tried, condemned to death, and beheaded. Anna was never interrogated, I received a bonus from the man in the trench coat—after all, I had set the Scholls up for the arrest. I was never able to supply them with any other really useful information but I was—ah, in their pockets from then on. Not only did they know about Anna and Heinrich but now they could hold my treachery over me, all wonderfully subtle, never any open pressure. Sometimes I couldn't quite believe it had all happened to me. . . .

"Anna was eventually killed in the bombing of Munich, an accident of the war, and my friend in the trench coat was very comforting. He came to visit me in my flat, drank an occasional schnapps with me, built up a peculiar bond of friendship with me. His Munich assignment to uncover the White Rose had been only an interlude—he was a liaison officer, very young, but favored at the highest levels. When he passed through Munich he always stopped in. He saw to it that Anna received a very nice funeral, though he never met her.

"Heinrich grew up a healthy, intelligent lad. Today he is an architect, lives in Rome, has his own family, remembers nothing of his mother. As a matter of fact, Mr. Cooper, he is just about your age. And my friend —he and I have remained friends through the years. He knows the truth about me and I have had certain opportunities to aid him at various times since I still have access to certain circles from which he is excluded. After all, I have served the new Republic, I have served on certain European commissions relative to scientific planning, I have led an active life as a writer and at times a diplomat *manqué.* . . . I am a survivor of the White Rose, you see, and there aren't many of us left. I am an honored personage, understandably so. But my friend from those afternoons long ago in the English Park has remained . . . and I have never failed to exhibit my gratitude for what he did for me. Again and again, I have been grateful.

"As one of the White Rose, I was even a member of the committee which arranged for the plaque at the university which commemorates the sacrifice made by Hans and Sophie and Professor Huber. Future generations should be aware of their dead heroes, shouldn't they? We made sure they were remembered. The university stands at the top of the Ludwigstrasse and the square is cut in half by the road—on the left is the Geschwister-Scholl Platz, on the right Professor-Huber Platz. Quite fitting.

"How ironic, you say? Of course, ironic—life is, I find, continually more and more ironic. I had coffee there just last week with my old friend in the trench coat—he was leaving for a business trip to London and wanted to know if he could take any particular message to Heinrich, who is there working on a new Italian-financed housing project. My old friend, always thoughtful. He is, as you have doubtless guessed by now, Gunter Brendel . . . my old friend." Roeschler smiled out from behind his spectacles. A bit of tape held them at the side and his eyes crinkled. He offered Peterson the bowl of nuts.

"Why in the world are you telling us all this?" Peterson asked. "First you know who I am—then you tell us what I assume must be your deepest personal secret. Why?"

"That, I regret, is the question I must not answer. But listen, because, for whatever reasons I may have, I am a friend of yours. You can trust me." He smiled benignly. Behind him the cats appeared in the doorway to the kitchen, tongues darting out at cream clinging to whiskers.

He settled back in the old rocker, snapped his fingers for the cats, and tasted more schnapps.

"The arrival of Lise on the scene concerned me from the very beginning. She was a strangely passive young woman when I first met her, at a small dinner party at Brendel's. Gunter had never married and was well into middle age; Lise was in her mid-twenties. She came to the party almost by accident as I was given to understand at the time—although I've often wondered about that.

"Well, Gunter was quite taken with her—surprisingly so, I assure you, since his sexuality had always been a matter of some doubt in my mind. Now he was in hot pursuit of this Lise. And for her part? She seemed innocent, even virginal, inexperienced, masking her limited experience with the remoteness which Gunter seemed to find so appealing. She never really responded to my offer of friendship until after the wedding. Which came inevitably about six months after they met. It was a social event of some magnitude here in Munich—Gunter was a man of substance and Lise was of a good family, solid Bavarian stock. Large wedding. They moved into the big house near Nymphenburg, took a large flat here in town, she quickly began to do the sort of things his wife should do. With a real cultural bent. The opera, dance, art shows, film societies—she was always involved . . . very busy but quiet, still, and withdrawn.

"My concern for her was greater than it might have been if she had not seemed so troubled. Gunter even spoke to me about her—he always remembered my ambitions from my days in Vienna. She was unhappy, stayed in her room for days at a time, stayed silent, would only come to life when she was required to entertain. He asked me if it could be a sexual matter—he trusts me, you see, as only a man who knows the truth about another can trust, and he confessed what he called his sexual inadequacies.

"He wondered if perhaps she should come more into contact with some younger people. Perhaps then she would not have such a quiet life, would not seem so isolated—I told him it was a risk, throwing a lovely young woman into contact with young men, surely he understood that, and he said yes, he understood that but he didn't really care." Roeschler spread his hands, palms up. "What to do? I told him that some variety among her friends might do her a world of good. Then he did what seemed to me a remarkably stupid thing. He gave her a very great shove in the direction of Siegfried Hauptmann. I would never have countenanced that, but it never occurred to me that Gunter could have had Siegfried in mind. He was actually drawing her into the greatest secret of all. It was unthinkable. But, by God, he did it."

Roeschler got up again, walked the worn carpet to the window, and drew the curtains back. He turned back to us. "Let's get some air."

He set off at a steady pace, keeping to the quiet side streets. It was cold but his wind was good. His voice carried in the night.

"Siegfried Hauptmann is very rich, very handsome, and the leader of a small but powerful group of elitists centered here in Munich. They are Nazis. But no one really knows how extensive their operations are. What is known is that they are young. And they have formed their cell around Siegfried Hauptmann.

"And this is the man Gunter chose to be Lise's new friend." He shook his head. "It was a purely political move on Gunter's part—perhaps a *rapprochement,* reconciling his own political interests with Siegfried's. After all, Gunter represents the *real* Nazis in Germany these days—perhaps he feels the competition between the old and the new has gone on long enough. Perhaps, to take another more pragmatic view, he is trying to lull Siegfried's people into relaxing their vigilance. Perhaps Gunter is preparing another night of the long knives for his young friends. He is certainly capable of it. But I only see the outlines of it, I don't know the details."

We walked a bit farther. Peterson was puffing in the cold. My mind raced, imprecise, driven by fear and curiosity. Roeschler was so calm.

"Did Lise tell you to tell us this?"

"No, Mr. Cooper, certainly not."

"Does she even know about her husband's political activities? Or Siegfried Hauptmann's? I can't remember who knows what around here," he muttered.

Roeschler stopped in the middle of the street and took hold of both our arms, his grasp firm.

"I don't know," he said. "I don't know how much she knows. I think, quite frankly, that she is almost totally egocentric. I don't know if she is aware of anything beyond the limits of her own being. I don't even know if she is altogether sane." He gave me a wintry smile and was quiet during the walk back to his home.

We sat in one of the Schwabing coffeehouses an hour later, staring at one another over bitter espressos. Snow had begun to sift down through the soft glow of the paraffin lamps and there was an ache behind my eyes. Peterson stared dolefully into the night and absentmindedly applied the Benzedrine inhaler to his nose. I shook my head.

"Two groups of Nazis—there's no end to it, it's like a children's game, fighting over whose bat and ball it is. I'm punchy, I can't even remember what he said."

"It's not *what* he told us," Peterson said. "It's that he told us at all that's so amazing. And he knew I would be with you. And he expected us to swallow all that stuff. Poor Anna, dear little Heinrich, sad and bewildered Lise, rich and dashing Siegfried, and good old Gunter, the only sane one in the bunch. He's right about that, it's a madhouse, Cooper, a madhouse, and that's what makes it so hard to figure out. It's a goddamn playpen. Steynes is a nut, Dawson is a robot, Lise is a manic-depressive having an identity crisis.

Shadow Nazis are running around all over the field and then we run into a comic-opera killer like Milo Keepnews and I wind up killing him in a toilet. Everyone seems to die but you, no matter how hard they try they can't seem to nail you, an absurd situation if they know what they're doing."

"It's real enough for me," I grunted. "I keep thinking they'll get me eventually. I'm so tired of it—I just don't want them to get me until I see her tomorrow. That's all I'm waiting for at this point, beyond that I'm beginning not to care. . . ."

Peterson was grinning more widely with each minute. "I've been trying to figure them out, see their plan, get a bead on what was going on. Well, goddamn it, they don't know what's going on. They don't care who dies but they're very sloppy about their methods. It explains a lot. They're bunglers and they're amateurs. Christ!" Glee curled around his cigar like a Christmas wreath. "Roeschler!"

"Roeschler what? Don't you believe him?"

"It doesn't make any difference. He's playing a game of his own. Steynes is playing his game. Brendel his. They are all playing their own games and we've been trying to fit in, play all the games at once because we thought there was just one game. But that's wrong—lots and lots of games. When I faced up to it with Keepnews we began to play ours. When you called Lise we were still playing ours—now we can't start backsliding."

"But what is our game?" I asked.

"Your game is to find out if she's your sister—let me worry about the rest of it."

By morning Munich had turned white. The snow was dry and fine. When I went outside the wind sprayed it on my face like old memories of anticipation and beautiful women. Skaters with their scarves unfurling behind them slid noiselessly through the snow, carving their paths on the ice of the small lake. The English Garden was eerie, quiet, sound hugged to the earth by the layers of snow. I was early, stood watching the figures gliding with their hands clasped behind their backs, tried to take Peterson's advice and play my role as the innocent American searching for a possible connection. Pretending Cyril and Paula and Dolldorf and Campbell and Keepnews were not dead at all but going about their business as usual. It was like being a man with normal sight trying to give the impression of blindness and it was confusing.

The serenity of the park swept across the lake, lapped at my failing nerves, soothed me. If only I could have strolled without reflection into the swirling whiteness, across a tiny arched bridge and into sheer nothingness—then, at that moment, I'd have sighed and gone without a good-bye. Looking back at it, I suspect that I was very far gone in those moments: I was alone, it was quiet and cold, there was no one trying to kill me, the world was as white as an abstract painting, an enormous canvas into which I could step and slowly watch myself dissolve as if I were in two places at once. I felt the way I remembered John Garfield had been in a movie I saw as a kid at the little theater in Cooper's Falls. He was sitting at the bar on a steamship sailing on an endless sea and Faye Emerson told him he was okay but he was a washed-up newspaperman who drank too much. He was bitter and he was tired out and he didn't know it but he was already dead, everybody on the ship was dead. John and Faye and Paul Henreid and Eleanor Parker and Edmund Gwenn—they were all dead and they didn't know it and I was thinking about that movie, remembering that it had been called *Between Two Worlds* and Cyril and I had been taken to see it by our grandfather and one of his guards. Eleanor Parker knew she was dead, she and dapper Paul figured it out, and they asked the steward, Edmund Gwenn, where they were sailing and he said, why, you're sailing for heaven . . . and for hell, too, because it was all the same place in the end. It was almost thirty years later and I was sure I hadn't thought about that long voyage out, with our popcorn and our Dr. Pepper, in all that time, but I was thinking about it when I saw Lee standing on the little humped bridge, the outline of her blurred through the snow, and she was watching me. . . .

Then she came down the bridge and around the

gentle curve of the lake toward me, purposeful but not hurrying, she was just walking toward me through the snow and I couldn't move. There was snow in her hair and her hands were jammed down into the pockets of her leather coat. She was wearing dark brown corduroy pants and her long legs ate up the distance between us until she was standing in front of me, smiling at me levelly, gray eyes straight and for a moment it was there, she looked exactly like my father's portrait of my mother; she was looking at me and past me at the same time, as if you could never have quite all of her attention.

Her voice was businesslike, faintly clipped and British. "I've been watching you, wondering what to do— I've been nervous about seeing you." She turned to me, slid her arm through mine, and shoved her hand back into her pocket, locking me against her and heading off around the lake path. "I'm Lise Brendel . . . or at least I am until you can prove I'm someone else." She stuck the tip of her tongue between her lips, caught a snowflake. She wasn't smiling when I looked.

"I can't prove anything," I said. "I have no evidence. Nothing. Intuition, hope, curiosity . . . but I am a little short of proof."

"So was your brother."

"You look like our mother." A man in a red jacket sat down abruptly on the ice, looking about to see if anyone had been witness to his fall.

"Yes, he told me that, and a good deal more. He told me about your little sister and the Blitz and that the body of the little girl was never found." She kicked at a tiny snowbank, pulling on my arm. The tension was easing away.

"I do quite want to know who I am. I try to treat this with a certain amount of bravado, I tried it with your brother and he wore me down   and I suppose you're the same way, aren't you?" She pushed on, said: "What were you thinking about when I first saw you? Me? Were you thinking about me?"

"No, I was thinking about a movie I saw with my brother Cyril when we were children . . . a fantasy. A bunch of people on a ship, they didn't know they were dead but finally Judgment Day comes and they have to answer to Sydney Greenstreet."

Arm in arm we walked through the snow.

"Paul Henreid comes back to life in the end. So does Eleanor Parker."

"Not an easy trick," she said, somber, eyes ahead.

"Love conquers all."

"I rather doubt that."

"Well, you should see more movies."

We walked a path leading out of the park, across the street, with snow to our ankles. Down a few narrow, snowy steps from the sidewalk there was a small coffee shop. A rotund woman with gray braids and a red nose welcomed us effusively; the place smelled of baking sweetcakes and fruit warming and strong coffee. Lise was obviously at home there.

I helped her out of the tight-fitting leather coat: it creaked in my hand. She moved to a table by a window which faced into a tiny patch of garden which ended some ten feet away with a brick wall rising six feet to the sidewalk. The garden was slowly filling with snow; huge flakes fluttered past our window. A fire leaped in the grate. From upstairs came the sound of a piano, elaborating on "Laura." I was Paul Henreid and she was Hedy Lamarr and outside there was a continent in flames, the Nazis reached for the world.

"You like the music?" she asked.

I nodded.

"It's the proprietress' son. He's blind and plays in a jazz club I sometimes go to."

"With Siegfried?"

Irritation flared like a signal in the night.

"Yes, with Siegfried."

She took a Camel out of a crushed pack and lit it with a paper match. Her tiny bag matched her coat. She leaned her elbows on the table, narrowing her square shoulders; the tight, ribbed sweater made her seem terribly thin, tiny-breasted and boyish. She wore no jewelry, all very plain, and her gray cat's eyes were large and luminous. Her cheekbones were high and prominent, the mouth wide, the cold light reflected from the snow took the color from her cheeks and hollowed them out, gave her a gaunt cast. "Is there really

much point in going on about my social life? I am very
fond of my husband and Siegfried is a close friend.
Doctor Roeschler is a kind of father. I lead a very
quiet, very circumscribed life. I teach my ballet class,
I consult with the children's mothers, I read books, try
to keep my English up, try to understand why there
isn't more to life. I wonder what other people's lives
are like, what gives them meaning, what draws them
on from day to day. . . ." She regarded me coolly. "I
am not a very interesting person, I'm afraid, Mr. Cooper. I'm not even sexually responsive . . . I'm alive. I
think I could be interesting perhaps—if only I knew
the trick. I'm sure there's some sort of trick to it. Perhaps, if I'm someone else—" There was no hint of a
smile, just the tight-lipped, cool voice. "Then maybe I
would find myself interesting. I don't know. So, if I am
your sister, that's all I amount to. A neurotic, not very
happy, exceedingly bourgeois woman on the wrong
side of thirty."

The strudel smelled of hot raisins and apple and
cinnamon, caramel melted across expanses of nut
buns.

Lise poured coffee, added cream and sugar in large
quantities without consulting me, severed a large
chunk of bun, spread it with butter, and ate it, leaving
a dusting of crumbs on her protruding lower lip.
"Good," she said, licking the tip of a finger. "Go
ahead, it's bad for you," and she smiled. "Most German women get fat asses and arms in time from just
this sort of eating." She took another bite. "Want to
avoid that if possible. Not easy." She sipped coffee,
leaving a faint mustache of foamy cream. The blind
boy switched to "You and the Night and the Music"
and a gust of wind blew snow in a flurry against the
window.

"Tell me about my brother," I said, "how he behaved. . . ."

She looked at me blankly.

"Well, you know him. He came to me with the story
straight out, saw that it disturbed me, saw that I was
unsure of my own lineage and he kept pushing at me
about it. He was making inquiries around Munich,
stirring certain people up, newspapermen and city rec-

ords officials. I was sorry that Gunter was upset because that meant he'd see to it that your brother left town. And I liked your brother—he had freckles. Your brother and I shared a sense of what was funny —he once said that what was funniest was what just missed being tragic." She chewed on the bun, stared out the window for a moment as if remembering something. "I liked that. He said that wherever I actually came from my soul dwelled in the Black Forest. I thought he was rather poetic."

Wind whistled in the little garden. The piano had slid into "Smoke Gets in Your Eyes" and I was trying to envision this version of Cyril.

"Did my brother ever mention your husband's political involvement?"

She smiled, almost chuckled. "The Nazi thing, you mean? Roeschler again, wasn't it? Well, that's something which struck us, Cyril and me, I mean, as rather funny—you know, just short of tragic. I'm aware of some of the friends my husband has, some of the games he plays with his friends . . . but it's impossible to take seriously, isn't it?"

"But did my brother express an interest?"

"All right, yes, he mentioned it. Look, he was curious about me. Me. Not my husband. Not Nazis. There were no political overtones."

"Did he meet with your husband?"

"At his office."

"And?"

"My husband was irritable, annoyed. He wanted your brother out of our lives."

"Did he threaten my brother?"

"My husband doesn't threaten people, Mr. Cooper."

"Look," I said, working up to my maximum wounded-sincerity level. "Look, I'm not myself—stop eating for a minute, for God's sake, and please listen to me. I'm not here as a troublemaker, please believe that—I'm overwrought, I admit it. But I have a hell of a reason." Her interest was with me now, a handful of bun had come to a halt halfway between plate and mouth.

"Yes? What reason is that, Mr. Cooper?"

"When my brother left you here in Munich he

didn't think the Nazi thing was a joke. He thought it was serious enough to follow it all the way to Buenos Aires. And he had your picture with him all the time." Her eyes were fixed on mine. "And I never did get to talk to him about you, about anything."

"Why not?"

"Because when he got back home somebody murdered him, Lise—and I don't think it would have happened if he'd never found you. I think you are the reason my brother is dead." I stared her down.

"You are really quite cruel, Mr. Cooper."

"Not as cruel as someone was to my brother."

She swallowed hard, sniffed.

"How could I have known—"

"That's what I want to know—did you know? Does anybody here know? I'll tell you, you're goddamn right, somebody here knows—either your husband knows . . . or that blond dreamboat Siegfried knows—"

"You've met Siegfried?" She jerked her breath back like an escaping mistake.

"I saw him with you in London. I followed you—I watched you—"

"You are ridiculous!"

"My brother is dead. A bunch of other people have died and I am a lot of things but I'm not ridiculous. I'm frightened. I'm tired. I'm incredibly angry. . . . And my voice is shaking."

She reached across the table and pressed my hand flat against the cloth.

"Your hand is shaking, too, Mr. Cooper." Her grip was strong, veins stood out on the back of her hand. The tiny breasts brushed the edge of the table, a muscle jumped in her cheek. My performance was over and reality was getting at me like an old war wound, throbbing in the memory. "Are you all right?"

"Look, either we can talk or we can't. You've no obligation to me, but I do. Do you understand that, do you understand what's going on here?"

"No, I don't understand," she said softly. She released her hold on my hand. "But I'll try to help you."

"Tell me the absolute truth about what happened with my brother."

"There is no such thing," she said quietly. But she tried.

Later, when she left me by the pagoda in the English Park, I stood in the snow watching her walk away, alone, straight, purposeful, growing dim behind the snow, and then I walked back again around the lake.

She said she'd told me all she knew. I think I trusted her but what I felt for her was so confused, so blurred by my curiosity about our possible relationship —now I could add to it a purely personal reaction: I was fascinated by her, by the circuitous ramblings of her mind, her egocentrism, her appetite for pastry, her hopelessness about her own life, her tiny breasts and her cool gray eyes, by the transparent way she seemed to be measuring her own heft in this peculiar situation. Her first concern, or so it seemed to me, was for herself, and yet, knowing that, I could believe that I might sacrifice myself for her. She offered little and the response to her own aura of selfishness was to make allowances, give her more. I didn't know if I wanted her to be my little sister Lee, after all.

The story she related with that solemn, unsmiling, determination was this:

Brendel had been taken off guard by Cyril's arrival and subsequent determination. And Cyril's digging had done far more than annoy him: she admitted she had never seen her husband so obviously upset and concerned. Cyril had quickly mapped out the relationship between Lise and Siegfried Hauptmann, confronted her with it—but primarily in terms of the political conflict between the two men, the old Nazis trying to head off and yet engage the support of the new. She insisted that fanciful splinter-group politics were of no interest to her or to anyone else with any sense. Cyril had doggedly insisted that she had no conception of the depth of their involvement.

Brendel made clear to her that she was not to see him again under any circumstances. Intuitively, she felt that Cyril was in danger. She took protective action.

Running a substantial risk, she arranged to meet him by the pagoda in the English Park after one of her ballet classes. Naturally she had turned to

Roeschler to help save the situation and it was decided that Cyril would go to ground immediately, disappear before any harm could befall him. It was, she insisted, a strong intuition on her part, though she could hardly associate her husband with anything so violent, so unpleasant.

She had to bet that Roeschler was more her friend than her husband's; it was a chance but again her instincts guided her. Cyril spent two nights at Roeschler's flat and made his exit by automobile through the Alps on the third day. Then he was gone and her husband and Siegfried had never discussed him again.

Having told me that version, Lise had stopped with a perplexed air. "So, I admit I am not pleased with my husband's political hobbies. And I am not at all taken by Siegfried's playing at being a Nazi—but really what difference does it all make? Why is it all so important? Who could possibly care? And why would my husband care if it turned out that I were in fact someone else? It's me he loves, whoever I am. Don't you see that? Doesn't anyone understand that? Me. It's me he married, not a name on paper. . . ."

But, of course, that was the point.

"Let's say, purely for the sake of argument," I'd said, "that there is some doubt about your real identity —let's say you're not Lise von Schaumberg at all. Then, Cyril's inquiries would have had some real relevance to your husband. If you are who you appear to be, why would Brendel have been driven so far—so far that you felt you had to arrange a hideaway for my brother?

"But what if there is something to hide, something they didn't want Cyril to know, what would it be? Why would they be so disturbed?

"I can only work my way round to one conclusion: that Cyril was right. Not just about the Nazi thing— from what I can tell that could be effectively denied, nobody in Germany wants to hear depressing things like that—but about who you are. Your real identity somehow frightens them."

She shook her head, not so much in disagreement, but slowly, as if in amazement. Absentmindedly, she stirred her coffee, rattling the spoon in the cup.

"You tell me, Lise"—I pressed her—"give me a better interpretation. Why else would they really care so much who you are? And why would Cyril go home to find his murderer after he'd gone so far to find you?" And why, I might have asked, would one of the men who tried to kill me turn up following me in Glasgow and London and wind up dead in a toilet? I had a hell of a lot of evidence, enough for me, connecting Brendel to the mess—but how could I explain it to her? And all of my evidence, which could convince me of so much, really couldn't convince me that Lise was Lee . . . only that Cyril thought she was.

"I don't know," she said. "You confuse me, you're so certain of so much. I believed my husband, why wouldn't I? Now . . . I don't know." She lit another Camel.

"Politics, the movement," I insisted, and she seemed to flinch, shrink back. "What do they really value? You? Do you believe they value you so much?"

She shrugged faintly.

"Finding out that you were someone else, that surely wouldn't make you leave your husband. If he was worried about that. All right—then what else is it that they value?" I paused like a schoolboy debater clinching his point. "They value their political involvement whether you think it's a joke or not. It's no joke to them. We *know* your husband is a Nazi—a real Nazi working beneath the surface of society. And it's that movement, that conspiracy which he values."

As I spoke to this subdued woman my mind wandered for a moment, remembering Ivor Steynes' photographs of Brendel through the years, remembering the attack on Steynes' fortress by men obviously connected with Brendel. Proof. Absolute proof and all the skeins of truth stretching back to the blizzard-swept highway in Wisconsin finally now being pulled together in the cold and snow and icy bleakness of Munich.

"And Siegfried, too, a Nazi from the other end of the continuum. So the real question now is this: Why and how do you threaten them politically? What does it matter to them if you are Lee? Where the hell do you lead?"

Of course, we had no answers, only questions, but

[272]

I was hopeful that she was grasping the significance of the questions. All I could think of was Peterson telling me to be aggressive, push a bit on the situation.

"I think I should see your husband."

Lise took it from there, made it easy for me—was she making it too easy? That thought squirmed out of the snow later, after she was gone.

"We're having a party tomorrow night. Why don't you come?"

"I have a friend with me."

"Roeschler told me. You must bring him, make a pair."

"Will Brendel know we're coming?"

"Do you want him to?"

"No. I think we should surprise him."

"How do you want to be introduced?"

"As Cyril Cooper's brother, John. I would very much like to see your husband's face. I want to surprise him."

"I'm very passive, Mr. Cooper, in almost every way you can imagine. I'm willing to let it all just happen and if there's a shoot-out in the dining room, well, that will be an improvement on what usually goes on in the dining room." Her face was calm, expressionless, and for an instant I thought how very peculiar it would be to have to cope with that face on a regular basis.

"All right," I said. "We'll be there."

That was when we left and she made that familiar gesture, locking her arm through mine. When we parted she stopped and leaned up to kiss me, the snow in her face, and left me to walk back through the park, to puzzle it out for myself. It struck me that, in contrast to her outward repose, there had been an almost feverish glaze to her eyes.

I tried to convey to Peterson not only the content of our conversation but my estimate of Lise Brendel. The content was no particular problem; the rest was not a success. I threw my impressions into the beetle-browed face which regarded me with alternating concern and amazement. He didn't understand. He never understood.

"You're not describing your sister, Cooper—at least I hope not. You're talking about a woman and what you're saying doesn't sound very brotherly." He frowned.

"I know," I said.

"Sounds like the Spider Lady to me. Spooky." He began to smile, unbuttoning his vest. "The party, though. Now that's a masterstroke, hers, I'm afraid, not yours. But at least you didn't decline." He unzipped his trousers, revealing black, hairy legs fit for a linebacker. He really was mindful of a coiled spring. He looked up from his trouser folding and gave me a quick grin, teeth bared.

It occurred to me that in all probability the strain or exhilaration of our adventures had driven Peterson clear around the corner into homicidal madness. Was that a comfort?

"Come with me," he said, giving me the hairy unshirted back. I followed him into the bathroom, where the water was running. The tub was full of bubbles. He clambered in among them, slid down, until only his head seemed to float on the cloud of foam. "Sit down and I'll tell you a story about your solemn Lise."

It was hot. The mirror was steamed over and I was sweating. I sat down on the toilet cover and prepared myself. He was grinning like a starving shark.

Before he began, he had me light a cigar for him. He took it with a soapy hand. My God: Edward G. Robinson in *Key Largo*. We were crossing ever deeper into make-believe and Peterson was taking a bubblebath and smoking a cigar. I grabbed a towel and wiped my face.

"Your Lise Brendel is not exactly a shrinking violet. And she has been something of a problem for her husband and other staid, conservative members of Munich society. She is, in fact, looked upon as a bit of a scandal in certain quarters—quarters which are normally very important to Herr Brendel. Old friends, aristocracy, family connections. They don't really approve of this girl with the shadowy antecedents—yes, that's right, Cooper, they're not all so damned sure who she is either. Out of nowhere palmed off as a von Schaumberg, over twenty years younger than Brendel.

[274]

Hell, most people thought he'd never get married at all and the rest apparently hoped he'd settle for one of their daughters. Then, wham, along comes Lise and he's bowled over, as if it were all preordained. Hand me the backbrush, Cooper."

He kept on talking with his arm bent backward, ash sprinkling onto the foam.

"And your Lise did damned little to win these people over. She was standoffish, uninterested in their social whirl, bored by the groups she was expected to join, utterly unconventional, got a job teaching kids ballet, ran around in Levis and looked like a pouting starlet . . . very bad in the eyes of old-time Munich bluebloods. Sponge, Cooper," he said, handing me the wooden-handled back scrubber. I threw the sponge into the suds. A cloud of soap landed on his cigar.

"But in time people would have gotten used to Frau Brendel's little idiosyncrasies—they were getting used to them until she took up with Siegfried Hauptmann. That little liaison, carried on in full public view, convinced them that everything they'd thought about her in the first place was true. More than true. The general feeling is that this scarlet woman has ruined Gunter Brendel, made him a laughingstock to some and a proven decadent to others—and that she has found a perfect mate in Hauptmann, rich, perverse, chaser of celebrities of both sexes, jet-setter, and God only knows what else, child molester, dope fiend, cat burglar, rapist, and on and on. He's not well liked, you see."

"How about being a Nazi?" I suggested.

"Oh, hell." He waved his hand. "No one gives a damn about that. Half of these people, more, probably, figure Hitler got a raw deal. They just don't much care. Not caring, they don't really know. They figure there are Nazis still lurking but they're harmless old men or raving perverts like Siegfried. I'm not saying they're right—I'm only telling you what they think." He splashed merrily.

"How the hell do you know all this?"

"Cops, Cooper, cops everywhere know other cops. Old school ties. Plumbers go someplace, they talk to other plumbers. Insurance salesmen, they talk to other insurance salesmen. Cops are always willing to talk to cops. If you do it right—and I always do it right."

I watched him soap under his arms.

"Peterson, is all this steam going to make your hair come loose? No, seriously, will it melt the glue or something?"

"No, Cooper, it won't melt the glue, for Chrissakes —have you gone mad?"

"I just wondered, that's all."

He soaped sulkily for a moment.

"Anyway, once she started screwing Siegfried everyone thought the marriage was over. But Brendel seemed relieved, not in the least bothered by it. The three of them began appearing in public together— and all the observers began to assume the, heh heh, worst—that is, that Siegfried was servicing both of them." He cocked an eye to see my reaction.

"Well? Is he?"

"Nobody knows for sure. How could they? But that's all gossip anyway, isn't it? Who cares who's screwing whom, right, Cooper? Scarlet women, raving perverts, the whole works—who the hell cares? We're not Masters and Johnson, are we? We're Peterson and Cooper, one of the great comic teams, and we don't give a shit about rumors. We're on the trail of the Master Race.

"And that's where my friends, over enough schnapps to pickle a regiment of Hessians, began to lay it on me. Roeschler was right—Siegfried is the leader of a strong new Nazi group, latter-day Nazis with no ties to the past. Nobody really knows how serious they are, but they have pots of money and are developing an enthusiastic youthful following.

"The theory seems to be that Brendel very calculatedly unloaded a troublesome wife on Siegfried and used her to build a bridge between the old guard and the new. She became a symbolic uniting of the old and new. It's not quite as nutsy as it sounds. These guys are not elves from the Black Forest, they're police officers and they're not nuts. Towel, Cooper, and stand clear, I'm coming out." The splashing was absurd.

Leaving footprints, he wandered into the bedroom.

"Any theories about who she is?" I asked.

"No. They don't know who the hell she is, wouldn't offer an opinion one way or the other. Nobody ever really asked them—until your brother came along. And he planted the idea in their minds but then he never followed up."

He wrapped the towel around himself and dropped onto the bed. He lit another cigar and told me to sit down, for God's sake.

"I called Cooper's Falls again," he said, "talked to Bradlee. He says Brenner is stronger every day, out of the coma, not talking much but he thinks he's going to pull through all right. Said the Feds are still all over the place. Can't find a damn thing, of course." He pushed back against the pillow. "If they knew what Steynes told us . . . can you imagine it? They'd go mad. If they knew what my man at Columbia knows, all the stuff that was in those boxes, their brains would turn to Alpo, Cooper. Alpo." He sighed the sigh of the just. "Did you ever think about what we're going to do with all this stuff? Will anybody believe us?"

"Will we live to tell anybody? That's the question."

"I also called Buenos Aires, talked with your little man there—he had a head cold, made my eyes water. He doesn't know where the hell Kottmann and St. John, the pilot or the plane went to. Sounds like he's beginning not to give a goddamn but that was probably just the cold.

"And finally I called Ivor Steynes. I wanted to find out who the killer sent to get Brendel is—I know, I know, faint hope. No answer, nobody home. Frankly, I don't think we can save Brendel anyway short of kidnapping him. Somebody's wandering around with Brendel's name on a bullet."

He got up from the bed and began to poke through our baggage, finally emerged with a bottle of brandy.

"So, my young friend, you've got more to worry about than my hair coming unglued." He poured brandy into a tumbler and handed it to me, poured another for himself. "If Deadeye Dick shoots old Brendel before tomorrow night, you and I are going to miss a hell of a party."

Peterson hired a Mercedes sedan and we drove through the snowy streets, leaving the center of Munich farther behind with the slow minutes. The snow had continued, was banked high at roadside, and the night was still as if calmed by a great gloved hand. We wore rented dinner clothes and Peterson was carrying a gun. The only time he spoke was to bitch about having to wear a rented garment. The armholes were tight.

Snow swept across the hood, the wind hammered at the car, there was no world beyond the edge of the roadway. It reminded me far too much of that first night in the snow, the night I met Milo Keepnews and the gaunt man. Peterson reached into an inside pocket. I expected to see the gun. He withdrew a round lollipop on a white stick and began to suck it, his cheeks bulging. He knew I was staring at him.

"When I was a kid," he said, eyes intent on the road, talking past the ball of candy, "I used to say that prayer about what I wanted to have happen if I died before I woke up. I was just a little kid, of course, and I prayed the Lord my soul to take. Well, I got older, went into several nights knowing I might not come out again in the morning, and I began to have doubts about the Lord taking my soul. He might not care—or he might be busy with some other guy's soul, I mean you couldn't count on it. And one time, faced with such a night, I got to thinking about very simple pleasures which meant a lot to me. You know how you can't explain certain things that sort of lodge in your memory? Well, I remembered my father taking me to a Chicago Cubs baseball game at Wrigley Field. I must have been eight or nine. I worshipped Big Bill Nicholson and Phil Cavaretta and we went to the game and —this'll kill you, Cooper: I can't even remember who won the game. I remember two things about that game. Nicholson hit a homer and my father bought me one of these suckers, the round ball with the white pasteboard stick coming out of it. It was grape and I could remember the taste with fantastic clarity. And I loved that taste. Yet I hadn't had one since I was a little kid. And the thought struck me that if I died during the night, why then I'd never get to taste one of those suckers again. I've kept a bunch of them with me ever since, when I go out to do something danger-ous—and at just the right times I haul them out and taste that grape again. It's very comforting, very com-forting."

I wanted it all to be over. I prayed the Lord my soul to take. I didn't have a sucker.

The house was a square, flat-walled thing, well back from the road, with a front lawn of gravel and a statue standing in the middle of it creating a huge turnaround. A hunter's moon slipped out from behind the screen of cloud cover for a moment, cast an icy-blue silver light, and then was gone, leaving us in the maelstrom of snow.

We were helped from our car by a pair of uniformed attendants who gave Peterson a ticket and drove the Mercedes away to the rows of other Mercedes which stood like tanks waiting in the order of battle. Peterson hustled me along. "Come on, it's a party. Have a good time." He was distracting me from the groping terror in my chest. We were in the doorway, more servants were helping us out of our coats, there was the rumble of a large party, people everywhere, a sea of German being spoken. I understood nothing, floated almost deliriously like a man strapped to a table and rolling groggily toward the operating room. I heard Peterson chuckle and I turned, knowing I was pale. "What are they gonna do, Cooper? Kill us?" His grin snapped at me beneath his mustache. "Hell, everybody dies." I nodded. "Introduce me to your sister, Cooper. Then we'll surround the bastards."

The faces were all worn by strangers who seemed to see through us. Men wore either black tie or military uniforms, women were mostly in long dresses with bare shoulders. Diamonds caught light from the chandeliers.

We stood unnoticed by an urn full of ferns and sev-eral palms. A string quartet was at work at tho far end of the room: you could see the bows flashing over the tide of heads and hear the music behind the blur of conversation, laughter, cries of Germanic greeting. Peterson whisked two glasses of champagne from a passing silver tray. He fingered a palm frond. "I want my sucker."

I was grinning numbly as I turned, saw a startlingly pale woman with cropped black hair, short like a raven's feathers on the nape of her neck. Her dress was black, her eyes were heavily outlined, her skin almost deathly in contrast. Her eyes were pale gray behind round steel-rimmed spectacles. There was a puckered wound at the corner of her right eye, small but strangely obvious, a false note, strangely theatrical. She was wildly out of place and coming toward us, looking past us, and I tugged at Peterson's sleeve.

"I beg your pardon—"

It wasn't Peterson. A tall man in an American general's uniform peered down at me over Ben Franklin half-glasses.

"Ah. . . ." I said. "Well, you're not my friend, are you?"

"I'm mighty sorry to hear that, son," he drawled. A large gray-haired woman with arms like draperies of spaghetti gritted her teeth at me. "Are you all right, boy?"

"He looks drunk," spaghetti arms said and began reeling him in.

"Get some air, boy," the general said, drifting away from me.

I turned away, caught a tailing of fern in the eye, and heard my name. "Mr. Cooper, good evening. You needn't cry out, you know."

It was the black-haired woman with the glasses that not only failed to disguise the mouse by her eye but drew attention to it.

"Well, I didn't mean to shout, but the general, you see—" She was looking slightly past me at the room over my shoulder. She raised her hand as if to slap me. I flinched and she brushed the fern from my face.

"Mr. Cooper, you don't look well at all."

The glasses magnified her gray eyes. I hadn't recognized her. It was Lise Brendel.

"Surprise," she said calmly.

I lifted my champagne and dribbled it over my hand.

"Are you enjoying yourself?"

"I just got here—"

"I know. I heard." Her mouth was red, like a forties

[280]

pinup queen. I shuffled my feet nervously; any rapport that I had expected was utterly nonexistent.

"What happened to your eye?"

"Why are you so frightened, Mr. Cooper?" A smile wormed its way onto her face, a trace of gloating. "Still thinking about your Nazis? Well, the place is crawling with them. And has Gunter found you yet?"

"You said you weren't going to tell him?" I didn't know this woman and it occurred to me that she might be on something.

"I changed my mind and I told him. I told Siegfried, too. I thought his reaction was quite amusing until he hit me in the eye." She sighed self-consciously. "Do close your mouth. And while you're doing that I shall attend to my guests."

I watched her walk away. Her feet were bare beneath the dress, and several heads, male and female, turned to watch her go. Mouths began moving, faces contorted: she attracted their hatred.

Peterson appeared from behind the cluster of palms.

"What in hell was that?"

I wondered how to break it to him.

He began to shake his head.

"Oh, no," he said. "You're not going to tell me—"

"But she's not the same as she was," I said. "I didn't even recognize her. She told Brendel. She said she wouldn't but she did." Peterson's eyes traveled slowly to the foyer, to the door where several servants, large servants, stood at ease.

"Cooper, do you see those men by the door? If they were any bigger their knuckles would drag on the floor. If men that size don't want you to leave, then you don't leave unless you're prepared to shoot them full of holes. You are not prepared to do that. I am. So don't try to leave without me."

He looked back at me. "And if you see me beating your goddamn sister into chopped liver, I'm telling you that you interfere at your own risk. I'm getting very survival-oriented all of a sudden. Brendel should not have been told ahead of time. That changes everything. Our only advantage is gone." He thrust a hand past me and I flinched again, Walter Mitty to the end. "Doctor Roeschler," he said, shaking hands with

Roeschler, who managed to look like Carl Sandburg even in evening dress. "It's nice to see a familiar face." Peterson was glazed with the phoniest smile I had ever seen. He was fully capable of shooting some people, pulling the trigger instead of shaking hands, and Roeschler seemed so gentle, a man whose compromises had been made so long ago.

"Well, you've certainly gotten inside the battlements," Roeschler said. I kept looking back into the crowd for a trace of Lise. I couldn't quite believe the way she had behaved; it made no sense to me. How could she have betrayed me?

"You've seen Lise," he said, his voice rumbling, Adam's apple bobbing behind the black tie. "I can tell."

"I didn't recognize her. Very confusing, Doctor Roeschler."

"Absolutely nuts," Peterson said. "God, it's hot in here."

"Mr. Peterson has a point," Doctor Roeschler said so softly that I had to incline toward him. "It's her style and in certain cases style is another name for madness. There is more than one Lise. . . ." He paused and touched my arm pointedly. "She is schizoid—I couldn't tell you that until you'd seen it for yourself. Not a psychosis, but pronounced nevertheless. She just comes and goes, one mask after another. She will never be sure who she is, Mr. Cooper," Roeschler said sadly. It was impossible to tell how figuratively he was speaking.

"We will, though," Peterson said. He was tense.

"One wonders," Roeschler said. He moved away, leaned for a moment against a chair, took a glass of champagne, drained it off, and walked slowly away into the crowd.

"He's an old man," Peterson said. "I wonder what's left for him?"

"What's left for her?" I couldn't get hold of the evening.

"I don't know, but she's trouble, John. You can't trust her. Do you hear me, John—don't make a bad mistake."

The music swept across the crowd. Peterson went to find the buffet. The vast, immense men stood by the front doors chatting, looking surly. The knot in my stomach tightened.

It was all so uncertain. We were there, but why? What was supposed to happen? Lise had turned out so badly: that was no ally, no friend in the enemy camp. I couldn't shake my terrible fear. Fear. Cowardice. What difference did it make?

It was all so serious, but I found myself awaiting the arrival of Porky Pig and Bugs Bunny and it didn't make sense. The room, the people, the fear were all tightening on me, squeezing me, and I kept wanting to giggle and go to the toilet from fright. I turned toward a French window which stood slightly ajar, wiped my face with a handkerchief, felt the draft cold on my sweat.

When I looked back the scene reminded me of one of Hieronymus Bosch's lesser canvases. For an instant it seemed a rioting madhouse and then there was Lise sailing toward me. I recognized Gunter Brendel following in the wake. She was smiling, the geometry of her face somehow off-center. I didn't realize that Siegfried Hauptmann was with them until they were on top of me.

"Ah, Mr. Cooper," she called airily, heads turning as she approached, "here you are at last! We've been searching so diligently for you and here you are all by yourself enjoying the music!" Brendel stared at me levelly through this absurd recital, waiting.

"My husband, Gunter Brendel," she said, turning first to one, then to the other, "and my dear friend, Siegfried Hauptmann both of whom have been dying to meet you all evening. Haven't you, darling?" She lobbed the ball into her husband's court.

He bowed a fraction. "How do you do, Mr. Cooper. I remember your brother very well." He smiled thinly, turning to Siegfried.

"Mr. Cooper." His eyes were like windows onto a bright sunny sky, his hair yellow as straw.

Lise burst out laughing, a false laugh which skirted the last outposts of real mirth. Her husband regarded her warily. "Well, you three must have so much to talk about!" she exclaimed loudly.

"Please, Mr. Cooper, you must forgive my wife's

high spirits. Parties frequently have this effect on her. She becomes overexcited—"

"No, not actually," she said stridently. "As a matter of fact I behave this way for a very specific reason."

"I'm sure you do, my dear," Brendel said. He was, suddenly frightened of her, squeezed her hand in his. "I'm so glad you could join us, Mr. Cooper. Lise is right—I have much to discuss with you. Perhaps you will remain long enough to join Herr Hauptmann and me for a brandy later—"

She interrupted, pulling her hand away. Her glasses slid down her nose. Siegfried looked on with vague amusement as if it were an old, weary, but still faintly diverting act.

"And the reason I behave this way," she said with exaggerated English diction, "is that I am so fucking bored by this whole stupid world! These lumpish slugs you call your friends—" Her voice dropped as two startled matrons peered quizzically from behind a fern of their own. I shrank back, felt the edge of the open door in the center of my back. She hissed: "And all your tired old Nazis. . . ." Brendel reached for her arm again but he was too late; she jerked away, knocked Siegfried's champagne glass to the floor, leaned groggily against him. A thick vein bulged in Brendel's neck. But his eyes told me he'd been through it before.

"Siegfried," he said, tight-lipped, "will you please see Lise upstairs?"

Lise's voice was thick. "He knows the way, doesn't he, darling?" She grinned, off-center, at her husband, eyes heavy-lidded, hooded, crafty. "But then we all have so much in common—" She switched into German and lost me. Brendel turned to me, ignoring her, as Siegfried began to move away with her. He spoke as if we were old friends.

"My wife is not particularly well, Mr. Cooper. She has an overworked imagination and too much free time —a very modern woman, I'm afraid." He shrugged, went on in his perfect English: "And this is the result —I'm terribly sorry. She was right about my wanting a word with you. She told me how far you'd come to see her and that you were asking the same questions your brother had. I knew it would upset her. Your brother had upset her. And now"—another stiff shrug —"here you are and it starts all over again." He stopped walking, released my arm. "This cannot go on, Mr. Cooper. My wife's stability is too insecure, too easily unsettled. And she also mentioned your interest in our political activities." He paused to survey his guests, squared his shoulders. Without looking at me, a fixed public smile on his smooth, tanned skier's face, he said: "We're going to lay all this to rest tonight, Mr. Cooper, absolutely to rest. Please enjoy the party, by all means enjoy the party, and we will have a long talk with Siegfried later. Don't even think of leaving here." He smiled at me. "I won't hear of it." He gave me that abbreviated bow. "Excuse me."

Across the room I saw Roeschler watching us. Ponderously, he moved off behind Brendel, ever faithful, the healer who tried to help him understand his wife. Across the years, their wives helped to bond them together.

I wondered where Peterson had gone, when he was coming back.

But I was seriously wondering if even Peterson could do me any good anymore. I had come all this way, I knew that this man Brendel was trying to kill me, I had no idea whatsoever if Lise was my sister, and I had willingly come to this party, this house. . . . It was incomprehensible when I thought about it: I just couldn't have done it. I had sweat in my eyes, the back of my neck was wet, my shirt clung stickily. I took another glass of champagne and pushed through the crowd. Long draperies swayed and I moved slowly on into other rooms until I found myself staring eye to eye with Martin St. John.

His hair hung like a dirty flag across his forehead, his dinner clothes were rumpled, and a morsel of crab dip reposed neatly on his lapel. He swiped at his face with a red bandanna and grinned puckishly when he saw me. He winked broadly, stuffed the red cloth into a hip pocket. With his other hand he stabbed a stub of cigarette into his mouth, puffed laboriously, and ran his tongue over thick lips.

"Mr. Cooper," he said. "How good to see you again! Your researches have taken you a very long way."

"What are you doing here?" Roca was scouring Tierra del Fuego for him and he was enjoying the party in Munich and he was smiling at me: these people didn't seem to mind being caught in their lies. He was chortling and sweating, the aging soldier of fortune up to his ears in his last big caper.

"A bit of this, a bit of that. Always working on something. Things always happening, deals to make. What are you doing here, my boy? Still looking for that girl?" He smiled broadly. The piece of crab came unstuck, rolled down his coat. He puffed at the cigarette and nudged me with his elbow. "Found her at last, haven't you?" He had the sly grin of a man dealing in pornographic films, changed from the opera board man in Buenos Aires.

"Yes, I found her at last."

"And you're thinking badly of me, I know, I know." He guided me past a potted tree of some sort and pulled me down on a settee out of the line of traffic. "And I can't blame you, thinking ill of old St. John, but you really shouldn't, not really. We're all soldiers under the surface, aren't we? We've all got our marching orders, don't you see? Our lives are not quite our own, we're all merely cogs—egad, what a boring speech, what? Reminds me of a sergeant major I once knew in Singapore, poor man eventually died—one of Wingate's men, of course. But I'm rambling." He patted my knee and dropped the cigarette into yet another tree pot. He fumbled for another, scratched a match on the urn.

"You lied to me," I said. "I can't help wondering why."

"Well, now, about what?"

"I don't even know anymore. But you could have helped me."

"Why, I did help you—I sent you to Kottmann, I gave you the picture. Now if that isn't helping you, old Martin St. John doesn't know help when he sees it."

"Part of the truth. Why not all of it?"

"And whoever knows all the truth, Mr. Cooper? I

[286]

told you what I could. We all have our orders, don't we?"

"Whose orders do you follow, then? Who's your master?"

"Ah, well, there you are—that would be telling, wouldn't it?" His jowls shook, he pushed the hair back, pursed his fat lips. "And I can't do that, Mr. Cooper. You'll have to do without that." He sighed. "But you've come so far, perhaps you'll go on a bit longer."

"I rather doubt it. I don't think I'm going much farther." I stood up. He watched me amiably, dribbled ash on his cummerbund. "Are you in this with Brendel? Are you all in it together? *Die Spinne*—the Spider?"

"Die Spinne?"

"You bet your ass," I said.

"I'm amazed," he said slowly.

"That I know?"

"No. That you'd tell me that you know." All the cordial bonhomie had bleached out of his voice. "Just offhand that strikes me as not particularly bright."

"Well, then it's in character, isn't it? I haven't been bright at all. Just sort of vaguely human."

"Not enough, old boy. A man's got to be a good bit more than that these days. Any days. I'm sorry—I find myself sorry about things more often the older I get. Do sit down, this is hurting my neck, looking up. . . ."

"Are you all in it, then?"

"More of us than anyone really thinks, I suppose. Enough of us, certainly." He was becoming his old self again. But there was an arctic waste stretching out behind his eyes. Something had changed.

"Is this the center of it? Here in Munich?"

"Here in this house," he said, "is closer the mark. There is apparently one more stop after this, too—even Brendel is a soldier who takes his orders. But this is where it stops for me. In this house. With this man."

He stood up and brushed ashes off his lapels.

"Well, Mr. Cooper, it has been . . . fascinating talking to you again." His hand was warm and dry, his smile automatic. He had always been human, warm, lying. Now he was remote.

"Am I going to get out of here alive?"

The thick lips pursed.

"I shouldn't count on it, Mr. Cooper. Not realistically, don't you see?" His weary eyes met mine. "Don't think badly of old St. John. I'm only a soldier. And I am truly sorry." He turned his back at the last moment. "For whatever comfort it may be, once you're my age you find yourself looking back and wondering what the point was . . . if there was a point at all. You won't be missing anything worthwhile, I assure you." He seemed to be bearing a heavy burden.

Alone, a pariah, one of the dead, I moved slowly back through the maze of rooms, corridors full of urns and statuary and paintings and plaster cherubs beaming indolently down from the molding. The level of noise was rising as the party gathered life and rhythm of its own. Near a bookcase, standing in close conversation with a tall man in evening clothes, a man with slicked-back, dyed black hair, whose bearing was military and whose face was strangely familiar, was Alfried Kottmann, the other half of the famed Buenos Aires comedy team. Boffo in Munich!

Kottmann must have felt my eyes boring into him. He looked up and saw me, returned my stare coldly, inclined his head minutely, expressionlessly. He kept talking to the familiar-looking man who seemed to have had a successful face-lift which gave him a slightly plastic, unseamed quality, a counterfeit youthfulness.

Across the room, through one of the French windows, Peterson appeared, brushing a sprinkling of snow from his shoulders. I got to him before he disappeared.

"We're going to die," I said abruptly.

"Who told you that, for God's sake?"

"Oh, hell"—I waved my hand—"all of them. Brendel, Siegfried. . . ." I laughed a trifle hysterically "Martin St. John. I just talked to him. He said he was sorry about it but that was the way it was. He was really quite nice."

"Cooper, listen to what I'm saying. You are about

half drunk right now. If you don't sober up you won't have to worry about these people killing you—because I'll kill you." He paused for effect while I blinked; it was entirely possible that he meant it. "Now where the hell did you see him?"

"Back there." I motioned over my shoulder. "He told me that he's just a soldier and that he takes his marching orders from Brendel. He said that this house is the center of it all, the headquarters of *Die Spinne.* He told me there was one other source, the place Brendel's orders come from—he didn't know where that was, though." I sighed. Peterson took my champagne away from me, emptied it into yet another urn.

Snow was melting in his hair. "The amazing thing about it all is the structure, like a piece of sculpture, spokes, and curves all intersecting and when you step back from it you realize the shape—we've been so close, just seeing pieces of the skeleton. But step back and you see what it is. . . ."

"What is it?"

"A globe, I think. And to think that your brother just stumbled into it." He cocked his head at me. "Think how it must drive them crazy when they think of it. One man just wandering into their work of art and breaking first this piece, then bending that, fucking it up. . . ." He shook his head vigorously, as if it rested on top of a coiled spring, "Think of it, think of how important it is to them . . . and this poor son of a bitch wanders in looking for his sillyass sister and blows the whistle on them. Jesus, it's quite a world, ain't it?"

He seemed to be forgetting our immediate problems. Among other things I had to go to the bathroom.

"Where have you been, anyway?" I asked.

"I went and got the car. Put it at the end of the walk, bullied those imbeciles, said I didn't want it parked in the rows with the others doors might get scratched. It's out in front now. Proves the attendants haven't been told about us."

"I've got to find the bathroom."

"Upstairs." He moved beside me to the foyer where we'd entered. It was nearly midnight and the rheostats had been turned down dramatically, dimming the lights

in the crystal chandeliers. Servants were moving un-
obtrusively along the walls lighting candles in ornate
fixtures. Shadows flickered, the people milled all the
more, enjoying themselves in the lateness of the hour.
Wrinkles faded, baldness no longer gleamed, and chests
full of medals glinted and gleamed, diamonds spun
webs of fire as gestures grew languid.

"Is that man your friend St. John?" He gestured
with a cigar. I nodded.

"My God," he said with generous disgust. "The man
is covered with food. Well, he and I have a few things
to discuss. You go find the bathroom—ah, there's Doctor Roeschler. Doesn't look any better than he did before. He worries me, talk to him if you have the
chance. . . ." He was somewhat distracted, watching
St. John, who was holding a plate of food and chatting
with a young woman whose long blond hair kept
brushing his salad. He patted my arm and abruptly
sneezed. "That's what I get for running around in the
goddamn snow. I'll always associate you with snow."

As the stairway curled around, there was a room-
sized landing with heavy draperies at the sides of immensely tall windows which disappeared in darkness
like mountaintops in the clouds before they reached
the ceiling. Candles in heavy sconces cast a warm, dim
glow. My legs were weak with fear and I sat on a
broad old couch beneath the window, out of sight from
the foyer, quite alone. There was a writing desk, a
huge leather chair, and a bookcase on the landing. Behind the couch, with its high, tufted leather back
cracked with age, there was a bay window seat and a
view of a lengthy, apparently six-car garage. Snow was
falling heavily through the penumbra of the driveway
lamps; the lawn was smooth, like deep white frosting,
without a trace of a footprint. It was a lovely scene
but I had to find a bathroom.

The second floor was quiet, insulated from the
sounds of the party, which was after all a considerable
distance away. Tapestries clung to the walls, hunting
scenes perceived vaguely in the dark, a boar cornered
against a great thick tree trunk, woodsmen in quaint
caps and gear closing in. Shadows crossed them,

brought them to life, and all that was missing was the anguished screech and snort of the beast.

A bathroom door stood slightly ajar. It reminded me of a locker room: a huge shower stall, a separate tub, a locked door leading to a bedroom, a toilet, a double basin, a bidet, a full-length mirror, a riot of towels. The light switch produced a dim, roseate glow and I sank onto the commode, leaned forward to hang my bleary-eyed head between my knees. Cary Grant, it occurred to me, had never had to use the bathroom in *Notorious* when he went to Claude Rains' party. But I wasn't Cary Grant and I was ten seconds from throwing up in Gunter Brendel's bidet.

I didn't know how long the voices had been going on when I finally calmed down enough to notice them. They were coming from the other side of the locked door.

"I ask you, what's left for me to do with you? What?" It was Brendel, I was sure, and he was speaking English. He was trying to keep his voice under control and it was strangling him. "Answer me!" He was losing the battle: I couldn't tell whether she was laughing or crying but she wasn't satisfying him. My head throbbed: I was an alcoholic and Peterson had been right, I was perilously near drunkenness. "Goddamn you, answer me! Tell me what you want me to do!" A piece of furniture slammed against a wall, she screamed in sudden fright: "Don't, Gunter, please—"

He hit her, the sound of the blow was punctuated by a grunt of exertion from him and a sob from her.

"You . . . you slut," he gurgled. "You have everything, you have your lover, you have freedom, you have my adoration . . . and you are a slut in return. A disgrace. Rotten, perverted—" He ran out of breath.

There was silence and I could picture the scene: he was stung by guilt, he went to her, held her, his voice was soft, muffled in her hair. I could hear her faint sobs, and slowly they turned to a wacky kind of giggle, as if there were something loose in her head.

"Lise—" He sounded fearful; he knew her well.

"Don't touch me again," she said through the compulsive giggling. "Be careful. Or I'll kick you where your nuts ought to be. Fairy! Fucking old fairy—" She was hissing and laughing. She wasn't the girl in the park.

"This has all happened too often, Lise. I'm lost. . . . Please, change your clothes, put on shoes, don't take such pleasure in disgracing me."

"How could I disgrace you? You disgrace yourself —did you have his brother murdered?"

"What did you say?"

"Did you have John Cooper's brother killed?" She gulped back laughter and tears, half choked.

"You have spoken with him about this?"

"Of course. I met him in the English Park—he knows about you, he knows more than his brother did . . . if it's true, of course."

"This is not to be discussed. I don't know what you're talking about. And how could you thrust him upon me, here in this house? How, Lise?"

"I'm feeding him to you." Ice tinkled in a glass. "He says you're a wicked man—I told him you were harmless. Which is it? Really?"

"You know what I am, Lise."

"No, I don't know what you are at all. And I don't know who I am. . . ."

"Nonsense—you're drunk. You're mad."

"You're the one who's mad, Gunter. You're the liar, the murderer, the disgusting pervert. . . ." She was working herself up. "You're turning purple, quite purple." She laughed loudly.

"Be quiet!"

"Fuck yourself, will you? For me?"

He hit her again. I heard her hit the floor. My legs shook uncontrollably.

"I loved you," he said. "Now I want to throw you away. Garbage. . . ." He began to sob.

She was breathing hoarsely. I imagined her on the floor, shaking her head, blood running out of her nose. She sounded as if he'd broken her nose and she was trying to talk through blood and the pain. "Siegfried even hits harder than you do—" The voice was lost as her stomach turned and she retched, gagging on vomit, and I saw it gushing down her dress, across her pale boy's chest, soiling herself. She gagged and tried to speak and couldn't stop vomiting.

"God, I loved you," he said, almost moaning.

"I never loved you. . . ."

"You have loved only yourself."

"No, you're wrong. As usual. I hate myself, too."

I heard the bed groan. He was helping her onto the bed. She had begun to weep by then, steadily. "Wipe me off," she said. "Clean me off, I can't stand the smell. . . ."

"No. You wear it well, Lise. It suits you."

I heard the door close softly and I slipped the bolt on the locked door and pushed it open. A bedside lamp cast deep shadows across the room. She lay huddled on the bed, knees drawn up, her back to me. The smell triggered a flashback in my overloaded memory and I saw Milo Keepnews lying by the filthy toilet, slowly dying in his own stink. I shut the door and went back to the hallway door on tiptoe, switched off the light, and opened it a crack.

Brendel stood at the railing at the top of the stairs, holding to it with both hands extended before him. leaning slightly forward. His head had slumped forward as if he were studying the crease in his trousers.

Finally, he moved to the stairway and began to descend. I slipped out of the bathroom, crossed to the far wall, and made my way cautiously along in his footsteps, praying that no one would find me and shoot me to death for the sport of it. It was a madhouse. But fear was sobering me up.

I stood in the deep shadows by the tapestry at the top of the stairs. It was quiet, only the string quartet sawing on a long way off. Brendel stood on the immense landing, passed a hand across his forehead. Candlelight reflected on his stiff white shirt and cuffs. With exquisite grace and sorrow he slumped onto the huge couch, rested his elbows on his knees, and dropped his head into his hands.

A movement caught my eye on the stair below the landing. A man—another watcher—stood in his own shroud of shadows, then moved slowly into view, a tall man, stooped, tired. He climbed the few stairs to the landing. He must have spoken: Brendel's head came up slowly and nodded his recognition. The stooped man went to him, sat down beside him, and put his hand on Brendel's shoulder, a consoling gesture.

It was Gerhard Roeschler.

The bond between them was almost visible, two men with so much of their lives behind them, so many secrets shared and hidden in the shadows of decades. Roeschler offered him a cigar and a match flared, smoke billowed upward. I couldn't hear a word, only a faint rumble of deep, guttural voices, and I thought that it would have been nice, better than nice, a godsend, to have such a friend to comfort me in my own time of trial.

At last Roeschler levered himself out of the deep couch and touched Brendel's shoulder. Brendel's head hung down and I could hear Roeschler's voice, soothing him, as if he were telling him a bedtime story.

Slowly Roeschler's left hand came out of his coat pocket. He was patting Brendel's back with one hand and there was something in the other, something I couldn't quite make out. He reached forward, slowly, pressing something to Brendel's temple and I heard a muffled coughing sound from their shadowy tableau and only then, remembering the sound in the Glasgow hallway, in the shadows where I'd found Alistair Campbell, only then did I realize that Doctor Roeschler had just put a bullet in Gunter Brendel's brain.

Brendel jerked sideways, collapsed against the back and arm of the couch. Methodically, Roeschler hoisted the inert body into his arms and rolled it over the back of the couch. I watched it disappear between the couch and the window-seat. It took perhaps thirty seconds from the sound of the silencer coughing to the last of my host slipping out of sight. Roeschler straightened his coat, sat back down on the couch, and I saw the tip of his cigar flare in the darkness. I couldn't swallow, I couldn't blink, I felt my eyes drying out and I couldn't remember how to make a sound. But I didn't want to make a sound. I stood paralyzed, leaning against the tapestry, the dying boar's golden eyes peering into my own.

Roeschler came up the stairway toward me. I smelled the cigar. He stopped beside me and looked into my eyes. We might have been alone in the world; the wind howled beyond the high window where Brendel rested.

"You saw?" he asked quietly.

I nodded.

"It had to be done. There were a great many reasons. There was revenge, for one thing. He had used me for a very long time, had blackmailed me for such a long time that he thought I was his friend—and I was, I was his friend until the time came when I could turn on him and my hate was stronger than our friendship."

"You don't have to explain to me," I said. My tongue had turned dry, sticky.

"Well, there's something you should know. I didn't simply decide to kill him on my own. It wasn't murder —a fine distinction. . . ." We had turned at the railing where Brendel had stood, steadying himself. "It was an assassination. Do you understand?"

I shook my head blankly.

"I am Ivor Steynes' man in Munich, Mr. Cooper. I had my orders, he told me to expect you and told me to help you." He inspected his cigar carefully before going on. "He made it clear to me that I was to reveal my identity only after the mission was completed." He sighed. "Now I feel much better. But I'm afraid we have a long night ahead of us. We must be very careful."

Roeschler. . . . We had never had the slightest chance of protecting Brendel: everyone always knew so much more than we did, we were always floundering, groping, playing fools.

"Cheer up," Roeschler rumbled. "It's not so bad— you could be an old man like me, nothing left to fear, but little left to live for." My mind was rewinding like a tape recorder and I heard St. John telling me that I'd miss so little if I died before morning. Everyone was so philosophical about my death.

"Your friend Peterson—he's downstairs. He was watching me for a while as if he expected me to suffer a stroke imminently. Go and get him, Mr. Cooper, and bring him to Lise's room."

"They just had a fight. I heard it—I was in the bathroom."

"I know, he told me. He was distraught. In a way, he wanted to die just then. He really loved her, you know. Now I'm going to go speak to her, tell her what has happened." He stopped on the verge of moving away. "You do understand that Steynes was right, that Brendel had to be stopped—"

"Stopped from what?"

"I'm not absolutely certain, Mr. Cooper. But something is about to happen, something very . . . important. I don't know if this will affect it, but it won't help it. Now, I must see to Lise."

Alone on the landing I felt faint and was drawn ghoulishly to the couch; what if he were still alive? I couldn't help it. I knelt on the couch and leaned over the back. Brendel's remains lay unnaturally bent, barely visible in the darkness, no vista of blood and brains, just a lump of dinner clothes.

"What in the name of God are you doing? Puking in the windowseat?"

It was Peterson. It was always Peterson at times like those.

He peered over the back of the couch.

"Oh, God," he whispered at last. "There's a body back there. . . ."

"Our host," I said. "Steynes' man got to him about fifteen minutes ago. I watched it happen."

Peterson looked at the body again. "Who killed him?"

"Roeschler."

"He was Steynes' man?" Incredulous, the realization dawning painfully.

"Yes. He told me."

"And he shot him here on the couch?"

I nodded. "Well, son of a bitch," he whispered.

"He's upstairs now with Lise. He sent me to find you and bring you up."

"And I naturally discover you with another stiff." He sighed at length. "Well, I guess we'd better go see him, then. But I'm beginning to wish this thing would stop moving for a minute." He jerked his compact little head at the couch. "Christ, nobody's going to find him till they nose him on the stair, right? That's *Hamlet,* Cooper, a literary allusion."

He started off up the stairs, teeth bared like Bogart in the old days.

Lise was standing before her dressing table mirror. I could still smell the vomit but it was losing ground to her perfume. A wet towel lay at her feet. Roeschler sat in a wicker chair. We stood in the doorway. Nobody moved, the wind scraped at the windows.

She was wearing slacks and a brassiere, the strap narrow and white across her thin, fragile back. She reached down, picked up a sweater, and slid it over her head, rolled the turtleneck beneath her chin. Her black hair lay like a dead rat on the rumpled bed. Her black dress was wadded up and thrown halfway into a wastebasket. She ran a long comb slowly through her own hair, which hung limply shielding her face.

She finally turned. She had changed back into the woman I'd met in the park. Her gray eyes connected with mine and she wet her dry lips, spoke as if she were dehydrated. Her voice was furry.

"Hello, John." She looked around the room at the mess and shrugged helplessly. "I don't know what to—" She swallowed dryly, produced a clicking sound. "I'm sorry about—" She shrugged and picked up the towel and walked very slowly, one hand out to touch bits of furniture for balance, toward the bathroom with it. I smelled it as she went past me: Brendel had said it suited her, his last words to his wife. Her face was terribly pale, her lower lip split at its center, her nose cut across the bridge where he'd hit her. Her breath whistled unhealthily in her clogged nasal passages. She said, "Excuse me," as she pushed slowly past Peterson. She went into the bathroom and left the door open a few inches.

"Did you tell her?" I asked.

"I gave her an injection, a very strong tranquilizer," Roeschler said. "I told her that Brendel was dead, that's enough for now. She's very sedated, really sleepwalking, but the fact is registering in her brain right now—but she's much too exhausted to react." He stood up and looked out the window. "She's fully aware of severe changes and the tranquilizer will allow her to go along with whatever we must do yet this evening."

"Will she stay awake?" Peterson was stroking his mustache.

"As long as we keep her awake, yes. She's had a great ingestion of chemicals in the past twelve hours or so, getting herself speeded up to handle the stress of the party. Oh, she brings it on herself, setting up confrontations between all the concerned parties, utterly self-destructive, egocentric, not caring who gets hurt as long as she satisfies her own curiosity." He saw our disconcerted expressions, and turned back to the window, spreading the curtains. "It's so complex . . . but you must try to understand that she is not like the rest of us, that she is obsessed by her own identity. Or lack of it. The result is that she is unpredictable—or that all you can predict is her inconsistency, her lack of concern for the consequences of her acts. She really doesn't see anything particularly wrong with what she does. She has no self-pity." He finally turned back and blew his nose. "But she has no pity for anyone else either. She just doesn't give a damn about anything but finding out what in the world is the point of her own existence. It's still snowing outside, gentlemen, and we've got to get you out of here."

"I don't give a damn how crazy she is," Peterson growled, "she's coming with us. Finding their master stuffed behind the couch is going to make some of these people very angry. There's always the chance that his wife will be some kind of insurance for us. She's valuable to both sides, Brendel's and Siegfried's, right?"

"Oh, yes, she's valuable. She has her protectors. You're right in wanting to take her with you. And what's kidnapping compared to your other crimes?"

"Which crimes are those?"

Roeschler smiled bleakly. "The murder of your host, for one. They're obviously going to hold you responsible for that. They certainly won't think I did it, will they?"

"So, the crazy lady comes with us, then," Peterson said.

"I'm not crazy, Mr. Peterson." She was leaning

heavily in the doorway. "I'm terribly tired but I'm not crazy."

I led her across to a chair. "Thank you, John." Her eyes were closed, her face battered, the words forced their way past her puffed, dry lips. She folded her hands in her lap, her lashes fluttered. I stood beside her, watching her. She leaned back in the chair, breathing with difficulty. Peterson and Roeschler were conferring quietly across the room.

"Could I have some water . . . John, please, some water." She opened her eyes but couldn't focus properly. She touched her breast again, as if seeking proof that she was still there. I held the glass to the cut lip but she didn't open her mouth and it ran down her chin. I held a tissue to her, soaking it up, covered my fingers with water, and moistened her split, parched lip. She was almost out. I remembered the touch of her mouth in the park, the snow drifting down on her face.

Peterson was standing over us, impatient.

"We're going out now," he said. "The four of us are going down the stairway, across the foyer, and out the front door. Roeschler says he can get us past the storm troopers at the door. If he can't a lot of people are going to get hurt. But crazypants here is coming along like the hostages in the movies. She's our ticket out of the madhouse. Now get her up and let's haul ass." He went to the door and looked into the hallway.

Roeschler brought a sheepskin coat from a closet for Lise. "We've got to keep her warm," he said. "She has no resistance to anything right now."

Peterson came back, snapping his fingers.

"Let's go, let's go and get this over with. Thank God for the candles, no one will really notice her face—Christ, she looks like she just went through fifteen minutes with the Swedish Angel. Roeschler, you get our coats, we can't go tear-assing out into a blizzard without our coats."

We went down the stairway like Cary Grant and Ingrid Bergman in *Notorious*. Peterson was in the lead, Roeschler at the rear, and he veered off to get the coats while we moved along the wall beneath the candles. We stopped well short of the door. They were there, blocking our exit. Siegfried stood with them, watching us, his blond hair dulled in the gloom. People moved sluggishly on all sides, laughing and chatting wearily, queuing up for their wraps. It was almost one o'clock.

Roeschler loomed up with coats. He helped me on with mine, trying to camouflage Lise's indisposition. We wedged her between us as I struggled into the sleeve. I smelled her perfume again in the close, hot crowd. Peterson got into his coat and turned to Roeschler.

"Okay, do it," he said and Roeschler took the lead as we moved toward the door.

Siegfried finally made a move, bypassing Roeschler and confronting me and Lise.

"Where are you going, Lise? Where is Gunter?" His voice was too high. "You are not to leave," he said to me.

Roeschler was at the door talking with the oversized palace guard. They were listening. He gestured back to us and looked worried and the men looked our way, too. One shook his head, frowning. Peterson kept pushing us forward, pushing us into Siegfried, who was also looking very worried.

"You must not leave," he said. He was becoming shrill and an elderly couple turned, taking notice with arched eyebrows. "Lise," he said insistently. "Where is Gunter?"

Peterson had had enough. He reached around and grabbed at Siegfried's waistcoat, his hand out of sight, and yanked him tight against us, smiling into the matinee idol face.

"Get lost," he said. "Understand? Just go away. We're leaving. She's coming with us and if there's any problem your balls will be the very first casualty."

Peterson shoved hard below eye level and Siegfried stepped back, mouth open, gasping.

We were at the door and Roeschler turned, confusion on his strong features. It wasn't working. The guards weren't buying it. We stood staring at an impasse.

"Do these people understand English?" Peterson asked.

Roeschler nodded. Siegfried stood with his back to the wall deciding if foolish bravery were required; no one knew quite what was happening. Except Peterson.

"I'll negotiate," he said. We were knotted closer, Peterson staring at the Adam's apples of the three men who didn't want us to leave. I heard every word because he was speaking very slowly.

"If we don't go out that door four people are going to die in about two seconds. First, my friend here"— he indicated me—"is going to kill Frau Brendel. While he's doing that I'm going to kill all three of you. Bang. Bang. Bang. I've got nothing to lose. You can buy back your lives by letting us out the door. You follow us—and the nice lady dies anyway."

The three impassive faces stared ahead at Peterson. "It's up to you."

Peterson motioned to me to go through the door. He was right. We were out of alternatives and I was glad. I walked Lise to the door. Roeschler opened it. Outside it was cold and white and clean and I didn't look back.

Lise turned her face toward me and shielded herself from the blowing snow. It was slippery and we took tiny, cautious steps. I didn't know what was happening behind us, I just kept walking the length of the way to the parking lot. Where the hell was the car?

I looked back at last. Roeschler, Peterson, and the three men were behind us, the three being marched along between. Snow was covering their dreary black suits. They didn't know what to do.

The parking attendants took a step toward our procession and stopped. Peterson smiled as he reached them, dangled his keys, and said, "It's all right, I've got the keys. It's the first car." He called to me as they went back to their shelter and cigarettes, ignoring us: "Cooper, over there, to your left, first in the rank."

The seven of us, including the three coatless and shivering men, stood by the car while Peterson unlocked the front and back doors. The lights popped on inside. When he turned back to us he was holding a gun with a bulbous canister on the end of the barrel.

"Okay, Roeschler, get in back, move it." Roeschler hunched clumsily in the back seat.

"Cooper, load her in next to him." Peterson's gun steadied against the three men, who moved from foot to foot, rubbed their white hands. "If you follow us, if you do any goddamned thing in the world to interfere with us, Frau Brendel dies. Do you understand?"

They nodded in unison.

"This is not what you think it is," Peterson said. "Before you make a terrible mistake, find Herr Brendel. When you find him, then ask him what to do—Herr Brendel will explain the whole thing to you. Have you got that? Now, come on, give me a great big smile. Come on, let's all smile together." He motioned with the gun. "Smile. I'm going to smile." He gave them the bared teeth, wolflike.

Finally they smiled, teeth chattering.

Peterson cuffed one on the shoulder, comradely.

I climbed in, slipping on the ice and snow, grabbing the door for support. He slammed the door. I pressed the button to lower the window. Peterson was enjoying himself.

He handed me the gun. "Hold it in your left hand, rest it on the window. They're going to wave bye-byes." He moved gingerly around the front of the car, slid in behind the wheel, and started the engine. Bending toward me, he flapped a hand at them.

They were backing away, waving.

"Fucking Katzenjammer Kids," he said. "You gotta have a good time, it keeps you from realizing what you're doing." He chortled in the dark. "There's a paper bag on the seat, Cooper. Reach in and get me a sucker." He sighed heavily. "Go ahead, take one for yourself. Celebrate."

As we drove back into Munich, Roeschler explained to us what lay ahead. First, the death of Brendel would go undiscovered for at least a few hours, enough time for us to make our getaway—the same escape route he had provided for my brother. It entailed a drive southward and on up through the Alps to a schloss well out of the way.

Second, no guilt must attach to Roeschler. After apparently killing Brendel, we kidnapped him to make good our escape. The following morning, his house-keeper would find him roped to his bed.

Third, we would remain at the mountain retreat until he got word to us.

"As to the rest of their movement," Roeschler went on, "I simply can't be sure. Brendel's death will confuse them—momentarily. They took their orders from him but he was like any other leader. Replaceable. Alfried Kottmann may assume leadership or, and this is the problem, Siegfried may make his move." He sniffed in the cold and blew his nose. The headlights poked warily into the billowing clouds of snow. "Siegfried is difficult to evaluate—he is a mercurial young man, but is he a dilettante or does he have real strength behind him? What kind of money does he have access to? Surely not the Madrid sources. I doubt if it will stand up now that Brendel is dead. Without Brendel, Siegfried may find life's realities a bit harsher than he expected. I'm rather worried about Siegfried's reaction to all this."

"What do you mean?"

"I expect he will add up his situation and see that the connection to Brendel was his main pillar of support. Which may turn him to a last resort, namely, Frau Brendel, the widow of the great man. He may or may not have feelings for her—he is a very modern fellow, whether or not he has feelings at all I cannot even guess—but he may choose to make her a symbol. If he can recover her, he may feel he can reestablish his role. He knows that Kottmann has no time for him and St. John is in Kottmann's camp, the sly old bastard.

"They may try to get rid of Siegfried themselves. They may want to shore up the situation and stay on schedule, forget Lise and erase Siegfried. After all, what do you need either of them for? They've got their timetable and men die—but timetables are made to be kept. Siegfried may realize they are his natural enemies. If he does, he'll either go underground or try to recover Lise and pose as the hero, the new Siegfried Germany has been waiting for." He sneezed, trying to muffle it.

Peterson found the narrow street and Roeschler directed him to a side street, intersecting an alley which ran behind his house. Lise stumbled groggily, but made it down the slender thread of snow and into Roeschler's warm, sweet-smelling kitchen. She mumbled distantly, tears welled in pink corners of her eyes, and I touched her hair in a frail attempt to comfort her. Peterson was watching me grimly. There was blood caked beneath her nostrils and speckles on the white fleece lining of the coat. I sat down, hungry and tired, my eyes burning, and watched her.

I must have dozed. Peterson was shaking my shoulder.

"Come on, John. We've changed license plates on the car. Now we're just another black Mercedes. But we've got to get moving. We're not safe here." He was pulling on his gloves. "Everything's in the car. All the bags, everything. It's all taken care of."

Lise had slumped across the table and Roeschler was getting her ready to go. The room smelled of coffee. Peterson slopped brandy into a mug and shoved it at me. I sipped it and it burned my tongue.

"Good-bye, Mr. Cooper," Roeschler said, shaking my hand firmly. He bowed slightly, dignity about him like a cape.

Peterson handed me the keys to the Mercedes.

"Take your sister"—he grimaced at that—"take that crazypants with you." He followed Roeschler out of the kitchen. I heard them on the stair.

I put her in the back seat and started the car, got the heater switch into the On position, got back out, and slid in beside her. She leaned against me. Helpless, reduced to her simplest animal self. I put my arm around her. But when I tried to think about her, the masks she wore, I kept seeing Roeschler pressing the silencer to Brendel's head.

I heard Peterson stomping down the steps into the snow. He got in and peered back at us. "Okay," he said. "We go."

We stopped in Bad Tolz at something past four in the morning. It was dark and the snow was fine and dry, whipped down the empty streets by a sharp wind. The houses were gabled and painted brightly but there was little light of any kind and no movement. We got out to stretch, left Lise in the snug rear seat. Peterson clenched and unclenched his hands.

The cold felt good. We sheltered in a doorway.

"How did you get us out of Brendel's house?" I asked.

He brushed the snow out of his mustache and turned up his coat collar. Snow blew down the street in clouds, like ghosts.

"It's a matter of leverage more than anything else. It was more important to us to get out than it was to the goon squad to keep us there. Now the goons, they were supposed to keep us there, but if we told them they might die trying to keep us there, their choice became one of choosing to let us go and living for sure or keeping us there and maybe dying." He snuffled and clapped his hands for circulation. "Now you give a man that kind of choice between living and dying and most of the time he'll choose to live. The leverage, of course, is the guns. You've always got to be able to back up your threats. If we'd said, let us out of here or we'll beat on you with our tiny fists, forget it. They'd have fed us to the dog for breakfast."

He pointed the Mercedes on through the town, which was nothing but a blur behind the snow.

"Roeschler's map says we angle off this main road and head back up into the mountains. We stop short of Austria but we get pretty well hidden in the Alps. We're about halfway there. The place we're going, this schloss, belongs to Brendel and it's deserted now. Roeschler says there's a tiny village where the road becomes impassable and a man named Lindt will take us the rest of the way."

Light comes quickly to the Alps, even the gray blur of that morning with the fir trees like black cones and the snow banked higher than the top of the Mercedes. It comes up out of Russia and the East and unaware the world takes shape, even the blunted gray-white crags and the endless towers of snow and tree and rock fading, disappearing in the snowstorms high in the mountain passes.

There were road signs posted frequently, jutting out of the snow, barely visible.

Frostschaden

Schlechte Wegstrecke
Verengte Fahrbahm

We were somewhere between Bad Tolz and Garmisch, where they do all the skiing. By the looks of it outside I couldn't believe anyone would be out skiing. It would have been so simple to simply glide off into the snow and be gone forever.

A small castle, stubby and squat, rose up quickly like an apparition and Peterson said, sighing with evident relief, "That's it. We're here." He pitched a sucker out the window and slid the car to a quivering halt before the largest of several smallish structures clustered around the foot of the castle.

He hurried off to knock on the door with all the gingerbread around its frame. It opened immediately and he ducked inside.

I woke Lise, who came to like a child, rubbing her eyes with her fists and moaning in a tiny voice. For an instant there was a glint of terror in her eyes, then she recognized me.

"John," she said slowly, as if learning again how to control her tongue, "I have to use the toilet, please."

I helped her up to the doorway and pushed inside. Peterson was talking with a gray-haired, gray-bearded man of fifty or so who wore a red-and-black checked shirt. Wind whistled in a large, blackened fireplace where coals smoked. Lise went away.

"Herr Lindt is ready to take us to the schloss. He says the snowmobiles have been rented but that we will be much warmer and more comfortable in the sleigh. I said okay. We couldn't keep crazypants on a snowmobile anyway."

Lise came back and Peterson went to the bathroom. Lise took my hand and held it to her face, smiling.

Lindt threw a log on the kitchen fire. She drank coffee from a huge chipped mug. Lindt went outside to ready the sleigh. Peterson came back and I went to the bathroom. I wondered if she even remembered that her husband was dead. The monster of the night had turned into Goldilocks and the problem was I wanted to hold her and kiss her.

Someone pounded on the door.

"Get your ass out here," Peterson said. "It's time.

Donner and Blitzen and Cupid are chomping at the bit."

Peterson rode in front with Lindt. Lise and I burrowed in back beneath blankets which covered our faces. We could hear the horses snorting and the runners hissing and the wind moving on the crust. Her hair was in my face and she turned her face up, her cheeks fresh and dark glasses over the mouse by her eye. She grinned. Her mouth was wide and impudent. I kissed her. Her mouth didn't move, she didn't kiss me back, and I knew I was making an awful mistake.

I don't know how many times I pressed my mouth to hers, how many times I wanted her to respond. But she didn't and I kept touching her face with my lips, the scab on her lip, the marks where she'd been struck, the snow on her forehead.

The sleigh finally stopped and I heard Lindt and Peterson get down, puffing, staggering in the snow. Peterson opened the tiny door for us to climb down and he went off with Lindt. The schloss had a balcony and looked like something from a guidebook. I stood up and saw an incredible panorama stretching below, beyond the line of fir trees. Far below, with the sun glinting on gray ice and snow, lay a lake. Great tufts of snow and fog hung above it but there it was, miles away and a long way below, huddled among the mountains like a picture from a jigsaw puzzle box, and it occurred to me that Gunter Brendel would never see it again.

I pulled Lise up and she saw what I saw. She shrugged and lowered her eyes.

"But am I your sister, John?"

A fire blazed in the grate. The stone fireplace took up half of an entire wall and heated the large room. The electric lights didn't work. Lindt was carrying logs in from a shed outside and Peterson had opened several cans of stew and canned brown bread. He was doing the cooking on the stove, which drew propane from tanks. The house was warm enough to shuck our coats. Lise was curled on a couch before the large fire, her sheepskin coat thrown across her lap and legs, a brandy snifter in her right hand. Lindt began carrying logs up to the bedroom, which opened onto the balcony circling the main room on three sides. It was very hard to believe it was anything but a vacation.

Peterson heard me come in and spoke without turning to look at me.

"Delicacy is not my strong suit, Cooper. You know that by now, right? Right?"

"Sure. You're insensitive. It's too bad but you have other good qualities."

"So let me get it right out there. The lady you've been necking with has two big strikes on her for sure, before you even start looking at her hard. One, she may be your sister. Two, she is a nut case. Am I right?"

"The question is, is it any of your business?"

He plunged a long wooden spoon into the pot on the stove.

"Nobody likes a smartass, Cooper." He dropped the spoon on the stove and ground pepper from a mill into the pot. "So I'm suggesting, man to man, that you think twice before messing around with the widder lady. That's all." He turned and looked at me. "I'm talking to you as a friend. I guess I've come to think of you as a friend of mine. I just think you should leave her alone. Treat her like the sister you thought she was. That's all. Otherwise, she's all trouble, and a mile wide."

"Look, I'm having a hard time handling this—it wasn't what I meant to do."

"She can make it worse for you, believe me."

"What if I said I just can't help it?"

"I'd understand that and I'd be sorry. Because right now, regardless of what she means to you, she's dead last on my list of priorities." He sighed and rubbed his stubble of beard. "And you're a nice guy, an innocent. I want to see you come out the other end of this nightmare. I don't care if she makes it through the afternoon."

Lise came to the kitchen table and the three of us sat like deaf and dumb mountain dwellers, scraping the bottoms of our bowls.

Lise fell asleep on the couch in the afternoon. I sat in a deep chair watching her for a while, wondering where her mind was, remembering that I'd seen her husband die quite violently only a bit over twelve hours before. The fire was warm and the party seemed a long time ago, acted out by another cast altogether.

Peterson went upstairs after our lunch and was gone an hour. When he came back down his face was freshly shaven and his mustache was trimmed. He wore a heavy turtleneck sweater and Levis, all from the bags which Lindt had dutifully loaded onto the sleigh from the trunk of the Mercedes. He looked reasonably fresh and he was carrying two rifles from a case on the balcony. Both were mounted with telescopic sights and rested over one forearm. In his hand was a large box of ammunition. He sat down at a long trestle table behind the long couch where Lise slept and laid the rifles lengthwise. He began to play with them but I didn't want to know why.

It was dark when I woke up. Lise lay on her side asleep, her mouth slightly open, an arm jutting outward from the couch toward the fire. The rifles lay on the table.

He looked up when I went back to the kitchen.

"Stew," he said. "Brendel must have loved stew. There's enough in the cupboard to feed the entire Fourth Reich." He tossed the corkscrew to me. "Open another bottle."

"What about Lise?"

"Let her sleep."

We ate quietly, exhaustion everywhere. Peterson had developed a low cough and had a row of pills arranged on the tabletop.

"Can I take these with wine, do you think?" He picked them up, rolled them in his palm like dice. "Roeschler gave them to me for my throat and cold and incipient pneumonia."

Later, we took a bowl of stew to Lise and the three of us sat in the firelight talking. He was quite civil to her and she seemed reasonable if impersonal. We were all tired and said nothing of the events of the previous evening. Less than twenty-four house before, Peterson and I were setting off for the party.

Peterson and I smoked cigars and drank Brendel's port and stared sleepily into the fire. Finally Lise took a candle and said goodnight, climbed the stairs, and disappeared into one of the bedrooms. I watched her go.

"How long do you think we'll have to wait?" I asked.

Peterson shrugged. "I don't know. Tomorrow, the next day. There may not even be a way to reach us. It would be easier to say if I knew who to trust."

"What do you mean? We're the good guys, they're the bad guys."

"But who's who? All we know is what people tell us. St. John told you things, Kottmann told you things, Alistair Campbell and Ivor Steynes and Roeschler and Lise—they've all told us things. But who the hell knows what's true? We keep hearing about things, a plan, coming to a head. Money in Madrid. Magical submarines, plans to take over the world, a group of conspirators called the Spider.

"What I want to know is just this: If this is so god-damned big and powerful and menacing, why hasn't someone else, the CIA or the Russians or somebody, discovered it and stopped it? Why Cyril? Why us? We're accidents, Cooper, not spies. We weren't looking for any of this, we stumbled into it. I'm beginning to wish we could just stumble on out. But they won't let us. It's all very strange. An accident."

"Maybe that's the explanation. Accident. It's hard to prepare for accidents."

"Sure, sure. We may have penetrated by accident. But why the hell didn't they just kill you? Or us?" A log fell, sprinkling sparks on the hearth.

"Somebody up there likes us."

Wind ate away at chinks in the chimney.

"I think you've got it," Peterson said. "Somebody somewhere is watching over us."

It was pitch-dark when I opened my eyes. Someone was speaking to me but I couldn't make sense of it. The square window took shape, the fire took glowing form, the smell of the smoldering embers made sense, jogged my memory. I looked up at the figure leaning over me, the hair draping down. It was Lise. She was speaking German, her voice edging toward hysteria.

She was wearing the sheepskin coat. It hung open, the lining brushing my face.

"What's the matter?"

She shivered. Her legs were bare. She pulled the coat tight.

"I woke up, all alone. I didn't know where I was. I called for Gunter, then I realized I was alone, and I began to cry. I didn't know where anybody was and I thought I heard someone outside." She sniffled. "I was thinking about Gunter. Is he all right? Someone told me he was dead, maybe in my dream. I'm so confused, I'm so tired. I woke up thinking he was dead and then I couldn't remember how I got here. Someone had hit me, Gunter I think, and then someone told me he was dead—" She peered at me.

I lit a match on the bedside table and fired the stubby candle I'd brought with me from the kitchen. She was covered with goosepimples, her arms, her legs.

"Where is he? Please . . . John."

"He's dead, Lise. He was killed at your party."

"Your brother is dead, too. Isn't he?"

"Yes, he's dead, too."

"What are we going to do?"

"I don't know."

She sniffled again and touched her lip.

"Who cares, anyway? Do you know?"

"When I found my brother dead, I cared then. And then, each time someone else died, maybe I didn't care quite so much. Now I don't know . . . I cared about finding you."

She looked at me. Her eyes were wide, remote, vacant.

"I had to find you," I said. "If you were my sister it was worth anything and I just wouldn't stop looking until I found you." I reached out and took her hand. Christ, who was she?

"Why?" she asked tonelessly, her hand limp and cold. "I don't know who I am, I don't know why I'm here, my husband is dead." She slumped inside the heavy coat. "You kissed me in the sleigh. . . . And was it all worth it?"

"I don't know."

"Are you glad you found me?"

"I don't know."

"Why did you do it? What was the point?"

"My brother was dead. And he had your photograph."

"So was it worth it?"

"Are you my sister?"

There were tears on her cheeks, like icicles. "Maybe I never knew—"

"If you are, it was worth it."

"Why would you kiss your sister that way?" She was watching the candle's twitching flame.

"I couldn't help it, that's all."

"Do you want to make love to me, then?"

"Yes . . . I don't know, Lise."

She pulled back the comforter and got into bed, lay straight beside me. She was ice-cold, quaking, rigid. There was no desire in me. I looked at her face, white, stark, staring at the ceiling. Her eyes were open, fixed like something in marble. She lay like a corpse, unnerving, inanimate. I leaned across her, felt her bare leg next to me, felt her breath on my neck. I blew out the candle. What a waste it all was. I kissed her cold, dead lips. I put my hand on her thighs, felt the smoothness and the wiry hair between her legs. A tremor shook her body.

"You were right," I said at last.

"What do you mean?" She spoke to me from some other place.

"It doesn't make any sense."

We slept. We didn't touch. It was like being dead and knowing it, being awake in the box and hearing the dirt being shoveled in on top of you. I was too tired to cry out for help.

When I woke up it was still deep night. Lise was gone. I got up, put on pants and shirt, and sat by the fire, huddled inside the comforter. I wrapped it around me and went to the window. The clouds had broken and the moon dangled like a coin over the mountains. Snow blew noisily in the trees and stretched away unmarked. Below, past the trees, the lake lay like a second coin, a reflection of the first.

My Rolex said 5:10 and I was trying to get the chronology of the past thirty-six hours straight in my mind. Twenty-four hours ago we were driving away from Munich toward the mountains and Roeschler's housekeeper must have found him later that morning, say, twenty hours ago. Once they found him, what would have happened? Would the police have been notified of Brendel's violent death? Or would the Nazis have hushed it up, attributed it to natural causes, and arranged for a certificate of death from one of their own doctors—perhaps even Roeschler himself? The irony fit so beautifully. I smiled stupidly in the night, staring out my icy window. To think that Roeschler had been Colonel Steynes' man all along. Nothing was what it seemed, nothing from the very beginning. Not even my little sister Lee.

And now, what must be happening in Munich? I poked the coals, watched sparks flare and shower, threw another log on the fire. Even if the Munich police were not looking for us, Brendel's associates surely must have assumed we'd murdered their leader and kidnapped his widow; surely, they must be looking for us—we'd penetrated their operation and we were loose somewhere and they couldn't know what we planned to do. As long as they couldn't find us, they had to fear us.

At first I thought it was a log slipping in the grate, a rustle of bark. But it continued and it was coming from outside on the balcony overlooking the main room. There was a shuffling and a sob and I went to the door, listened again. Quiet. I opened the door an inch and it was shoved hard against me, the knob smashing into my stomach, the flat wood ramming against my face. I felt my nose erupt, blood gushing back through the tunnels into my throat and flowing down my upper lip. I slipped backward and fell on the hardwood floor, the edge of a chair taking a bite out of my back.

Siegfried Hauptmann was standing in the doorway, the dim light behind his golden hair. One of his arms was clamped around Lise, who was dressed in worn Levis and a denim shirt. Cradled in the other arm was a machine gun sort of thing with a stick clip of ammunition protruding below the barrel and a metal handle like a gunstock in outline with no wood. I touched my nose, trying to stop the blood.

"Up," he said, whispering, gesturing with the gun. "Stand up and shut up." Lise moaned and he yanked her tighter. "Please," he said to her. "Please, Lise, be quiet—" She sucked in her breath, her mouth shaking like a child's, fighting back the urge to whimper. I stood up on rubbery legs.

"Downstairs," he said.

I staggered out of the room. Candles were lit along the balcony railing and the fire downstairs was roaring and bright but the light died as it hurtled toward the corners of the room.

They followed me down the stairway and across to the fireplace.

"Sit down," he said. I sat on the couch and Lise crumpled into a large chair. She fumbled with a box of matches, lit a candle on the table beside her.

"Where is your friend?" His hands were shaking, the gun's muzzle fluttering in a rather terrifying manner.

"I don't know." I put my bloody hands on my knees and bent my head back the way my nanny had taught me in the nursery and the blood slowed to a trickle.

He put the machine gun down on the mantelpiece and took a pack of Camels from the inside pocket of his costume. He was wearing a silver snowmobile suit. He clicked a lighter and immediately inhaled, relaxing.

"It was all I could think of—this place. A possibility that she might bring you here if you took her with you. I drove as far as I could with the snowmobile on the rack behind. I left it in the trees and walked the rest of the way." He frowned dramatically, blew smoke out through his flared nostrils.

Lise got up and went to the kitchen. He watched her but made no move to stop her.

"What are you going to do?" I wanted to keep him talking. Where the hell was Peterson?

"You don't know what I've gone through since you left the party. They found Gunter's body in the morning, early, and I was still there. It's been awful—" He was letting himself lapse into a chatty mode. He was very female in some ways. "They got tough with me, as if the special relationship Gunter and I had built could be wiped away in an instant. They made it clear I was unwelcome—"

"They?"

"All the old ones, Kottmann, St. John, and those idiotic old medal-bearers, broken-down generals who lost a war . . . lost the world thirty years ago." He was boiling over, hate racketing inside his pipes. "Those greasy South Americans, all shiny black hair and gold braid. . . . Suddenly they were in charge and I was alone."

He shook the cigarette ash onto the floor and touched the gun reassuringly. Lise came back and hovered over me, standing behind the couch. She pressed a cold towel to my forehead.

"So what have you come here to do?" she asked coolly.

"I'm going to take you back. They'll listen to me if I bring you back." His voice betrayed him.

"You are an idiot," she snapped. "What do they care about me? Without Gunter what am I to them? Nothing. You have come all this way for nothing. Idiot!"

"You're wrong, Lise," he said, controlling himself. "You'll see. When I bring you back they'll have to think. My people are not insignificant. They'll see how much we can add to the movement. You'll see. . . ." He lit another Camel.

Lise leaned possessively on my shoulders. His eyes followed her hands, watched them touch my shoulders, narrowed.

"Why do you think I'd come back with you? What is there for me in Munich? My husband is dead, you are a ridiculous, posturing fairy . . . a complete waste, a mistake. . . ."

"You will come."

"I'm going with John, wherever he goes—" Her voice was growing shrill: she was grasping, playing another game, using me. Siegfried walked back to the mantelpiece and stood looking into the flames. She wheeled and went to stand behind him. "Go away. Leave us alone. Face all the other pederasts alone." And she went on in German, her hands up clawing at his back.

He turned without a word and slammed the machine gun into her side, cutting off her breath, cracking the metal against her rib cage. His face was blank as she

[315]

dropped to the floor, gagging, mouth gaping. He was fumbling for the trigger, trying to turn the gun around: he was going to shoot her. I threw myself forward buckling his legs from behind, dropping him to his knees with a cry as his kneecap hit the edge of the slate hearth. The gun swung around, the barrel scraped across my nose, and the tears brimmed over, blurring my vision. The front door flew open as we lay near the fire and I heard Peterson begin to laugh.

I lay on my back, half across Siegfried. Lise lay sobbing a few feet away. Peterson looked benignly down.

"Amateur night," he said. Siegfried tried to right himself. Peterson kicked him in the crotch, swiftly and economically, and he curled into a shrimplike crescent, saliva foaming a few inches from my face. Peterson kicked him again and the eyes floated back in their sockets, showing nothing but whites, and then they closed and the head lolled against the slate.

Peterson reached down and pulled me up.

"You've got a bloody nose," he said. He bent over Lise. "Are you all right?" he asked briskly.

She tried to sit up and winced, her face gray and pinched at the corners of her eyes. "It hurts." I knelt beside her.

"Leave her alone," he snapped. "She's probably got a cracked rib from this slimy little shit I've just turned into a soprano. Just let her lie there. She'll get up when she has to go to the toilet." He picked up the wet towel and threw it to her.

"Thank you," she moaned.

Peterson ignored her.

"Where were you?"

"Outside freezing my ass. I saw this idiot coming across the snow from the woods. He was carrying the gun like a bottle of champagne. I went outside and waited because I wanted to find out what he had on his mind—I listened at the door, but my God, he was so slow." He regarded the slowly reviving victim of his boot. "Creep," he muttered.

Siegfried cupped his crotch tentatively, dragged himself into a sitting position. Peterson approached and he flinched, cowering near the fire. Lise said: "Don't kick him again."

"Shut your goddamn mouth. You've got problems of your own. This asshole's past worrying about."

He reached down and yanked Siegfried to his feet like a man jerking weights. Siegfried hung forward over his groin. Peterson took a handful of the gold hair and dragged him to the couch and dropped him. Tears poured down the weak, pretty face. The matinee idol was aging fast.

"What do you want?" Peterson asked.

"Lise," he gasped. "I'll make a deal. Give me Lise and I won't tell them you're here. You'll get away—"

"What deal? You're the one sitting here holding your nuts, not me. You're crazy. Here's the deal and listen hard. You tell us what's going on in Munich and maybe I won't kill you—how's that for a deal?"

Peterson went into the kitchen. We waited. Finally he came back.

"Are they looking for us?"

"I don't know."

"Are they sending men out to look for us?"

"I don't know."

Peterson took Siegfried's hand in his own and turned it palm up. His other hand slid across the palm and Siegfried drew back, sucked his breath in. A paring knife had sliced a deep, straight line across the open palm and it was turning a rich, thick red. I stood up, holding on to the arm of the couch. Lise watched with horror-stricken eyes. Blood welled in the creases of his palm.

"Are they sending men to find us? Were you followed, Siegfried?" Peterson was speaking patiently. I was in enough pain to keep me from worrying too much about Lise's ribs or Siegfried's flesh wound. After all, that's what it was. It just looked so awful and he'd done it so calmly.

"Well, now," Peterson was saying, "what else? Who is taking Herr Brendel's place?"

"Kottmann, I think," Siegfried croaked. His hand was covered with blood. When I got close I could smell it.

"And what about your own happy band—"

"Kottmann and his people, they're trying to force us out."

"I daresay that shows good judgment."

"You don't understand."

"And you wanted to take Frau Brendel back with you, a trophy, to prove what serious fellows you all are." He shook his head. "God, how dreary."

He went back into the kitchen. I followed. Peterson was making coffee.

"It all gets so messy," he said. "There's no point in trying to keep it clean because it always gets messy, like this." He put cups on the counter. "People are so fragile."

"Everybody but you," I said.

"Ah, me. I'm a predator."

Peterson tied Siegfried's hands behind him and stretched him out on the couch. We all went to sleep after we had our coffee. It was past seven. I woke up at a sound: Peterson's eyes were open and he was watching Siegfried, who had gotten up, hands still trussed behind him, blood caked on his silver suit, and was pulling the front door open.

Peterson put his finger to his lips. Siegfried got the door open and lurched out. We got up and went to the door. He was moving away, staggering in the deep snow, breaking clumsily through the crust. With his hands tied behind him he was finding balance difficult to maintain. The sun was shining somewhere behind the gray clouds and his silver suit reflected what little of the sun that seeped through. He shone like a new toy soldier, an astronaut on the surface of another world. He was drifting toward the cover of trees. He fell several times, thrashed about on his knees like a wounded beast, struggled on. We watched until he made the trees and was obscured by the shadows and the windblown snow which hung everywhere in wisps.

"Let him go. He'll come wandering back. No way he can get his hands loose, poor bastard." He yawned and stretched his arms high. "I'm too damn tired to go running after him."

He went in and stood looking down at Lise.

"She's been through a lot," I said.

"She thrives on it," he said sourly. "She loves it. Beat her up, break her ribs, give her an eyeful of some

[318]

good clean sadism. Keeps her mind occupied. She'd adore the death of a thousand cuts."

"Why don't you shut up."

"Did you screw her?"

"Does it make any difference?"

"Hard to say anymore." He paced to the far wall, peered at the contents of a huge built-in bookcase, ran his finger along the shelf, gathering dust. He picked out a thick, worn volume and blew dust from its spine. "Freud. Freud would have loved you and Lise. A field day for the old boy."

"Bullshit," I said.

"My God, you're a monster." Lise was awake.

"Oh, look who's awake. How are you, crazypants?"

"John, make him be quiet." She straightened up painfully.

"Which game is it now?" he asked. "Shall we play John off against Olaf? You bore me, madam. You're a tedious neurotic woman who may or may not be old Cooper's sister. I have ceased to give a damn one way or the other." He came back and dropped the book in her lap. "I just want to get rid of you." He pointed to the book. "Read it. Kill some time."

He went upstairs.

"Fucking monster," she said and began to cry. She needed her pills, uppers or downers or a little hemlock, something. "My husband is dead. He cut Siegfried with a knife. I'm hurt, John, my side hurts, something is hurting inside."

In the afternoon it had begun to snow again and the wind was up, blowing down from the top of the mountains.

Lise was sitting by the kitchen fire smoking a cigarette. She was looking into the fire, her face blank, empty.

"Well, we'd better go look for him," Peterson said. "If he's out there when it gets dark he may not be able to get back."

We put on Brendel's sweaters, got into our coats, wrapped mufflers over our mouths and noses. Snow cut at our eyes, burned any exposed skin. I could hear Peterson swearing. We slogged off toward the trees where we'd last seen Siegfried. It was getting dark quickly and trying to move fast left us wheezing and sweating by the time we reached the treeline.

It didn't take long to find the snowmobile, but Siegfried wasn't with it. It sat drifted under, a handlebar sticking out. Any tracks he might have left were filled in by the wind.

The next thing we found wasn't Siegfried.

Twenty yards farther on in the trees there were three more snowmobiles parked in a row, faintly dusted with powdery snow. It was too dark and the woods were full of people.

Peterson tugged at his muffler, pulled it away from his mouth.

"I think we just lost the game," he said. "I didn't hear them." He watched the three snowmobiles intently as if he expected them to make a break for it. He kicked the closest one and turned his back on it in frustration.

Moving through the dark trees, with the sun gone behind the mountains, we found Siegfried.

Peterson tripped over him. His hands were still tied behind him. He was frozen in a kneeling position. Peterson tipped him over like a big stuffed animal and he moved in a piece, stiff, a once-human ice cube. Peterson flicked a match with his thumbnail and cupped it close to Siegfried's head. The back of it was gone: the coup de grace. "An execution," he said.

They were waiting for us. Their snowmobile suits were thrown across the long table behind the couch and a huge khaki dufflebag stood on the floor. Three men, sturdy, fair, square-jawed, even-voiced, very proper. They were waiting quietly, chatting among themselves. Lise sat in her big chair, remote and pale, not looking well.

One of the men, short-haired, blue-eyed, stood up when we came in. He waited while we got our coats off.

"Good evening," he said. "You'll be wanting some brandy." One of the other men handed us each a snifter. "Please sit down." We sat down.

The first man, who seemed somewhat older, took

a pipe out of his hip pocket and smoothed an oilskin pouch on the table. He filled the pipe methodically and struck a match, sucked it into life. Once he got it going he used it to gesture like a self-conscious professor. They all looked like astronauts, the same prefabricated faces, blank and impersonal like automatons.

"Gentlemen," he said, folding his arms and trying to talk through teeth clenched around his pipestem, "we're here to take you—and Frau Brendel—back to Munich. My associates and I have provided the proper attire for the first part of the journey. We will be met by limousine for the major part of the trip." He took the pipe out of his mouth. "You will have to trust us."

"Who sent you?" Peterson asked.

"No comment, sir."

"You're not Germans, are you?"

"No comment, sir. I'm sorry." He applied another match to the bowl of the briar. "Now enjoy that brandy before we go."

"Stick your brandy up your ass, Sunny Jim." Peterson stood up and went to hold his hands out to the fire.

"There's no point in being abusive, Mr. Peterson. We're just doing our job." He must have been about thirty, all of him but his eyes: they were roughly two thousand years old. He'd rolled dice at the foot of the Cross, just carrying out his orders, just doing his job, and he'd stoked the furnaces at Dachau and kept the rack turning in the bad old days.

"Well, Sunny Jim, you're doing a mediocre to piss-poor job. We found a big piece of litter out in the woods. He'll be a mess when he thaws out in April."

"Oh, no. . . ." Lise turned to me again, choking. "Oh, no. . . ."

The three men looked blank.

Peterson turned to Lise. "Oh, yes, oh, yes, crazy-pants. You may have lost a husband but you've also lost a fairy." She began to cry again, hands pressed to her sore ribs.

I drained off my brandy.

One of them unzipped the khaki bag and took out

a dark blue snowmobile suit. I took it. He handed one to Lise. Peterson looked at his.

"We'll leave in half an hour." He put down his pipe and the three of them checked their wristwatches. Peterson went upstairs and two of them followed him.

"Help me," Lise said. We were alone by the smoking remains of the fire. She was struggling with her suit, brushing tears from her face. She was short of breath. "John," she whispered, "who are they? What's going to happen to me?"

"I don't know."

"Will they hurt us?"

"I don't think so."

"Did you see Siegfried?"

"Yes."

"Did they kill him?" There was a tic in her cheek.

"I suppose they did."

She clutched my arm, nails digging in.

"I'm afraid," she said, panting.

"So am I."

The limousine was waiting as promised, a Mercedes of indescribable length and opulence. The night was cold and wet, fog seeped across the mountain road. The headlights flicked on to guide us. The moon sneaked in and out among the clouds like a searchlight. We made the switch into the car with a minimum of talk. Lise huddled against me.

I was tired but I couldn't sleep. Peterson was snoring lightly. I watched the night sliding by. Near Munich it began to rain. The waiting was almost over.

Rain was drumming in the streets, dirtying the snow and finally washing it away in the gutters. There was a familiar quality about what I saw but it took a moment to place it. The paraffin lamps were glowing, fuzzy, and as we passed they were being snuffed out. We were in Schwabing.

Suddenly I was hyperventilating and I turned to Peterson, who stared into the night at the other window. "They're taking us to Roeschler. We're safe—they're the good guys."

Peterson finally turned, pulled at his mustache, nodded.

"It all fits somehow," he said. "It all comes together and makes sense. It has to—but I don't quite see how, yet. Roeschler sends his men to bring us back safe and sound, that's fine, but why kill Siegfried? Why do Kottmann's job for him?" He shook his head and rubbed his nose with a knuckle. "I suppose we'll see."

We were moving slowly down the alleyway behind Roeschler's house. The three men were out of the car immediately after it stopped, opening the back doors and helping us out. Rain rushed on the bricks, spattered from the rooftops, slashed at us in the wind trapped in the alleyway. I had my arm around Lise, helping her up the steps to the back door. From inside a shadow moved and opened the door. The kitchen light shone on his benign, smiling face. It was Roeschler and he was clucking over us, helping us inside to warmth and safety. Lise and I went on through the snug kitchen to the sitting room, where Peterson and I had first met him. A fire crackled, the cats stretched sleepily, awakened by the commotion. The rain slanted on the windows. The lamplight was yellow and dim seeping out from beneath the fringed shades.

Lise and I were alone. The bags were being carried into the kitchen and no one was paying any attention to us for the moment. I helped her out of the suit and she stopped me, held me close to her. I felt her breath on my face.

I shook involuntarily. She stepped back and stood by the fire in her Levis, looking like a slender boy. Her profile was fine and sad with the flames licking up behind her. Watching her stare into the fire, I knew that it didn't make any difference, that I loved her enough to know I'd never quite get over it. Whether she was good or bad, or insane, or Lise or Lee, it didn't make any difference anymore.

It was past midnight when we'd all settled down. Peterson stood by the fire. Lise sat on the floor beside an overstuffed, ramshackle chair with a worn slipcover. And Roeschler, in his immense, droopy cardigan sweater sat in his rocking chair with a pair of tortoiseshell cats warming his lap, nuzzling his dry, wrinkled hands. He'd poured schnapps for us all. The air was full of cat hair.

"Well, I am delighted to have you all back safe and sound," Roeschler said, his voice rumbling. "Are you all right, dear?" She nodded.

"She may have a cracked rib," Peterson said. "The late Herr Hauptmann beat on her with a grease gun for a while. Grand girl, though," he concluded sourly, "came through like a trooper. Didn't you, crazypants?"

Roeschler stroked the cats. The rocker creaked.

"Let me assure you all that you are quite safe here. The crisis which began with the discovery of Herr Brendel's corpse—I'm sorry, Lise, my dear—the crisis has run its course. Ah, let me explain."

Peterson was in a truculent mood. There were no more options. His manner conveyed it, the bitterness in his voice, the slouch. "I've got the feeling we'd better brace ourselves."

"I'm afraid that you're right, Mr. Peterson. But trust me."

Peterson laughed and went to the window, stood staring into the black rain. "Roeschler, you ask for miracles. Trust. The moon. An honest man."

"Mr. Peterson has a feel for all this," Roeschler explained for our benefit. "And he is right, in his own way. He has guessed by now, I suspect, that I have been less than absolutely candid with you." He took a deep breath. "Lise, I am the one who killed your husband, my old friend. He was an evil man. He had to die, it was the only way to stop him." He looked at her, stroked his cats.

"You?" she said tonelessly. "You murdered him?"

"I executed him."

"That is lost on me, I'm afraid." I had expected her to fly apart; instead she seemed uninvolved.

"And to you, John, I must admit that I am not merely the tool of Ivor Steynes, not quite the doddering old victim I painted myself." I held on to my chair. "In the vernacular, I am a double agent—forgive me the melodrama. At least these Nazis believe I am with them, Brendel considered me an ally. Trust. He trusted me—only in this way can I be of any real use to Colonel Steynes. I am not only an observer of the movement: they believe me to be a part of it."

"And what about all the White Rose bullshit," Peterson said to the window. "What about your poor little Jewish wife?"

Roeschler's grip tightened on the cat. Its eyes clicked open, tiny white fangs popped into view, a claw arched up.

"That is neither here nor there at present, Mr. Peterson. Suffice it that I am a Janus, I face both ways, doing what I can in a society which is dominated by Nazis, old and new. Judges, police officials, elected officeholders, directors of companies, educators all the way from kindergarten to graduate studies—there are Nazis everywhere and to function among them, I surely had to seem to be one of them." His face, the Carl Sandburg visage, had grown harsh. All the comfort was gone.

"With that in your minds, let me explain what has happened. Once Brendel's corpse was discovered, once my housekeeper found me tied to my bed, I was summoned to a meeting at your home, Lise, a meeting convened by Alfried Kottmann. He is an ambitious man whose reach habitually exceeds his grasp." He sipped his schnapps and reached for the bowl of nuts, fitted one into the nutcracker, and shattered its shell. "Kottmann assumed leadership of the Brendel faction without serious challenge, St. John at his side, of course. Alfried's great virtue is craftiness. He has lasted a long time. Although it was assumed without question that you two gentlemen had murdered poor Gunter and escaped with Lise and myself as hostages, he immediately saw an opening—namely, that nothing stood in the way of blaming the murder on Siegfried. The motive? Siegfried wanted to assert the primacy of his faction, or possibly a personal conflict centering on Lise, jealousy. The motive wasn't really important. What was important was the opportunity Brendel's murder afforded the Old Guard to purge Siegfried and thereby defuse the dilettantes, as Kottmann called them."

"Are you quite serious?" Lise's manner was hardening, growing more analytical. "There was actually a power struggle going on? What fools they are. . . ."

"Precisely, a struggle, but hardly foolish. Kottmann convinced the others that Siegfried had been the weak link, the only flaw in the movement. And he was ambivalent about Lise's importance—perhaps she should disappear, too. Why risk her continued existence? Who knew how much she might know and might decide to tell? There was always the off chance that someone might listen to her—and believe her.

"I was instructed to make arrangements regarding Siegfried. And I was in a unique position to handle that because before going to the meeting I had received a call from Siegfried. He was on the verge of hysteria. He was desperate, he wanted to find Lise, he was babbling precisely the nonsense I expected. I sent him to the schloss, I encouraged him to go, have it out with you, make a deal, and bring Lise back in triumph."

Peterson was laughing again. Who the hell was who?

"The poor fool accepted it. You see, if Kottmann hadn't suggested the Siegfried operation I would have. Whether from the Nazi viewpoint or my own, Siegfried was the weak link, a danger to us all.

"Kottmann was less concerned about you two, however troublesome you might be. When you weren't turned up through normal channels he was willing to assume that you'd finally been frightened off and had gone to ground. He was ambivalent about Lise when I argued against harming her. It seemed overly cold-blooded to the others so he backed away from it, said we'd discuss it later if I managed to bring her back to Munich." He faced Lise. "I repeat, my dear, you are safe. Absolutely safe—but I'm ahead of myself.

"By sending some of my own men to undo Siegfried I could protect all of you from any wild ideas Kottmann might have and I could get you back here as quickly as possible." He stood up with a cat in each fist and placed them carefully on the chair cushion. He took a cigar from the thermidor on the sideboard and carefully bit the end, spat it onto the worn carpet. He struck the match, let the phosphorus burn away, and leisurely applied it to the tip, enveloping himself in billowing, fragrant smoke. The old clock ticked like footsteps in a quiet hallway.

[326]

"As it stands now," he went on, moving to the clock and opening its glass cover, "Brendel has been temporarily replaced as German leader of the movement by Kottmann. Siegfried is dead and the young bunch is far less significant. Kottmann is pleased." He permitted himself a dry chuckle and corrected the hands on the clock's face. It was three minutes to one. "The South American adventure will occupy his time. He will be returning to Buenos Aires shortly. St. John will remain here for a time, I believe. He pulls Kottmann's strings like a master of puppets and Kottmann, pompous ass, hasn't the faintest idea." He slowly closed and fastened the glass and turned back to us, rubbing his hands.

"Which brings us to you three, doesn't it?" He beamed his Father Christmas smile, which faded as he came closer. "And I'm afraid that you are all in for some difficult moments which are simply unavoidable. Inevitable. And it falls to me to clear up the questions which we all must have."

I watched Lise and smiled, but she looked past me, beyond my shoulder as my mother had done in my father's painting. She was thinking about herself. It was the way she was and nothing was ever going to change that.

"Who is Lise?" Roeschler said it slowly. His eyes moved to Lise; one of her hands traced a design on the faded denim thigh.

Peterson's eyes flicked up from one of Roeschler's cigars and he batted them for effect.

"Lise Brendel is Lee Cooper," he said.

"Ah, Mr. Peterson," Roeschler said, rocking.

Peterson lit the cigar and turned back to the window.

Roeschler drummed his nails on the arms of the chair for a moment.

"Your father, Edward Cooper," he said to me, "was an exceedingly brave man, far braver than you can possibly imagine. Through the intervention of a friend, a Mr. Arthur Brenner, who had known him even as a boy and was involved in certain United States government agencies, your father was accepted in the Royal

Air Force. He was a trained pilot, of course, and had very strong reasons for wanting to get into the war."

"My father wanted to—atone, is perhaps the best word—for his own father's advocacy of the Nazi war aims. He was deeply ashamed, psychologically wounded by the experience of being Austin Cooper's son." I was speaking too quickly, feeling my face flush. "He believed that by flying for the RAF he would prove that being a Cooper was not synonymous with being a traitor."

"And also with the aid of special influence," Roeschler went on, nodding, "he was joined by his wife, who was at the time pregnant. Foolhardy, perhaps, but the young couple wanted to be together when the new baby was born. You, Mr. Cooper, were left in Cooper's Falls with your nanny, the servants, and your grandfather. As a result, you never saw your father, your mother, or your new little sister again. The tides of time and war, John." He sighed, swallowed more schnapps, and held it out empty. Peterson filled it while the clock ticked.

"Edward Cooper was commissioned and took his place as an officer in the RAF. He distinguished himself in the Battle of Britain, was decorated by Prime Minister Winston Churchill in a ceremony which was publicized all over the world—not only was he one of America's first heroes of World War II, he was a symbol, a crucial piece of propaganda in the campaign to bring his country into the war. He was the perfect patriot."

I was very tired. He'd been dead such a long time.

"When the time came for him, he died. His Spitfire trailing smoke, he was last seen pursuing a wounded Messerschmitt trying to escape into a fog bank. His plane was never found, he was never heard from again.

"But what of the wife and daughter?"

"They chose to stay in England for the duration of the war," I said. "It wasn't safe to try to come back. So they stayed."

"They were rich," Roeschler said, "and well connected. Beyond the sorrow of her husband's death, life for mother and daughter was pleasant enough. I know nothing of the details of their life—only that one day a stray stick of bombs clattered down in Belgravia and their home was destroyed." He sighed and coughed. "Enough of the mother was found to identify without question. The daughter was something else, I'm afraid. Her body—like her father's—was never found. Some clothing was found, scorched and ragged, a favorite doll blown to pieces, bits of rather circumstantial evidence that the little girl, your little sister Lee, had perished with her mother. There were many casualties that day, no great amount of time was expended on the search for proof of two deaths. They were quite logically assumed and recorded.

"But," he said, eyes flickering from one of us to the other, "they were mistaken. The little girl did not die."

Lise looked up, asked calmly: "You know this to be true?"

Roeschler nodded.

"And I was never told?"

Roeschler raised a hand.

"The air raid warden who was the first on the scene following the bomb blast in that quiet street never reported what he saw, perhaps because he did not realize its significance at the time. But two men were seen taking a small child away from the wreckage. They were associates of Edward Cooper. They were Englishmen . . . who were German agents working within the English bureaucracy." He looked at me, waiting. "Nazi agents," he said.

"I don't understand—" I was sweating and I could feel it trickling down from my armpits. Peterson and Lise were watching me. "What do you mean, Nazi agents associating with, with . . . my father. . . ." My voice was shaking. "Talk sense, for Christ's sake," I shouted, slamming my palm down on the arm of the chair. "Tell me the truth." By then there was nothing left but a whisper.

"I said that your father was an exceedingly brave man, John. He was. He risked his life in a Spitfire. He fought in an enemy country. And he posed as something he wasn't. He spoke out against his father—and all that took a great deal of courage. John, your father, Edward Cooper, was a German agent, by birth, by training, by inclination—he was truly his father's son. And he believed in what he was doing. He believed in it enough to reject his father before the world, to pose as what he felt to be a traitor—an American patriot. . . ."

Roeschler stared at me from beneath those eerie white brows, from heavy-lidded eyes, firelight on the narrow ribbons of pupil. I felt myself sinking back, faint, sick.

"Is he all right?" someone said. My father had been a Nazi. I had come from a rattling, hissing nest of them. My father, my grandfather. My little sister Lee.

"He's tired, defenseless. It's a terrible shock, coming this way."

I heard the voices and I opened my eyes. It was like looking through the wrong end of a telescope. Everyone seemed small, out of focus, far away.

"When's it going to be over?"

"Soon," he said. "It's almost over, John. Sip this."

It was brandy, harsh and burning. I snapped my head, shook like a dog.

"I'm sorry," Roeschler said, rumbling. "I'm truly sorry, John. Can you hear me? Well, this had to come out—you got so far into it. No one ever thought you would. But you did and this is where it led. Can you hear me? Do you understand what I'm saying to you?"

I nodded. "I hear you . . . understand you? Not so sure."

"Go on, Doctor." That was Peterson, pushing on. "Cooper's all right now. He's my boy. He's okay."

"Edward Cooper was a key German agent," Roeschler resumed. "He prevailed on Mr. Arthur Brenner to place him in a useful spot; he used Mr. Brenner, who acted out of friendship. Once he was inside the Royal Air Force he became a conduit of information for Air Ministry secrets. He had reported to the two men who were calling at his home on the day it was bombed." Roeschler coughed and relit the cigar.

"Your father, you see, did not die over the English Channel. He flew the Spitfire to the coast of France, landed it at a prearranged site, and was met by some useful German agents—one of whom was, of course, young Gunter Brendel. And he took your father to

Germany. The details of what happened during the remainder of the war are not known to me. Your father was for a time in Norway working with Quisling; later he was sent to the Balkans, then to Madrid. He was a phantom, now here, now there, the son of Austin Cooper, the American who had been the perfect inside agent-in-place. To a very few he was known as a kind of legend. Why didn't the Nazis make a huge propaganda success of him? Why wasn't he paraded about as the American hero who was in fact a Nazi spy—a Nazi hero?" He smiled at me, at the slowly grinding wheel of history, fate.

"There was a very good reason. His work was not done, not by any means. They were saving him for the postwar years. They were saving him for the time when the movement would be reborn years later. That was when he would be of greatest use." Roeschler peered at me. "Are you hearing me, John?"

I nodded. The clock was ticking like a sledgehammer. My perceptions were distorted, but I was hearing it.

"There was a long-term plan," he went on. "And your father was part of it. It all depended on when the final victory came. If the war had been won—then it would have been your grandfather, Austin Cooper. He would have become the party deputy in the United States. But the war was lost and it became necessary to wait, to build again. And your grandfather's role was passed to your father. He was still young. He was absolutely safe—the world *knew* that he was dead. The Nazis had given him a new identity for as long as he needed it. And when the time came, he would be revealed and returned to his own country. Don't shake your head, Mr. Peterson. Of course it's farfetched. Many things are farfetched . . . until they actually happen. People adapt to the farfetched with amazing alacrity. History is always being rewritten. Truth is relative, at best. And when Edward Cooper got his hero's return to America there would have been an entirely new truth, history would have been entirely reconstructed, and he most certainly would have been called something other than a Nazi.

"These things are infinitely subtle, don't you see?

He might have been called a Republican or a Democrat, or a Socialist even, or he might have begun a new movement, the All-American Party—names mean nothing. He might have the support of the Jews . . . or the blacks . . . or labor . . . or business. What matters is the underlying continuity. Believe me, the South American plan about to begin is not being thrust upon the world as the second coming of the Nazis. Nor the African movement already under way. The control of Middle Eastern oil reserves—do we hear of Nazis? Certainly not. Everyone knows that the Nazis are all but gone from the face of the earth."

Roeschler's eyes were closed. He was smiling faintly, stroking the purring cats.

"Where is my father?"

"Your father spent some time in Cairo, working there with survivors of the war, and in Paris and in Algeria." Roeschler sniffed, sneezed in the cat hair, rubbed his nose vigorously with a rumpled handkerchief. "Edward Cooper died of cancer in Sweden three years ago. Someone else took his place. Who?" He shook his head. "What does it matter? There will always be someone else. . . ."

I stared into Lise's pale-gray eyes. There were infinite distances in them, places I was sure I'd never been and would never go. In her eyes there was a kind of animal shock, the kind that is dealt with, absorbed into the subconscious, and forgotten. She protected herself that way, perhaps that was the key to survival. I dwelled on the anguish. My chemistry acted up and it didn't surprise me. But the pain in Lise's eyes was incalculable because she was, I thought, impervious to such agonies. Now it struck me that the shock to her was more harrowing even than my own and it snapped me back; I shook off Peterson's comforting hand and went to her.

"Lee," I said and held her against me. "Don't cry," I whispered, feeling her tears on my cheek, feeling the flutter of her eyelashes. "Don't cry." She held me, her body jerking against me. Somehow her pain was my responsibility, I was down deep at the root of it.

"You've left us hanging, Doctor," I said. "You've cleared up the story of my father—but that wasn't really the point, was it? Not to begin with, anyway. What happened to the little girl? The last time we saw her she was being spirited away into the fog by two mysterious strangers—"

"Not strangers—fellow agents, associates—they took her away. And this was an accident of fate. They happened to be there when the bombs fell; otherwise the little girl Lee would have perished with her mother. Instead, she was taken away, to Ireland, where there were many sympathizers, many homes open to a tiny guest. And there she remained for two years, rusticating, too small to remember it later in her life. Then she was taken to Bergen, Norway, with an Irish identity. Then to Austria and to the von Schaumbergs, where she was given a final identity—Lise von Schaumberg."

She was sobbing and sank from my arms into the chair.

"Where was my father?" She tore the question from her throat, brutally.

"It was terribly difficult for him, my dear," Roeschler said soothingly. "He had his own new life and continuing responsibilities to the movement. As I have told you, Edward Cooper *believed*. He was making his final commitment, acting out his own destiny. Once his wife was dead he decided that his children must be given the opportunity to live without the shadow of his own life hanging over them. He would never see any of you again and you would never be faced with either accepting or rejecting him." He paused, looking from me to Lee. "He was a very strong man and a very good man. He loved you all. As it turned out, his plan for you, John, and for Cyril worked out as he intended. Your lives were lived as he'd hoped, insulated by an ocean and the myth of his patriotism and the passage of years. He knew that you and Cyril had grown to manhood, lived your own lives." He sighed heavily, an old man in the middle of a long night. "For his little daughter Lee, it was not quite so simple. . . ."

The clock reached two and chimed sedately. Peterson went to the kitchen and came back with coffee in mugs. The cats' eyes blinked as he passed, the rain drove against the windows. My life was unfolding, at least the life behind my life, the underpinnings.

"Lise," Roeschler said, "knowing what I have known about you all these years has troubled me. Sitting in the church the day you and Gunter were married, I exhausted myself wondering if you knew what you were becoming involved in. Later Gunter told me you knew nothing at all."

"Why wasn't she simply returned to Cooper's Falls after the war, to her grandfather?" Peterson looked up from the fireplace, holding the poker in his large fist.

"Let me tell you the story," Roeschler said. "We have the time now before you must leave. Your father had no idea what he would be called on to do once he reached England—he certainly could not have known that he would be required to escape to Germany and devote his life to the movement—"

"You make him sound like a priest," Lee said.

"Yes, I do. He was—it's not an unfitting comparison. Had he served out the war under cover, if he had never been revealed, the family would have remained intact. Perhaps husband, wife, and daughter would have returned to the United States—everyone might have lived more or less happily ever after. But then he was called to Germany to serve the Reich . . . and the bombs fell on the little family in London. The German agents didn't know what to do with the little girl. They improvised, got her to Ireland, not an easy task for a couple of spies. . . .

"So again fate, destiny, call it what you will, takes a hand in the story. It took time for the Nazi command running Edward Cooper's mission to learn what had happened and they were unable to contact Cooper for advice regarding what should be done with the little girl who was, after all, legally dead in London. Consequently they went ahead, sequestered her. Finally, when Cooper surfaced again upon completion of one of his sorties, he was told of the death of his wife and the curious survival of his little daughter. What happened when he learned the fate of one and the good fortune of the child? I don't know—I know only that he decided there was no way to care for her himself, that she should instead lead as normal a life as the times would permit and in the country that he himself had chosen. Thus, my dear, you became Lise von Schaumberg and your father made certain that although he would never know his daughter personally he would be kept informed as to your life. He retained the interest of a father but denied himself the joys."

"Gunter knew my father," Lise said.

"Of course. He met him when he flew the Channel. He worked with him."

"Have I ever seen him?"

"No, I think not."

"Did my father approve of my marriage?"

"He was pleased with your life. He had respect for your husband."

"Oh, my God," she said, her fingers clawing at her face, covering her eyes. She threw her head back and forth, sounds issuing but not words, a convulsion of terror and sorrow and disappointment, lost hopes, a forlorn life. Peterson looked at her disinterestedly. As her cries subsided her shoulders heaved, frail and adolescent; she seemed tiny and sad and without hope.

"Until last fall," Roeschler went on, turning to look at the clock, "everything was going as planned. You and Cyril were utterly uninvolved with any of this. Lise was reasonably content, a confused modern woman perhaps, but no more confused than most. She had no interest in her husband's political activities, there was no threat at all to the movement. Gunter knew that his marriage was far from perfect but he saw his relationship with you, Lise, as important in two ways—he loved you and he looked upon you as very important in the sense of continuity within the movement. It didn't matter that you were unaware of your true identity—he *was*. You meant even more to him than a wife. South America was working perfectly; Africa and the Middle East were, if anything, slightly ahead of schedule."

Peterson said: "Doctor, let me take a crack at this."

"Don't dawdle, Mr. Peterson. Time is running out."

"Fate again, the little grindings of fate—bone on bone. Gunter Brendel goes to the Glasgow Trade Fair to make a deal to market some new scotch in Germany. Christ," he said, slamming his fist into his

[335]

palm, "it's so goddamn beautiful! Fucking, pure, sheer chance—he doesn't know that Cyril Cooper could have anything to do with some sillyass booze he's trying to get on the cheap! How could he know? Cyril's name never appears on anything. So Brendel goes to Glasgow and does he just take a nice, normal business trip? Hell no, he takes his poor confused young wife—she's depressed, she needs a holiday, what the hell—let's go to Glasgow, get out of the old rut!" Peterson was dripping with sweat, the grin fierce as the jungle night. "Well, by God, they got out of the rut. Now the next fateful step. Jack Dumfries makes a deal with Alistair Campbell, a nosy, drunken little newspaperman, to have a picture taken of his hotshot German guest, a very nice public relations move by Mr. Dumfries—a shot in the arm for Old Tennis Sock Scotch, a feather in his own cap he can show Cyril, a little ego massage for the kraut. Perfect. And Frau Brendel—she's a goddamn movie star, gorgeous, let's get her in the picture, too.

"Fate again! It gets better and better." He beamed at us, teeth shining behind the bandit's mustache. "Does Dumfries even know when Cyril Cooper is likely to drop by the Glasgow office? Chance . . . if Cyril had come a week later, a month later, Dumfries might have forgotten his momentary coup and the newspaper would never have reached Cyril Cooper's breakfast table. But, by God, Cyril hit Glasgow the day the photograph appeared . . . and when he looked at it he didn't see a public relations triumph for Jack Dumfries. Do you know what he saw? Jesus Christ, can you imagine it? He saw his mother!"

Roeschler regarded him with something approaching awe. Lee stared openmouthed. He winked at me.

"So Cyril Cooper went to Germany. What was in his mind? I don't know. He was presumably innocent of the political convolutions of Gunter Brendel. He just had that photograph and the nugget of an idea. And what harm would it do to simply inquire?

"He contacted you, Lee. He made a nuisance of himself and he knocked the stilts out from under your life. He asked you if you knew for certain who you were . . . and you decided that just maybe you didn't.

He spoke with you, Doctor, and he got himself run out of town. But he was on to something. God only knows exactly how he put it together, but he listened and he did make sense out of it . . . he may even have somehow gotten wind of the involvement of your father. Remember that telegram, John, something about the family tree needing some work. After shaking hell out of everybody here, this son of Edward Cooper wound up in Buenos Aires talking to Kottmann and St. John —I'm telling you, he had figured it out!"

"Why didn't they kill him then?" Lee looked like death, eyes red, face splotched from crying, but it was her life and nothing could have been more important.

Roeschler answered: "Because he was Edward Cooper's son. Kill him and you would have to answer to someone."

"So he lit a fire under them in Buenos Aires, sent the telegram to John in Cambridge and John sets out for home. By car. Cyril flies home and goes to the family home in Cooper's Falls to wait for John's arrival." Peterson held up a hand and began to tick the items off, one by one.

"So here comes John across country from the East. Cyril is home waiting on the last night. Two men attack John on the road and leave him for dead . . . and someone kills Cyril, poisons him. John survives the attack and arrives home the next day or late the next night. Nobody home, so he sleeps in the guesthouse. The next day he finds Cyril Cooper dead—dead about twenty-four hours, murdered right about the time John was arriving home. The murderer was, in fact, probably in the house when John arrived and thought it was empty.

"Somebody, Doctor Roeschler, wasn't worrying about having to answer to anyone. And they've been trying to kill John Cooper ever since . . . with an incredible incompetence.

"And these were Brendel's men. There's no point in going into all that now, but a bunch of them have died recently—"

Roeschler's eyebrows raised.

"I killed one in London, a man named Keepnews who was one of the two men who waylaid John on the highway. And John himself killed the other one in Cooper's Falls." He heaved an immense sigh and went back to lean on the mantle. "All because Lise Brendel was really Lee Cooper—John's sister, Cyril's sister. . . ."

"That's not quite right," Roeschler said. "It never made any difference whose sister she was. It was whose daughter she was—that was the problem."

My sister had dried her tears with the denim shirttail. I saw her tiny naked waist, saw the tremor in her hands. In the silence, she looked up.

"What will happen to me?"

No one knew what to say.

An hour later my sister and I were alone in the room, sitting on the floor staring at the fire. Roeschler had wrapped tape around her rib cage in case there was a hairline fracture. While he wrapped her at the kitchen table, he told us what was going to happen right away, why he had been looking at the clock. Lee sat on the table, naked to the waist, her tiny nipples erect on the small mounds of her breasts as he wound the white tape tight. Her shoulders were held back, her eyes closed, her face set and wounded and very tired.

He told us that he had arranged for our passage to the United States on a commercial flight, connecting from the air terminal in Munich to London, Shannon, and New York. We would be met by "friends" in New York and they would take us the rest of the way. He told us that we really had no choice, that our search for my little sister was finished, that it was time to go home.

"Are you telling us that this is it? It's all over?" Peterson asked.

"Exactly, Mr. Peterson." Roeschler looked up from his tape. "And you will do precisely what you are told. Without my help, you are dead men and there will be no incompetence, not anymore." The smile was gone, the Doctor Roeschler we had known was gone: he was ordering us and Peterson knew it.

Lee shifted before the fire, moaned. The house was quiet. Roeschler and Peterson had retired upstairs to grab a couple hours of sleep. Our plane would leave at seven, with dawn.

"What to do?" I said. The fire had burned low and the sound of the rain and wind came down the chimney.

"You will be home this evening," she said quietly.

"I meant what about you. All of it, from the time I saw the newspaper photograph in Buenos Aires, all of it has been to find you. I forgot everything else, I forgot about finding whoever killed my brother, I thought only of finding you . . . seeing you for myself, seeing if you were my sister."

"You succeeded. I asked you before if it was worth it, I asked you if it made any difference. . . ." She took a deep, painful breath.

"Is this it, then? I found you. People have died. . . ."

"My husband and my lover are dead because of you."

"I'm sorry."

"Of course you are. But you can go back to your old life, you see. I don't have one, there is nothing waiting for me—unless it's Alfried Kottmann and his toy soldiers."

"There's Roeschler, isn't there?"

"He will try to keep me from taking too many pills. He will protect me from anyone who wants to hurt me. There are my ballet classes. I can fill my days with the little girls. I will go back to the house in the country where my husband was . . . executed. The servants will have cleaned up my party, there will be fresh flowers in the vases and in the spring we'll open the windows and clean the house."

"Why don't you come with us?"

"What do you mean?"

"You're a Cooper. Come back with me. To Cooper's Falls."

"What in the world for?"

"We would be together. We could get to know each other."

"John, listen to me. I don't want to know you any better. Do you hear me? You may think I'm a Cooper, you may want to have me around to get to know me

[339]

—you may want many things. You wanted to find me, you had to find me at any cost. You got what you wanted. Because of you my life is now barren, I have no one. Not you, not Gunter, not Siegfried, no one. You have demolished my life—no, listen to me. You'll only hear this once. When you leave here, I will be alone. Try to understand—that's the way I want it. I don't want you here, anywhere near me. I don't hate you, I simply want to forget about you. I won't ever be able to forget what you and your friend have done to me and to my life but I am a German and I am strong because I have no choice. I have done nothing to regret. You have, if you are at all sane. You live with what you have done to me. I won't help you, I won't forgive you, I will only try to keep living and re-build my life. Do you understand me?"

I couldn't answer.

"There is no comfort for you in me. None. You've lost a brother. I have lost so much more. . . ."

"He was your brother, too," I choked.

"Perhaps you actually are insane," she said calmly. "You call him my brother. He was your brother. He was nothing to me. You are nothing to me. Only something evil that happened. I can survive, I can will my survival, I can recover. I have already begun to re-cover. Don't cry. Don't be so foolish. You're em-barrassing me. Please, help me get up."

I stood up and took her arm, helped her to her feet. Her face was utterly without expression. She was re-turning my look, she was standing beside me, but I was alone, as I'd been when we'd lain in bed together. I felt the tears on my face.

"Now, good-bye, John."

Impulsively, she pulled my head down and I felt her lips on mine, unhurried, passionless, but thought-ful, as if she were making a single concession. I held her shoulders gently so as not to hurt her, kissed her soft dry cheek and her eyes and her hair. Finally she pulled away, slowly, and freed herself completely. There was no smile.

"You should get some sleep," she said, moving away. "I won't be awake when you leave."

She stopped in the doorway to the hall.

"Will you be all right?"

"I should think so. Yes." She sounded so English, so distant.

I nodded. "Good."

"Good-bye, John."

I watched her leave, heard her on the stairs.

"Good-bye, Lee."

There was no one left to hear me. My sister Lee was gone.

The morning was dark and the rain beat steadily. The snow was almost gone. Water rushed in the gutter. A car waited under the overhang. The headlights shone through the rain; the stone alleyway glistened. I was holding my bag and Peterson was talking to Roeschler.

"If he asks for the pills," Roeschler was saying, "don't worry about it—just give him one of the yellows. It'll relax him, let him sleep. About half an hour before you reach New York give him one of the red and green ones, it will pep him up and induce a slight euphoria." They were talking about me. I felt Roeschler's hand on my coat sleeve. "You need rest and time to get all of this into perspective. You'll see —you'll be amazed at how well you'll feel after a week's rest. Now"—he slapped my back gently—"the sooner you're away the better." He shook hands with Peterson.

I was thinking about her, somewhere in the house, in her bed, lying awake and shivering in the cold. I thought of what she had said and of what I had done to her and I swallowed against the knot in my throat.

"Help her," I said to him.

The driver opened the door of the Mercedes and I moved into the shelter of his black umbrella. Peterson had climbed into the car already.

"I will."

Roeschler was standing on the steps while we moved slowly up the narrow alley. The wipers beat across the windshield. At the top of the alley I looked back. On the third floor of his narrow, spindly house a light clicked on behind the glass, the white curtains parted, the car turned into the street, and that was all.

The air terminal was shiny and metallic and bright, like schoolrooms on rainy days of childhood. I was vague and disoriented, I knew, and without Peterson I would probably have bungled it all and missed the plane. But he was quietly in charge, saying as little as possible, attending to the luggage and boarding checks and passports. I let myself go, let him take care of me, and my mind wandered helplessly in the memories crowding the present out of my consciousness. I settled back in a window seat, watched the tears of rain bead up and spin along the glass as the plane gathered speed on the runway, and I ate my breakfast like a good boy as we climbed up out of the clouds and rain into a molten sky with the rays of sun like sticks of glowing gold. Germany was behind us.

Home

SOMEWHERE over the Atlantic, hours later, I came to and felt a bit more like a human being. The ocean looked like metal in the sunlight and the sky was pale blue, cloudless. Peterson was reading *Playboy*. He saw that I was awake.

"How do you feel?" he asked.

"My teeth are wearing socks."

"Do you feel like a drink?"

"You forget I'm an alcoholic," I said.

"You can have tomato juice and fixings, no booze."

We took the little stairway up to the lounge. We settled back in black leather chairs and listened to the piped-in music. It was a pianist playing "Where or When." I sipped my tomato juice and fixings and tried not to remember where I'd last heard the song.

"Well, your health," he said, sipping.

"Your wealth," I replied and he grinned, shook his head.

We sat in silence for a while longer.

"Well, John," he said at last, "we didn't accomplish much, did we?"

"I don't know. I suppose we didn't."

"I wonder if Milo Keepnews killed your brother?"

"Maybe we'll never know. But he sure as hell tried to kill me."

Peterson nodded.

"What do you think Cyril was going to tell me?"

"I think he'd figured out most of it. He probably felt like we do."

"And how do we feel?" I asked.

"Like who the hell can we tell? He could tell you and that was going to be a relief to him. But who the hell is there for us? Can you imagine trying to explain all this? It isn't that people would laugh at us—no, they just wouldn't be able to make any sense of it. The conspiracy theory of history, rampant paranoia. How would we blow the whistle? Produce the bodies? Blow Steynes' cover? Try to get Roca to talk in Buenos Aires? Or Maria Dolldorf?"

I thought of her, remembered the golfers in Palermo Park and the fire in the night.

"Nobody would talk. It's too big, it's too audacious, and it's too well camouflaged." He sighed philosophically. "They know we're handcuffed . . . they know we can't really expose it. But still—"

"What?"

"But still, why take the chance? Why let us go?"

"You forget," I said. "I'm one of the family. Who would want to take the responsibility of killing Edward Cooper's son?"

"But who would they have to answer to? Who the hell is at the top?"

"Another thing we'll never know," I said.

"But why were they willing to risk killing you for a while and not now? There's always some kind of logic in a paradox. Why then and not now? Someone is protecting you, Cooper, that thought just won't go away."

"Well, what difference does it make?" I said.

"None, if it's all over. No difference at all."

"What do you mean, if it's all over? What could be left?"

"Nothing, I didn't mean anything."

I looked out of the window for a long time.

"It's not worth it," he finally said.

"What?" I came back slowly.

"Crazypants. I didn't say she's not worth it—she's probably okay if you like crazy women. I said it's not worth it. You're sitting there thinking about her, wondering if you'll ever find her again, racking your brain to figure out where it all went wrong. Well, let me tell you, it could never have gone right. It was a mess from the beginning, I knew it was the first time I heard about her."

"You don't understand," I said. My face was hot and I was beginning to sweat.

"Bullshit I don't understand," he said softly. "I understand. The problem was, once you saw her, you never treated her like a sister. You came on telling her she was your sister but you were obsessed with her as a woman. You fell in love with her. You came back from your walk in London, the day you tailed her, and you were in love with her already. You were in love with just looking at her. But, goddamn it, what could I do? She was the key to it—by then there was a lot more to it than just finding out if she really was your sister.

"And look at it from her point of view. She didn't know if you were brother and sister, but she was a woman, an unhappy woman, and she must have sensed your feeling about her. Now what was she to make of that? Say she finds herself attracted to you—but she's got her own identity crisis, her own set of problems. Like I told you, Cooper, she's just a woman. . . . And little men keep dropping in on her, telling her they're her brothers. But you're not acting like a brother. She doesn't know what to do because she doesn't know what's going on—no more than you did. Then, wham, last night any doubt is erased. She finds out she is your sister and she realizes that you're in love with her regardless of who she is." He shook his head, drained the glass, and the ice cube slid down and hit his nose. "No picnic. I don't know what went on between you two last night. I don't want to know. But I'd advise you to look at it from her point of view.

[344]

Stop feeling sorry for yourself, Johnnie, and think about the lady you left behind."

"I'm thinking about her," I said.

"Ah, what the hell," he said.

"What difference does it make?"

Peterson looked at me balefully.

"There is an old belief," he said, and I could tell he was quoting, "that on some distant shore, far from despair and grief, old friends will meet once more." He cleared his throat. "I read that once. Somewhere."

"Well," I said, "it's all right with me."

New York sparkled in the night.

The 747 settled down through the night, floating through wisps of cloud like ack-ack from Long Island battlements. It was warm when we came down the corridor into the Kennedy receiving section for international flights. People swarmed around us. Rain streaked the vast windows. Two men in brown suits and narrow ties and tan, wet raincoats picked us up on our way out of the customs area. They looked like very strong accountants, faceless, like the men who had come to the schloss, killed Siegfried, and brought us back to Munich.

"Mr. Peterson? Mr. Cooper? Will you please step this way? We'll only be a moment." One of them went ahead of us, one brought up the rear, and we marched quickly into a small office fronting a concourse. A pale-tan curtain was drawn across the window. The walls were pale-green, needed paint, and a modern steel and formica woodgrain desk faced the door. An empty room, a dead room. "Please sit down. We'll be very brief. You both must be tired."

"Right. We're tired. Now who the hell are you?" Peterson asked.

"I'm Mr. Jackson, he's Mr. Whitney." Mr. Jackson flipped open a fake-alligator wallet and showed it to Peterson, who scowled, peered at the small, gilt-edged document encased in a plastic shield. "And these are your new tickets." He handed us each a folder. Mr. Whitney quickly attached luggage tickets to our bags. "Washington, official business," Mr. Jackson said pleasantly, imperturbable, businesslike, as though he spent a good deal of time spiriting people from air-planes and explaining who the hell he was.

Peterson flipped his folder. "Eastern Airlines," he muttered. Mine was United, the friendly skies and all.

"I believe you'll find them in order, gentlemen. Time is short. Are there any questions?"

"You're goddamn right," Peterson said. "I'm not going to Washington. I'm going with him—" He grabbed my folder and opened it, ran a finger along the ticket. "Minneapolis. I'm going to Minneapolis with Cooper."

"Please, Mr. Peterson, let's not make a problem here." It was Mr. Whitney. He had a determined voice and a terribly dirty raincoat which shot his neat, efficient image. I wondered who they were but I really didn't give a damn: Roeschler had said we'd be met. What difference did it make?

"You're due in Washington this evening, Mr. Peterson. Now, let's move it—no shit."

"Look, no need for unpleasantness. We're all on the same side here. Mr. Peterson, it's really essential, the whole show is set. If you don't trust us, trust Doctor Roeschler." Mr. Jackson smiled reassuringly.

"Come on, George," Mr. Whitney said. "I don't give a flying fuck if he believes you or not. He's coming." He reached for Peterson's arm, which was a mistake. Peterson reached up and closed his fist around the arm.

"Mr. Jackson, do you value the life of this silly bastard?"

Mr. Whitney's eyes were wide and the color was draining from his face.

"Of course I do," Mr. Jackson said. "Really, we are off on the wrong foot, aren't we? Please, Mr. Peterson, do come along to Washington and try not to hurt Mr. Whitney."

"Identify yourself then, Mr. Jackson."

"I'm sorry, I can't. I have very specific instructions. It will all be explained in Washington."

"What about Cooper?"

"He goes on to Minneapolis alone. You'll be joining him within the week. Scout's honor."

Then Peterson dropped Mr. Whitney's arm. Mr.

Whitney leaned against the door, wiped his forehead. Peterson broke into a loud hearty laugh.

"Jesus! Scout's honor! Okay, okay, Jackson. What the hell. . . ."

"Well, then, let's go." He opened the door. Peterson put his hand on my shoulder.

"I'll call you when I get back. And remember this —everything's going to be all right."

I watched them walk away. I had an hour to wait. I went and had coffee and looked at the stuffed animals and the junk you used to prove to your kids you'd been in New York. But then I didn't have any kids and I hadn't been to New York.

When I arrived in Minneapolis I heard my name being paged. It was late. There weren't many people, footsteps echoed. I'd have to find a cab.

"Mr. John Cooper, passenger John Cooper, please report to the Northwest Airlines information counter for a message. John Cooper to Northwest Airlines information."

Northwest was the only ticket counter that seemed to be inhabited. The tired-looking man pushed his glasses back up his stubby nose and fumbled under the counter. He came up with a plain white business-size envelope with my name printed on it in thick black pencil.

I took the envelope. It had a large bulge. My hand was shaking; it was the tiredness, nervous strain.

There was no message. Only the keys to the Lincoln I'd left with the car at the garage in Cooper's Falls. And a piece of paper: "Row 9, Slot 5." It was obviously where I'd find the car. But no one had known I was coming. It was curious. But what difference did it make? The hell with it. I wasn't worrying about understanding things anymore.

I got my bag on the lower level, which was all but deserted. It was wet and cool outside, stars shining after the rain. A jet whooshed up, hissing and roaring, past the slanting ramps, huge and effortless, red and white and climbing. I was back in God's country and it was going to be all right. Nothing was going to go wrong now.

The car was immaculate, a new slab side, new paint, gleaming wax on the silver with rain standing in big shining drops. Everything was going to be fine. I packed my pipe and lit it while I waited for the engine to warm up.

It was a pronounced euphoria, the sense of well-being which I knew perfectly well was the companion of people who'd undergone an overdose of strain, people who'd finally slipped off the old rocker. But since I couldn't control it I let it be, let myself feel good as I drove out of the parking lot, eased it out along 494, went north on 35W, toward the lights of Minneapolis, left on 194 toward St. Paul, sweeping north again on 280, moving through the false spring night and the cool moist wind along the highways I knew, moving east on 36 toward the St. Croix and then north along the river road toward Cooper's Falls. Not the menacing, unknown roads winding through the night to Land's End and Cat Island, not up through the mountains past Bad Tolz. I was going home.

Finally, the gates were ahead of me, then I was through them, winding up the driveway. I wasn't as well as I'd thought. I wiped my wet forehead with my glove and sat for awhile behind the steering wheel. I turned the lights out, shut off the engine, opened the window. It was quiet. I got out of the car and took a deep breath. The moonlight was bright and there were shadows everywhere. I saw the low railing circling the driveway, heard for an instant the awful tearing sound as the snowmobile skis caught under it and ripped apart. . . . But it was quiet and when I turned to look at the spot where he'd died and frozen, the gaunt man wasn't there.

They say that careful, methodical, routine behavior is either a symptom of or an antidote for incipient madness. The choice was in my mind when I woke up in the morning. I was in the guesthouse and for an instant I thought that maybe it was the first night home, that I'd just driven in from Boston to meet Cyril. For a moment I thought I was waking from a bad dream. But then, of course, it began to come back to me. It wasn't the first time around: it was the second and I hadn't been dreaming.

So I got out of bed and showered and cleaned up very methodically, gritting my teeth under the cold spray, watching ice melt on the lake and the icicles drip on the eaves outside the kitchen window. I made instant coffee, found a jar of strawberry preserves, and ate them with a spoon. The sun was shining on the lake and the ice reflected it like fire.

I got dressed and went outside and ran my hands over the Lincoln. The false spring made the air balmy and wet, good to breathe. There was heavy, deep snow ahead, there always was, but it was lovely and youthful just then, a hint of the annual rebirth. What snow was left was thin, sinking into the moist earth.

I went back inside, rinsed out my cup, screwed the lid back on the jam, rinsed the spoon, put everything away. I went into the bedroom and straightened the covers on the bed, made sure that the coals from the fire I'd apparently made before retiring were contained in the grate. Method equals sanity so I was being as methodical and orderly as possible.

Slowly, admiring the morning, I drove into town. The courthouse was a wet black ruin, snow clinging in patches like moss. It was cordoned off with sawhorses and slat fencing which buckled every few feet from the kids in town hanging on it. I parked the Lincoln and went to Doctor Bradlee's office.

He was alone, bending over an appointment book. He looked up and saw me over the top of his glasses.

"Well, John," he exclaimed, straightening up, tall and stoop-shouldered in a four-hundred-dollar blue suit. "What a surprise! When did you get back?" He was glad to see me and I was glad to be back.

"Last night," I said.

"Olaf back too, eh?" He motioned me into his private office and followed me in, leaving the door to the reception room open.

"Why, no," I said. "He had some business in Washington."

"Washington," Bradlee said, nodding sagely. "We haven't seen those fellows for awhile but when they were here they were here in force. FBI men, security officers, heaven help us—when the courthouse went all the town records went with it." He shrugged, frowned. "Then they were gone and everything was back to normal, the smoking ruins, that was all we had to remind us. It was quiet and calm, like a demon had been exorcised." He smiled again. "And how's your poor head? Have you had any headaches?"

I reassured him and when he asked me what in the world we'd been doing I didn't know what to say.

"Traipsing around Europe," I said, "getting nowhere."

"Do you know who murdered Cyril?"

I shook my head, wondering what to say. How do you tell someone about *Die Spinne,* giant submarines, a man like Ivor Steynes, and a man like Brendel . . . a man like my grandfather? And what would he have said if I'd told him about my father? It all spun out like filament from an enormous, ever-moving, always-twitching spider. The web was infinite and infinity has never been easy to describe.

"A senseless killing—" he began, then blinked. "But of course it wasn't senseless. I don't know what to make of it and I don't suppose it amounts to a hill of beans if I can, one way or the other." He unwrapped a piece of Christmas candy, a round disk with red and white spokes. "Keep these around for kids," he said, crumpling up the cellophane wrapper. "But there aren't many kids in Cooper's Falls anymore. Time flies, John."

"Look, Doctor Bradlee, what I wanted to see you about—how's Arthur? Can I see him?"

Bradlee folded his hands across his vest and tilted back in the leather swivel chair behind his massive desk. He put his size 13 wingtips on the edge of the blotter and moved the candy into his cheek.

"It's funny about Arthur. A man his size and age has a heart attack and it's not good—too much weight, arteries wearing out, the oldest story. He collapsed at the hotel one day in the middle of his lunch, just fell forward into his Cheddar omelet. I'd told him to lay off the eggs, but he had to have his omelets, his big cigars, and you can't blame him, I guess. Anyway, we got him to the hospital and I did all the usual things.

On top of it all we found out he had pneumonia—walking around in the cold, you get pneumonia."

"But how is he? Is he alive?"

"Well, yes, he's all right now, as all right as he can be—he was a long time coming around. He was in a deep sleep for days but his life signs kept coming back. He was resting up, you might say. Lots of stamina, what people like to think of as the will to live. He just lay there fighting it and one day he woke up." Bradlee's eyebrows went up and he shrugged. "First thing he said was—you'll be amused by this—the first thing he said to his nurse was, 'Where's John? Is John all right?' Came out of it and asked how the hell you were. . . ."

"I wonder why that was on his mind?"

"Well, I suppose he'd been thinking about you when it happened—you know, thinking about all the goings-on around here before you and Peterson went your separate ways. He woke up thinking about whatever he'd been thinking about when he fell into his omelet. Nothing surprises me anymore, John, not a thing. . . ." He peeled off his glasses and plucked a Kleenex from a container on his desk. He carefully folded it and breathed on the lenses and began to polish.

"He went home yesterday, took him home myself. Seems fit enough. He's on borrowed time now, of course. He knows that. But with reasonable discretion, he could live for years." He hooked his glasses back over his ears. "He'll be glad to see you, John."

"I'll be glad to see him," I said. "There's not much left to believe in. Arthur's something."

Bradlee looked at his watch.

"I've got a fellow coming in with a bad arm, John. Said he could use a painkiller. At least I think that's what he said—while I'm dispensing medications can I give you something? Some Valium, anything for your head?" He stood up and I got up and walked into the outer room.

"Valium," I said.

He went back to his office, returned with a plastic bottle.

"Directions are on it," he said. "Say, are you going to see Arthur? Now?"

"I thought I would."

"Let me call him. The fewer shocks the better."

I was sitting in the car when I saw the man come around the corner. His arm was in a sling. There was something vaguely familiar about him but he was in the door before I could place him. Someone I'd once known, someone from out of the past. Cooper's Falls was full of people who looked vaguely familiar, who somehow bore the last traces of their childhood after all the years.

I was thinking about my father while I drove out to Brenner's house. What would Arthur have thought about the truth of my father's life? But it was immaterial. There was certainly no point in telling him at this late date, was there?

There was solace and contentment that afternoon, a rest for the weary spirit and body. Arthur Brenner met me at the door, thinner and strained about his eyes, but warm and reassuring, enveloped my hand in his.

I told him the story while we walked in the warm afternoon, the country lanes and matted grass wet underfoot, the earth fragrant, ice melting. We walked in the woods among the tall, barren trees which flourished on Arthur's estate and we stood watching the fragile, thin shields of ice on the ponds and low spots where the weeds and cattails poked up through. It reminded me of hikes I'd taken long ago with Cyril, of high-topped boots with knife pockets on the sides, of the roar and the rush of Cooper's Falls tumbling down white and choppy. . . .

Arthur's mood of quiet support was such that I went ahead and told him of my father's treachery, his devotion to the philosophy which had made my grandfather a pariah. I tried to apologize to him for the abuse of his trust, his help, but he marched impassively on in his great brown overcoat which flapped low near his ankles. He wore a brown cap pulled low on his broad forehead, looked older and more tired than I had ever seen him. His age was against him. He tightened the muffler at his throat.

As I'd talked, I hadn't been aware of the course

we'd taken, and then I heard it, the falls, and we stood at the precipice on the flat slippery rock looking down at the water rushing over the ledge, white frothy plumes increased by the melting snow. It roared as it tumbled and crashed and spray crystallized in a cloud hanging above it. The hills rose up around it, the firs pointed and dark green. The sun was an orange-pink glow rolling on the horizon.

"When I wonder what it all means," Brenner said, his voice giving the lie to his frail-seeming appearance, "I come here and watch the falls and remember that it was here long before me and will be here long after I'm gone, that the sound of the falling water has never ceased in all the years. We're all one with nature. All of us. . . ." He turned his back on the falls and looked off across the fields toward the setting sun. We were at peace and I wasn't haunted by any ghosts. It was lonely, as if Arthur and I were the last two men on earth. Finally, he hooked his arm through mine and we set off together on the path winding back toward the house.

"Don't apologize for your father," he said as we made our slow way through the gathering gloom. "Never apologize for any of the Coopers, John. It's a strong line, stronger than you may be thinking just now."

"Nazis, Arthur," I said. "A nest of them."

"It may not be what it seems," he said, his voice still strong and rich from the great chest. "The Orientals may have something in the worship of their ancestors. Continuity, John. We're all in this together and nobody has ever gotten out of it alive. Belonging to a line, being part of the great whole. In the end, it may be everything."

It was as if the rocks and the ages were speaking to me, telling me of the immutability of time and how everything goes on and friends and enemies finally become one in the infinite past.

"There is an old belief," I said, "that on some distant shore far from despair and grief, old friends shall meet once more."

Arthur looked at me and from deep in his eyes, sunken with his illness, he smiled.

We were both tired when we got back to the house. We ate a light meal, eggs and bacon and tea, and he prevailed on me to stay the night. I agreed, as much for him as for myself: I was worried about him in a vague, undefined way.

Before we went upstairs to bed he took me down to his workroom, where he did his porcelain.

Flowerdieu's Charge was finished, fired, painted, gleaming. It shone in the light, a complete and perfect thing. Flowerdieu's Charge, a last hopeless, doomed gallantry.

In the morning we settled in the bright, cheerful sitting room. He had prepared trays of breakfast, scrambled eggs and muffins with butter and honey and steaming cups of tea. The sunlight drenched the green and white flowered chintz chairs and couch, flowers winked brightly in vases, and a fire burned in the grate. Bach was playing in another room. I thought of the distant shore.

"You presented me with a difficult choice, John," he said, "after I had some time to reflect on what you told me yesterday. I couldn't sleep for a long time last night. I was thinking. . . ."

"I didn't mean to upset you," I said. I stared into the steam, stirred my pale tea while watching stray leaves swirl up to the surface, then sink.

"No, no, you didn't upset me. You presented me with a problem, a choice, and I wondered what to do. I could lie there in my bed listening to my heart beating and I thought, how many more times will it beat? How long before I slip quietly into the past? And I also considered how much you'd found out on your travels, how many lives had been lost. And I thought how much despair there was in your voice and your eyes. I'm old now, John, I know that despair is a waste and a joke, I know that politics and war and the struggles we engage in are nothing more really than something to keep us busy while we're here. . . ."

"What are you saying, Arthur?"

"I haven't seen God suddenly at the end of my life, I have no evidence of the existence of Satan, or evil or good. I sometimes doubt even right and wrong. God is so often a justification for the worst of what we want to do. God is always on our side—and what matters in the end?" He sipped the scalding tea; sunshine played on the craggy side of his massive head, with its well-combed white hair. He smelled of Yardley. "Personal worth, your integrity, character—no matter what your cause. Decency, a vision of the greater good whatever the greater good may be, the eradication of pain. . . ."

"I know," I said, but I wasn't sure.

"All of the reason why Nazism as we once knew it came to such failure," he said. "The lack of decency and integrity and reason and the scales tipping out of control toward pain. Fighting a war is one thing, losing a war is yet another, but the Nazis under Hitler redefined bad judgment." He sighed and gave me a tired smile. "It is best they lost," he said softly.

"Yes, it's best," I said. My mind fluttered like wings, brushed at Lee, and I saw the curtains on the third floor parting, parting. . . . I was tired of Nazis. They could have the world as far as I was concerned.

"But I was thinking about your father, John. I was remembering what a man your father was. A great man, John, a man of very considerable honor. I lay there in my bed and I was bothered by the immense amount of information you had discovered about him, about all of them. You knew almost all of it—"

"What do you mean, Arthur? Almost all of it? You mean you know . . . more?"

"Of course. I know more than anyone else." He kept chewing on muffin while I stared at him. I was having a fear reaction, like a shellshock victim.

"So I decided," he said quietly, "that perhaps, before it's too late and I'm gone, you'd better hear all of it, the entire story. You have so much to live with now, such a great burden and so much of what you know is off-center, so wrong. If you're going to bear the burden, I asked myself, why not the truth?"

He looked at me benevolently, with the calm of a man no longer a participant. He was going to die soon. He knew it. And I didn't want to hear the truth: I'd been told so many lies and so many versions of the truth that I didn't want to hear Arthur Brenner's. He went right on talking and I didn't know how to stop him.

"Your father was a Nazi, as you know, but that's only a very small fragment of the picture, John, a startling corner but far from the center, far from the truth. Yes, he was a Nazi—but he was also an American patriot, a very real American hero—the kind who must wait, perhaps for generations, for their proper role to be defined by history."

"What are you trying to tell me? He was a Nazi. And a patriot. . . ."

He clasped his hands across his broad chest and settled into the chintz chair. "Many of us in this country saw the strengths and even the virtues of Nazism in the thirties and were dismayed by the manner of its misuse by Hitler's people. And, of course, by Hitler himself. Your grandfather was one, of course, and since he was in an independent position, he could state his feelings openly. Others were not able to do so openly. But, believe me, the strong feelings were there in the thirties and in some rather surprising places.

"Well, then, when the war began to go badly for the Germans, when we had begun to apply some very significant pressure, there were several plans put forth in Washington and London about how best to use the situation—"

"Use the situation?" I asked. "We were winning the war, for God's sake—"

"Winning the war," he repeated. "Wars are almost never won on battlefields, John. Many other places . . . seldom battlefields. Planning rooms, war rooms, council chambers of one kind and another—in any case, there were good men within the Nazi system, men who could bring order and reason to the postwar chaos, men who could be absolutely trustworthy in the inevitable struggle against the encroachments of Communism."

"You're joking," I said. "We hadn't even defeated the Germans!"

"I am not joking," Brenner said.

"No," I said slowly. "No, I can see you're not."

"It was decided in Washington that your father would develop liaison with these cells inside Germany, these cells of able and gifted men we found sympathetic. Your father was a Nazi, yes, but he had always been operating, or run, by Washington and London—that is, by the governments of the United States and the United Kingdom, by highly placed officials operating at the most secret authorizations, by men who knew that Hitler was mad, a barbarian perverting a usable system.

"For these men, John, the war was fought to rid the world of Hitler and his people, just as it was for all, ah, right-thinking people the world over." He smiled comfortingly and poured more tea for both of us. "But not to destroy the movement, you see. The nucleus was to remain strong, active, but rid of its debauchers. After all, Russia had to be contained. But first Russia, the greater enemy, had to be used to defeat the lesser. Don't look so amazed, John. Think about it." He poured cream into his tea and stirred sugar in tight little circles. "Think—we already knew that even Hitler's atrocities against European Jewry were dwarfed by what Stalin had been doing to Jews for years. We knew that bad as Hitler was, the world could recover from him. But Stalin was a scourge, a plague, unparalleled in recorded time. You see," he said, carefully sipping so as not to scald his mouth, "it was a bit of a quandary—Hitler had to be stopped first because he controlled for the moment the movement we knew was rightfully our own. Once Hitler was removed there would be plenty of time to deal with Comrade Stalin."

"Arthur," I said, "level with me. Where do you fit in?"

"I am a Nazi, too. And I am no traitor. Surely, you can't imagine that I would betray my country?" He smiled tightly, eyes narrowed.

"No, of course not," I said. "I'm not questioning your loyalty . . . I don't know what I'm questioning. . . ." I didn't understand what was happening. "What do you mean, you're a Nazi?" Outside the window, a globule of water gathered at the tip of an icicle and hung, stretching, growing heavier, defying gravity. "You were a government official—you were always in Washington."

"Precisely," he said. "You see the connection, John?

The two halves of my life have not been in conflict. Washington and the Nazi movement; one, the same, John—that's what I am explaining to you now." He saw my face. "I can't, I don't expect you to accept all this yet. But you will, John, you will. . . .

"I have been in constant touch with Europe all through the years—or, I should say, they've been in touch with me. Sometimes through Washington, the Pentagon, sometimes through your grandfather, but always in close touch. It was I, John, who arranged for the giant submarines to unload our people on the East Coast. I funneled our agents into key positions in our own government, in Canada, all through Central and South America—all our people. We chose which ones would escape from Germany, which ones would take over the postwar government there and in the other free countries of Europe, which ones would stand in the dock at Nuremberg. Obviously, we didn't want to keep the most famous ones, the symbols, and we didn't want the monsters, the real war criminals—those we would either send to Nuremberg or feed to Simon Weisenthal or later to Colonel Steynes. We wanted to make sure the able men got out, got to safety. The only one we really failed with, the only one we really wanted and didn't get was Albert Speer. We couldn't get to him in time, and once the Russians had him in Spandau we couldn't get him out.

"In any case," he went on with a motion of the huge, pale paw, "we have made great use of the scientists, the administrators, the intelligence operatives. Gehlen is only the most famous and Allen Dulles wanted him badly, particularly in the years immediately after hostilities ceased, when we knew so little about the Communist apparatus and he knew so much. There have been many others—we could not have contained the Communists without our German friends."

He went away to replenish the tea and I sat staring out the window. I wasn't sure it was all registering. Layer after layer was being built up and the complexity was by now a self-fulfilling prophecy. I couldn't begin to imagine where it went now, or even where it had been. It had been so simple: at least it had seemed so simple. But that was a lie. It had never been simple. Never. Arthur came back. There was a can of Twining's breakfast tea on the tray and he sat down, measured tea into the strainer, carefully poured the boiling water from the kettle into the lovely ceramic pot. He began measuring his words like the tea.

"What will be difficult for you to understand, of course, John," he said like a gentle schoolmaster, "is that what I am discussing with you is not a mad plot to rule the world—"

"But a perfectly serious, rational, right-minded plan to rule the world," I said.

I felt lightheaded, like giggling. Or crying. I tightened my grip. I was fighting the icicle.

"Not a mad plot, John, but United States policy, a continuing policy, but beneath the surface. Elected officials have seldom been involved or even informed of the movement. We don't need figureheads, you see—all we need are the intelligence people, the operations people, the diplomats, the professors, and a handful of Congressmen at key points, on the proper committees and so on. You see, we don't operate on four- or eight-year plans according to whoever may be occupying the White House—we are methodically ordering the world our way, on our own timetable, stopping Communism and bringing it all under a single unifying umbrella of power. Sinister?" He smiled his characteristic avuncular smile and nodded. "To some people, surely, terribly sinister, or it would be if anyone knew, anyone in the public at large. But the point is, we see no other way, no other line of defense against the Russians and the Chinese. It's their way or ours, John—the survival of the mass, the group, as robot life, or the triumph of the will, of the individual, and it is a long struggle. . . ."

"What if you're wrong?" I asked numbly.

"We'll never know we'll all be gone, we're gambling with other lives a long time from now. For now, we're staying busy, keeping ourselves occupied. When their time comes, they can stay busy too, as best they can."

Finally I said: "Why were they trying to kill me? Why did they kill Cyril? And Paula?"

"The problem was with those documents, the things in that box in the library—the whole thing there for anyone who could understand it." His eyebrows arched up and he held his hands out, palms up. "Well, a problem. And why run the risk of making it all public, bring all the old Nazi rigamarole back to life? Too much would have been stirred up, wouldn't it? Would anyone have believed it? Who knows? Almost certainly not. But it would have gotten people talking again . . . and then someone else would have begun digging and the trail would have led back to Germany and Herr Brendel and Siegfried and just maybe someone would have remembered Edward Cooper, son of Austin, and so on back to poor little Lee. There was that chance and there was no point in risking it. Then, when we realized that Olaf Peterson had taken the documents to the government, some very high-level strings had to be pulled, and we pulled them, but our Mr. Peterson is a resourceful man. He went to New York and of course we were watching him all the time. Finally we decided to send a CIA man to deal with the man at Columbia, who badly needed some money for alimony payments and his son's education at Exeter and he fancied a new car, I believe. So now he's doing a certain amount of contract work for our cryptographic center. He has enough money to meet his obligations and have a luxury or two, and his lips are sealed on the subject of those documents. We can always fall back simply on the interests of national security—national security covers a multitude of, oh, well, not-quite sins, you know—and that puts an end to it, particularly if there's a bit of money involved. So, you see, we've completely neutralized Olaf's friend." He looked at me, his fingers laced across the old cardigan.

"But the killing," I said.

"The attempts on your life—they should never have been allowed to happen." He looked sad, chagrined, kept on. "They were CIA men, Keepnews and Reichardt, and they were authorized by Herr Brendel. Who was panicking—"

"CIA men!" I exploded, scalp prickling. "Brendel had that kind of power, for God's sake?"

"Of course, John. CIA men. And yes, unfortunately Herr Brendel had the power to send them on their way. Since they were CIA men, all records of their existence could be concealed, repressed. There were no answers forthcoming from Washington because the government had been set the task of investigating itself. Very useful—the result, no records of such people exist." He balanced the teacup on his knee as if to demonstrate his control. "When you killed the gaunt man, Reichardt, that upset them. Keepnews was recalled at once, to Buenos Aires, which was his regular base."

The sky outside had lost the sun, and gray clouds flattened out against the landscape. The trees were stark, as if they had been burned, and snow dripped like a hundred metronomes from the eaves.

"Did Milo Keepnews kill Cyril?"

"No." Arthur breathed heavily, rubbing his nose with the flat of his hand. His hair was combed back so neatly, silvery and straight with pink scalp beneath. "He didn't kill Cyril and he didn't kill Paula. Once the man at the top of our little pyramid realized what Brendel had taken upon himself and that he had turned assassins loose on you—why, then the attacks stopped and Keepnews was recalled. By then it was too late for Reichardt."

"Peterson killed him in London," I said.

"I beg your pardon?"

"Keepnews."

"You were present, I take it?"

"Yes. In a filthy public toilet."

"Well, well. Keepnews." A grudging respect flickered at the corners of his mouth. "I must say I'm not surprised. Mr. Peterson is a very hard case. I admire him. He's in Washington now, as you may know, being told more or less what I'm telling you."

It was increasingly difficult for me to talk coherently. The numbness was shared equally by my body and my brain. The front of my mind was perfectly aware that I had been battered mentally and physically and that the stress on my mind had been much the worse. Stress: it was like an inquisitor's pincers pressing on my temples, crushing everything behind my eyes into a single mangled sludge of fear, incomprehension, disgust. I sat in the chair for what seemed a long time and when I looked at the clock on the mantlepiece it was the afternoon and a spring rain had begun falling sluggishly outside. The snow seeped away, revealing the wet, dead, brown leaves like huge flattened beetles. The ticking clock reminded me of Roeschler's parlor and my thoughts swiveled to Lee.

I remembered as I sat by the darkening window the day we had met in the snowy park, how we had strolled and talked of old movies, of passengers on a ship sailing away into eternity. I rambled endlessly through my times with her, the touch of her mouth in the sleigh and her visit in the night, her cold thighs spreading beneath my hands and the unfeelingness. Would I ever see Lee again?

"You've had a hard time, John," Brenner said. He poked at the dying fire and bent stiffly, placed a couple of more logs on it, shook up the remains until flame licked up at the loose bark.

"I was thinking about Lee," I said. I saw the square of window, the light clicking on as we drove away. I knew what I wanted to believe.

"She'll be all right," he said. "I promise you. She'll be taken care of. She's a Cooper."

"They started trying to kill me again in Glasgow. . . ."

He nodded. "Yes, yes, another silly, ill-advised move and once again attributable to Brendel's panic. He knew by then that you had been to Buenos Aires, he knew you'd seen the photograph and talked to Kottmann and St. John. Kottmann, a meticulous and prudent man, was terrified—but he did not wish to overstep the boundaries of his actual authority, which surely did not extend to include the killing of Edward Cooper's only living son. St. John, a singularly amoral man, found it all rather amusing—after all, he takes no sides, makes no commitments, though he knows perfectly well that behind the Nazi movements stands the government of the United States and he has no wish to trifle with Washington.

"Brendel decided once more to avoid the proper channels," Brenner said, with a flaking of distaste.

"He turned his dogs loose again when he realized that you were in Glasgow, tracking back on Cyril's path, which would evenually lead to Munich. He didn't think about it, he didn't consult anyone—he merely wanted you dead before you found your little sister alive and relatively well." He sighed again, a wheeze: the strength of the long talk couldn't be doing his heart any good but he seemed steady, calm, the final authority.

"The job he tried to have done on you was, I am told, hideously bungled—fortunately for you, thank God. And again Brendel had failed to consult the top man—he knew that such a matter, involving tying off the son of Edward Cooper, would have to have final approval and he knew it would not be forthcoming. So he didn't go to the top. In fact, he knew he couldn't go to the top, that it was not possible at just that time—so Herr Brendel just went ahead and did it."

"But why," I asked, "why couldn't he have asked the man at the top? Why was it impossible?"

Arthur looked at me for a long time, weighing it all up.

Finally he said: "I had suffered a heart attack, John. I was unconscious."

My dinner was untouched, but the wineglass had twice been emptied. It was a dark night and candles flickered in silver on the large dining table with its old lace cloth. I sat in my chair and listened to the rain and watched it blow across the stone patio and the white wrought-iron furniture and watched the fire. I was desperately tired, without will or determination or hope. Without a future, held tight by the past.

Arthur lit a cigar from the candelabra and swallowed sherry. A cut-glass decanter stood before him. In the flickering light he looked older, cheeks hollowed, eyes set flat on the skull, but his voice was strong and his mind nimble.

"I am Barbarossa, John, I have always been, ever since the war was obviously going to be lost. Hitler had botched his chance and they turned to me. I was a government official at the time, in the State Department, I was honored and respected, I was thought to have real 'bottom' as my Southern colleagues called it. I was utterly sane and quiet and sound in my thinking—and was know to be uncommonly effective. The council made known to me their joint will—that I was the man they wanted.

"I was at my desk in Washington at the time. It was spring, and I said that I would have an answer by evening of the same day. I knew the risks and I knew the stakes. I went for a long walk beneath the cherry blossoms and I considered what it meant, what a long-term undertaking it was. It was not an easy choice but it wasn't so terribly difficult either; it was more a matter of coming to grips with what it meant. And that evening, in a lovely Georgetown home, in a library full of leather and brandy and cigar smoke, I accepted, and when it was clear what my decision was and I had been wished well—why, then we rejoined the ladies for bridge." He smiled distantly, memory sweeping over him. "Almost thirty years ago . . . and, of course, the character of the movement changed completely. We let the war run its course because we knew it would condition the world properly —Nazis had lost the war and the hope for domination of Europe and the Far East; they would vanish in disgrace from the face of the earth. . . ." He looked up and through the smoke and the candlelight caught my eye. "But only the name would die, John. Only the name.

"In any case, to return to our discussion of this afternoon, while I was incapacitated by my heart problems, Herr Brendel went ahead with his attempts to protect himself from you. He'd face up to the worry of dealing with me later . . . if I even survived my illness. He may have thought I was a dead man, hanging on by an unraveling thread. In any case, the man was out of his mind with worry, not only over the movement being revealed but with the fear of losing his wife—he saw you as the final, awful threat to his entire existence. You had to be stopped whether you were the last of the Coopers or not. And I was no longer able to protect you."

I listened and remembered the pale gray eyes like flat stones and the serious face only infrequently visitd by a smile.

"They lost you when you went to Cat Island. Very few of us know about Colonel Steynes and Brendel had no idea at all, neither did Kottmann. I know about the mad Colonel; he has been useful to us from time to time—throw him the bait and watch him and his man Dawson, they're very quick on the scent. Gerhard Roeschler knows of him, and has gained his trust over the years, done some work for him. Which is, in light of his most recent assignment, rather an understatement. But only a few of us know—your father was one, John.

"Steynes has never really been a problem to us and he has helped us, unwittingly of course, rid the movement of the sort of people we want no part of. He'd always held off on Brendel. After all, Brendel was not covered in gore by any means, not the sort of creature Steynes was interested in—'New Nazis' the mad Colonel called Brendel and his people, and he wasn't interested. Yet you got him interested, you and Peterson, and he went to Roeschler . . . and Roeschler killed him."

"Will you have to kill Roeschler, then?" I asked.

"Ah, no, I think not," Arthur said patiently.

"But Roeschler works for Steynes—he helped us escape from Brendel. . . ." My voice was trailing off because I was beginning to catch the rhythm of the motives and realities.

"He helped you because I ordered him to, John. I ordered you sent back here, I arranged for Peterson to be briefed in Washington. John . . . listen carefully. Doctor Roeschler is one of us. He is head of our European enterprises."

"But the White Rose?" Nothing was what it seemed. "What about his Jewish wife?" I heard my voice cracking, the voice of another man I no longer knew or cared to know.

"All true," he said, "all true. He hates the old Nazis, hates their butchery of Jews. He was happy to accept his commisions from the mad Colonel."

"Does Steynes know about Roeschler?"

"No, no, Roeschler's identity is exceedingly well guarded. He, like me, is a secret—a very important secret. I am his only superior in the movement. He is number two, John."

He got up from the table and came around and stood beside me.

"My God, Arthur—my God."

"I know, I know," he said, his heavy hand on my shoulder. "I'm sorry you ever had to learn the truth. A good deal of effort has been spent to keep it from you." He shrugged. "But this is the way it is. Come on, John. Let's go outside. A walk will do us good, settle our stomachs and ease our burdens. Come on, son."

We put our coats on and went outside. It was wet but the rain had stopped. In the quiet night, if you strained, you could hear the falls a soft roar muffled by the cliffs.

"What happens now?" I breathed the cold air and it reminded me of the night we went out in the snow and found Siegfried, kneeling and manacled and frozen like a boulder in the trees.

"Well, I will be gone soon. I won't see it happen. Of course, you don't actually know it all. You don't know our timetables, you don't know how we will go about our operations, how we plan to deal with this country. You don't know who our man is in this country nor the men we are considering for my place and Dr. Roéschler's when he is gone. And you don't know the man we'll eventually put in the White House. Oh, you know his name, everyone knows his name—you just don't know he's our man." He was walking with the help of a cane, his free hand shoved deep in his coat pocket. I watched him out of the corner of my eye: he was leaning into the moist breeze. As I heard his last words, I felt myself cringing inside.

"What I want to know now," he said, "is what you think about it, about all that you've heard today. I need an idea of your attitude, John. Do you understand? I need to know." He coughed and pulled his hand out of his pocket, tugged his muffler up to his chin, and pulled the collar tighter. God only knew where he got his strength.

"What do you expect me to think, Arthur?" I sighed and tried to get my breath. "Everything I believe in

[366]

has been proven a lie, everything I had ever looked to as an anchor in my life. Nothing is what it seemed. There's just nothing left—my brother is dead, my sister rejected me after I caused the deaths of several people while I tried to find her, I learned that my father was a Nazi agent instead of a war hero. Roeschler, the one man I met in my travels whom I truly trusted, is one of them, or one of you if you prefer." I got my breath again and went on: "I have been told with some authority that my own country is part of a worldwide conspiracy or plot or movement, the goddamn Fourth Reich—and now, Arthur, the one final sure thing in my world, the last thing I clung to—you, Arthur—you're one of them, too. What do I think, Arthur? I want out. I don't want to know any more, I don't care, take the world and good luck with it, it doesn't matter to me one way or the other. I feel dead, Arthur. I'm not going to tell anybody, I just don't care, and who the hell would I tell? The FBI? the CIA? For God's sake, who? The New York *Times?* The Washington *Post?* Hell, I'd be better off telling *Punch.* You're telling me that this is the way it is and the way it's going to be and I say okay. It's all right with me." I put my arm on his sleeve and stopped him in the muddy road. The falls was louder now and somewhere far away I heard the sound of a car. "The trick for me, the one thing left for me is to try to put my world back together again. You're safe from me, you've succeeded. I just don't care. All of you, you're just another big corporation. What do I care now?"

He moved on. I was slightly behind him. He was a huge shape and above us the moon came and went, low in the sky. The quiet night was really full of sounds.

"If only Cyril had felt that way."

"What do you mean?"

"I wouldn't have had to kill him, John. If only he'd accepted what I told him, if he'd only said, The hell with it, what difference does it make to me? The whole thing would have been avoided, no one would have died, life would have gone on—"

"Arthur, what are you saying to me?"

"But he didn't believe I'd kill him, he didn't be-

[367]

lieve I could bring myself to do it, he told me he would have to tell you and then he'd have to find a way to get the truth out." He was speaking into the night, as much to himself as to me. Maybe he was trying to settle accounts with the infinite. Maybe he was insane. It didn't really matter.

"We were sitting in the bedroom, the fire roaring, drinking our brandy, and I told him the whole story. And he was outraged, he didn't see the logic and the inevitability behind it all. We talked for a long time but I couldn't dissuade him. He said he was going to talk to friends he had in the press, he was going to drag it all out again. Do you see, John?" His voice was growing weaker. "I had no real choice. He died painlessly, he didn't know it was happening. And I had to do away with poor Paula, too. You thought I was napping at the hotel but I went to the library and killed her."

He turned to start back. I couldn't speak. My eyes burned and I was covered with cold sweat. Nothing had been this bad. The best was last. Sweat turned to ice on my forehead.

"I can't tell you how horrible it was, not in a way that would make you understand. I'd never killed anyone." He was speaking erratically, more and more to himself, as if I weren't there. "I was upstairs in the bedroom when you got home. I held my breath, not knowing what I'd do if you came upstairs. Cyril was dead or at least unconscious and dying—I prayed—and then you went away. I waited for a while and then I walked back to town to the hotel. The snow was blowing and I knew it would fill in my tracks. No one saw me on the road, it was so cold no one was out in it, no one saw me come in the private back door at the hotel; it was darkest morning." He coughed again, deep and rattling in his throat and lungs. "I knew I was ill. Then, when I had to walk to the library, I knew it was getting worse . . . and the attack on my house, the explosion, we rigged it to convince you and Peterson, Milo and I did before he left—I'd hidden him in my house, in the attic. It was all so absurd, I felt so foolish, so melodramatic, God knows it never

[368]

occurred to me that I'd ever have to kill anyone and now I'd killed poor Cyril—"

He broke off, held onto my arm, his weight heavy. I staggered. He was shaking, the great hulk trembling. He wept and I watched him.

"I had killed Cyril Cooper . . . and now you were in it, too, and so help me I wanted you out of it. I never thought you'd hang on so . . . but you insisted. I was lost—but my word was final in the movement. I thought I could still protect you wherever you went. I thought you'd find a dead end in Buenos Aires—then St. John gave you the picture from the newspaper—he didn't know," he gasped, "he didn't know what he was doing, there'd been no communication. How could he know what it meant? No one knew everything. Not even I. . . ."

I helped him walk. The story was over at last. I was empty and sick and tired. Life had gone to the rim, then one step more.

Neither of us saw the black Cadillac parked behind my silver Lincoln. We didn't know it was there until the rear door swung open and the lights snapped on.

"What?" Arthur said, a great white hand up to shield his eyes. "What?—Cyril!" He called my dead brother's name. "John! What's happening?" He was dazed, jerked away from me.

"Get away, Cooper!" I couldn't see who spoke and I slipped on a patch of ice, flailed my arms for balance, and felt myself going down.

There was a terrible flash from the car and a roar that enveloped me as I hit the ground. I'm dead, I thought, thank God, I'm dead. . . .

Above me Arthur's coat flew away, shreds of cloth in the arcs of light, and the great body surged backward. Another flash and roar and Arthur collapsed backward, bent in half at the middle, bent backward like an enormous rag doll. I felt ice cutting my knees and my hands. I was on all fours in the wet and somebody was coming toward me. I hung my head waiting. I had no breath, no sense of anything but pain. I dug my palms into the ice, cutting my flesh like jagged glass.

An enormously strong arm took hold of me, pulled

me upright, moved me toward the car. Whoever it was had only one arm. The other was in a sling. The sound of the gun blasts had demolished my hearing, my eyes were blurred with sweat and pain and fear. The man with the sling pushed me heavily into the car. I sprawled into the back seat, in the dark, and I felt my face on someone's leg. I gagged, grasped for a hold on the seat, and pulled myself up.

"Good evening, Mr. Cooper."

The voice was metallic and there was the hint of a smile in it. I looked toward the voice in the front seat. Colonel Steynes was looking back at me. Dawson was sliding in behind the wheel.

I hauled myself all the way up onto the back seat.

"Well, Cooper, it's good to see you."

I turned and he was staring at me.

"Olaf," I said.

Epilogue

WRITING of London, T. S. Eliot had called it "the brown fog of a winter dawn," a phrase which always appealed to me. I was thinking of it as I braked and moved the silver Lincoln into a parking place on Marlborough Street in front of the four-story town houses which peer somewhat warily down the single flights of stairs to the sidewalk and the everyday world. The morning fog had pretty well burned off and behind the clouds the autumnal sun glowed like a reflection from burnished brass. The leaves were amber and crimson and crackled dryly underfoot. It was a good clean morning, late October, and I felt fit in a tweed jacket and gloves. I had covered myself in normality, including my shiny cordovans and blue button-down shirt from Brooks and my rep tie. Doctor Moss, whom

I see three times a week in Boston, tells me that a performance of normality is well along the road to actually being normal. She may be right. Between my Harvard associate professor costume, and long walks by the Charles, and work on the book about the tame agonies of murder amid college unrest, and regular dosages of Thorazine, I can act as normal as the next man, if that is reassuring. I was thinking about being normal as I stood on the corner of Arlington Street, taking deep breaths and trying to be glad to be alive.

Across the way, near the Frog Pond, a woman in a blue cloth coat sat on a bench reading a book. A small boy in a harness attached to the bench had gotten to the end of his tether, as far from her as possible, and was peeing into the leaves, a beatific smile on his round face. I noticed the scene, the world around me, and when I did I'd been told to make a point of it to Doctor Moss. That inevitably brought a reassuring smile from Doctor Moss. She had been worried about me through the summer: I hadn't been much in contact with the world. Now I was noticing things like the weather and the smell of the leaves and the pastels revealed far across the Public Garden and the Common as the fog lifted. She'd told me to get back in touch with the world and I was trying.

I saw him standing in front of the Ritz. It was so like him to come to Boston and matter-of-factly stay at the Ritz. I made a point of noticing what he wore, the light gray herringbone suit, the white shirt, the foulard tie in red and blue, the silver collar pin. He turned as if telepathically controlled and saw me coming toward him. He faced me and waited, smiling a bit off-center.

"Cooper," he said, and self-consciously shook my hand. "How are you?"

"Normal," I said. "My shrink tells me I'm normal. Or almost normal. She tells me that's the way she wants me."

Peterson grunted, his face swarthier than I'd known it. He'd spent a summer in the sun.

"It's overrated, this normality stuff." He was checking me out, looking into my face to see what he could see, looking for scars on the old psyche.

"How the hell would you know? You've never spent a normal day in your life."

We laughed together, not quite friends but at the least a couple of people who had been together during a time of stress. It was like war buddies meeting when the war which had held them together was finally over. There wasn't much common ground and what there was lay there, brooding and dark, in the past.

"My wife has gone shopping with an old friend," he said. "I've got to meet them for lunch, probably some goddamned tearoom with doilies and little old ladies in mob-caps." We were crossing the street. "Shopping," he muttered. "Thank God she's rich, thank God for that."

The grass was brown and the ground was hard from frost. There were always people in the Public Garden and on the walkways of the Common. I could smell pipe smoke. You could always smell pipe smoke in Boston. We walked in silence for a while and I felt healthy. No psychic shocks from seeing Peterson again. I remembered what had happened, what I'd seen him do, and it was all right. It was a test. Doctor Moss would have had a fit if she'd known I was seeing him even now. But I was all right.

"Tell me about Cooper's Falls," I said.

"Oh," he said after a lengthy pause. "Oh, it's back to normal. They're talking about a new building where my office used to be, they've got to have something. Aho is running around making little impromptu speeches. Same with the library. You know how it goes. They'll build some glass box, put some shelves in it, a bunch of modern furniture, call it a library. But it won't be the same."

"No, it won't."

"Otherwise, everything's pretty . . . normal." He glanced at me. The mustache drooped, the eyes flickered like pieces of anthracite.

"Did they ever find out who killed Cyril and Paula? And poor Arthur?"

"No, they—we never have. Not a clue, or what clues there were went just so far and came to dead ends. The Feds were with us again but they weren't worth anything either—just an isolated footnote to history, I

[372]

guess. World's full of them, I hear. People getting killed all the time, nobody ever gets caught. Happens all the time."

There was a Salvation Army band at the top of the hill. We stopped to watch it for a moment, our reflections bigheaded in the immaculate flowering of the tuba. The man who played it had his eyes closed. He must have known his part by heart. His face was turning purple. Peterson tugged my sleeve.

"Let's go up there." He pointed to a bench at the top of the rise commanding a view of the Common and the city of Boston rising up on the other side. Sitting down, he took out a case and offered me a cigar. I took it and we puffed for a moment, watching the people and feeling the sunshine on our faces.

"Have you heard from our friends?" I asked.

"No, not since the Colonel and Mr. Dawson left."

"How did it happen, Olaf? I'm curious. I don't think it will bother me now, not anymore."

"All right," he said from behind a cloud of smoke. "Then let's not talk about it again—"

"We may never see each other again," I said.

"Well, be that as it may. Let's get it out of the way once and for all. If we live long enough we'll talk it over in our old age. I don't know. Anyway, I'll give it to you briefly.

"They took me to Washington and gave me pretty much the same story Arthur gave you. I oohed and aahed on cue and didn't know if they were all nuts or if I was or if the world was. It turned out to be the world, by the way, but that's neither here nor there at this point, is it? Well, when they were finished I told them that it was all right with me—I mean, what are you gonna say at a time like that? The whackos are running the world, that's their problem—I've got my wife's money and you don't live forever, right? Okay. Fuck it, I told them, more or less. They clapped me on the back, said that they had faith in me—can you imagine that?" He shook his head. "They said Arthur has assured my welfare, sort of signed for me or some goddamn thing and I winked and said I understood. . . . God, telling this for the first time—it's government by the Marx Brothers." He stopped to reflect.

"I don't know, though. We're reelecting an invisible President in a week, we've had a summer of Watergate and Eagleton and God only knows what else. The loonies are at it, Cooper. Well, anyway." He turned back to the subject, forcing himself away from the fantasies of the front pages and back to our own world.

"When I left Washington I was picked up by one of Roeschler's people. Now, you've got to remember, these people in Washington are not autonomous—in the end they answered to Arthur. And Roeschler was Arthur's second-in-command. So, when Roeschler's people took me for a ride I had to execute a little triple think. Roeschler had had us watched on the flight back after all and now he was pulling a little end run on the Washington office. He was circumventing Washington and his little men told me that I'd be meeting an old friend with a very serious mission—that I would cooperate with him or I would die without further discussion, and that you would die." He looked me square on. "And they told me that if I needed any more inducement to behave appropriately I should be aware that Lee Cooper—that's what they called her—would die, as well.

"I told them it was all right with me, anything they said was fine. The old friend, of course, was Steynes. Roeschler told Steynes the truth about Brenner and the movement, everything but his own involvement. Roeschler told him that unless Brenner were neutralized at once it would be too late. Steynes went for the bait and made the trip himself. I was the guide. There was just no choice. Steynes pulled the trigger on Brenner himself. He looked upon it as the culmination of his work.

"It was a setup, Cooper.

"Roeschler knocked off the one man above him in the hierarchy and no one can possibly pin it on him since everyone else in the movement who knew of Steynes' existence is dead. And no one but Brenner knew Roeschler worked for Steynes on suitable occasions." He beamed at me, as if he'd finally finished the impossible all-white jigsaw puzzle. "It's perfect!" He couldn't help admiring the scheme.

"One loose end," I said. "Steynes."

"Steynes is dead."

"Dead? Roeschler?"

"No, no, he was dying, had six months at the out-side when we saw him on Cat Island. Worked out to just over four. Roeschler knew that, of course, and knew the temptation to cap his career would be so great that Steynes couldn't resist doing it himself. So Roeschler is at the top of the heap now. The top. Pulling the strings."

"Dawson? What about Dawson?"

Peterson laughed.

"He's in Munich. Works for Roeschler. Is paid through Brendel's old firm, handles English interests. Sound man, Dawson. A mercenary. But fiercely loyal." He puffed and leaned back, glad that is was over.

"It's all tied up then, isn't it?"

"Yes. We're safe. Everybody's safe. It's the world that's in danger . . . and maybe the world can take care of itself Who the hell knows?"

"Have you heard anything from Munich?"

"No. I don't expect to. You shouldn't expect to either. It's all behind us now, Cooper."

Together we walked back the way we'd come.

At the sidewalk in front of the Ritz Peterson looked at his watch and shrugged.

"Well, it's time for me to go," he said.

"Me, too," I said.

"Well, then," he said. A breeze swirled down the street and tugged at his wig. He put his hand up re-flexively, smoothed it down. "Always think the damn thing's going to blow away." He laughed. "You were the first person who ever just spotted it, you bastard."

He grabbed my arm.

"Look," he said, "this is getting silly. Stay well, John. And try to forget it." He was shaking my hand, squinting in the bright sunshine, backing away from me.

"Everybody dies," I said.

I don't know if he heard me.

"I'll be in touch, Johnnie." He waved and we both turned around and went our own ways.

I went back to my flat. I'd moved: I no longer lived where I'd been when I got the telegram from Cyril.

Now I was high up in a tower overlooking the Charles River Basin and the Boston skyline with the Hancock Building where the windows keep getting blown out by the wind.

I sat at my desk looking out past the window and the balcony at the river turning into something shiny, gun-metal, as the sun sank. Car lights came on and I watched them trace their little paths so far below.

On my desk here was a delicate, colorful ceramic depiction of Flowerdieu's Charge. I had the only one in the world and I used it to hold piles of manuscript paper down when I opened the sliding doors onto the balcony.

And when I sat at my desk and looked the length of the room I could see the huge painting my father had done so many years before. My mother was there, looking just past you as if something interesting was happening just beyond your shoulder.

But I didn't have the picture there to remind me of my mother.

Sometimes, when I am in just the right mood, I can look into her eyes, which never seem to be quite paying attention, and if I look long enough I can see the great house on the outskirts of Munich. The wind is blowing there, sweeping across the empty driveway and worrying at the windows. There's a light on inside and the night is quiet. There may be a shadow at the window. But then again . . . maybe there isn't. It really doesn't matter.